*Heresy*

S. J. Parris is the pseudonym of the *Sunday Times* No. 1 bestselling author and journalist Stephanie Merritt. It was as a student at Cambridge researching a paper on the period that Stephanie first became fascinated by the rich history of Tudor England and Renaissance Europe. Since then, her interest has grown and led her to create this series of historical thrillers featuring Giordano Bruno.

Stephanie has worked as a critic and feature writer for a variety of newspapers and magazines, as well as radio and television. She currently writes for the *Observer* and the *Guardian*, and lives in Surrey with her son.

www.sjparris.com

@thestephmerritt

# S.J.PARRIS

Heresy

HarperCollins*Publishers*

This novel is entirely a work of fiction.
The names, characters and incidents portrayed in it are
the work of the author's imagination. Any resemblance to
actual persons, living or dead, events or localities is
entirely coincidental.

HarperCollins*Publishers*
1 London Bridge Street,
London, SE1 9GF

www.harpercollins.co.uk

This paperback edition 2011
1

First published in Great Britain by
HarperCollins*Publishers* 2010

A catalogue record for this book is
available from the British Library

ISBN 978 0 00 840561 8

Set in Sabon by Palimpsest Book Production Limited,
Falkirk, Stirlingshire

Printed and bound in Great Britain by
CPI Group (UK) Ltd, Croydon, CR0 4YY

**MIX**
Paper from
responsible sources
**FSC** C007454
www.fsc.org

PROLOGUE

# Monastery of San Domenico Maggiore, Naples 1576

The outer door was thrown open with a crash that resounded along the passage and the floorboards shook with the purposeful marching of several pairs of feet. Inside the small cubicle where I perched on the edge of a wooden bench, taking care not to sit too close to the hole that opened over the cess pit beneath, my little candle flickered in the sudden draught of their entrance, sending wavering shadows growing and shrinking up the stone walls. *Allora*, I thought, looking up. They have come for me at last.

The footsteps halted outside the cubicle door, to be replaced by the furious hammering of a fist and the abbot's throaty voice, strained beyond its usual placid tones of diplomacy.

'Fra Giordano! I order you to come out this instant, with whatever you hold in your hands in plain sight!'

I caught a snigger from one of the monks who accompanied him, swiftly followed by a stern tutting from the abbot, Fra Domenico Vita, and could not help smiling to myself, in spite of the moment. Fra Vita was a man who, in the ordinary course of events, gave the impression that all bodily functions offended him mightily; it would be causing him unprecedented distress to have to apprehend one of his monks in so ignominious a place as this.

'One moment, Padre, if I may,' I called, untying my habit to make it look as if I had been using the privy for its proper purpose. I looked at the book in my hand. For a moment I entertained the idea of hiding it somewhere under my habit, but that would be fruitless – I would be searched straight away.

'Not one moment more, Brother,' Fra Vita said through the door, a quiet menace creeping into his voice. 'You have spent more than two hours in the privy tonight, I think that is long enough.'

'Something I ate, Padre,' I said, and with deep regret, I threw the book into the hole, producing a noisy coughing fit to cover the splash it made as it fell into the pool of waste below. It had been such a fine edition, too.

I unlatched the door and opened it to see my abbot standing there, his heavy features almost vibrating with pent-up rage, all the more vivid in the gusting light of the torches carried by the four monks who stood behind him, staring at me, appalled and fascinated.

'Do not move, Fra Giordano,' Vita said tightly, jabbing a warning finger in my face. 'It is too late for hiding.'

He strode into the cubicle, his nose wrinkled against the stench, holding up his lamp to check each of the corners in turn. Finding nothing, he turned to the men behind him.

'Search him,' he barked.

My brothers looked at one another in consternation, then that wily Tuscan friar Fra Agostino da Montalcino stepped forward, an unpleasant smile on his face. He had never liked me, but his dislike had turned to open animosity after I publicly bested him in an argument about the Arian heresy some months earlier, after which he had gone about whispering that I denied the divinity of Christ. Without a doubt, it was he who had put Fra Vita on my trail.

'Excuse me, Fra Giordano,' he mouthed with a sneer, before he began patting me up and down, his hands roaming first around my waist and down each of my thighs.

'Try not to enjoy yourself too much,' I muttered.

'Just obeying my superior,' he replied. When he had finished groping, he rose to face Fra Vita, clearly disappointed. 'He has nothing concealed in his habit, Father.'

Fra Vita stepped closer and glared at me for some moments without speaking, his face so near to mine that I could count the bristles on his nose and smell the rank onions on his breath.

'The sin of our first father was the desire for forbidden knowledge.' He enunciated each word carefully, running his tongue wetly over his lips. 'He thought he could become like God. And this is your sin also, Fra Giordano Bruno. You are one of the most gifted young men I have encountered in all my years at San Domenico Maggiore, but your curiosity and your pride in your own cleverness prevent you from using your gifts to the glory of the Church. It is time the Father Inquisitor took the measure of you.'

'No, Padre, please – I have done nothing—' I protested as he turned to leave, but just then Montalcino called out from behind me.

'Fra Vita! Here is something you should see!'

He was shining his torch into the hole of the privy, an expression of malevolent delight spreading over his thin face.

Vita blanched, but leaned in to see what the Tuscan had uncovered. Apparently satisfied, he turned to me.

'Fra Giordano – return to your cell and do not leave until I send you further instructions. This requires the immediate attention of the Father Inquisitor. Fra Montalcino – retrieve that book. We will know what heresies and necromancy our brother studies in here with a devotion I have never seen him apply to the Holy Scriptures.'

Montalcino looked from the abbot to me in horror. I had been in the privy for so long I had grown used to the stink, but the idea of plunging my hand into the pool beneath the plank made my stomach rise. I beamed at Montalcino.

'I, my Lord Abbot?' he asked, his voice rising.

'You, Brother – and be quick about it.' Fra Vita pulled his cloak closer around him against the chill night air.

'I can save you the trouble,' I said. 'It is only Erasmus's *Commentaries* – no dark magic in there.'

'The works of Erasmus are on the Inquisition's Index of Forbidden Books, as you well know, Brother Giordano,' Vita said grimly. He fixed me again with those emotionless eyes. 'But we will see for ourselves. You have played us for fools too long. It is time the purity of your faith was tested. Fra Battista!' he called to another of the monks bearing torches, who leaned in attentively. 'Send word for the Father Inquisitor.'

I could have dropped to my knees then and pleaded for clemency, but there would have been no dignity in begging, and Fra Vita was a man who liked the order of due process. If he had determined I should face the Father Inquisitor, perhaps as an example to my brethren, then he would not be swayed from that course until it had been played out in full – and I feared I knew what that meant. I pulled my cowl over my head and followed the abbot and his attendants out, pausing only to cast a last glance at Montalcino as he rolled up the sleeve of his habit and prepared to fish for my lost Erasmus.

'On the bright side, Brother, you are fortunate,' I said, with a parting wink. 'My shit really does smell sweeter than everyone else's.'

He looked up, his mouth twisted with either bitterness or disgust.

'See if your wit survives when you have a burning poker

in your arsehole, Bruno,' he said, with a marked lack of Christian charity.

Outside in the cloister, the night air of Naples was crisp and I watched my breath cloud around me, grateful to be out of the confines of the privy. On all sides the vast stone walls of the monastic buildings rose around me, the cloister swallowed up in their shadows. The great façade of the basilica loomed to my left as I walked with leaden steps towards the monks' dormitory, and I craned my head upwards to see the stars scattered above it. The Church taught, after Aristotle, that the stars were fixed in the eighth sphere beyond the earth, that they were all equidistant and moved together in orbit about the Earth, like the Sun and the six planets in their respective spheres. Then there were those, like the Pole Copernicus, who dared to imagine the universe in a different form, with the Sun at its centre and an Earth that moved on its own orbit. Beyond this, no one had ventured, not even in imagination: no one but me, Giordano Bruno the Nolan, and this secret theory, bolder than anyone had yet dared to formulate, was known to me alone: that the universe had no fixed centre, but was infinite, and each of those stars I now watched pulsating in the velvet blackness above me was its own sun, surrounded by its own innumerable worlds, on which, even now, beings just like me might also be watching the heavens, wondering if anything existed beyond the limits of their knowledge.

One day I would write all this in a book that would be my life's work, a book that would send such ripples through Christendom as Copernicus's *De Revolutionibus Orbium Coelestium* had done, but greater still, a book that would undo all the certainties not only of the Roman Church but of the whole Christian religion. But there was so much more that I needed to understand, too many books I had yet to read, books of astrology and ancient magic, all of which were forbidden by the Dominican order and which I could never obtain from the library at San Domenico Maggiore. I knew that if I were to stand before the Holy Roman Inquisition now, all of this would be pricked out of me with white-hot irons, with the rack or the wheel, until I vomited my hypothesis out half cooked, whereupon they would burn me for heresy. I was twenty-eight years old; I did not want to die just yet. I had no choice but to run.

It was then just after compline; the monks of San Domenico were preparing to retire for the night. Bursting into the cell I shared with Fra Paolo of Rimini, trailing the cold of the night on my hair and habit, I rushed frantically about the tiny room, gathering what few belongings I had into an oilskin bag. Paolo had been lying in contemplation on his straw pallet when I flung the door open; now he propped himself up on one elbow, watching my frenzy with concern. He and I had joined the monastery together as novices at the age of fifteen; now, thirteen years later, he was the only one I thought of as a brother in the true sense.

'They have sent for the Father Inquisitor,' I explained, catching my breath. 'There is no time to lose.'

'You missed compline again. I told you, Bruno,' Paolo said, shaking his head. 'If you spend so many hours in the privy every night, people will grow suspicious. Fra Tomasso has been telling everyone you have some grievous disease of the bowel – I said it would not take long for Montalcino to deduce your true business and alert the abbot.'

'It was only Erasmus, for Christ's sake,' I said, irritated. 'I must leave tonight, Paolo, before I am questioned. Have you seen my winter cloak?'

Paolo's face was suddenly grave.

'Bruno, you know a Dominican may not abandon his order, on pain of excommunication. If you run away, they will take

8

it as a confession, they will put out a warrant for you. You will be condemned as a heretic.'

'And if I stay I will be condemned as a heretic,' I said. 'It will hurt less *in absentia*.'

'But where will you go? How will you live?' My friend looked pained; I stopped my searching and laid my hand on his shoulder.

'I will travel at night, I will sing and dance or beg for bread if I have to, and when I have put enough distance between myself and Naples, I will teach for a living. I took my Doctor of Theology last year – there are plenty of universities in Italy.' I tried to sound cheerful, but in truth my heart was pounding and my bowels were turned to water; it was somewhat ironic that I could not now go near the privy.

'You will never be safe in Italy if the Inquisition name you as a heretic,' Paolo said sadly. 'They will not rest until they see you burned.'

'Then I must get out before they have the chance. Perhaps I will go to France.'

I turned away to look for my cloak. There flashed into my memory, as clear as the day it was first imprinted, the image of a man consumed by fire, his head twisted back in agony as he tried in vain to turn his face from the heat of the flames that tore hungrily at his clothes. It was that human, fruitless gesture that stayed with me in the years afterwards – that movement to protect his face from the fire, though his head was bound to a stake – and since then I had deliberately avoided the spectacle of another burning. I had been twelve years old, and my father, a professional soldier and a man of orthodox and sincere belief, had taken me to Rome to watch a public execution for my edification and instruction. We had secured a good vantage point for ourselves in the Campo dei Fiori towards the back of the jostling crowd, and I had been amazed at how many had gathered to make profit from the event as if it were a bear-baiting or a fair: sellers of pamphlets, mendicant friars, men and women peddling bread and cakes or fried fish from trays around their necks. Neither had I expected the cruelty of the crowd, who mocked the prisoner with insults, spitting and throwing stones at him as he was led silently to the stake, his head bowed. I wondered if his silence were defeat or dignity, but my father explained that an iron spike had been driven through his tongue so that he could not try to convert the spectators by repeating his foul heresies from the pyre.

He was tied to the stake and the faggots piled around him so that he was almost hidden from view. When a torch was held to the wood, there was an almighty crackling and the kindling caught light immediately and burned with a fierce glow. My father had nodded in approval; sometimes, he explained, if the authorities feel merciful, they allow green wood to be used for the pyre, so that the prisoner will often suffocate from the smoke before he truly suffers the sting of the flames. But for the worst kind of heretics – witches, sorcerers, blasphemers, Lutherans, the Benandanti – they would be sure the wood was dry as the slopes of Monte Cicala in summer, so that the heat of the flames would tear at the offender until he screamed out to God with his last breath in true repentance.

I wanted to look away as the flames rushed to devour the man's face, but my father was planted solidly beside me, his gaze unflinching, as if watching the poor wretch's agonies were an essential part of his own duty to God, and I did not want to appear less manly or less devout than he. I heard the mangled shrieks that escaped the condemned man's torn mouth as his eyeballs popped, I heard the hiss and crackle as his skin shrivelled and peeled away and the bloody pulp beneath melted into the flames, I smelled the charred flesh that reminded me horribly of the boar that was always roasted over a pit at street festivals in Nola. Indeed, the cheering and exultation of the crowd when the heretic finally expired was like nothing so much as a saint's day or public holiday. On the way home I asked my father why the man had had to die so horribly. Had he killed someone? My father told me that he had been a heretic. When I pressed him to explain what a heretic was, he said the man had defied the authority of the pope by denying the existence of Purgatory. So I learned that, in Italy, words and ideas are considered as dangerous as swords and arrows, and that a philosopher or a scientist needs as much courage as a soldier to speak his mind.

Somewhere in the dormitory building I heard a door slam violently.

'They are coming,' I whispered frantically to Paolo. 'Where the devil is my cloak?'

'Here.' He handed me his own, pausing a moment to tuck it around my shoulders. 'And take this.' He pressed into my hand a small bone-handled dagger in a leather sheath. I looked at him in surprise. 'It was a gift from my father,' he whispered. 'You will have more need of it than I, where you are going. And now, *sbrigati*. Hurry.'

The narrow window of our cell was just large enough for me to squeeze myself on to the ledge, one leg at a time. We were on the first floor of the building, but about six feet below the window the sloping roof of the lay brothers' reredorter jutted out enough for me to land on if I judged the fall carefully; from there I could edge my way down a buttress and, assuming I could make it across the garden without being seen, I could climb the outside wall of the monastery and disappear into the streets of Naples under cover of darkness.

I tucked the dagger inside my habit, slung my oilskin pack over one shoulder and climbed to the ledge, pausing astride the window sill to look out. A gibbous moon hung, pale and swollen, over the city, smoky trails of cloud drifting across its face. Outside there was only silence. For a moment I felt suspended between two lives. I had been a monk for thirteen years; when I lifted my left leg through the window and dropped to the roof below I would be turning my back on that life for good. Paolo was right; I would be excommunicated for leaving my order, whatever other charges were levelled at me. He looked up at me, his face full of wordless grief, and reached for my hand. I leaned down to kiss his knuckles when I heard again the emphatic stride of many feet thundering down the passageway outside.

'*Dio sia con te*,' Paolo whispered, as I pulled myself through the small window and twisted my body around so that I was hanging by my fingertips, tearing my habit as I did so. Then, trusting to God and chance, I let go. As I landed clumsily on the roof below, I heard the sound of the little casement closing and hoped Paolo had been in time.

The moonlight was a blessing and a curse; I kept close to the shadows of the wall as I crossed the garden behind the monks' quarters and, with the help of wild vines, I managed to pull myself over the far wall, the boundary of the monastery, where I dropped to the ground and rolled down a short slope to the road. Immediately I had to throw myself into the shadow of a doorway, trusting to the darkness to cover me, because a rider on a black horse was galloping urgently up the narrow street in the direction of the monastery, his cloak undulating behind him. It was only when I lifted my head, feeling the blood pounding in my throat, and recognised the round brim of his hat as he disappeared up the hill towards the main gate, that I knew the figure who had passed was the local Father Inquisitor, summoned in my honour.

That night I slept in a ditch on the outskirts of Naples when I could walk no further, Paolo's cloak a poor defence against the frosty night. On the second day, I earned a bed for the night and a half-loaf of bread by working in the stables of a roadside inn; that night, a man attacked me while I slept and I woke with cracked ribs, a bloody nose and no bread, but at least he had used his fists and not a knife, as I soon learned was common among the vagrants and travellers who frequented the inns and taverns on the road to Rome. By the third day, I was learning to be vigilant, and I was more than halfway to Rome. Already I missed the familiar routines of monastic life that had governed my days for so long, and already I was thrilled by the notion of freedom. I no longer had any master except my own imagination. In Rome I would be walking into the lion's maw, but I liked the boldness of the wager with Providence; either my life would begin again as a free man, or the Inquisition would track me down and feed me to the flames. But I would do everything in my power to ensure it was not the latter – I was not afraid to die for my beliefs, but not until I had determined which beliefs were worth dying for.

# PART ONE

# London, May 1583

# ONE

On a horse borrowed from the French ambassador to the court of Queen Elizabeth of England, I rode out across London Bridge on the morning of 20th May 1583. The sun was strong already, though it was not yet noon; diamonds of light scattered across the ruffled surface of the wide Thames and a warm breeze lifted my hair away from my face, carrying with it the sewer stinks of the river. My heart swelled with anticipation as I reached the south bank and turned right along the river towards Winchester House, where I would meet the royal party to embark upon our journey to the renowned University of Oxford.

The palace of the bishops of Winchester was built of red brick in the English style around a courtyard, its roof decorated with ornate chimneys over the great hall with its rows of tall perpendicular windows facing the river. In front of this a lawn sloped down to a large wharf and landing place where I now saw, as I approached, a colourful spectacle of people thronging the grass. Snatches of tunes carried through the air as musicians rehearsed, and half of London society appeared to have turned out in its best clothes to watch the pageant in the spring sunshine. By the steps, servants were making ready a grand boat, decked out with rich silk hangings and cushions tapestried in red and gold. At the front were seats for eight oarsmen, and at the back an elaborate embroidered canopy sheltered the seats. Jewel-coloured banners rippled in the light wind, catching the sunlight.

I dismounted, and a servant came to hold the horse while I walked towards the house, eyed suspiciously by various finely dressed gentlemen as we passed. Suddenly I felt a fist land between my shoulder blades, almost knocking me to the ground.

'Giordano Bruno, you old dog! Have they not burned you yet?'

Recovering my balance, I spun around to see Philip Sidney standing there grinning from ear to ear, his arms wide, legs planted firmly astride, his hair still styled in that peculiar quiff that stuck up at the front like a schoolboy hastened out of bed. Sidney, the aristocratic soldier-poet I had met in Padua as I fled through Italy.

'They'd have to catch me first, Philip,' I said, smiling broadly at the sight of him.

'It's *Sir* Philip to you, you churl – I've been knighted this year, you know.'

'Excellent! Does that mean you'll acquire some manners?'

He threw his arms around me then and thumped me heartily on the back again. Ours was a curious friendship, I reflected, catching my breath and embracing him in return. Our backgrounds could not have been more different – Sidney was born into one of the first families of the English court, as he had never tired of reminding me – but in Padua we had immediately discovered the gift of making one another laugh, a rare and welcome thing in that earnest and often sombre place. Even now, after six years, I felt no awkwardness in his company; straight away we had fallen into our old custom of affectionate baiting.

'Come, Bruno,' Sidney said, putting an arm around my shoulders and leading me down the lawn towards the river. 'By God, it is a fine thing to see you again. This royal visitation to Oxford would have been intolerable without your company. Have you heard of this Polish prince?'

I shook my head. Sidney rolled his eyes.

'Well, you will meet him soon enough. The Palatine Albert Laski – a Polish dignitary with too much money and too few responsibilities, who consequently spends his time making a nuisance of himself around the courts of Europe. He was supposed to travel from here to Paris, but King Henri of France refuses to allow him into the country, so Her Majesty is stuck with the burden of his entertainment a while longer. Hence this elaborate pageant to get him away from court.' He waved towards the barge, then glanced around briefly to make sure we were not overheard. 'I do not blame the French king for refusing his visit, he is a singularly unbearable man. Still, it is quite an achievement – I can think of one or two taverns where I am refused entry, but to be barred from an entire country requires a particular talent for making yourself unwelcome. Which Laski has by the cartload, as you shall see. But you and I shall have a merry time in Oxford none the less – you will amaze the dullards there with your ideas, and I shall look forward to basking in your glory and showing you my old haunts,' he said, punching me heartily again on the arm. 'Although, as you know, that is not our whole purpose,' he added, lowering his voice.

We stood side by side looking out over the river, busy then with little crafts, wherries and small white-sailed boats crisscrossing the shining water in the spring sun, which illuminated the fronts of the handsome brick and timber buildings along the opposite bank, a glorious panorama with the great spire of St Paul's church towering over the rooftops far to the north. I thought what a magnificent city London was in our age, and how fortunate I was to be here at all, and in such company. I waited for Sidney to elaborate.

'I have something for you from my future father-in-law, Sir Francis Walsingham,' he whispered, his eyes still fixed on the river. 'See what a knighthood gets me, Bruno – a job as your errand boy.' He drew himself upright and looked about, shielding his eyes with his hand as he peered towards the mooring-place of our craft, before reaching for the oilskin bag he carried and pulling from it a bulging leather purse. 'Walsingham sent this for you. You may incur certain expenses in the course of your enquiries. Call it an advance against payment.'

Sir Francis Walsingham. Queen Elizabeth's Principal Secretary of State, the man behind my unlikely presence on this royal visitation to Oxford; even his name made my spine prickle.

We walked a little further off from the body of the crowd gathered to marvel as the barge was decked with flowers for our departure. Beside it, a group of musicians had struck up a dance tune and we watched the crowd milling around them.

'But now tell me, Bruno – you have not set your sights upon Oxford merely to debate Copernicus before a host of dull-witted academicians,' Sidney continued, in a low voice. 'I knew as soon as I heard you had come to England that you must be on the scent of something important.'

I glanced quickly around to be sure no one was within earshot.

'I have come to find a book,' I said. 'One I have sought for some time, and now I believe it was brought to England.'

'I knew it!' Sidney grabbed my arm and drew me closer. 'And what is in this book? Some dark art to unlock the power of the universe? You were dabbling in such things in Padua, as I recall.'

I could not tell whether he was mocking me still, but I decided to trust to what our friendship had been in Italy.

20

'What would you say, Philip, if I told you the universe was infinite?'

He looked doubtful.

'I would say that this goes beyond even the Copernican heresy, and that you should keep your voice down.'

'Well, this is what I believe,' I said, quietly. 'Copernicus told only half the truth. Aristotle's picture of the cosmos, with the fixed stars and the six planets that orbit the earth – this is pure falsehood. Copernicus replaced the Earth with the Sun as the centre of the cosmos, but I go further – I say there are many suns, many centres – as many as there are stars in the sky. The universe is infinite, and if this is so, why should it not be populated with other earths, other worlds, and other beings like ourselves? I have decided it will be my life's work to prove this.'

'How can it be proved?'

'I will see them,' I said, looking out over the river, not daring to watch his reaction. 'I will penetrate the far reaches of the universe, beyond the spheres.'

'And how exactly will you do this? Will you learn to fly?' His voice was sceptical now; I could not blame him.

'By the secret knowledge contained in the lost book of the Egyptian sage Hermes Trismegistus, who first understood these mysteries. If I can trace it, I will learn the secrets necessary to rise up through the spheres by the light of divine understanding and enter the Divine Mind.'

'Enter the mind of *God*, Bruno?'

'No, listen. Since I saw you last I have studied in depth the ancient magic of the Hermetic writings and the Cabala of the Hebrews, and I have begun to understand such things as you would not believe possible.' I hesitated. 'If I can learn how to make the ascent Hermes describes, I will glimpse what lies beyond the known cosmos – the universe without end, and the universal soul, of which we are all a part.'

21

I thought he might laugh then, but instead he looked thoughtful.

'Sounds like dangerous sorcery to me, Bruno. And what would you prove? That there is no God?'

'That we are all God,' I said, quietly. 'The divinity is in all of us, and in the substance of the universe. With the right knowledge, we can draw down all the powers of the cosmos. When we understand this, we can become equal to God.'

Sidney stared at me in disbelief.

'Christ's blood, Bruno! You cannot go about proclaiming yourself equal to God. We may not have the Inquisition here but no Christian church will hear that with equanimity – you will be straight for the fire.'

'Because the Christian church is corrupt, every faction of it – this is what I want to convey. It is only a poor shadow, a dilution of an ancient truth that existed long before Christ walked the earth. If that were understood, then true reform of religion might be possible. Men might rise above the divisions for which so much blood has been spilled, and is still being spilled, and understand their essential unity.'

Sidney's face turned grave.

'I have heard my old tutor Doctor Dee speak in this way. But you must be careful, my friend – he collected many of these manuscripts of ancient magic during the destruction of the monastic libraries, and he is called a necromancer and worse for it, not just by the common people. And he is a native Englishman, and the queen's own astrologer too. Do not get yourself a reputation as a black magician – you are already suspicious as a Catholic and a foreigner.' He stepped back and looked at me with curiosity. 'This book, then – you believe it is to be found in Oxford?'

'When I was living in Paris, I learned that it was brought out of Florence at the end of the last century and, if my advisor spoke the truth, it was taken by an English collector to one of the great libraries here, where it lies unremarked because no one who has handled it has understood its significance. Many of the Englishmen who travelled in Italy were university men and left their books as bequests, so Oxford is as good a place as any to start looking.'

'You should start by asking John Dee,' Sidney said. 'He has the greatest library in the country.'

I shook my head.

'If your Doctor Dee had this book, he would know what he held in his hands, and he would have made this revelation known by some means. It is still to be discovered, I am certain.'

'Well, then. But don't neglect Walsingham's business in Oxford.' He slapped me on the back again. 'And for Christ's sake don't neglect me, Bruno, to go ferreting in libraries – I shall expect some gaiety from you while we are there. It's bad enough that I must play nursemaid to that flatulent Pole Laski – I'm not planning to spend every evening with a clutch of fusty old theologians, thank you. You and I shall go roistering through the town, leaving the women of Oxford bow-legged in our wake!'

'I thought you were to marry Walsingham's daughter?' I raised an eyebrow, feigning shock.

Sidney rolled his eyes.

'When the queen deigns to give her consent. In the meantime, I do not consider myself bound by marriage vows. Anyway, what of you, Bruno? Have you been making up for your years in the cloister on your way through Europe?' He elbowed me meaningfully in the ribs.

I smiled, rubbing my side.

'Three years ago, in Toulouse, there was a woman. Morgana, the daughter of a Huguenot nobleman. I gave private tuition to her brother in metaphysics, but when her father was not at home she would beg me to stay on and read with her. She was hungry for knowledge – a rare quality in women born to wealth, I have found.'

'And beautiful?' Sidney asked, his eyes glittering.

'Exquisite.' I bit my lip, remembering Morgana's blue eyes, the way she would try and coax me to laughter when she thought I grew too melancholy. 'I courted her in secret, but I think I always knew it was only for a season. Her father wanted her to marry a Huguenot aristocrat, not a fugitive Italian Catholic. Even when I became a Professor of Philosophy at the University of Toulouse and finally had the means of supporting myself, he would not consent, and he threatened to use all his influence in the city to destroy my name.'

'So what happened?' Sidney asked, intrigued.

'She begged me to run away with her.' I sighed. 'I almost allowed myself to be persuaded, but I knew in my heart that it would not have been the future either of us wanted. So I left one night for Paris, where I ploughed all my energies into my writing and my advancement at court. But I often wonder about the life I turned my back on, and where I might have been now.' My voice trailed away as I lowered my eyes again, remembering.

'Then we should not have had you here, my friend. Besides, she's probably married to some ageing duke by now,' Sidney said heartily.

'She would have been,' I agreed, 'had she not died. Her father arranged a marriage to one of his friends but she had an accident shortly before the wedding. Drowned. Her brother wrote and told me.'

'You think it was by her own hand?' Sidney asked, his eyes dramatically wide.

'I suppose I will never know.'

I fell silent then, and gazed out across the water.

'Well, sorry about that,' Sidney said after a few moments,

clapping me on the back in that matter-of-fact way the English have, 'but still – the women of King Henri's court must have provided you with plenty of distractions, eh?'

I regarded him for a moment, wondering if the English nobility really did have as little fine feeling as they pretended, or if they had developed this manner as a way of avoiding painful emotion.

'Oh yes, the women there were beautiful, certainly, and happy enough to offer their attentions at first, but I found them sadly lacking in worthwhile conversation,' I said, forcing a smile. 'And they found me sadly lacking in fortune and titles for any serious liaison.'

'Well, there you are, Bruno – you are destined for disappointment if you seek out women for their conversation.' Sidney shook his head briefly, as if the idea were absurd. 'Take my advice – sharpen your wits in the company of men, and look to women only for life's softer comforts.'

He winked broadly and grinned.

'Now I must oversee the arrangements or we shall never be on our way, and we are to dine at the palace of Windsor this evening so we need to make good progress. They say there will be a storm tonight. The queen will not be present, naturally,' he said, noting my raised eyebrows. 'I'm afraid the responsibility of entertaining the palatine is ours alone, Bruno, until we reach Oxford. Steel yourself and pray to that universal soul of yours for fortitude.'

'I would not be the one to boast, but my friends do consider me to be something of a poet, Sir Philip,' the Palatine Laski was saying in his high-pitched voice, which always sounded as if he was voicing a grievance, as our boat approached Hampton Court. 'I had in mind that if we tire of the disputations at the university' – here he cast a pointed glance at me – 'you and I might devote some of our stay in Oxford to reading one another's poetry and advising on it, as one sonneteer to another, what say you?'

'Then we must include Bruno in our parley,' Sidney said, flashing me a conspiratorial grin, 'for in addition to his learned books, he has written a comic drama in verse for the stage, have you not, Bruno? What was it called?'

'*The Torch-bearers*,' I muttered, and turned back to contemplate the view. I had dedicated the play to Morgana and it was always associated with memories of her.

'I have not heard of it,' said the palatine dismissively.

Before our party had even reached Richmond I found myself in complete agreement with my patron, King Henri III of France: the Palatine Laski was unbearable. Fat and red-faced, he had a wholly misplaced regard for his own importance and a great love of the sound of his own voice. For all his fine clothes and airs, he was clearly not well acquainted with the bath-house, and under that warm sun a fierce stink came off him which, mingled with the vapours from the brown Thames at close quarters, was distracting me from what should have been an entertaining journey.

We had launched from the wharf at Winchester House with a great fanfare of trumpets; a boat filled with musicians had been charged to keep pace with us, so that the palatine's endless monologue was accompanied by the twitterings and chirpings of the flute players to our right. To add to my discomfort, the flowers with which the barge had been so generously bedecked were making me sneeze. I sank back into the silk cushions, trying to concentrate on the rhythmic splashing of the oars as we glided at a stately pace through the city, smaller boats making way on either side while their occupants, recognising the royal barge, respectfully doffed their caps and stared as we passed. For my part, I had almost succeeded in reducing the palatine's babble to a background drone as I concentrated on the sights, and would have been content to enjoy the gentle green and wooded landscape on the banks as we left the city behind, but Sidney was determined to amuse himself by baiting the Pole and wanted my collaboration.

'Behold, the great palace of Hampton Court, which once belonged to our queen's father's favourite, Cardinal Wolsey,' he said, gesturing grandly towards the bank as we drew close to the imposing red-brick walls. 'Not that he enjoyed it for long – such is the caprice of princes. But it seems the queen holds *you* in great esteem, Laski, to judge by the care she has taken over your visit.'

The palatine simpered unattractively.

'Well, that is not for me to say, of course, but I think it is well-known by now at the English court that the Palatine Laski is granted the very best of Her Majesty's hospitality.'

'And now that she will not have the Duke of Anjou, I wonder whether we her subjects may begin to speculate about an alliance with Poland?' Sidney went on mischievously.

The palatine pressed the tips of his stubby fingers together as if in prayer and pursed his moist lips, his little piggy eyes shining with self-congratulating pleasure.

'Such things are not for me to say, but I have noticed in the course of my stay at court that the queen did pay me certain *special* attentions, shall we say? Naturally she is modest, but I think men of the world such as you and I, Sir Philip, who have not been shut up in a cloister, can always tell when a woman looks at us with a woman's wants, can we not?'

I snorted with incredulity then, and had to disguise it as a sneezing fit. The minstrels finished yet another insufferably jaunty folk song and turned to a more melancholic tune, allowing me to lapse into reflective silence as the fields and woods slid by and the river became narrower and less noisome. Clouds bunched overhead, mirrored in the stretch of water before us, and the heat began to feel thick in my nostrils; it seemed Sidney had been right about the coming storm.

'In any case, Sir Philip, I have taken the liberty of composing a sonnet in praise of the queen's beauty,' announced the palatine, after a while, 'and I wonder if I might recite it for you before I deliver it to her delicate ears? I would welcome the advice of a fellow poet.'

'You had much better ask Bruno,' Sidney said carelessly, trailing his hand in the water, 'his countrymen invented the form. Is that not so, Bruno?'

I sent him a murderous look and allowed my thoughts to drift to the horizon as the palatine began his droning recital.

If anyone had predicted, during those days when I begged my way from city to city up the length of the Italian peninsula, snatching teaching jobs when I could find them and living in the roadside inns and cheap lodgings of travellers, players and pedlars when I could not, that I would end up the confidant of kings and courtiers, the world would have thought them insane. But not me – I always believed in my own ability not only to survive but to rise through my own efforts. I valued wit more than the privileges of birth, an enquiring mind and hunger for learning above status or office, and I carried an implacable belief that others would eventually come to see that I was right; this lent me the will to climb obstacles that would have daunted more deferential men. So it was that from itinerant teacher and fugitive heretic, by the age of thirty-five I had risen almost as high as a philosopher might dream: I was a favourite at the court of King Henri III in Paris, his private tutor in the art of memory and a Reader in Philosophy at the great university of the Sorbonne. But France too was riven with religious wars then, like every other place I had passed through during my seven-year exile from Naples, and the Catholic faction in Paris

28

under the Guise family were steadily gaining strength against the Huguenots, so much so that it was rumoured the Inquisition were on their way to France. At the same time, my friendship with the king and the popularity of my lectures had earned me enemies among the learned doctors at the Sorbonne, and sly rumours began to slip through the back streets and into the ears of the courtiers: that my unique memory system was a form of black magic and that I used it to communicate with demons. This I took as my cue to move on, as I had done in Venice, Padua, Genoa, Lyon, Toulouse and Geneva whenever the past threatened to catch up; like many religious fugitives before me, I sought refuge under the more tolerant skies of Elizabeth's London, where the Holy Office had no jurisdiction, and where I hoped also to find the lost book of the Egyptian high priest Hermes Trismegistus.

The royal barge moored at Windsor late in the afternoon, where we were met by liveried servants and taken to our lodgings at the royal castle to dine and rest for the night before progressing to Oxford early the next day. Our supper was a subdued affair, perhaps partly because the sky had grown very dark by the time we arrived in the state apartments, requiring the candles to be lit early, and a heavy rain had begun to fall; by the time our meal was over the water was coursing down the tall windows of the dining hall in a steady sheet.

'There will be no boat tomorrow if this continues,' Sidney observed, as the servants cleared the dishes. 'We will have to travel the rest of the way by road, if horses can be arranged.'

The palatine looked petulant; he had clearly enjoyed the languor of the barge.

'I am no horseman,' he complained, 'we will need a carriage at the very least. Or we could wait here until the weather clears,' he suggested in a brighter tone, leaning back in his chair and looking about him covetously at the rich furnishings of the palace dining room.

'We have no time,' Sidney replied. 'Bruno's great disputation before the whole university is the day after tomorrow and we must give our speaker enough leisure to prepare his devastating arguments, eh, Bruno?'

I turned my attention from the windows to offer him a smile.

'In fact, I was just about to excuse myself for that very purpose,' I said.

Sidney's face fell.

'Oh – will you not sit up and play cards with us a while?' he asked, a note of alarm in his voice at the prospect of being left alone with the palatine for the evening.

'I'm afraid I must lose myself in my books tonight,' I said, pushing my chair back, 'or this great disputation, as you call it, will not be worth hearing.'

'I've sat through few that were,' remarked the palatine. 'Never mind, Sir Philip, you and I shall make a long night of it. Perhaps we may read to one another? I shall call for more wine.'

Sidney threw me the imploring look of a drowning man as I passed him, but I only winked and closed the door behind me. He was the professional diplomat here, he had been bred to deal with people like this. A great crack of thunder echoed around the roof as I made my way up an ornately painted staircase to my room.

For a long while I did not consult my papers or try to put my thoughts in order, but only lay on my bed, my mind as unsettled as the turbulent sky, which had turned a lurid shade of green as the thunder and lightning grew nearer and more frequent. The rain hammered against the glass and on the tiles of the roof and I wondered at the sense of unease that had edged out the morning's thrill of anticipation. My future in England, to say nothing of the future of my work, depended greatly on the outcome of this journey to Oxford, yet I was filled with a strange foreboding; in all these rootless years of belonging nowhere, depending on no one but my own instinct for survival, I had learned to listen to the prickling of my moods. When I had intimations of danger, events had usually proved me right. But perhaps it was only that, once again, I was preparing to take on another shape, to become someone I was not.

I had been in London less than a week, staying as a guest of the French ambassador at the request of my patron, King Henri, who had reluctantly agreed to my plea to leave Paris indefinitely, when I received a summons from Sir Francis Walsingham, Queen Elizabeth's Principal Secretary of State. It was not the kind of invitation one declined, yet the manner of its arrival gave me no clue as to how a statesman of such importance knew of my arrival or what he wanted of me. I rode out the next day to his grand house on the prosperous street of Seething Lane, close by the Tower in the east of the City of London, and was shown through the house by a harried-looking steward into a neat garden, where box trees in geometric patterns gave way to an expanse of wilder grass. Beyond this I saw a cluster of low fruit trees in the full swell of their blossom, a magnificent canopy of white and pink, and among them, gazing up into their twisted branches, stood a tall figure dressed all in black.

At the steward's nod, I stepped towards the man under the trees, who had turned to face me – or so I believed, for the late afternoon sun was slanting down directly behind him, leaving him silhouetted, a lean black shape against the golden light. I could not gauge his expression, so I paused a few feet away from him and bowed deeply in a manner I hoped was fitting.

'Giordano Bruno of Nola, at your honour's service.'

'*Buonasera, Signor Bruno, e benvenuto, benvenuto*,' he said warmly, and strode forward, holding out his right hand to clasp mine in the English style. His Italian was only faintly coloured by the clipped tones of his native tongue, and as he approached I could see his face clearly for the first time. It was a long face, made the more severe by the close-fitting black cap he wore over receding hair. I guessed him to be about fifty years of age, and his eyes were lit with a sharp intelligence that seemed to make plain without words that he would not suffer fools. Yet his face also bore the traces of great weariness; he looked like a man who carried a heavy burden and slept little.

'A fortnight past, Doctor Bruno, I received a letter from our ambassador in Paris informing me of your arrival in London,' he began, without preamble. 'You are well known at the French court. Our ambassador says he cannot commend your religion. What do you think he could mean by that?'

'Perhaps he refers to the fact that I was once in holy orders, or the fact that I am no longer,' I said, evenly.

'Or perhaps he means something else altogether,' Walsingham said, looking at me carefully. 'But we will come to that. First tell me – what do you know of me, Filippo Bruno?'

I snapped my head round to stare at him then, wrong-footed – as he had intended I should be. I had abandoned my baptismal name when I entered the monastery of San Domenico Maggiore and taken my monastic name of Giordano, though I had reclaimed it briefly while I was on the run. For Walsingham to address me by it now was clearly a little trick to show me the reach of his knowledge, and he was evidently pleased with its effect. But I recovered myself, and said,

'I know enough to see that only a fool would attempt to hide anything from a man who has never met me, yet calls me by the name my parents gave me, a name I have not used these twenty years.'

Walsingham smiled.

'Then you know all that matters at present. And I know that you are no fool. Reckless, perhaps, but not a fool. Now, shall I tell you what else I know about you, Doctor Giordano Bruno of Nola?'

'Please – as long as I may be permitted to separate for your honour the ignominious truth from the merely scurrilous rumour.'

'Very well, then.' He smiled indulgently. 'You were born in Nola, near Naples, the son of a soldier, and you entered the monastery of San Domenico Maggiore in your teens. You abandoned the order some thirteen years later, and fled through Italy for three years, pursued by the Inquisition on suspicion of heresy. You later taught in Geneva, and in France, before attracting the patronage of King Henri III in Paris. You teach the art of memory, which many consider to be a kind of magic, and you are a passionate supporter of Copernicus's theory that the Earth rotates around the Sun, though the idea has been declared heretical by Rome and by the Lutherans alike.'

He looked at me for confirmation, and I nodded, bemused.

'Your honour knows much.'

He smiled.

'There is no mystery here, Bruno – when you stopped briefly in Padua, you became friends with an English courtier named Philip Sidney, did you not? Well – he is shortly to marry my daughter, Frances.'

'Your honour could not have found a worthier son-in-law, I am sure. I shall look forward to seeing him,' I said, and meant it.

Walsingham nodded.

'As a matter of curiosity – why *did* you abandon the monastery?'

'I was caught reading Erasmus in the privy.'

He stared at me for a moment, then threw back his head and guffawed; a deep, rich sound, such as a bear might make if it could laugh.

'And I had other volumes on the Forbidden Index of the Holy Office. They would have sent me before the Inquisitor, but I escaped. This is why I was excommunicated.' I folded my hands behind my back as I walked, thinking how strange it seemed to be reliving those days in this green English garden.

He regarded me with an inscrutable expression and then shook his head as if puzzled.

'You intrigue me greatly, Bruno. You fled Italy pursued by the Roman Inquisition for your suspected heresy, and yet you were also arrested and tried by the Calvinists in Geneva for your beliefs, is it not so?'

I tilted my head, half-assenting.

'There was something of a misunderstanding in Geneva. I found the Calvinists had only swapped one set of blind dogma for another.'

Again he looked at me with something approaching admiration, and laughed, shaking his head.

'I have never met another man who has managed to get himself accused of heresy by both the pope *and* the Calvinists. This is a singular achievement, Doctor Bruno! It makes me ask myself – what *is* your religion?'

There was an expectant pause while he looked at me encouragingly.

'Your honour knows that I am no friend of Rome. I assure you that in everything my allegiance is to Her Majesty and I would be glad to offer her any service I may while I remain under her sovereignty.'

'Yes, yes, Bruno – I thank you, but that is not an answer to my question. I asked what is your religion? In your heart, are you papist or Protestant?'

I hesitated.

'Your honour has already pointed out that both sides have found me wanting.'

'Are you saying that you are neither? Are you an atheist, then?'

'Before I answer that, may I know what the consequences of my answer might be?'

He smiled then. 'This is not an interrogation, Bruno. I only wish to understand your philosophy. Speak frankly with me, and I will speak frankly with you. This is why we are walking here among the trees, where we will not be overheard.'

'Then I assure your honour that I am not what is usually meant by the word "atheist",' I said, fervently hoping that I was not condemning myself. 'In France, and here in her embassy, I call myself a Catholic because it is simpler not to make trouble. But in truth, I do not think of myself as Catholic or Protestant – these terms are too narrow. I believe in a greater truth.'

He raised an eyebrow.

'A greater truth than the Christian faith?'

'An ancient truth, of which the Christian faith is one later interpretation. A truth which, if it could be properly understood in our clouded age, might enlighten men instead of perpetuating these bloody divisions.'

A pregnant silence fell. The sun was low in the sky now, and in the shade of the trees the air was growing cool Birdsong became more insistent with the gathering dusk, and Walsingham continued to pace through the grass, the shoulders of his black doublet flecked with white petals of blossom that fluttered from the branches overhead.

'Faith and politics are now one and the same,' he went on. 'Perhaps it was always so, but it seems to have reached new extremes in our troubled century, do you not think? A man's religion tells me where his political loyalties lie, far more than his place of birth or his language. There are many stout Englishmen in this realm with a greater love for Rome than you have, Bruno, or than they have for their own queen. Yet, in the end, faith is not merely politics. Above all else it is a matter of a man's private conscience, and how he stands before God. I have done things in God's name that I must justify before Him at the last judgement.' He turned and fixed me with an expression of sorrow then. When he spoke again his voice was quiet and expressionless. 'I have stood by and watched a man's beating heart ripped from his living body at my command. I have coldly questioned men as their limbs were pulled from their sockets on the rack, and the very noise of that is enough to bring your stomach into your mouth. I have even turned the wheels myself, when the secrets that might spill from a man's lips as he stretched were too sensitive for the ears of professional torturers. I have seen the human body, made in the likeness of God, forced to the very limits of pain. And I have visited all these horrors and more on my fellow creatures because I believed that by doing so I was preventing greater bloodshed.'

He passed a hand across his forehead then, and resumed walking.

'Our nation is young in the new religion, and there are many in France and Spain who, with the backing of Rome, seek to kill Her Majesty and replace her with that Devil's bitch, Mary of Scotland.' He shook his head. 'I am not a cruel man, Bruno. It gives me no pleasure to inflict suffering, unlike some among my executioners.' He shuddered, and I believed him. 'Nor am I the Inquisition – I do not imagine myself responsible for men's immortal souls. That I leave to those ordained to the task. I do what I do purely to ensure the safety of this realm and the queen's person. Better to have one priest gutted before the crowds at Tyburn than he should go free to convert twenty, who might in time join others and rise up against her.'

I inclined my head in acknowledgement; he did not seem to expect debate. Beneath the largest and oldest tree in the orchard a circular bench had been constructed to fit around its trunk. Here Walsingham motioned to me to sit beside him.

'You are a man who knows first-hand the persecutions Rome visits on her enemies. The streets of England would run with blood if Mary of Scotland found her way to the throne. Do you understand me, Bruno? But these conspiracies to put her there are like the heads of the Hydra – we cut off one and ten more grow in its place. We executed that seditious Jesuit Edmund Campion in '81 and now the missionary priests are sailing for England by their dozens, inspired by his example of martyrdom.' He shook his head.

'Your honour's task is not one I envy.'

'It is the task God has given me, and I must look for those who will help me in it,' he said simply. 'Tell me, Bruno – does the French king provide for you, other than your lodgings at the embassy?'

'He supports me rather with his good opinion than with his purse,' I said. 'I had hoped to supplement my small stipend with some teaching. To that end I planned to visit the famous University of Oxford, to see if they might have some use for me there.'

'Oxford? Indeed?' he said, a spark of interest catching in his eyes. 'Now there is a place mired in the mud of popery. The university authorities make a show of rooting out those who still practice the old faith, but in truth half the senior men there are secret papists. The Earl of Leicester, who is its chancellor, makes endless visitations and orders enquiries, but they scurry away like spiders under stones as soon as he shines a light on them. Then, once our backs are turned, they go on filling the heads of England's young men with their idolatry – the very young men who will go on to the law and the church, and into public life. Our future government and clergy, no less, being turned secretly to Rome under our very noses. Her Majesty is furious and I have told Leicester it must be addressed with more vigour.' He pressed his lips together, as if to suggest things would not be so lax if he were in charge. 'The place has become a sanctuary for those who trade in seditious books, and most of these missionary priests coming out of the French seminaries are Oxford men, you know.' Then he thought for a moment, and moderated his tone. 'Yes, you should go to Oxford. In fact, I shall be glad to recommend you if you wish to visit. There is much you might see of interest.'

He paused as if contemplating some idea, then his thoughts appeared to land briskly elsewhere.

'When you told me you wished to serve Her Majesty in any way she saw fit to use you – was this offer sincere?'

'I would not make such an offer in jest, your honour.'

'Her Majesty has money in her treasury for those willing to be employed under my authority, to aid in protecting her person and her realm from her enemies. And she would show her gratitude by other means as well – I know how important patronage and preferment can be to you writers. This would be the greatest service you could perform for her, Bruno – living at the French embassy, you will be privy to a great many clandestine conversations, and anything you hear touching plots against Her Majesty or her government, anything that concerns the Scottish queen and her French conspirators' – he spread his arms wide – 'letters you may glimpse, anything that you think may be of interest, no matter how small, would be of great value to us.'

He looked at me then, eyebrows raised in a question.

I hesitated.

'I am flattered that your honour shows such faith in me—'

'You have scruples, of course,' he cut in, impatiently. 'And I would think the less of any man who did not – I am asking you to present a false face to your hosts, and an honest man *should* pause before taking on such a role. But remember, Bruno – whenever you feel the wrench between conscience and duty, your care should always be for the greater good. The innocent among them will have nothing to fear.'

'It is not quite that, your honour.'

'Then what?' He looked puzzled. 'Philip Sidney told me you were so much an enemy of Rome that you would gladly join the fight against those who would bring the Inquisition to these shores.'

'I am an enemy of Rome, your honour, as I am opposed to all who would tell men what to believe and then execute them when they dare to question the smallest part of it.'

I was silent for a moment while he regarded me through narrowed eyes.

'We do not punish men for their beliefs here, Bruno. Her Majesty once eloquently declared that she had no desire to make windows into men's souls, and no more do I. In this country, it is not what a man believes that will lead him to the scaffold, but what he may do in the name of those beliefs.'

'What he *may* do, or what he can be proved to have done?' I asked pointedly.

'Intent is treason, Bruno,' he replied impatiently. 'Propaganda is treason. In these times, even distributing forbidden books is treason, because anyone who does so does it with the intent of converting those into whose hands they place them.

And converting the queen's subjects means seducing their loyalties away from her to the pope, so that if a Catholic force invaded, they would side with the aggressors.'

We sat in silence for a moment, then he placed a hand on my arm.

'Here in England, a man of progressive ideas such as yours, Bruno, may live and write freely, without fear of punishment. That, I presume, is why you came here. Would you have the Inquisition return to threaten those freedoms?'

'No, your honour, I would not.'

'Then you will consent to serve Her Majesty in this way?'

I paused, and wondered how my answer would change my fortunes.

'I will serve her to the best of my ability,' I replied.

Walsingham smiled broadly then – I caught the glint of his teeth in the dusk – and clasped my hand between both of his, the skin dry and papery.

'I am exceedingly glad, Bruno. Her Majesty will reward your loyalty, when it has been proved.' His eyes shone. Around us the garden was almost in darkness, though a few streaks of gold light still edged the violet banks of cloud behind the trees, and the air had grown chill, the plants releasing sweet scents into the evening breeze. 'Come, let us go inside. What a poor host I am – you have not even had a drink.'

He rose, with an evident stiffness in his back and hips, and began making his way over the grass.

A servant had lit a series of small lanterns along each side of the path through the knot garden, so that as we approached the house our way was lit by two rows of flickering candles; the effect was charming, and as I took a deep breath of the evening air I felt again an intimation of new possibilities, a future that I could grasp. The long days of travelling through the mountains of northern Italy, staying in filthy roadside inns infested with rats, where I would force myself to keep awake all night with one hand on my dagger for fear of being murdered for the few coins I carried, seemed very far distant; I was entering the intelligence service of the Queen of England. Another of my life's unexpected turns, but part of the great map of my strange journey through the world, I thought.

Walsingham halted just before the lanterns and leaned towards me.

'I will arrange for you to meet with my assistant, Thomas Phelippes,' he said. 'He organises the logistics – devises ciphers, delivery points for correspondence, that side of business. He is the most skilled man in England for breaking codes. I hardly need to say that you should not breathe a word of our meeting to anyone except Sidney,' he added, in a low voice.

'Your honour, I was once a priest – I can lie as well as any man.'

He smiled.

'I rely upon it. You could not have outwitted the Inquisition for this long without some talent for dissembling.'

So it was that I became part of what I later learned was a vast and complex network of informers that stretched from the colonies of the new world in the west to the land of the Turks in the east, all of us coming home to Walsingham holding out our little offerings of secret knowledge as the dove returned to Noah bearing her olive branch.

A sudden crack of thunder overhead jolted me out of memory, back to the room where I sat pressed up against the rain-slick window of a royal palace, watching a courtyard illuminated by sheets of light. In England I had hoped to live peacefully and write the books that I believed would shake Europe to its foundations, but I was ambitious and that was my curse. To be ambitious when you have neither means nor status

41

leaves you dependent on the patronage of greater men – or, in this case, women. Tomorrow I would see the great university city of Oxford, where I must ferret out two nuggets of gold: the secrets Walsingham wanted from the Oxford Catholics, and the book I now believed to be buried in one of its libraries.

# PART TWO

# Oxford, England, May 1583

# TWO

We left for Oxford at first light the following morning on horses that Sidney procured from the steward at Windsor, fine mounts with elaborate harnesses of crimson and gold velvet, studded with brass fittings that jingled merrily as we rode, but we were undoubtedly a more solemn party than had set out the day before on the river amid music and gaily coloured pennants. The storm had broken but the rain had set in determinedly, the warmth had evaporated from the air and the sky seemed to sag over us, grey and sullen; it would have been impossible to travel by river without being half-drowned. The palatine was much quieter over breakfast and sat with his fingers pressed to his temples, occasionally emitting a little moan – Sidney whispered to me that this was the penance for a late night and prodigious quantities of port wine – and my mood was much improved accordingly. Sidney was cheerful, as his winnings from the night's card games had grown steadily in direct proportion to the palatine's drinking, but the weather had dampened our bright mood and we spent the first part of the journey in silence, broken now and again by Sidney's observations of the road conditions or the palatine's unapologetic belches.

To either side, the thick green landscape passed unchanging, bedraggled under the rain, the only sound the muted thud of hooves on the wet turf as Sidney drew his horse alongside mine at the head of the party and allowed the palatine to fall behind, his head drooping to his chest, flanked by the two bodyservants who attended him, their horses carrying the vast panniers containing Laski's and Sidney's finery for the visit. I had only one leather bag with a few books and a couple of changes of clothes, which I kept with me, strapped to my own saddle. By the middle of the afternoon we had reached the royal forest of Shotover on the outskirts of Oxford. The road was poorly maintained where it passed through the forest and we had to slow our pace so the horses would not stumble in the puddles and potholes.

'So, Bruno,' Sidney said, keeping his voice low, when we were out of earshot of the palatine and his servants, 'tell me more about this book of yours, that has brought you all the way from Paris.'

'For the last century it was thought lost,' I replied softly, 'but I never believed that, and all through Europe I met book dealers and collectors who whispered rumours and half-remembered stories about its possible whereabouts. But it was not until I was living in Paris that I found real proof that the book could be found.'

In Paris, I told him, among the circle of Italian expatriats that gathered around the fringes of King Henri's court, I had met an aged Florentine gentleman named Pietro who never tired of boasting to acquaintances that he was the great-great-nephew of the famous book dealer and biographer Vespasiano da Bisticci, maker of books for Cosimo de' Medici and cataloguer of the Vatican library. This Pietro, knowing of my interest in rare and esoteric works, recounted to me a story passed down to him by his grandfather, Vespasiano's nephew, who had been an apprentice to his uncle in the manuscript trade during the 1460s, in the last years of Cosimo's life. Vespasiano had assisted Cosimo in the collection of his magnificent library, making more than two hundred books at his commission and furnishing the copyists with classical texts, so that the book dealer became an intimate associate of the Medici circle, and in particular a friend of Marsilio Ficino, the great humanist philosopher and astrologer whom Cosimo had appointed head of his Florentine Academy and official translator of Plato for the Medici library. As Pietro's grandfather, who was then the young apprentice, told it, one morning in 1463, the year before Cosimo died, Ficino came to visit Vespasiano at his shop, clearly in a state of some distress, clutching a package. He, Ficino, had already begun work on the Plato manuscripts when he had received word from his patron that he must abandon them and turn his attention as a matter of urgency to the Hermetic writings, which had been brought out of Macedonia some three years earlier by one of the monks Cosimo employed to adventure overseas in search of books from the libraries of Byzantium, but which had yet to be examined. Perhaps Cosimo knew he was dying and wanted to read Hermes more than he wanted to read Plato in the last days of his life, I can only speculate. In any case, the story goes that Ficino told Vespasiano, ashen-faced and trembling, that he had read the fifteen books of the Hermetic manuscript and knew that he could not fulfil his commission. He would translate for Cosimo the first fourteen, but the final manuscript, he said, was too extraordinary, too momentous in its import, to put into the language of men hungry for power, for it revealed the greatest secret of Hermes Trismegistus, the lost wisdom of the Egyptians, a secret that could destroy the authority of the Christian church. This book would teach men nothing less than the secret of knowing the Divine Mind. It would teach men how to become like God.

47

Ficino had brought this devastating Greek manuscript to the shop with him, carefully wrapped in oilskins; here he handed it over to Vespasiano, exhorting him to keep it safe until such time as they could decide what should be done with it while he, Ficino, would tell Cosimo that the fifteenth book had never been brought out of Byzantium with the original manuscripts. This was the plan, and the remaining books were duly translated; after Cosimo died the following year, Ficino and Vespasiano met to discuss the fate of the fifteenth book. Vespasiano saw the opportunity for profit and favoured selling it to one of the wealthy monastic libraries, where experienced scholars would know how to keep it safe from the eyes of those who might misinterpret or abuse the knowledge it contained; Ficino, on the other hand, had begun to regret his earlier delicacy and wondered whether it might not be better to translate the book after all, bringing its secrets into the light by revealing them first to the eminent thinkers of the Florentine Academy, the better to debate the impact of what was effectively the most blasphemous heretical philosophy ever to be uttered in Italy.

'So who won?' Sidney asked, forgetting to keep his voice down, his eyes gleaming through the stream of rainwater dripping from the peak of his cap.

'Neither,' I replied bluntly. 'When they came to take the manuscript from the archive, they made a terrible discovery. The book had been sold by mistake some months before with a bundle of other Greek manuscripts that had been ordered by an English collector.'

'Who?' Sidney demanded.

'I don't know. Nor did Vespasiano.' I lowered my eyes and we rode on in contemplative silence.

Here Pietro's story ended. His grandfather, he said, knew no other details, only that an English collector passing through Florence had taken the manuscript and that Vespasiano was never able to trace it, though he tried through all his contacts in Europe until the end of his long life, in the dying years of the last century. It was little enough to go on, I knew; there had been numerous English collectors of antiquities and rare books travelling through Italy in the past century, and there was no knowing whether the man who had acquired such a book by accident might have sold it on or merely abandoned it to gather dust in some corner of a library, not realising what fortune had dropped into his hands.

'Then why do you believe it is in Oxford?' Sidney asked, after a while.

'Process of elimination. The English collectors travelling through Europe in those years would have been educated men, probably wealthy, and I understand it is the custom of English gentlemen to leave books as a bequest to their universities, since precious few can afford to maintain private collections like your Doctor Dee. If the Hermes book ended up in England, it may well have found its way to Oxford or Cambridge. All I can do is look.'

'And if you find it . . .?' Sidney began, but he was interrupted as his horse suddenly shied sideways with a sharp whinny; two figures had appeared without warning in the middle of the road. We pulled our horses up briskly, the palatine and his servants almost running into the back of us as we looked down at two ragged children, a girl of about ten years old and a smaller boy, barefoot in the mud. The girl's right cheek was livid with a purple bruise. She held out her small hand, palm upwards, and addressed herself to Sidney in an imploring voice, though her stare was one of pure insolence.

'Alms, sir, for two poor orphans?'

Sidney shook his head silently, as if in sorrow at the state of the world, but reached at the same time for the purse at his belt and was drawing out a coin for the child when there came a sharp cry from behind us. I wheeled around just in time to see one of the palatine's servants dragged from his horse by a burly man who had emerged silently, along with two others, from among the shadows of the trees to either side. The palatine gave a little shriek, but gathered his wits remarkably quickly and spurred his horse forwards into a gallop, crashing between Sidney and me and almost trampling the two children, who dived into the undergrowth just in time to watch him disappearing around the bend. I jumped from my horse, pulling Paolo's knife from my belt as I launched myself at the back of one of the assailants, who was swinging a stout wooden staff at the second servant to knock him out of his saddle. Sidney took a moment to react, then dismounted and drew his sword, making for the men who were now trying to cut the straps holding the packs to the horses.

The man I had attacked roared and lashed at me as I clung to his arm, diverting his blow, so that the servant was able to urge the horse forwards, out of harm's way; another of them ran at me with a crude knife, just catching me on the leg as I tried to kick him away. Incensed, I dropped to the ground and struck out towards him with my own knife but, distracted by a movement from the corner of my eye, I whipped around just in time to see the larger man lifting his stick to aim it at me; I thrust the knife upwards into the fleshy underside of his upper arm and he let out a howl of pain, his arm crumpling to his side as he clutched at the wound with his other hand. I took advantage of his lapse to drive my knife home again, this time into the hand that held the stick, which fell to the ground with a dull thud as I turned to face his friend, who crouched, holding out his rusted knife towards me, though with less conviction now. Shouting curses in Italian, I lunged at him but feinted, so that, wrong-footed, he slipped in a rut and fell to the ground, still flailing at me with the knife. I kicked him hard in the stomach, then stood astride him as he lay, doubled over and groaning, my blade against his cheek.

'Drop your knife and get the hell back to where you came from,' I hissed, 'before I change my mind.' Without a word, he stumbled to his feet, slipping again in his haste, and scurried away into the trees as a chilling scream rent the air; I looked up to see one of the men Sidney was fighting fall slowly to his knees as the poet withdrew his sword from deep in the man's side. The remaining assailant looked for a moment with horror at his friend's body slumped in the mud and scrambled for the undergrowth as fast as he could. Sidney wiped the sword on the wet grass by the side of the road and sheathed it, his breath ragged.

'Is he dead?'

Sidney gave a dismissive glance over his shoulder.

'He'll live,' he said, pressing his lips together. 'Though he'll think twice before he tries that trick again. This road is notorious for outlaws, we should have been better prepared. You acquitted yourself well, Bruno,' he added, turning to me in admiration. 'Not bad for a man of God.'

'I'm not sure God counts me as such any longer. But I did not spend three years on the run through Italy without learning to defend myself.' I cleaned Paolo's knife on the wet grass, thanking my old friend silently for his foresight; it was not the first time this blade had kept me from danger.

Sidney nodded thoughtfully.

'Now that I remember – when we were in Padua, you mentioned you'd had some trouble over a fight in Rome.' He looked at me expectantly, a half-smile hovering on his lips.

I didn't answer immediately, turning the knife in my hands as the rain continued to course down my neck inside my collar. This was one of the darker moments in my fugitive past that I would prefer to bury. In England I wanted to be known as the eminent philosopher of the Parisian court, not the man who lived underground, pursued through Italy on suspicion of heresy and murder.

'In Rome, someone informed the Inquisition against me for money. But I had already fled the city when his body was found floating in the Tiber,' I said quietly.

Sidney gave a sly smile.

'And did you kill him?'

'The man was a notorious brawler, I understand. I am a philosopher, Philip, not an assassin,' I replied, sheathing the knife at my belt.

'You are not a typical philosopher, Bruno, that much is certain. Well, I will hear more of this story later. I suppose we had better find the Pole,' he said, suppressing a sigh.

The servant I had saved was still mounted, a little way ahead of us, holding with difficulty the reins of our two horses, who were stamping and snorting, their eyes rolling back in alarm; the other servant had taken a bad blow to the head as the robbers first sprang upon us, and he had to be helped back into his saddle, where he slumped forward and clung to the horse's neck, his eyes unfocused. Fortunately we had fought them off before they had been able to sever the straps binding the horses' panniers, but one hung precariously from its saddle and had to be retied before we could continue. We found the palatine cowering under a tree around the next bend; Sidney muttered an apology for the brutal interruption, though I could not help thinking that it was the Pole who should be apologising for his cowardice.

We rode on, bruised and bedraggled; though the cut on my thigh was only shallow, it stung as the wet cloth of my breeches chafed against it. I was more deeply shaken by the attack than I cared to let Sidney see; though it was true that my eventful past had taught me how to keep my wits in a fight, I had spent the past year in soft living at King Henri's court, and my reactions felt slow and unpractised. The water drove relentlessly down my neck and into my eyes, and even when we reached the brow of Shotover Hill, which Sidney said should have afforded us a magnificent view over the city of Oxford, the curtain of rain all but obscured it from sight.

We descended towards the bridge that crossed the river by the College of St Mary Magdalen and saw that a small crowd had gathered there; as we drew closer Sidney announced that this was the delegation of university dignitaries and aldermen waiting to greet us. A rider had gone out from Windsor that morning to notify those preparing for the palatine's visitation that we would not now be arriving by river, but so much of the road had become waterlogged that our progress had been slow, and it seemed the poor welcoming party had been waiting for us for some time in the rain, which now dripped from their velvet caps and the sleeves of their black and scarlet gowns.

The vice-chancellor stepped forward and introduced himself, bowing low and kissing first the palatine's bejewelled hand and then Sidney's; I saw his eyes widen at our bruised and dishevelled appearance, but he graciously made no mention of it. He explained that they would be guests at Christ Church College, the grandest of all the Oxford colleges and the one for which the queen herself had special charge; Sidney had himself been an undergraduate at Christ Church, so it was natural that he should return there. I was to be lodged separately, and here a round-faced, balding man stepped forward and extended his hand to me in the English fashion as he tried stoically to ignore the water streaming from the peak of his hat.

'Doctor Bruno – I am John Underhill, Rector of Lincoln College. You are most welcome to Oxford and I hope you will do us the honour of accepting our hospitality at the college.'

'Thank you, I am very grateful.'

'You and I are to be adversaries in the disputation tomorrow night and will face each other across the floor of the Divinity School, but I hope that, until then, we may regard one another as friends.' He smiled as he said this, but it died quickly on his lips.

So this was my Aristotelian opponent. He had a fussy air and there was something brittle about his expression of hospitality, but I was determined to make a good impression in Oxford, so I smiled broadly and shook his proffered hand.

'I certainly hope so too, Doctor Underhill.'

We entered the city through the East Gate, a small barbican in the high walls that encircled the main body of the town, and as we passed under its battlements so a concert of musicians struck up, their instruments sounding bravely through the noise of rain and wind. The palatine roused himself from his sulk just enough to wave unenthusiastically as our party progressed along the High Street past rows of little timber-framed houses, which gave way as we neared the centre to the ornate blond stone façades of one or other of the colleges. Outside these stood groups of students of all degrees, decked out in their formal dress and shivering as they huddled under the eaves to salute us as we passed, flanked by the doctors and aldermen. At length we came to a halt beside a narrow street that turned off to the north, where I was informed I would depart with the rector. After I had dismounted and handed the care of my horse to a young groom, to be taken to the rector's private stables, I walked across to Sidney, who reached down and clasped my hand.

'I shall see you tomorrow for your moment of glory, Bruno,' he said, smiling. 'Do not let anything throw you off the scent – but spare a charitable thought for me at dinner.' He nodded in the direction of the palatine, who was complaining loudly to one of the university officials about the advanced state of his saddle-sores. I would not be sorry to lose his company, though I was disappointed to be separated from Sidney. Tonight, however, I wished only to retire early and prepare myself for the public debate and knew I would not be best disposed for company; once the disputation was over and I had acquitted myself as best I could, I would be able to relax and enjoy the convivial atmosphere of the college hall, and turn my attention to my other missions.

The rector stood at the entrance to the narrow lane, his robe drenched, but smiling resolutely. I pulled up the collar of my cloak as we made our way along between buildings for a few yards, until the wall on our left rose up into a squat rectangular tower of that same buttery yellow stone. The rector pushed open a smaller wooden door the height of a man set into the heavy iron-studded timber of the high arched gateway and held it for me to pass through, followed by the servant who carried my bag.

'I'm afraid that here I must relieve you of your dagger, Doctor Bruno,' he said, apologetically, lowering his eyes to the sheath at my side. 'It is one of the first laws of Oxford that no man may carry weapons within the university precincts. We must have a care for our young men's persons as well as their minds and souls. Don't worry, we will keep it quite safe for you.' He gave a self-conscious laugh as I reluctantly unstrapped the knife and handed it over.

I stepped past him through an archway that led beneath the tower to a neat quadrangle paved with stone flags. The buttressed range immediately opposite the gatehouse tower I guessed to be the college's hall, by its high mullioned windows and the smoke louvre in the centre of the roof. Ivy grew along the stonework there, though not on the ranges to my right and left. At the corners of each range in the quadrangle an archway led to a narrow passage. The rector appeared beside me and took off his sodden hat, passing a hand across his shiny pate.

'Forgive my appearance, Doctor Bruno – this sudden regression to winter has taken us all by surprise, and just as we thought summer on its way. But that is what you must expect in England, I'm afraid. You must long for the blue skies of your native land.'

'At times, though I must say that I find the weather of northern Europe suited to my temperament,' I replied.

'Ah. You are of a melancholy humour, then?'

'Like all of us, Doctor Underhill, I am a mixture of contradictory elements. Equal parts earth and fire, melancholy and choler, I fear. But it is more that warmth and blue skies stir the blood, do you not think? I find it easier to write when I am not tempted to other pursuits.'

Underhill nodded doubtfully; he had the expression of a man whose blood had not been stirred in many years.

'You are right, it is hard to bend the students to study during the summer months. Now – I have arranged a room for you in the south range, where you will be adjacent to my own residence.' Here he waved a hand at the mullioned bay windows next to the hall. 'And directly opposite, across the quad, you will find our very fine library, which you must feel free to make use of at any time.'

'Have you many books?' I asked, shaking the water from my cloak.

'Some of the finest of any college,' he said, swelling with a pride I could forgive, since it was on behalf of his manuscripts. 'Largely works of scholastic theology, but the nephew of our founder, Dean Flemyng, left as a bequest to the college a remarkable collection of literary and classical texts, many of which he copied in his own hand. He studied in Italy, you know, and brought many manuscripts back from the corners of Europe at the end of the last century,' he added.

'Really? I should very much like to see your collection,' I

said, my pulse quickening. 'Do you know if Dean Flemyng visited Florence at all during his travels? Around the 1460s?'

The rector gave a little swagger with his shoulders. 'He certainly did – a number of books in our collection bear the inscription of the great Florentine bookseller Vespasiano da Basticci, dealer to Cosimo de' Medici, as I'm sure you know. Does this period particularly interest you?'

I took a deep breath, trying to keep my face neutral, and clasped my hands together so that their trembling would not betray my excitement.

'You know, every Italian scholar must be fascinated by Cosimo's library – at that time he had envoys travelling through all Europe and the Byzantine empire in search of undiscovered texts to augment his collection. I knew a descendant of Vespasiano once, in Paris,' I added lightly. 'I should be extremely interested to see which of these rare treasures Dean Flemyng brought back to Oxford with him, if I may.'

Was it my imagination, or did the rector look slightly uncomfortable?

'Well, you must ask Master Godwyn, our librarian, to show you the collection – he will be delighted to share his knowledge, I'm sure. But for now you must be longing to change your clothes and take supper. And if you want to have a shave first –' here he cast a critical eye over my hair and beard – 'we have a barber in the college. The porter will let you know where to find him. Usually the senior Fellows and I dine in hall with the undergraduates, but it is a noisy affair and for your first evening in Oxford I thought you might prefer something more sedate. Therefore I would like to invite you to join my family and a few select guests to dine in my own lodgings, which you see there next to the hall, abutting the south range.'

'Your family?' I said, surprised. 'You are not a bachelor, then?'

'We are no longer a community of clerics here in Oxford, Doctor Bruno,' he said with a modest laugh. 'Priests of the Church of England may marry – in fact, Her Majesty positively encourages them to do so, to further distinguish themselves from those of the Roman faith – and likewise for the heads of colleges here, though I admit we are still very much in the minority. I suspect it is not a life to tempt many wives – university society is somewhat limited for ladies – but my dear Margaret is a rare woman and professes to have been happy enough here these past six years, excepting . . .' Here he broke off and it was as if a cloud passed over his face, before he resumed, in a lighter tone. 'She does not dine with us in hall, according to the regulations, so she is always delighted to be able to entertain guests in our own rooms. I shall go now and tell her you are arrived, and call a servant to show you to your room. Perhaps in an hour you would like to make your way over – just go through that right-hand archway beside the hall and you will see a wooden door off the passage.'

We had no sooner moved out from the shelter of the gatehouse arch to venture through the rain across the quadrangle than we were interrupted by an urgent cry.

'Rector! Rector Underhill – wait, I pray you!'

From the north side of the quadrangle a figure was running towards us, a tattered black scholar's gown fluttering behind him, with a paper in his hand which he brandished as if there were some imminent emergency. I noticed the rector's face set tight for a moment in annoyance. The young man slid to a halt in front of us on the wet flagstones and I saw that he was perhaps twenty years of age, and very shabbily dressed, his shirt and breeches patched and his shoes thin and worn through at the toe. He looked from me to the rector with an expression of great anxiety and said, breathlessly,

'Rector Underhill, is this your esteemed visitor from the court? I beg you, give me leave to speak to him.'

'Thomas,' the rector looked supremely irritated, 'this is neither the time nor the place. Kindly show some decorum before our guest.'

To my surprise, the boy then turned to me, dropped to his knees there on the wet ground and clutched the hem of my cloak in one hand, pressing his scrap of paper into my hand with the other.

'My lord, I beseech you, take pity on one whom God has forgotten. Give this letter to your uncle, I beg of you, and ask him to pardon my poor father and let him return, please, my lord, if you have any Christian compassion, grant me this favour and take his suit to the earl, tell him Edmund Allen repents of his sins.'

There was a wildness in his eyes, and his evident distress moved me. Guessing his misunderstanding. I laid a hand gently on his head.

'Son, I would gladly help, but my uncle was a stonemason in Naples, I cannot imagine he would be much use to you. Come.' I took his hand and helped him to his feet.

'But . . .' He started at my accent, then his face reddened violently and he looked at me in an anguish of confusion as he realised his mistake. 'Oh. I beg your pardon, my lord. You are not Sir Philip Sidney?'

'Alas, no,' I said, 'though I am flattered you should mistake us – he is a good half-foot taller than I, and six years younger. But I will see him tomorrow, most likely – is there some message I might convey to him?'

'Thank you, Doctor Bruno, that is kind but it won't be necessary, this is no more than an impertinent intrusion,' the rector cut in brusquely. Then he turned to the boy with barely suppressed anger. 'Thomas Allen, have some care for your manners. I will not have you assaulting guests of the college. Must you be disciplined again? Do not forget how fragile is your position here. Back to your studies, Master Allen – or else I'm sure you must have some servant's duties to attend to. You will not trouble Doctor Bruno again during his stay, do you understand my meaning?'

The boy nodded miserably, lifting his eyes briefly to see if I was in agreement with the rector's harsh words. I tried to convey my sympathy in my face.

'And look to your dress, boy,' the rector called after him as he sloped away, defeated. 'You shame the college looking like a beggar as you do.'

The boy turned then, mustered what little scrap of dignity remained to him and said, with his head high,

'I cannot afford new clothes, Rector Underhill, and you well know why, so do not ask me to apologise for what is no fault of my own.' Then he disappeared into one of the staircases on the west range.

The rector stood looking after him for a moment, perhaps shamed by his own severity.

'That poor boy,' he said eventually, shaking his head.

'Why poor?' I asked, curious. 'Who is he?'

'Let us step inside your staircase here, it will not do for you to have another soaking,' he said, motioning to the furthest archway on the south range. We ducked into its shadows out of the rain. 'It is a sad story, that boy has suffered much for one so young. I am sorry you were troubled by him.'

I shook my head; I was intrigued by the boy's words.

'His name is Thomas Allen. His father, Doctor Edmund Allen, was a Doctor of Divinity here in Oxford and my sub-rector in the college last year.'

'Are all the Fellows permitted to live with their families?' I asked in surprise.

'Not at all, only the heads of colleges. Edmund had moved away and taken a living at one of the London churches when he married. He only returned to Oxford after his wife died and Thomas, being then too young to matriculate, lodged with a family in the town.' He shook his head again in a show of pious sorrow. 'Edmund Allen was a good man – appointed by the Earl of Leicester himself, you know, as was I.'

'The senior positions are not appointed through election by the Fellows?' I asked, affecting innocence.

'In normal circumstances, yes,' he replied, looking embarrassed. 'But there were many entrenched papists remaining in high office here – some of them appointed by Queen Mary herself and still unrepentant – so to weed them out, the earl began placing his own men to ensure loyalty to the English church, until such time as the canker of popery could be cut out altogether. I was his personal chaplain prior to my position here.' He smiled, and couldn't resist a little strut of pride.

'And this was a popular choice among the senior university men?'

'No, since you ask. But we must all rely on patronage, one way or another,' he replied, somewhat ruffled. 'Edmund Allen was also appointed by the earl at my recommendation – we had been undergraduates together here. So you may imagine our distress when it was discovered last year that he too was secretly practising the old religion – and not so secretly, neither, for he was discovered in possession of forbidden books and had for some time been corresponding with the Catholic seminaries in France.'

'Is this a crime?'

'If he could have been proven to have known about or aided the secret arrival of missionary priests from France, he would have been for the scaffold. But there was no evidence against him on that count, only hearsay, and no confession could be got from him under questioning.'

'Was he punished?'

'His questioning was hard, but his punishment light, in

61

the circumstances,' said the rector, pursing his lips. 'The earl was outraged, as you may suppose – Allen was deprived of his fellowship immediately, but the earl is merciful and he was offered safe passage to leave the country, not to return on pain of imprisonment. He went to France and took up residence at the English College in Rheims.'

'Rheims? I have heard of it. That was founded by a William Allen, was it not?'

'A cousin, yes. They are one of the old Catholic families. But Edmund Allen's son Thomas, whom you had the misfortune to encounter just now, was then in his first year as an undergraduate here. He did not follow his father into exile – Thomas wished to complete his studies, but there were many in the college who felt he should be expelled simply by connection with his father's disgrace.'

'It would seem harsh to punish a son for his father's beliefs. Does he share them?'

'One never knows. All students must swear the Oath of Supremacy acknowledging Her Majesty as the head of all religious authority in the realm, but you know as well as I that a man may sign a paper with his hand and hold something different in his heart. Thomas Allen was questioned hard about his doctrines, you may be sure.' The rector nodded significantly.

'He was tortured?' I said, appalled.

The rector stared at me in horror.

'Good God, no – do you think us barbarians, Doctor Bruno? It was merely questioning – though the manner of it was not pleasant, I will admit. He was pressed on points of theology even a Doctor of Divinity would find hard to answer, and every aspect of his responses held up to scrutiny. But his father's expulsion had been so public that the college authorities had to be seen to be utterly scrupulous with the son – we could not be accused of turning a blind eye to a known papist in our midst.'

'He passed the test, I gather, by his continued presence here?'

'Eventually it was decided that he could stay on, but at his own expense – his scholarship was withdrawn.'

'Did the family have means?'

The rector shook his head.

'Almost nothing after Edmund had paid his fines for religious disobedience. Young Thomas has done what many poor scholars in the university must do – he pays his board by acting as a servant to one of the wealthy commoners – sons of gentry and nobles who pay to study here.' The scornful curl of his lip expressed his opinion of these commoners.

'So one moment this Thomas is a scholarship student, the son of the sub-rector, the next he is living on crumbs, a servant to one of his friends? A hard reversal of fortunes for any man, especially one so young,' I said, with feeling.

'Such is the way of the world,' the rector said pompously. 'But it is sad, he is a bright boy and always had a cheerful disposition. He might have done well in the world. Now he is as you saw him. He writes endless petitions to Leicester to pardon his father – I find them pushed through the door of my lodgings and my private office. I have told him I've done all I can with regard to the earl, but he only grows more determined. It has become an obsession with him and I almost fear he may lose his wits over it. And I do pity him, Doctor Bruno – you must not think me stony-hearted. There was even a time I considered he might be a suitable match for my own daughter – his father wanted him to go into the law and his prospects seemed fair. Our families had been friends, and Thomas was certainly much taken with Sophia.'

I wondered if having a daughter of marriageable age in this cloister of young men might account for the slightly harried expression that permanently troubled the rector's face.

'Was your daughter interested?'

The rector's nose wrinkled.

'Oh, she has ever been troublesome on the question of marriage. Girls have foolish notions of love – I should not have allowed her to read poetry so freely.'

'She is educated, then?'

He nodded absently, as if his mind were elsewhere.

'Both my children were close in age – barely more than a year between them – and I thought it unfair that my son should have lessons and my daughter be left only to sew. Besides, young John always had trouble keeping his mind on his books, I thought it would do him good to have to compete with his sister, for she was always the sharper of the two and he hated being bested by her. In that I was correct. But now it seems I have spoiled her for marriage – she loves nothing more than to dally in the library arguing ideas back and forth with the students when she has the chance, and is much too bold with her own opinions, which is hardly seemly in a lady and no gentleman wants in a wife. So it was all for naught.'

He turned his face away then and, with a great sigh, looked out towards some point across the courtyard.

'Why for naught? Did your son not stick to his studies?'

His face convulsed, as if with a sudden bodily pain, and with some effort he answered,

'My poor John died some four years past, God rest him – thrown from a horse. He would have been turning twenty-one this summer, he was of an age with Thomas Allen.'

'I am sorry for your loss.'

'As for Sophia,' he continued briskly, 'she was fond of Thomas and thought of him as a friend, but now I have not thought it proper that they should associate, given the reputation of his family. His prospects are much diminished, of course.'

'Yet another loss for the boy, hard on the heels of so many others.'

64

'Yes, it is a shame,' the rector said, without much sympathy. 'But come, we must not stand here gossiping like goodwives – the servant will show you to your room, where I trust a good fire will be blazing for you to dry your clothes. By Jesus, that wind has grown cold, it is more like November than May. I shall look forward to seeing you at supper.'

He shook my hand and I turned to follow the servant up the dim wooden stairway to my room.

'Doctor Bruno,' the rector called, as I was almost out of sight. I leaned back to see his face looking anxiously up at me. 'Please, out of charity, I ask that you do not make any mention of Thomas Allen or what I have told you of my poor John at supper – my wife and daughter find both subjects quite distressing.'

'You must not worry on that count,' I replied, intrigued by the idea that in a short time I would meet this boldly opinionated daughter. The prospect of an intelligent young woman's company made the idea of supper with the rector considerably more enticing than it had seemed before.

# THREE

I dressed for dinner in a clean shirt with a plain black doublet and breeches and paused for a moment to consider myself in the mottled glass that had been left resting on my mantelpiece. My hair and beard were a little too long, it was true, and the weather had left them more unruly than usual, though I had long ago decided at the Parisian court that I had neither the time nor the vanity to compete with gentlemen of fashion in matters of dress. But at thirty-five, I thought, I could still make myself presentable. My reflection looked back from large dark eyes pooled in shadow; our scuffle on the road had left a graze on my cheek, but perhaps a young woman confined in a college cloister might find that intriguing. I knew that women found enough in my appearance to please them, even though I was no prospect for a serious attachment, having neither property nor title but only a dubious kind of fame to my name; for my part, I had made the most of such opportunities as came my way in Paris, but since Morgana's death I had met no woman with equal wit and spirit to catch my heart as well as my eye. But the rector's daughter sounded intriguing, and I must confess that the prospect of meeting her had piqued my interest, even though

I knew I could hardly afford distractions in Oxford with so much at stake and so few days.

I grinned at my reflection in the glass, ran my hands through my hair and shook my head briefly at my own foolishness, before making my way down my staircase to the archway in the east range where I had been told I would find the rector's lodgings. As I entered its shadows, my eye was caught by a glimpse of green from the other end of the passageway, which ran the width of the building; following it to the end I emerged through an open gate of iron bars into a walled garden at the back of the college, not over-cultivated but left as an orchard, the grass grown tall and thick with wild flowers under apple trees and wooden benches set at intervals along the path that ran around by the walls. In better weather this would be a pleasant place for scholars to sit and read, I thought, though it was empty now as the rain battered at the leaves. I returned to the passageway and found the door that proclaimed the rector's name on a plaque, straightened my clothes, and prepared myself for my first taste of Oxford hospitality.

The first thing I noticed as I waited to be admitted was that the animated conversation I could hear from behind the door was pitched slightly too loud, in the way that men in a group will compete to outdo one another if they want to impress a woman. An old servant with a pinched face opened the door and showed me straight through into a fine high room with tall arched windows in two facing walls, the rest panelled in dark wood and hung with portraits and tapestries. Immediately I understood the source of this braggadocio. At the far side of a long table set with grand sconces of candles sat a young woman of about nineteen years, dressed in a plain dove-grey gown with a straight embroidered bodice and with her long dark hair unbound. Like the rest of the guests already seated, she stopped her conversation and turned her attention to me as I approached, her eyes skimming me up and down with a mixture of curiosity and amusement. This, then, was Sophia Underhill, and I understood her father's urgent wish to marry her off; she had a striking, feline face with keen light brown eyes and her presence in the college must have proved a sore distraction for the young men trying to bend their minds to their books. The rector rose from his chair at the head of the table with bustling importance and reached out to shake my hand.

'Welcome, Doctor Bruno, welcome to my table. Please be seated, and I shall introduce you to some of the college's senior Fellows, and my family.'

He gestured to the seat on his left hand, which I was pleased to note was almost opposite his daughter's. I nodded politely to her in greeting before glancing around at the rest of the guests assembled at the table. We were ten in number, all men dressed in academic gowns, with the exception of the girl and a tired-looking woman of middle years seated at the other end of the table, opposite the rector.

'Allow me to introduce my wife, Mistress Margaret Underhill,' he began, gesturing towards her.

'*Piacere di conoscerla*,' I said, bowing my head. The woman smiled weakly; despite her husband's earlier words, she did not look especially delighted at the prospect of entertaining.

'And my daughter Sophia,' the rector continued, unable to keep the note of pride from his voice. 'You see that I gave her the Greek name for wisdom.'

'Then her suitors may truly call themselves "philosophers",' I replied, smiling at her. 'Lovers of Sophia.'

There was a sharp intake of breath from her mother at the end of the table and a suppressed laugh from the men present, but the girl returned my smile and blushed pleasingly before lowering her eyes. The rector forced a smile.

'Ah, yes, I was warned that the men of your country are experts in the art of flattering ladies,' he said tightly.

68

'Especially the monks,' grunted the elderly man seated to the right of Sophia, and the guests all laughed.

'*Former* monks,' I said emphatically, holding the girl's gaze. This time she did not look away, and something in the frankness of her look reminded me so sharply of Morgana that I had to catch my breath, caught off-guard by the resemblance.

'I must protest in defence of my countrymen,' declared the dark-haired young man seated to my immediate left, who did indeed look distinctly Italian, though he spoke with no trace of an accent. 'My father's countrymen, I should say. I do not know how we have come by this reputation among the English as great seducers – I have certainly not inherited any such talent, alas.' He held out his palms in a gesture of defeat and the company laughed again. I suspected the young man of false modesty in this regard – he was blessed with handsome features and obviously dressed carefully, his beard and moustache neatly trimmed. He turned to me and extended a hand. 'John Florio, son of Michelangelo Florio of Tuscany – I am pleased to make your acquaintance, Doctor Bruno of Nola. Your reputation precedes you.'

'Which one?' I said, to more laughter.

'Master Florio is a greatly respected scholar and tutor of languages, as was his father,' said the rector, 'and he is engaged in compiling a book of proverbs from various countries. I am sure that later he will not hesitate to regale us with some.'

'It is, and ever was, a woman's fashion / To love a cross, and cross a loving passion,' Florio said obligingly.

'He speaks the truth,' Sophia said, with feigned dismay, and Florio beamed at her.

'Thank you,' said the rector, his smile growing increasingly strained. 'I must confess, Doctor Bruno, I did not know how easily you would converse in English and I thought you might feel more at home with a fellow Italian speaker to hand.'

'That was kind of you,' I said. 'I learned my English from travellers and scholars over the years, but I fear it is unpolished.'

'My father also fled Italy in fear of the Inquisition after he converted to Reform,' Florio said eagerly, leaning in close. 'He came to London, ended up in Lord Burghley's household and was later Italian tutor to Lady Jane Grey and the Princess Elizabeth.'

'Not such a cursed exile, then,' I said.

'Exile is always a curse,' the elderly man next to Sophia cut in, with surprising vehemence. 'A cruel fate to inflict on any man, do you not agree, Roger?' Here he leaned around to glare at the man seated on the other side of Sophia, directly opposite me, a large, broad-featured man in his late forties, with a full beard just turning to grey and a ruddy complexion, who turned away uncomfortably. 'Particularly on one's friends,' the old man added. A tense silence descended over the gathering.

'My father was indeed fortunate in his patrons,' Florio continued hastily, attempting to cover the interruption, 'though we were exiled again from England when I was just an infant and Bloody Mary came to the throne.'

'God rest her soul,' interjected the elderly man, reverently. This time the rector moved to intervene.

'*Please*, Doctor Bernard.'

'Please what, Rector?' Doctor Bernard gestured at me, his wild white hair fanning out around his head like the crest of a bird. 'Must I guard my words for this renegade monk? Why – will he denounce me to the Earl of Leicester?' He turned to look at me and I understood that, though he had few teeth left and must have been at least seventy, his rheumy eyes still saw shrewdly. The hollows of his face seemed more pronounced in the flickering shadows of the candlelight; it was a face to frighten children. 'I was appointed by Queen

Mary herself, thirty years ago now, when those of the new faith were almost purged altogether from the university, and here I have remained through the storms, though my friends are all long dead or deprived of office, and I have long since renounced the old ways.' Here he laughed, as if in self-mockery, then pointed at me, suddenly grave. 'But I think you are of the Catholic faith, are you not, Doctor Bruno?'

'I am an Italian,' I replied evenly, 'raised in the church of Rome.'

'Well, I'm afraid you will find no one to say the Roman Mass with you here, sir. There are no Catholics left in Oxford, oh no. No man here cleaves to the old faith.' He shook his head solemnly, but his voice was filled with bitter sarcasm. 'Here we all sign the Declaration of Belief to save our skins, and swear our oath to the English Church as we are commanded, for we are all obedient subjects, are we not, gentlemen?'

There was an awkward murmur of assent; I saw that the rector was growing agitated.

'William, I beg you.'

'So we all seem. But no man in Oxford is what he seems, Doctor Bruno, keep that in mind. Not even you, I suspect.'

I looked up and met Doctor William Bernard's eye. This spiky and gnomic old man gave the distinct and alarming impression of being able to read the secret thoughts of others, and he was nearer to the truth than I liked, so I merely inclined my head and searched for a distraction as his pale grey eyes continued to bore into me. Fortunately, one was provided by the arrival of servants bearing plates laden with the first course: boiled capons with damsons and calves'-foot jelly accompanied by a good claret.

As they bustled around the table, heaping our plates from each dish, I leaned forward with the intention of engaging Sophia Underhill in conversation, but at the same moment the bearded man opposite addressed me, and I saw Florio take the opportunity to claim the girl's attention.

'Roger Mercer, Doctor of Divinity and sub-rector of the college,' the bearded man said in a rich baritone, with an accent that I believed came from the west parts of England. He extended a hand across the table. 'We are indeed glad to make your acquaintance, Doctor Bruno, and there has been much anticipation here for your disputation with the rector tomorrow night.'

'Now, now, Roger,' said the rector hastily, 'there is to be no talk of any matter touching the disputation at table. My esteemed guest and I must preserve our arguments for the debating chamber, is that not so, Doctor Bruno? We must, as they say, keep our powder dry.'

I nodded my assent. Roger Mercer held up his hand in protest.

'Fear not, Rector – I spoke only as a prelude to telling Doctor Bruno how I have been curious to meet him since I read his book, *On the Shadows of Ideas*, that was published in Paris last year.'

'Did not the sorcerer Cecco d'Ascoli, who was burned for necromancy, make mention of a book with the same title, a book of forbidden magic which he attributed to Solomon?' Doctor Bernard leaned around Sophia once more to make this interjection, his trembling extended finger pointing almost in her face, though aimed at me. She moved her chair backwards to accommodate him, flicking her hair over one shoulder while continuing her conversation with the irrepressibly enthusiastic Florio. From the odd phrase I could catch, he appeared to be treating her to further rhyming aphorisms. Reluctantly I turned my attention back to Bernard.

'The book Cecco mentions has never been found,' I said, raising my voice so that the old man might hear me clearly. 'It seemed a shame to waste a good title, so I borrowed it.

72

But mine is a treatise on the art of memory, based on the memory systems of the Greeks – no necromancy, gentlemen.' I laughed, perhaps too hard.

Roger Mercer eyed me thoughtfully.

'And yet, Doctor Bruno, your memory system makes use of images that seem to correspond precisely to the talismanic figures described by Agrippa in his *De Occulta Philosophia*, that he claims can be invoked in the rituals of celestial magic to draw down the powers of angels and demons.'

'But these are images that correspond to the signs of the zodiac and the mansions of the moon, familiar to many mnemonic systems,' I said, hoping not to betray my unease. 'They are popular because they are based on regular numerical divisions, which aids in recall, but in the end they are merely images.'

'Nothing is *merely* an image to the magician,' Bernard snapped back. 'All are signs pointing to hidden realities, as your title implies. Especially those images derived from the ancient astrology of the Egyptians – as Agrippa well knew, for he was quoting from his master, Hermes Trismegistus, who was condemned by St Augustine for summoning demons!'

His voice rose on this last word; a cold hand gripped the base of my spine. I drew myself up to answer, but before I could speak, Sophia Underhill pulled her chair nearer to the table, looked directly at me and asked, cutting off Florio in mid-sentence,

'Who is Hermes Trismegistus?'

The company fell silent; all eyes turned to me.

'I have read passing reference to his name in works of philosophy,' she continued, with an innocence I did not quite believe, 'but I can find none of his books in our library here, and I don't have permission to enter the university libraries.'

'Nor should you, since you are not a scholar,' chided her

73

father, looking around the table as if embarrassed by her boldness. 'I permit you to improve your mind by reading in our library as long as you keep your studies to what is fit for a lady's understanding.'

I felt he said this for the benefit of the company; Sophia appeared about to protest, but then swallowed her words into a petulant expression. Her mother tutted again, loudly.

'You will find no works of Hermes the Thrice-Great in Oxford now,' Bernard said in a sonorous voice, shaking his head. 'Before, we had them – before the great purge of the libraries in '69. Translated out of the Greek by the Florentine Ficino a century ago, at the dying request of Cosimo de' Medici. You know Ficino's version, Doctor Bruno?'

'I have read Ficino's translation,' I said. 'But I have also read the original Greek manuscripts, though the collection is incomplete. The fifteenth book was lost. Do you read Greek, Doctor Bernard?'

Bernard fixed me with those bright, accusing eyes.

'Yes, I read Greek, young man, we are not all barbarians north of the Tiber. But the missing book is a myth – it never existed,' he added briskly. Then he went on, in a softer tone, 'I read Ficino too, when I was young, and Agrippa. There was not such a fear of the ancient writers then. But so many books are lost to us now, carried off by the tides of reform. Centuries of learning, burned to ashes.' He tailed off and it seemed he had travelled deep into memory.

'Doctor Bernard,' said the rector, a warning note in his voice again, 'you know very well that the Royal Commission of '69 was sent to seek out heretical books acquired in the old monastic times, lest they infect the minds of our young men with their unholy ideas – a danger we senior Fellows must guard against still. I am sure you would not wish to disagree with such a prohibition.'

Bernard gave a short, croaking laugh. 'Books prohibited

to scholars? How then should men of learning sharpen their intellect, or learn to discern between truth and heresy? And do those who proscribe not have the wit to realise that forbidden books lure men more potently than the lewdest temptress?' Here he cast a sideways glance at Sophia. 'Oh yes – but a forbidden book will always find its way in through the cracks and the mouseholes, do you not know that, Rector? If one only knows where to look.' He cackled to himself as if this were a great joke, and I noticed his fellow scholars were shifting uncomfortably in their seats.

'What happened to the books that were purged from the libraries then?' I asked, perhaps too urgently, for my question seemed to provoke a sudden hostility from Bernard; his eyes narrowed and he pulled himself stiffly upright.

'It was a long time ago,' he said brusquely. 'Burned or taken away by the authorities – who knows? I am old now, and I have forgotten those days.'

He did not quite meet my gaze and I knew he was lying; a man who spoke so passionately about books one moment would surely have remembered a public bonfire of them, even if it had occurred many years ago. But if the forbidden books were not burned, they must have passed into someone's hands, and I wondered if the old man knew whose.

'Doctor Bruno, you have still not answered my question,' Sophia cut in, leaning across to tap my hand while fixing me with her wide-set, tawny eyes. The hint of a smile played around her full mouth, as if she too knew a great joke and was considering letting us in on it. 'Who *was* he?'

I took a deep breath, and returned her expectant gaze as steadily as I could, aware that the whole table had fallen silent, awaiting my answer, and that there was every chance my next words might be considered blasphemy.

'Hermes Trismegistus, called the Thrice-Great, was an Egyptian high priest of great antiquity,' I began, turning over

75

a piece of bread in my fingers. 'He lived after the time of Moses, long before Plato or Christ. Some say he was the Egyptian god Thoth, the divinity of wisdom. In any case, he was a man of unusual insight who achieved, through profound contemplation of the cosmos and experimentation with the properties of the natural world, the wisdom to unlock the secrets written in the book of nature and the heavens. He claimed to have entered and understood the Divine Mind.' I paused. 'He claimed he could become equal to God.'

Here there was a collective gasp from around the table; these men knew that this was indeed dangerous ground to tread, and I quickly added,

'He is called the first philosopher, the first theologian, and he was also a prophet – Lactantius credited him with foretelling the advent of the Christian faith, in the very words of the gospel.'

'And Augustine said he had his foreknowledge from the Devil,' Roger Mercer said eagerly, his face reddening further as half-chewed meat fell from his mouth and lodged in his beard, though he appeared not to notice. 'For does Hermes not write of how the Egyptians animated the idols of their gods in magical rites by calling down the powers of demons?'

'I have never believed the account of the demons and the statues,' I said lightly. 'Men have always created mechanical toys and automatons and claimed to have endowed them with the gift of life, like the brazen head possessed by Roger Bacon that was reported to prophesy. But this is merely conjuring and skilled craftsmanship.'

'Hermes Trismegistus was no magician, then?' Sophia said softly, still looking at me. She seemed disappointed.

'He wrote at length on the hidden properties of plants and stones and the arrangement of the cosmos,' I replied. 'There are some who call this alchemy or natural magic, and others who call it scientific enquiry.'

'When it is done for the purpose of seeking forbidden powers, it is called sorcery,' the rector put in, sternly.

'But did he discover any magic that worked?' she persisted, ignoring her father.

'How do you mean, *worked*?' I asked.

'I mean, was he able to use this natural magic to influence the world – to change people's thoughts or deeds, for example, and did he write of how it is done?' Her eyes were bright and impatient now as she leaned closer.

'Recipes for spells, you mean?' I laughed. 'I'm afraid not. The Hermetic magic, if you want to give it that name, is concerned with teaching the adept how to penetrate the mysteries of the universe through the light of the intellect. He cannot teach you how to make your sweetheart fall in love with you or keep him true – for that you had better consult some village wise-woman.'

There was some amusement at this from those at our end of the table, but the girl coloured violently and I suspected that my joke had accidentally struck the truth, so to cover her embarrassment I continued, hastily:

'But the German alchemist Henry Cornelius Agrippa does speak of such things, in his treatise on the occult sciences that Doctor Mercer mentioned earlier. He writes that, as well as the celestial images used in magic, we may create our own fitting to our purpose. For example, he says that to procure love, we may create an image of people embracing.'

'But how –' Sophia began, just as the rector coughed loudly and the servants entered to clear away the first course.

'Well, this has been a most illuminating discussion, Doctor Bruno – I knew your conversation and your unusual ideas would enliven our little college society,' the rector said, patting me on the shoulder with considerable insincerity. 'But I have devised that we should all change places for each course, so that you may become acquainted with some of the other important officials of the college. Much as I would like to continue with our theme . . .' he added.

Now he rose from his seat and fussed around the table, officiously rearranging the seating plan so that I found myself at the opposite end, surrounded by the three men to whom I had not yet spoken. The servants brought in silver dishes steaming with richly scented beef and a stew of vegetables, and in the course of all this activity, the rector's wife, who had barely spoken, took the opportunity to excuse herself with a headache, apologising profusely to me for being such a poor hostess. She seemed a melancholic and sickly woman, but I recalled what the rector had told me about their son; I had seen such symptoms previously in women who had lost a child, often years after the death, as if the mind itself had taken some wasting sickness from which it could not recover, and I felt profoundly sorry for her. It was hard to credit that such a forlorn creature could have been the author of the lively girl at the other end of the table.

The second half of the meal passed with considerably less interest than the first, now that I had been removed from Sophia's company. My new dining companions introduced themselves: opposite me sat Master Walter Slythurst, the college bursar, a bony, thin-lipped man of my own age with narrow, suspicious eyes and lank hair that fell in curtains around his face. Beside him was Doctor James Coverdale, a plump man of about forty with a great sweep of dark hair, a close-cropped beard and an air of complacency, who explained that he was the proctor, the official responsible for the students' discipline. To my right was Master Richard Godwyn, the librarian, who appeared older, perhaps fifty, and whose large, drooping features reminded me of a blood-hound, as though his skin were too big for his face, though his gloomy countenance was transformed when he allowed a brief smile to illuminate it as he shook my hand. All were courteous enough, but I could not help but wish I had been allowed to continue my discussion with Sophia. It was clear that the tenor of our conversation had angered her father; she was now seated next to him, on the same side of the table as me, so that I could not see her without rudely leaning around my neighbour Godwyn and drawing attention to myself.

'I fear you have had to suffer the sharp end of William Bernard's tongue up there, Doctor Bruno,' said James Coverdale, leaning across the table.

'He seems disappointed with the world as he finds it,' I observed, checking to see that Bernard had been moved far enough away to be out of earshot.

'It is often the way with old men,' Godwyn said, with a sombre nod. 'He has weathered a great many changes in his seventy winters, it cannot be easy.'

'If he continues to speak his mind as plainly among the undergraduates as he does among his fellows, he will soon go the way of his friend,' said Slythurst, in a clipped tone that suggested he would not be displeased at such an outcome. I do not like to judge men on appearance and so little acquaintance, but there was something about the bursar that did not invite respect. He had been staring at me intently from the moment I sat down, and I sensed that the look was not friendly.

'His friend?' I asked.

Coverdale sighed.

'It is a sorry business, Doctor Bruno, and a source of shame to the college – the former sub-rector, Doctor Allen, was deprived of office last year after he was discovered to have . . .' he hesitated, looking for a diplomatic expression '. . . perjured himself in swearing the Oath of Supremacy. It seemed he was still a devout communicant of the Roman Church.'

'Really? How was he discovered?'

79

'Denounced by an anonymous source,' Coverdale said, as if relishing the intrigue. 'But when his room was searched, he was found in possession of a quantity of banned papist literature. And of course the sub-rector holds the second highest office in the college, and is in charge whenever the rector is absent, so you may imagine the scandal. A number of us here had to testify against him in the Chancellor's Court.'

'The university holds its own legal sessions to enforce discipline,' explained Godwyn the librarian in a lugubrious tone. 'Though in a matter of such import the Privy Council also took an active interest. The Earl of Leicester – our chancellor, you know – has repeatedly charged the heads of colleges to rid themselves of all suspicion of popery so the rector had to be seen to strike swift and hard against Allen.'

'Doctor Underhill was formerly the Earl of Leicester's own chaplain, as he has no doubt boasted to you already,' added Slythurst. 'He could not have pardoned Allen and kept his own position.'

'Yet Allen hoped for a pardon,' Coverdale interjected. 'And for better loyalty from his friends. In that he was badly disappointed.'

'I think the rector did his duty with a heavy heart, James,' Godwyn said, with a meaningful look at Coverdale. 'Indeed it grieved all of us to have to bear public witness to his errors.'

'Roger Mercer gave his testimony quickly enough,' said Coverdale, glancing with barely concealed anger down the table to where Mercer was laughing merrily with Florio. I saw Slythurst roll his eyes, as if he had heard this grievance many times before. 'And he was supposed to be Allen's closest friend. Still, he got his thirty pieces of silver, did he not?'

'Silver?' I asked.

'His testimony was crucial to condemning Allen, and for

that he was given Allen's position when he was deprived,' Coverdale said bitterly.

'Perhaps I should clarify for Doctor Bruno that, traditionally, it is the proctor who succeeds as sub-rector, just as the sub-rector goes on to become rector,' Godwyn explained. 'This is the way it has always been done – there is a congregation of the Fellows, of course, but the vote is really a formal seal of approval on the established succession.'

'But since the present rector was placed here by the Earl of Leicester, to do his bidding,' Coverdale hissed, hunching down in his seat so that he would not be heard, 'he shows scant regard for tradition and appoints those he finds most pliable. And we all know why Leicester forced through Underhill's election,' he added significantly.

'James,' said Slythurst, a warning in his voice.

'I understood it was to enforce propriety in religion,' I said. 'Cut out the canker of popery.'

'Oh, that is the official reason.' Coverdale waved a dismissive hand. 'But the college owns substantial manors and parcels of profitable farmland in Oxfordshire, you understand – many of which are now leased at a most advantageous rate to friends of Leicester, are they not, Master Bursar?'

'You forget yourself, James,' Slythurst said smoothly. 'Doctor Bruno here is a friend of the Earl of Leicester.'

'Indeed, I have never met him,' I said hastily. 'I merely travel with his nephew.'

'In any case,' Coverdale continued, warming to his theme, 'the college loses valuable profit and must struggle to make ends meet by admitting legions of these so-called gentlemen commoners – paying students who have neither the inclination nor the talent to be scholars and gad about the town wenching and gambling and bringing the university into disrepute.'

'This is not an appropriate subject for the supper table,'

81

said Slythurst, in a voice thick with cold anger, bringing down his palm flat against the board just firmly enough to signal his displeasure. 'There is nothing improper about those leases, moreover the disbursal of college funds can be of no interest to our guest. A little discretion, if you please, gentlemen.'

The Fellows looked down, embarrassed; an uncomfortable silence loomed.

'Doctor Coverdale,' I said, turning to the proctor with a diplomatic smile, 'you were telling me about the trial of Edmund Allen – please do go on.'

Coverdale exchanged a look with Slythurst that I could not read, then folded his hands together.

'I was saying only that Mercer's testimony against Allen carried great weight in the trial, not least because he was Allen's closest confidant. The rector needed Mercer's co-operation, and in return he was given Allen's position.'

'Which should have been yours,' I prompted.

Coverdale placed a plump hand on his breast and assumed a face of unconvincing modesty.

'It is not for my own merits that I say an injustice has been done, Doctor Bruno,' he said, 'but for the violation to tradition. This university is founded on tradition, and if individuals feel that they are not obliged to respect it because their personal patronage carries more weight, the fabric of our community will crumble.'

'Edmund was friend to many of us,' Godwyn said, with an air of regret. A sombre mood had fallen on our group as once again I heard Sophia, Florio and Mercer erupt into laughter. 'He was greatly liked by the undergraduates, too – it was a pity that he could not in his heart renounce the errors of his old beliefs.'

'Exile seems a harsh punishment for owning a few books,' I ventured, helping myself to more beef and onions.

'He was lucky to leave England with his guts still inside

82

his belly,' said Slythurst dispassionately. 'Less favoured men have had harder punishments for less. You of all people, Doctor Bruno, should know that heterodoxy in religion is a most grave sin, against God and the established order.' He looked at me pointedly.

'It was not just the books,' Godwyn interrupted, in a confidential tone. 'He was suspected of being a courier for his cousin, William Allen, at the English seminary in Rheims. They took him to London and questioned him under cruel torture, but he never said a word and in the end they sent him abroad. Poor Edmund.' He shook his head sadly and drained his cup.

'I met his son today,' I remarked, tearing another piece of bread.

Coverdale rolled his eyes.

'Then I pity you,' he said. 'No doubt he was begging you to carry pleas to the court for his father's pardon?' Without waiting for an answer, he clicked his tongue angrily. 'That boy should never have been allowed to stay on after his father's disgrace. Thomas Allen holds dangerous beliefs, mark my words. Though I could not persuade the rector to act on my advice – he is too soft-hearted with that boy.'

I could not help thinking that if the rector's treatment of Thomas Allen was evidence of soft-heartedness, the boy's life must be harsh indeed.

'Once again, it behoves me to say that I do not think our eminent guest has travelled all the way here to listen to us griping about college matters,' Slythurst interrupted in a voice smooth as ice. He tucked a limp strand of hair behind his ear and turned to me, smiling with his teeth. 'Tell us, Doctor Bruno, something of your travels in Europe. I understand you have taught at many of the famous academies across the continent. How do you find Oxford by comparison?'

Returning his smile with equal insincerity, for the remainder of that course, and the almond custard and jellied fruits that followed, I told them of my wandering years as the candles burned lower, leaving out what I thought politic and subtly flattering my new companions with what they wanted to hear – namely, that none of the European universities could hold a candle to the great scholarship and wisdom of the men of Oxford.

'How long do you stay in Oxford, Doctor Bruno?' asked Coverdale, sitting back in his chair and wiping his lips as the servants cleared away the last plates and cups.

'I believe the palatine, in whose party I travel, intends to stay a week,' I said.

'Then I hope you will attend chapel with us here in the college. The rector is delivering a most erudite series of sermons on John Foxe's *Acts and Monuments*, are you familiar with it?'

'The *Book of Martyrs*? Naturally,' I replied, suspecting that this was some sort of test. 'Many consider it a most inspiring work.'

'Doctor Bruno is not genuine in his admiration, I fear,' said Slythurst, glancing from me to his colleagues. 'I never met a Catholic yet who admired Foxe's dreadful accounts of what was done to the Protestant martyrs.'

'Does he not also give many examples of Christian martyrs from the earliest centuries of the faith, when Christians suffered at the hands of pagans and unbelievers, before we began persecuting one another?' I replied. 'And are these not martyrs whom all Christians may honour, and whose sufferings may remind us of a time when we lived in unity?'

'That was not Foxe's intention,' Slythurst began, but Coverdale interrupted.

'Well said, Bruno. Believers on both sides have suffered for Christ, and only He knows who shall stand with Him at the Last Judgement.'

'That is the first time I have ever heard *you* advocate tolerance, James,' Slythurst said, his eyes narrowing even further. Coverdale ignored the provocation.

'Let us have some more wine here, ho!' he cried to a serving boy, clapping his hands. I declined another glass, for I wanted to reflect on my notes for the disputation before I went to bed and needed to keep a clear head.

By the time the meal was over, it was fully dark outside the windows and the guests all rose, taking their leave with much handshaking and compliments to the rector on the food, which I understood had been greatly superior to the usual fare of the college hall supper. The Fellows all shook my hand warmly, repeating their welcome to Oxford and wishing me a good night's rest in anticipation of the great disputation the following day, which they were all, they said, much looking forward to. Richard Godwyn invited me to make use of the library whenever I chose, for which I thanked him, John Florio expressed in perfect Italian his eager hopes that we might spend some time together before I left, and even Doctor Bernard rose unsteadily and clasped my fingers between his two bony hands.

'Tomorrow night, Sorcerer,' he hissed, with a toothless grin, 'you will contradict their pious certainties, and I shall be there in the front row applauding you. Not because I support your heretical notions, but because I admire men who are not afraid. There are too few left in this place.'

Here he glanced pointedly at the rector, who affected not to notice. Only Slythurst did not trouble himself to express a welcome, he merely acknowledged me with a curt nod as he disappeared through the doorway, and only then because I caught him looking at me with those cold eyes. I felt again his dislike of me, though I tried not to view it as a personal slight; I noticed that he left without saying goodnight to his colleagues either, and surmised that he was one of those men, common enough among academics, who was simply not blessed with an easy social manner.

When I said goodnight to Sophia, she extended her hand demurely and I kissed it respectfully under her father's watchful eye, but he was then distracted by Doctor Bernard loudly fretting about where he had left his coat, and while the rector was reassuring Bernard that he had not brought any coat, Sophia leaned close to me and laid a hand on my arm.

'Doctor Bruno, I should very much like to continue our earlier conversation – you remember? The book of Agrippa? Perhaps when the disputation is over, you may have more leisure to talk. I can often be found in the college library,' she added. 'My father allows me to read there in the mornings and the early evenings, when most of the scholars are attending lectures and disputations.'

'So that you do not distract them from their books?' I whispered back. She blushed, and gave me a knowing smile.

'But you will come? There is much I would ask you.'

She looked up at me with a surprising urgency in her eyes, her hand lingering on my arm; I nodded briefly as her father appeared at her shoulder and looked at me enquiringly. I shook his hand, thanked him for the meal and bade the company good night.

I was glad to emerge into the cool of the passageway; the rain had stopped and the night air smelled fresh and inviting after the heavy warmth of the rector's lodgings. I thought I might walk in the orchard garden to clear my head and digest before retiring, but before I reached the end of the passageway I realised that the iron gate had been closed. When I tried the ring set as a handle, I found it was firmly locked.

'Doctor Bruno!' called a voice behind me, and I turned to see Roger Mercer standing at the other end of the passage, by the rector's door. He took a few paces towards me. 'You wished to take a turn in the Grove?' He gestured towards the closed gate.

'Is this not permitted?'

'The Grove is for the use of the Fellows only,' he said, 'and only we and the rector have keys. It is kept locked at night, for fear the undergraduates would make use of it for all manner of improper trysts. No doubt they find alternative places, if they can slip past the main gate,' he added with an indulgent smile.

'They are not allowed out of the college at night?' I asked. 'That does seem a hard confinement on men in the prime of youth.'

'It is meant to teach them self-discipline,' Mercer said. 'Most of them find ways around the rules, though – I know I did at their age.' He chuckled. 'Cobbett the porter is a good old man, he's been here for years, but he is willing to look the other way for a few coins if the young ones come back from town after the gates are locked. He likes a drink, too, Cobbett – sometimes I think he conveniently forgets to lock the gate altogether.'

'Does the rector not discipline him?'

'The rector is severe in some matters, but in others he shows a shrewd understanding of how best to manage a community of young men. A rod of iron is not always the wisest course – sometimes good leadership is a matter of knowing when to turn a blind eye. Young men will go to taverns and whorehouses whether we like it or no, and the greater the force used in prohibition, the greater the allure.'

'As Doctor Bernard said about forbidden books,' I mused.

Mercer glanced at me sideways as we emerged from the other end of the passage into the open courtyard, where the clock on the north range proclaimed the hour to be almost nine.

'You must excuse Doctor Bernard some of his harshness,' he said, apologetically. 'He has had to change his religion three times under four different sovereigns. He was ordained priest in his youth, you know, before the queen's father broke with Rome. But he grows more and more outspoken of late, and I begin to suspect that he suffers that affliction of old men, where he is sometimes lost in memory and not clear to whom he speaks.'

'He seemed lucid enough to me. But angry.'

'Yes.' Mercer sighed. 'He is angry – at the world, the university, at what has been demanded of him and at himself for what he has done. And you must be wondering at his anger towards me.' He glanced at me again, almost timid.

'He spoke bitterly of exile.'

'He meant the trouble last year over our sub-rector, Edmund Allen, I expect you have heard. William was close to him, as was I, but I was obliged to testify against him to the Chancellor's Court for certain matters regarding his religious practices. William considers this an unforgivable betrayal.'

'And you?' I asked softly.

Mercer gave a small, bitter laugh.

'Oh, I acted according to my duty and to save my skin, and now I have the sub-rector's gown and his well-appointed room in the tower. William was right. I betrayed a friend. But I had no choice, and neither did he. You see the life we have here, Bruno?' He gestured at the windows of the rector's lodgings, still glowing with amber light from the candles. 'It is a good life, a comfortable life for a scholar – we are sheltered in many ways from the world. And I – I am not fitted for any work but the life of books and learning, I lack the worldly ambition to push myself forward. If I had not publicly condemned my friend for his perfidy in religion, I would have shared his fate and lost everything. And at that point his fate was not known – the Privy Council allowed the university to conduct his trial, but there was every chance the matter would be handed to them and Edmund might have been facing a worse punishment than exile.' He shuddered. 'So I am not proud of my actions, no, but William Bernard has no right to rail against me. When Her Majesty took the throne and ended her sister Mary's brief reconciliation with Rome, there was a great purge in the university – all the Catholic Fellows and heads of colleges appointed by Mary were deprived of office unless they renounced the pope's authority and swore the Oath of Supremacy. William swore it quickly enough, and that oath bought him twenty-five peaceful years in this place, while his more steadfast friends were scattered to the four winds.'

'And yet, in the winter of his life, it seems clear enough to anyone listening that his heart returns to the old faith.'

'I think, as he nears death, he grows less concerned with the fate of his body and more fearful for his soul,' Mercer said. 'Perhaps if we all saw our death so close at hand, we might choose a different course, but alas, while we breathe our fears are all for our poor, weak flesh and our worldly status.'

'Perhaps so. But it is the son who seems to suffer it most,' I observed.

'You have met Thomas? That poor boy. He is a very able scholar, you know. At least, he was.' Mercer ran both hands over his face as if washing it, a gesture of hopelessness. 'I have known him since he first came to Oxford at fifteen – before his father left for Rheims, he charged me to care for Thomas like a father in his absence. Edmund understood why I had to act as I did – he forgave me. But Thomas will not forgive me for my part in Edmund's trial. I have tried to help him – with such gifts of money as are in my power, I mean – but he would rather humiliate himself slaving for

89

that young peacock Norris than accept a penny. When I pass him in the courtyard he does not even acknowledge me, but I feel the hatred burning in him like a furnace.'

'That is hard,' I said. 'But he is young, and the passions of the young are often as brief as they are fierce. Perhaps he will forgive you in time.'

I bowed then and moved towards my staircase, keen to get to work before the hour grew too late. Mercer stepped towards me and grasped my hand.

'I hope we will have a chance to talk further, Doctor Bruno,' he said. 'I am truly glad to have met you, and I hope I did not sound too sanctimonious in my disapproval this evening when we spoke of Agrippa and the Hermetic treatises.'

'Oh, I am quite used to disapproval,' I said, waving away his apology with a smile.

'You mistake my meaning. The rector is a pious man and, as I say, he can be severe when he chooses – it is prudent for those whose position depends on his good opinion to express views that accord with his own when at his table. But I have long had a great interest in these works – as a scholar, I mean, for I believe that one can study the occult philosophies objectively yet still remain a good Christian. Is it not so, Bruno?'

'Ficino thought so,' I replied. 'And I hope he was right, Doctor Mercer, else I am damned.'

'Please – call me Roger,' he said warmly. 'Well, I shall look forward to our next discussion on these matters.'

With that, he bowed and strode away across the court-yard. I turned towards my room just as fat drops of rain began once more to fall from a brooding sky.

# FOUR

I read and revised my notes for the disputation until my lamp burned out, and afterwards I slept fitfully; the room was cold and the rain lashed hard against the panes as the timbers creaked. So it was that when I was disturbed by a great noise during a brief slumber I was at first not sure if it was morning or merely a hallucination of my confused dreams. Gradually, though, the noise became more insistent, and as I awakened to see that it was not yet dawn, I realised that the infernal riot outside my windows was the frenzied sound of a barking dog. I pulled the sheet closer around me, cursing the rector or whomever had thought to keep such a feral animal in the college grounds and curled up in the hope of recovering my ruined sleep, when a second sound joined that bestial dawn chorus, one that I have never forgotten and still, sometimes, hear in dreams. It was the blood-chilling scream of a human being in pain and mortal terror, and it rose in pitch and agony as the creature's barking grew wilder and more vicious.

As the horror of those combined sounds dispelled the last vapours of sleep, I realised that someone not far from my windows was in fear of their life; I supposed it must be some intruder, surprised perhaps by a watchdog, but I could not ignore it, so I hastily pulled on my breeches and a shirt and set out to find the source of this consternation and see if I might offer assistance.

I emerged from my staircase into the shadowy courtyard; the heavy clouds were broken with veins of pale light and the rain, for the moment, had abated, leaving behind a silvery mist that hung thick in the morning air so that I could barely make out the clock on the north range opposite and had to step forward to read its hands: almost five. The dreadful noise of the hound continued and from other staircases around the main courtyard figures appeared through the vapour as young men, with hose pulled on under their nightshirts and hair disarrayed, timidly gathered in groups, whispering to one another, unsure whether to come any closer. The din was unmistakeably coming from the passageway in the east range that led to the rector's lodgings and the Grove, the Fellows' garden I had explored the previous evening. Gathering my wits, I ran the length of the passage to the iron gate, where I found two young men pulling at the handle, to no avail, and peering into the misty depths of the garden. Hearing my footsteps, they turned, their faces ashen.

'Someone is in there, sir, with a wild beast!' cried the taller. 'I had just risen to wash when I heard his cries, but from here we can see nothing.'

'We do not have a key!' the other said frantically. 'Only the senior men do, and the door is fast.'

'Then we must wake one of the senior men,' I said, wondering how the rector, whose lodgings must have windows on to the garden, could possibly be sleeping through this tumult. 'You must know where their rooms are – quick, go and wake anyone who could open the gate. Is there another entrance?'

'Two, sir,' said the tall student, terrified, while his friend scuttled away up the passage in search of help. 'Another gate like this from the passage at the other end of the hall, by the kitchens, and a door in the garden wall from Brasenose Lane, but they are all locked at night.'

'Well, the man in there must have got in somehow,' I said, urgently, as a throttled voice unmistakeably cried, 'Jesu, save me! Holy Mother, save me!' Another scream rent the air, followed by mangled cries for help, then a ferocious growling and a truly inhuman sound, a strangled gurgling that seemed to last for minutes. A small crowd of curious and agitated undergraduates was forming behind us when I heard the rector's voice crying, 'Let me through, I say!'

His face was puffy and bleary with sleep, a coat thrown over his nightgown, and he carried in his hand a bunch of keys. He started when he saw me.

'Oh – Doctor Bruno – what is this ungodly disturbance? Who is within – can you see anything? I tried to look from my windows, but the mist and the trees hide all else from sight.'

'I can see nothing, but it seems that a wild animal is savaging someone in the garden. He must be helped, and quickly!'

The rector stared at me as if I had just told him a herd of cows had flown over the college; then he collected himself and stepped towards the gate with his keys, but just as suddenly he stopped and turned back to me, his face tight with fear. The terrible snarling and barking continued within, but the human sounds had tailed off. I feared the worst.

'But – but then it would be folly to enter without a weapon if a wild dog is on the loose!' the rector stammered. 'It must be killed – someone must fetch the constable or a serjeant-at-arms, who can bring a crossbow. One of you – quickly!' he snapped at the crowd of half-dressed boys who stood at the end of the passageway, staring, open-mouthed. 'Go for the constable – immediately!' They all looked at one another before a couple of them ran out to the courtyard.

'Could we not find a stick or a poker, anything? We must go in, Rector – I fear we may already be too late for the poor wretch trapped in there,' I urged, holding out a hand for the keys.

The rector looked around in panic.

'But – how could there be a *dog* in the garden?' he asked, as if to himself, his brows knit in perplexity.

'Is it not a watch dog, to keep out intruders?' I asked, now puzzled myself. 'Could it not be some thief who has scaled the wall, perhaps?'

'But there is no watch dog,' the rector said, his voice tight with panic. 'The porter has a dog, but it is an old, blind creature that has only the use of three legs and it sleeps in his lodge by the main gate. No one else in college is permitted to keep an animal.' He shook his head, unable to make sense of the evidence of his own ears; the beast in the garden went on making its hellish noise.

'Step aside there,' said a calm voice behind us, and the gaggle of students crowded in the passageway parted to reveal a tall young man with shoulder-length fair hair, dressed incongruously in a fine doublet and breeches, black silk slashed to show a rich crimson lining and topped with an elaborate ruff, looking for all the world as if he were off to a dance or a playhouse in London, not hastily risen like the rest of us in all the confusion. In one hand he carried an English longbow, of the kind the nobility use for the hunt, taller than himself and ornately carved with gilded inlays and green and scarlet tracery. In the other he held a leather quiver of arrows decorated with the same design of curlicued vines and gilt leaves.

'Gabriel Norris!' exclaimed the rector, staring at the longbow. 'What is this?'

'You must open the gate, Doctor Underhill,' commanded

the young man, 'there is no time to lose, a man's life is in danger.'

He spoke in measured tones, despite the urgency of the situation, as if he and not the rector held the authority here; half-dazed, the rector unlocked the gate and the young man stepped through, fitting an arrow to his bow as he did so. I followed him hesitantly, and the rector fell in behind me, keeping close to the wall.

The mist hung heavily between the twisted trunks of the apple trees, playing tricks on my eyes with its shifting shapes. Stepping cautiously through the blue shadows, I glimpsed suddenly towards the furthest north-east corner the movement of a large, long-legged dog – by its shape a wolfhound of sorts, I thought, though I could not see clearly. I kept close to the wall as this Gabriel, conspicuous in his gaudy clothes, advanced in steady paces towards the animal, which was still growling and shaking between its teeth a limp black object at its feet. As I moved closer, the mist thinned and I was able to see the animal clearly; its jaws were bloody and daubed with shreds of torn flesh. My heart sank then and my stomach convulsed, for I knew we were too late. The young man paused a few paces away; the dog, catching a scent or a sound, paused in the mauling of its prey and raised its head. For the briefest moment, its snarling ceased and it made a movement towards the young man; as it did so, he let the arrow fly. He was a good shot, despite the thick air, and the animal crumpled to the ground as the arrow-head tore through its neck.

As soon as it fell, Gabriel dropped his bow and we both rushed to the black heap that lay up against the wall, beside the animal's corpse. It was the body of a man, lying face down, his black academic gown spread out around him, the grass all torn and soaked with a quantity of blood around the body. I helped Gabriel roll the man over, and cried out suddenly in shock. Here was Roger Mercer, his head bent at a hideous angle, eyes staring to the sky, his throat quite torn out – a flap of flesh hung open, raw tissue protruding from the wound. Instinctively I reached out to staunch the blood that still seeped down his neck and breast, but it was too late – the eyes were motionless, fixed forever in a stare of terror. Gabriel Norris jumped back from the bloody corpse, checking anxiously to see that he had got no gore on his clothes, as if this were his only concern. Preening little peacock, I thought in disgust – then remembered where I had heard his name before; Mercer himself had referred to him the night before in exactly the same terms. I crouched in disbelief by the body, taking in the ravaged hands – two of the fingers near bitten off where he had tried to fight the animal away – the chunks of flesh torn from the legs and ankles where it had dragged him to the ground, that horrifically mauled gullet.

The rector came cautiously towards us, a handkerchief clutched over his mouth.

'Is he . . .?'

'We came too late, God have mercy on his soul,' I said, more from custom than piety. The rector moved close enough to identify the mutilated body of the man who had sat at his right hand only the night before at dinner, and was immediately sick. The young man called Gabriel seemed to have recovered himself, and was probing the corpse of the dog with his toe.

'A giant of a beast,' he said, with a note almost of pride, as if he were displaying it as a hunting trophy. Peering more closely, it struck me: hunting was the apt image.

'This is a hunting dog,' I said, kneeling beside it. 'And look, here.' I pointed to where its ribs protruded painfully under its wiry grey pelt. 'See how thin it is – it looks as if it was starving. And look at its leg.' A ring of raw flesh ran around the top of the dog's left hind leg where the skin had been brutally chafed by a tether of some kind. The fur around the wound was patchy and torn, as if the dog had tried repeatedly to tear off its fetter with its own teeth. 'It has been chained up, I think – you see? No wonder it went so crazed.'

'What was it doing in the garden, though?' the young man asked, looking at me expectantly. 'And why was Doctor Mercer here with a dog?'

'Perhaps he was walking his dog and it suddenly turned on him – dogs are sometimes unpredictable,' I suggested, unpersuaded by my own hypothesis.

'But Roger didn't have a dog,' the rector said in a weak voice, wiping his mouth with his handkerchief. 'I told you – no one in the college, save the porter, is allowed to keep an animal. No – no, gentlemen, there is nothing to see here!' he cried suddenly, as the scholars began crowding through the narrow gate into the garden, intent on seeing the spectacle. 'Back to your rooms, all of you! Chapel at six as normal – back to your rooms and make yourselves ready, I say!'

The students reluctantly turned and shuffled back through the gate, casting glances over their shoulders and murmuring among themselves in animated tones. The rector turned then to the young man, who stood contemplating the corpses, the quiver still dangling from his shoulder; an expression of disbelief spread over the rector's face, as if he were only now seeing the young man clearly for the first time.

'Gabriel Norris!' he exploded, flapping a hand frantically. 'What in God's name are you wearing?'

Norris looked down at his flamboyant doublet and hose, then shifted his feet as if embarrassed.

'I think now is not the time, Doctor Underhill,' he began, but the rector cut him off.

'You know perfectly well the Earl of Leicester's edict about the rules of dress for undergraduates! And I am charged with enforcing it – would you have us both disciplined by the Chancellor's Court, after all that has happened?' His face had turned the shade of beetroot, his voice strangulated; I could not help but think that this was an overreaction, in the circumstances. 'No ruffs, no silks, no velvets, no cuts in doublet or hose!' he continued, his pitch rising with every item. 'And no *weapons!* You deliberately flaunt every rule laid down regarding apparel! This is a community of scholars, Master Norris, not some ball at court for you to flaunt your wealth!'

The young man pursed his lips and looked surly. Even in this attitude of petulance, I saw that he was exceptionally handsome and was clearly used to having his own way.

'This community of *scholars* could not do without my wealth, as you well know, Rector. And you overcharge us as it is – I am forced to eat like a pauper here, must I also dress like one?'

The rector, chastened, lowered his voice.

'You must dress as the Earl of Leicester deems fitting for an Oxford man,' he said. 'Now please make haste and change – if you are reported we will both be in trouble and how shall I explain . . .?' He broke off there, looking around him helplessly at the two bodies, and I saw that his hands were shaking badly; I suspected he was in shock.

Gabriel Norris looked at me for a moment, as if reluctant to leave the scene of his heroism, then perhaps thought better of it and with some haste picked up his bow and turned to go.

'Master Norris!' the rector called after him.

The young man turned defiantly.

'Yes, Rector?'

'A *longbow*? Why in the Lord's name do you even have a bow and arrows in college?'

Norris shrugged.

'My father left it to me. It is a keepsake. Besides, hunting for sport is permitted to those commoners who have a licence.'

'It is *not* permitted to keep a longbow in college rooms,' the rector said weakly.

'If I had not had it in college, you would have had to wrestle that dog with your bare hands, Rector,' Norris replied drily. 'But I do not expect you to thank me.'

'Nevertheless, Master Norris, I insist that you take it to the strongroom in the tower where it can be held for safekeeping. Ask Master Slythurst or Doctor Coverdale to lock it away for you. Today, please!' he added, as Norris disappeared through the open gate.

The rector took a deep breath and then his legs seemed to buckle under him; I offered my arm and he leaned on me gratefully.

'Rector Underhill,' I said gently, indicating Mercer's body, 'a man has died in a horrific accident, and we must try to understand how this could have come to pass. If indeed it is an accident,' I added, for the circumstances troubled me the more I looked for an explanation.

The rector stumbled then, and almost fell against me, his face blanched.

'Dear God, you are right, Bruno. The reports will spread like wildfire among the students. But how can it be explained? Unless . . .' There was terror in his face and I felt sorry for him; his calm, ordered little kingdom upended in a few minutes.

'Well, let us look for the most likely causes first,' I said. 'If there are no dogs in the college save the porter's old hound, this one must have found its way in from the outside, most likely through this gate.'

'Yes – yes, that's it, some feral stray, found its way in through the gate.' The rector grasped at the suggestion gratefully.

Mercer had fallen and been savaged only yards from the wooden gate into the lane behind the college, but when I went to try the handle, it was locked fast. The rector stood as if transfixed by the bodies of the hunter and his prey. On the back wall nearby I noticed a scrap of black material spiked on the edge of a brick; below this spot the grass was churned to mud with boot and paw prints, and splashed liberally with Mercer's blood.

'It looks as if he tried to scale the wall, poor man,' I said, half to myself. 'That would account for the mauling of his legs. But it is twice the height of a man – why did he not simply run towards the gate to escape? Unless the dog was between him and the gate, meaning it must have come in from outside. But then, how is the gate locked?'

I glanced at the rector, who remained immobile, then I ran to try the second gate into the college, from the passage that ran between the hall and the kitchens. This too was locked. How, then, I puzzled, had the dog entered the garden? And how, for that matter, had Roger Mercer?

I walked back to where the bodies lay.

'Is it possible,' I ventured, as the reality of what I had seen began to solidify in my mind, 'that someone could have let the dog in deliberately?'

The rector turned to look at me incredulously.

'As a prank, you mean?'

'Hardly a prank. Whoever unleashed a half-starved hunting dog must have known it could kill.' I knelt down by Mercer's mauled body and patted the pockets.

'Doctor Bruno!' the rector exclaimed. 'What are you about? The poor man is still warm, if you please.'

Roger Mercer had been fully dressed, despite the early hour; in one of the pockets sewn into his breeches I found what I had been looking for.

'Here,' I said, holding up two iron keys attached to a single ring, one much larger than the other. 'Is one of these a key to the garden?'

The rector took the ring from my hand and examined the keys against the light.

'Yes, the larger would open any of the three gates.'

'Then either he let himself in and locked the gate behind him, or someone locked the gate through which he entered once he was inside,' I reasoned. 'Either way, he was trapped in here with a savage dog.'

'But we still don't know how the dog got in,' the rector said, uncomprehending.

'Well, we know it didn't jump the wall, and it didn't let itself in and lock the gate after it.' I looked him directly in the eye as I spoke, waiting for understanding to take effect.

The rector clutched my arm, his face twisted with panic; I could smell the bile on his breath.

'What are you saying, Bruno? That someone let that dog in and then closed every means of escape?'

'I can't see another explanation,' I said, looking again at the dog's fearsome teeth, through which its limp tongue now lolled, spittle hanging in tendrils from its jaws. Norris's arrow stuck upright from its gullet. 'Someone who knew Doctor Mercer would come here at this hour. But surely he never suspected any harm would come to him, else he would have armed himself.'

Then I remembered Mercer's strange remark the previous night, about how we might all live differently if we saw death approaching. I had dismissed it, but had he been revealing that he feared for his life? Unhappy coincidence only, I guessed; besides, he had spoken confidently of attending the disputation, and of conversing with me later. I felt a sudden awful sorrow; though I hardly knew the man, he had seemed warm and genuine, and I had stood by only minutes ago and listened to him die. To think that he might have been saved if I had acted quicker, if someone had had a key, if Norris had arrived sooner with his bow. One moment of indecision decides a man's fate, I thought, and realised that I too was trembling.

'Was it perhaps his regular practice to walk in the garden so early?' I asked. 'I mean, could someone have known to expect him here?'

'The Fellows often like to read in the quiet of the Grove,' the rector said. 'Though not usually at this hour, I grant you – it is too dark. The undergraduates usually rise at half past five to make themselves ready before chapel at six – morning service is compulsory. There is rarely a soul abroad in the college any earlier, not even the kitchen servants. I confess I have never walked in the garden at such an hour so I could not say if any of my colleagues had the habit of doing so.'

As I bent again to Mercer's body, separating the bloodied and torn clothes to see if anything on his person might explain his presence in the Grove so early, I remembered how he had joked about the garden being popular for trysts. Had he been expecting someone who never came, or who came and brought death with them? He carried no book, but a bulge inside his doublet suggested a hidden pocket; reaching in, I withdrew a fat leather purse that jingled with coins.

'If his purpose was a quiet, contemplative walk before sunrise, surely he would not have needed to bring this,' I said, untying the purse and showing the rector its contents. The English coins meant nothing to me, though there were clearly a lot of them, but the rector's eyeballs bulged at the sight.

'Good God, there is at least ten pounds here!' he exclaimed. 'Why would he carry such a sum?'

'Perhaps he expected to meet someone to whom he owed money.'

'And knowing he would be here, they set a dog on him!'

he exclaimed, his eyes wide. 'Revenge for a bad debt, that must be it.'

I shook my head.

'Then why is the money still in his pocket? If someone had wished to harm him for failure to pay a debt, surely they would have made sure to take the money first?'

'But who would ever have meant to harm Roger?' asked the rector in despair.

'I cannot say. But a wild dog does not get into an enclosed garden through locked gates by accident.' I brushed down my clothes, realising that they were now stained with Mercer's blood. 'I suppose now that this terrible thing has happened, Rector, you will want to cancel the disputation this evening?'

The rector's face filled with fear again.

'No!' he said fiercely, gripping my shoulders. 'The disputation must go ahead. We cannot allow this *incident* to disrupt a royal visitation – can you imagine the consequences, Doctor Bruno? Especially if it were rumoured to be –' he glanced around before whispering the word – '*deliberate*. The college would be tainted and my reputation with it, and we have already had so much trouble here lately, I fear Leicester's displeasure more than I can tell you.'

'But a man has been brutally killed – perhaps murdered,' I protested. 'We cannot go about our business as if nothing has happened.'

'Shh! For the love of Christ, do not repeat that dreadful word *murder*, Bruno.' The rector looked frantically about the garden and lowered his voice, though we were alone. 'We will have it announced that this was a tragic misfortune – we shall say . . .' he paused briefly to compose his story '. . . yes, we shall say that the garden gate was left open and a stray dog got in and attacked Roger, who had got up early to pray and meditate in the Grove.'

'Will this be believed?'

'It will if I say it was the case – I am the earl's appointed rector,' said Underhill, a touch of his old pomposity returning. 'Besides, it was dark and misty and no one saw clearly.' There was a hardness in his face now, and desperation; I saw then his determination to preserve the college's good name at any price, and imagined this same ruthlessness must have ruled him during the trial of the hapless Edmund Allen.

'But the locked gates—' I protested.

'Only you and I know about the locked gates, Bruno. I see nothing to be gained from mentioning them at present, if you wouldn't mind.'

'What about the porter? Will he not remember checking the gates at night?'

The rector gave a dry laugh.

'I see you are not acquainted with our porter. A clear head and a sharp memory are not his strong points. If I say a gate was left open, he could not for certain claim otherwise. No, I think this is our safest course.'

Seeing my look of concern, he squeezed my shoulder and added, in a lighter tone, 'If all suspicion is hushed up, it will be the easier to investigate what really happened here this morning. But if there is a great fuss, and all Oxford is abuzz with the idea that Lincoln is a place of savage murder, the perpetrator – if indeed there is a perpetrator – will surely disappear in the hubbub. If justice is to be served, we do best not to shout this tragedy from the tower. I would be most grateful for your help in this matter, Doctor Bruno.'

I was not sure whether he meant the matter of disguising the truth or of uncovering it, but I was sorely troubled by the thought that I may well have been the last person to see Roger Mercer alive, and that whoever had planned his vicious end was at that moment at liberty somewhere in Oxford, perhaps exulting in his success. The rector's cold briskness had shocked me, too; his human response to his colleague's awful death seemed swallowed up in fear for his office.

The sky had grown paler and the mist was thinning, lingering only in ragged shreds among the trees. The two corpses in the dewy grass had acquired a stark solidity with the grey light. The rector glanced up anxiously.

'Dear God – it is almost time for chapel! I must be there to speak, reassure the community. Already the story will be growing.' He twisted his fingers together until the knuckles turned white, speaking as if to himself. 'First I must order the kitchen servants to bring a sack for that carcass. It cannot stay here.'

I stared at him, appalled, until he noticed my expression.

'The dog, Bruno! But you are right – the coroner must be fetched before the body can be removed. Oh, there is too much to do! I will have to ask Roger—' Then he clapped his hands to his mouth and turned back to look at the corpse, as if only now comprehending the loss of his deputy.

'Oh, God,' he whispered. 'Roger is dead!'

'That's right,' I said, watching him absorb the truth of it.

'But then – this means there will have to be another congregation, another election for sub-rector, and there is no time to convene – but in the meantime I must have someone to act under me, and that will occasion all the usual petty jealousies and ill-feeling, just when we do not need them – oh, how could this have come to pass?' Trying to contain his mounting fears, he turned to me with an earnest expression, his hands flapping helplessly at his sides. 'Doctor Bruno – this is a dreadful thing to ask of a guest, I know, but would you stay with poor Roger's body until the coroner can be brought? I must make the sad announcement of this morning's events in chapel in such a way that quiets the reports of it, if that is possible. Keep the students out – we do not want them crowding in here to satisfy their ghoulish curiosity as if it were a bear-baiting.'

'Of course I will stay,' I said, hoping my vigil would not be a long one; though I am not superstitious about the dead, the empty stare of Roger Mercer's sightless eyes seemed to accuse me for my failure to help him. *Our fears are all for our poor, weak flesh,* he had said the night before. Now he had looked that fear full in the teeth; I still remembered his cracked voice crying to Jesus and Mary to save him.

The rector scuttled off across the grass in the direction of the courtyard, and I was left alone with the bodies and my whirling thoughts. While I waited for them to settle into some semblance of order, I bent again to Mercer's corpse and lifted what remained of his tattered gown to cover his ravaged face. Superstition says that the eyes of a murder victim retain the image of his killer, but as I looked at Mercer's terrified stare for the last time I thought: if such foolishness were true, would I see the image of the great dog? But the fact of the locked gates stubbornly persisted; the dog was not Mercer's true killer, only his agent. I moved again from the sub-rector's body to the dog's to examine it. It was a huge brute, the height of a man's waist upright with a long, narrow head. I noted again how thin it was, though it did not look otherwise abused. Whoever had loosed this dog in here must have planned the event carefully, increasing the force of the attack by keeping it desperately hungry for some days beforehand, by the look of it. And Mercer's heavy purse – which the rector had taken – suggested he had been expecting to meet someone to effect some kind of transaction. But if the money had been at the centre of some dispute in which Mercer had fallen out with someone so badly that they could wish to kill him, I could not fathom why the purse had been left. It would seem that the money had been less of a priority than the sub-rector's death, though it must have been key to the meeting he anticipated.

I considered again the layout of the garden. It was abutted on the north side by the kitchen part of the way, though I could see no door from the kitchens into the garden. On three sides it was enclosed by a wall at least twelve feet high, and on the fourth it adjoined the east range of the college, the side of the quadrangle that housed the hall and the rector's lodgings. I presumed Mercer had entered the garden through one of the two passageways either side of the hall, letting himself in with his own key. Had he then locked the gate behind him, so as not to be disturbed, or had someone waited for him to enter before locking the door from the college side, leaving him unwittingly shut in? Could that have been the same person who then opened the gate from the lane through which the dog – presumably muzzled until the last moment – had been released, locking that behind the animal? But it would have taken a good few minutes to run out of the main gate and around the side of the building, and anyone doing so would have been seen by the porter – assuming he had been awake.

From the courtyard a bell tolled dismally to rally the scholars to chapel, where the rector would spread his benign reassurance and dispel the young men's more lurid imaginings. As I rose to my feet, I wondered idly if James Coverdale would finally achieve his ambition of becoming sub-rector, and a thought struck me like a cold blade. The rector had asked, rhetorically, who would want to harm Roger Mercer, and I had replied that I had no idea. But now that I considered the proposition I realised that even I, a stranger who had not been in the college one full day, had already encountered two people who apparently hated him. Might there not be more? Perhaps one of them tried to extort money from him and decided instead to kill him. I had found him a genial enough man, but it seemed his part in the trial of the unfortunate Edmund Allen had aroused resentment; who was to say how many other enemies he might have made? But these resentments must have simmered for a long time; why wait until the week of a royal visitation to act on them? Unless—

I was interrupted in my pursuit of this new trail by the sight of a figure running towards me through the trees from the direction of the college; I stepped forward in the hope that the coroner had arrived to relieve me of my duties, and was surprised to recognise Sophia Underhill, dressed in a thin blue gown with a shawl around her shoulders, her hair flying out behind her. She halted a few yards away, looking equally surprised to see me.

'Doctor Bruno! What – what are you doing in here?'

'I was – waiting for your father,' I said, taking another step towards her in the hope of guiding her away from the two corpses.

'They said Gabriel Norris shot down an intruder,' she said, her face flushed with the drama of the moment. 'Is he still here?' Her eyes were bright with eager anticipation as she looked around wildly, but I noticed she was twisting her hands together in agitation in the same manner as her father.

'Not quite.' I almost smiled; despite the rector's best efforts, it seemed the tale was already growing in the telling. 'You have not spoken to your father?'

'He is at morning prayers in chapel – I heard the news from two scholars who were running there late,' she said, peering past me to where the shapes lay in the dense grass. 'Of course we heard all the noise from our windows but I never imagined – is that the thief's body there?' She seemed keen to take a look; I planted myself firmly in her path.

'Please, Mistress Underhill, you must keep back. It is not a sight you should see.'

She tilted her head and stared at me defiantly.

'I have seen death before, Doctor Bruno. I have seen my own brother with his neck broken, do not treat me like one of these pampered ladies who has never been out of a parlour.'

'I would not dream of it, but this is worse,' I said, holding my arms out absurdly as if this might obscure the sight. 'Well, not worse than one's brother, I don't mean – I mean only, it is very bloody, not something a woman should see. Please trust me, Mistress Underhill.'

At this she snorted, and placed her hands on her hips.

'How is it that men think women are too frail to look on blood? Do you forget we bleed every month? We push out babies in great puddles of gore, do you imagine we hide our eyes when we do that, in case it offends our delicate senses? I promise you, Doctor Bruno, any woman can look on blood with more fortitude than a soldier, though men think we must be treated like Venice glass. Do not be one more who wants to wrap me up in linen and keep me in a box.'

I was surprised by the ferocity of her argument, and conceded that she had a point; even so, I had been charged with protecting Mercer from prurient eyes, so I stepped forward again until I was standing directly in front of her, only a few inches away. It was disconcerting to find that she was almost as tall as me.

'I would not dream of it. Nevertheless, Mistress Underhill, I beg you not to go any closer – this body is badly mutilated. I fear it would be distressing, however strong your constitution.'

She stood her ground for a moment longer, and then her instinctive propriety dictated that she step back. The defiant expression was replaced by one of anxious curiosity.

'What happened, then?'

'A man was savaged by a wild dog. Norris shot the dog, not the man.'

Her brow creased.

'A *dog*? In the *garden*? Wait –' she shook her head, flustered, as if she had her questions all in the wrong order. 'Which man?'

'Roger Mercer.'

'Oh, no. No!' she repeated, one hand clasped to her mouth, the other to her breast. 'No!' Her eyes darted about wildly, resting nowhere, then she sank slowly to the ground, her skirt billowing around her, her hand still pressed to her mouth; I was unsure if she was about to cry or faint, but her face was drained of all colour. 'Oh God, it can't be.'

I crouched beside her and laid a tentative hand on her shoulder.

'I am sorry. You were fond of him?'

She looked up at me with a fleeting expression of puzzlement, then nodded emphatically.

'Yes – yes, of course – this is my home, the senior Fellows here have been like family to me these past six years,' she said, her voice shaky. 'I cannot believe something so horrible could happen here in college, just below our windows too. Poor, poor Roger.' She glanced past me to the heap in the grass and shuddered. 'If only . . .' she broke off, pressing the edge of her thumb to her mouth again.

'If only?' I prompted.

But she merely shook her head and cast her eyes around again frantically. 'But where is Master Norris?'

'Your father sent him to change. His attire was apparently unsuitable.'

She gave a soft, indulgent laugh then and I felt a sudden unexpected pang of jealousy. Was she fond of the dandyish young archer?

'A *dog*, though?' she mused, running her hands through her hair as if thinking aloud, her expression troubled again. 'Where did it come from?'

110

'The gate to the lane must have been left open during the night – it looks as if some stray found its way in and was so starving it would set upon anything,' I said, as evenly as I could.

Sophia's eyes narrowed.

'No. That gate is never unlocked. Father is paranoid about vagabonds and trespassers getting in at night, or undergraduates using it to meet the kitchen girls – he checks it every evening at ten before he retires. He would no more forget the gate than he would forget his prayers or his work. That cannot be.'

'Perhaps he left that task to the porter last night, as he had to attend to our supper,' I suggested, thinking how absurd it was that I should be defending the improbable falsehood when I wanted to compare her suspicions with my own. 'I hear the porter is an unreliable old drunk.'

She looked at me then as if she were disappointed in me.

'Cobbett is an old man, yes, and he likes a drop now and again, but he has been at the college since he was a boy and if my father had entrusted him with such a task he would rather die than let the rector down. He may be only a servant to you, Doctor Bruno, but he is a kind old man and does not deserve to be spoken of with contempt.'

'I am truly sorry, Mistress Underhill,' I said, chastened. 'I did not mean—'

'You had better call me Sophia. Whenever I hear Mistress Underhill called, I look around for my mother.'

'Your mother did not hear the commotion this morning?'

'I don't know, she is in bed.' Sophia sighed. 'She is in bed most of the time, it is her chief occupation.'

'I think she carries a great weight of sadness since your brother's death,' I said gently.

'We all carry a great weight of sadness, Doctor Bruno,' she snapped, her eyes flashing. 'But if we all hid under the

111

counterpane pretending the sun no longer rose and set, the family would have fallen apart. What do you know of my brother's death, anyway?'

'Your father made a brief account last night. It must have been unbearable for you.'

'It would be unbearable to lose a brother in any case,' she said, in a milder tone. 'But I was given unusual liberties while John lived, because he spoke up for me, he insisted that I should be his companion in all his pursuits and treated as his equal. Without him, I am forced to behave like a lady and I must confess I do not take to it at all.'

She laughed unexpectedly then and I was greatly relieved, but her laughter trailed off into silence and she began plucking at the grass distractedly.

'I suppose your disputation today will be postponed because of this?' she asked, gesturing vaguely towards the mound of Roger Mercer's body as if she did not much care either way.

'No indeed – your father is determined not to disappoint the royal guest. We shall go ahead as planned, he says.'

Her face lit up with anger again – her temper was as changeable as the weather over Mount Vesuvius, it seemed – and she rose to her feet, brushing down her dress with quick, furious strokes.

'Of course he does. No matter that someone has died, terribly – nothing must interrupt college life. We must all pretend nothing is amiss.' Her eyes burned with fury. 'Do you know, I never saw my father shed one tear when my brother John died, not one. When they brought him the news, he just nodded, and then said he would be in his study and was not to be disturbed. He didn't come out for the rest of that day – he spent it *working*.' She spat this last word.

'I have heard,' I said hesitantly, 'that Englishmen find this mask necessary to hide what they feel, perhaps because it frightens them.'

She made a small gesture of contempt with her head.

'My mother hides in her sheets, my father hides in his study. Between them, I am sure they have almost managed to forget they had a son. If only they did not have the inconvenience of my presence to remind them.'

'I am sure that is not the case—' I began, but she turned away and set her mouth in a terse line. 'What is this work in which your father buries himself?' I asked, to break the silence.

'He is writing a commentary on Master Foxe's *Actes and Monuments of these Latter and Perillous Days*,' she said, with some disdain.

'Ah, yes – the *Book of Martyrs*,' I said, remembering that someone at dinner had mentioned the rector preaching on this subject. 'Does it need a commentary? Foxe is quite prolix enough on his own, as I recall.'

'My father certainly thinks so. Indeed, my father thinks its need for a commentary is more pressing than any other business in the world – except perhaps his endless meetings of the College Board, which are nothing but an excuse for gossip and back-biting.' She pulled a handful of leaves from the branch overhead with special vehemence as she said this, then lifted her head to look at me. 'These are supposed to be the cleverest men in England, Doctor Bruno, but I tell you, they are worse than washerwomen for the pleasure they take in malicious talk.'

'Oh, I have been around enough universities to know all about that,' I smiled.

She seemed about to say more, but there was a noise from the direction of the courtyard, where two sturdy men in kitchen aprons approached.

'I had better go,' Sophia said, glancing once more with a

113

fearful expression at the corner where the bodies lay. 'I am sorry that I will not be able to attend the disputation, Doctor Bruno. I am not permitted, but I should have liked to see you best my father in a debate.'

I raised an eyebrow in mock surprise, and she smiled sadly.

'No doubt you think that disloyal of me. Perhaps it is – but my father has such fixed ideas about the world, and its ordained order, and everyone's place in that order, and sometimes I think he believes these things only because he has always believed them and it is less trouble to go on the same way.' She bit anxiously at the knuckle of her thumb. 'I would just dearly love to see someone shake his certainties, make him ask himself questions. Maybe if he can accept even the possibility that there might be a different way of ordering the universe, he might learn to see that not everything in that universe has to stay as it has always been. That is why I want you to win, Doctor Bruno.' With these last words she actually gripped my shirt and gave me a little shake. I nodded, smiling.

'You mean that if he can be convinced that the Earth goes around the Sun, he might also be persuaded that a daughter could study as well as a son, and that she might be allowed to choose her own husband?'

She blushed, and returned the smile.

'Something like that. It seems you are as clever as they say, Doctor Bruno.'

'Please, call me Giordano,' I added.

She moved her lips silently, then shook her head. 'I cannot say it properly, my tongue gets all tangled. I shall just have to call you Bruno. Win the debate for me, Bruno. You shall be my champion in this joust of minds.' Then she lowered her eyes to the bloodstained grass and her smile quickly faded. 'Poor Doctor Mercer. I cannot believe it.'

She cast a long look at the mounds of the bodies beneath

the trees, her expression unreadable, then turned and ran lightly over the grass towards the college, throwing me a last glance over her shoulder as the burly man who now drew level with me lifted up a capacious sack and said,

'Right, matey – where's this dog wants buryin' then?'

# FIVE

Relieved of my last duty of care to poor Roger Mercer by the arrival of the coroner, who came accompanied by the bustling figure of Doctor James Coverdale – the latter hardly bothering to disguise his self-importance in being asked to officiate over the removal of his one-time rival – I left the Grove gratefully and hurried through the passageway to the main courtyard. Chapel was over and groups of under-graduates in their billowing gowns stood about in animated discussion, many of them apparently thrilled to be so near to such calamity, even as they pressed hands to their mouths and opened their eyes wide in horror.

It was only just seven o'clock but I felt I had been awake most of the night; I wanted nothing more than to return to my chamber, change my clothes and try to recoup some of the sleep I lacked, before attempting to order my mind in time for the evening's disputation – an event which held little savour for me now. My shirt and breeches were stained with Mercer's blood, a fact Coverdale had taken pleasure in pointing out as I took my leave of him and the coroner. 'You'd better find some clean clothes, Doctor Bruno,' he had said, with a levity that seemed out of place, 'or people will think you the killer!'

I surmised that he was displeased to find me already on the scene, and had made an idle joke to puncture any illusion of my usefulness, but as I glanced around the courtyard at the scene of excited consternation, I wondered why he had used the word 'killer', even in jest, if it had been given out officially that the sub-rector's death was a tragic accident? Perhaps I was giving undue weight to thoughtless words; in any event, he was right about my clothes, I thought, looking down at my breeches and holding the fabric out to see the extent of the bloodstains. As I did so, I felt something in the pocket and realised that I was still carrying the keys I had taken from Mercer's body; I must have tucked them away in my own breeches without thinking.

I turned the key-ring over in my palm; the smaller key, I guessed, must open the door of the sub-rector's chamber, since it was a similar size to the key I had been given for my own guest room. I glanced around the courtyard again. The students were beginning to disperse, books in hand, some towards the staircase that led to the library in the north range, others towards the main gate; no one paid me any attention. I looked at Mercer's key. Might his room not hold some indication of who he had expected to meet in the garden, I wondered, and why he had taken so much money? I could take a quick look now, while the students were occupied, and return the keys to the rector later, claiming (truthfully) that I had pocketed them inadvertently.

Mercer had mentioned that he lived in the tower room above the main entrance. I glanced up at the tall perpendicular arches of the first-storey windows, presuming this must be the right place, then with a confident step I passed into the shadow of the first staircase on the west range that appeared to lead up into the tower.

Reaching the first landing, I arrived at a low wooden door

bearing a painted sign that read Doctor R. Mercer, Sub-Rector. After a fleeting glance to either side, I tried the key in the lock. It turned easily, and I slipped quietly into the room Roger Mercer had left only two hours earlier, never imagining he would not return. For a moment I thought I heard light footsteps quickening away overhead; I froze, my ears straining, but I heard no door open or close and there was no further sound.

I had not anticipated the sight that greeted me as I gently pressed the door shut behind me. The room was in turmoil: books, papers and maps pulled from shelves and flung in every direction with no care for their contents, garments pulled from chests and strewn across the floor. A thick tapestry rug that must have covered the floor was rucked up and pulled to one side, and marks in the dust suggested that someone had tried to prise a floorboard out of place. Either Mercer had left in a great hurry after ransacking his room for some lost object, or someone else was also searching for something connected with his death and had got here before me.

The room was long with a high ceiling and stretched the width of the range, the narrow leaded windows overlooking the quadrangle on one side and the street outside on the other. On the street side was a wide brick fireplace and, opposite, a large oak desk with delicately carved legs. At the far end, facing the door, were three steps leading up to another doorway, which stood open. Sweat prickled on my palms for an instant as I held my breath and listened for any sound other than the frantic pumping of my own blood as I remembered the footsteps I had heard; perhaps they had not come from the storey above, and someone was still in the room. Stepping as carefully as a cat, I grabbed the nearest thing the study offered to a weapon – an iron poker from the grate – and clutched it in both hands along with my courage as I tensed myself to approach the open door. I stepped through, raising the poker – but the small room, inside the tower itself, contained nothing more than a plain truckle-bed, a wash-stand and a heavy oak wardrobe with carved panels in the doors.

This little bedchamber had not been spared the searcher's attentions: sheets were roughly torn from the bed, an earthen-ware jug had been knocked from the washstand and broken in pieces, leaving a damp stain on the rushes that covered the floor. As I drew closer I saw that even the straw mattress had been slashed with a knife, its stuffing spilling out over the bed. In the corner of this square room was a small wooden door set into the wall. I tried the handle but it was firmly locked, though there was a hollow sound when I knocked on the wood; here, I presumed from the echo and the draught that whistled from the cracks, was the staircase to the upper floor of the tower. Gripping the poker, I checked behind the heavy window drapes and under the bed, but found no one; satisfied that I was alone, I returned to the main room and quietly locked the door behind me so that I could examine the scene in peace.

Where to begin amid such chaos? The room was crammed with furniture of assorted sizes and shapes, all made from good oak. Chairs had been turned over, a trunk dragged across the floor and forced open to reveal a cache of books. The apparent desperation of the searcher proved beyond any doubt that he believed there was something of significance to be found among Mercer's possessions; the question was whether it had already been found, and whether I would know it if I saw it.

I turned to the handsome writing desk, now littered with papers and quills. A little brass astrolabe had been knocked to the floor in the frenzy; I bent to retrieve it and set it back on its stand, but its rule was broken. As I crouched

I noticed a dark curling object under the desk; its shape was unusual, but when I reached to pick it up and brought it into the light, I saw that it was only a length of orange peel, long dried out, and threw it back to the floor. Lifting one or two of the top sheets, I skimmed the papers on the desk; it would be painstaking work to sift through the mass of leaves piled up there for any letter or jotting that might shed light on the former occupant's death. All the drawers of the desk had been pulled out; I reached into each one, feeling along the underside for any catches that would release secret compartments, but found nothing. I lifted out contents of the drawers abandoned in disarray, but already I felt daunted by the task; I had no idea what I hoped to find.

From the top left-hand drawer I withdrew a fine leather writing-case and briefly tensed with hope, thinking that perhaps Mercer's most recent correspondence might still be within and might reveal who he had lately fallen out with or any transactions that could explain his presence in the garden. I cleared a space on the desk for the case and, as I opened it, a thin, cloth-bound book fell out. Picking it up, I opened it at random and saw that it was a printed almanac for the year 1583, the pages marked into divisions for the days of the week, the month marked at the top of each page and annotated with the relevant astrological predictions. My pulse racing in my throat, I flicked hastily through to the page for today's date, wondering if there was the slightest chance he might have noted whom he had planned to meet this morning.

As I searched for the page marked 22nd May, I noticed an oddity about this calendar: each division was marked with two dates, one printed in black, the second marked in by hand in red ink. The red date was ten days ahead of the black. I knew immediately what this meant, because my host the French ambassador worked from such calendars in the embassy: the red number showed the date according to the new calendar introduced the previous October by Pope Gregory, now mandatory in the Catholic states by order of the Papal Bull *Inter gravissimas*. In a marked act of defiance to papal authority, it had not been adopted by England and the other Protestant countries of Europe, and I had often heard the ambassador complaining that it made correspondence between the officials of different countries extremely confusing because no one was quite sure which date was meant; usually he would use both, just to be sure. But why, I wondered, would an English Protestant like Roger Mercer need a calendar marked with the Gregorian dates?

I found the page I wanted and was moved to see that on 22nd May (1st June) he had written the time and place of my disputation in his elegant, sloping hand: *G. Bruno vs Underhill, Div. Sch. 5*, it read. Then, holding the book closer, I noticed another mark for today's date; in the top left-hand corner of the day's division there was a solitary letter J. I blinked in disbelief. Could J be the initial of the person he had arranged to meet? That could certainly narrow it down. I scoured recent dates for any other clues. The previous day, the 21st (31st) was marked only with a curious symbol, a circle with spokes like the wheel of a cart. Flicking back through the book, I noticed this symbol appeared on other pages at regular intervals; more or less once every ten days, though never on the same day of the week. It might have been a code, but I had no way of deciphering it. The J, though, did at least seem a concrete clue.

But as I had held the book up to my nose, I had noticed something else: a faint smell of oranges. I thought at first that it came from my own fingers, having picked up the peel from the floor, but as I sniffed I realised that the smell was coming from the almanac itself. Perhaps that was not unusual; if Roger Mercer liked to eat oranges, it was possible that he had spread the juice to the pages of his books; he had not been the most fastidious eater, as I had noted the night before. But something nagged at my mind, and as I sniffed the book again I suddenly cursed myself for being so stupid.

At that moment, the wardrobe door creaked a little further on its worn hinge, making me jump almost out of my boots; instinctively I hid the book inside my shirt, tucked into the waist of my breeches, and whipped around, but the door appeared to have moved under its own weight. Opening it right up, I saw at first only heaps of cloth, half pulled out by the hasty searcher, and then I made out a squat dark shape pushed up against the back of the closet, covered by an old blanket. When this was yanked away, it revealed a small wooden chest bound with iron bands and fastened with a sturdy padlock. Reaching in, I dragged the object into the light, but it tilted and landed with a resounding thud as it dropped between the ledge of the wardrobe and the floor. I paused, my breath held tight in my throat, to see if the noise had alerted anyone to my presence in the room, but all was silent. As the chest fell, I had heard unmistakeably the metallic clink of coins. So this was Roger Mercer's strongbox, his treasury, plainly full of gold. He had not taken much trouble to conceal it, and yet it had been left untouched by whoever had laid waste to his room.

This fitted with the full purse left on Roger's body; it seemed clear that whoever had killed him was not interested in taking money. But why else does a man kill, if not for money? Either for revenge, I thought, or because he fears the victim may do him harm. I decided I would have to visit the porter, Cobbett, and see what he could tell me of the college's system of gates and locks; the person who had turned this room upside down had evidently let himself in with a key and locked the room again behind him.

As I crouched beside the trunk brooding on the matter of keys, I heard the undeniable click of the lock in the room behind me turning smoothly and my heart almost froze in my chest. There was no time to hide; all I could do was watch helplessly as the door slid open just wide enough to admit the lanky figure of Walter Slythurst, the bursar I watched as his gaze slowly swept the tumult of the room with incredulity before eventually coming to rest on me. There was even a brief pause as his brain struggled to process the evidence of his ferrety eyes, before he gave a little cry and stared at me as if I were an apparition.

'Almighty God!' he exclaimed. 'You! What the Devil –?'

It was going to take a quite exceptional feat of invention to explain why I had locked myself into the recently ransacked room of a newly dead man and was now cradling his strongbox in my blood-soaked lap. I took a deep breath and affected nonchalance.

'*Buongiorno*, Master Slythurst.'

Slythurst's face, all planes and angles, was made for sneering cynicism rather than purple rage, but at this moment he appeared to swell up to a point where he could barely formulate his own language.

'What . . . ?' he began, before his gathered breath escaped in a squeaking hiss, and he inhaled for the next attempt, 'what *is* this?'

'I am assisting the rector,' I explained, exaggerating my accent, which I had found in the past to be a useful cover for apparently eccentric behaviour; people put it down to the oddities of a foreigner. 'I was with him this morning, we were the first to arrive at the scene of the terrible misfortune. And the clothes, you see, were badly destroyed, so I have come to find some replacements in which to dress the poor body of Doctor Mercer for his final rest.' I assumed a pious expression; never had I uttered so unconvincing a lie. In his place, I would not have believed me for a moment.

Slythurst narrowed his eyes until they were mere slits below his thin brows.

'I see. And did you have some trouble finding them?' The sweep of his hand mockingly took in the destruction that had been visited on the room.

His tone could have withered the spring leaves from the trees. I returned his look of contempt as levelly as I could.

'The room is as I discovered it.'

'Then why did you lock the door?'

'Force of habit.' I laughed self-consciously. 'Foolish, I know – but in Italy I lived for many years often in fear for my life. The places I travelled, you never left a door open behind you. Even now, this is something I do from pure instinct, I do not even notice that I am doing so.'

He appeared to consider the likelihood of this for a moment, then folded his arms as if to underline his distrust of me.

'Where did you get the key?'

'It was the set Doctor Mercer had with him. When the coroner arrived, I came here to see how I might help.'

'Hm.' Slythurst stepped forward and made a perfunctory assessment of the papers scattered across the desk. 'I am here, by the way, to make an inventory of personal effects to be returned to the family,' he added, not looking at me.

It was clear that he was lying, particularly since, as an official of the college, he was not obliged to explain his business to me. I rose and faced him, taking care not to let the book slip out from under my shirt; he turned, arms still folded, and we squared up to each other, each knowing the other had an unspoken intent but not quite daring to make an outright challenge. I wondered briefly if we might both

124

be searching for the same thing, before remembering that I did not know what I was searching for, only whatever might help to explain Mercer's presence in the garden. But were Slythurst and whoever had turned over the room before I arrived looking for the same item? I studied his pale, almost hairless face with distaste as he glared back at me with equal contempt. Could he have been the original ransacker of the room, disturbed in his first attempt and now returned to pick up where he left off? I doubted it; I had seen his expression when he first opened the door and the chaos had shocked him as much as it had me, I was sure. So more than one person believed that something they wanted was hidden in the dead man's room.

'What is that?' Slythurst eventually broke the silence by pointing to the chest at my feet.

'I believe it is Doctor Mercer's strongbox.'

'And what were you doing with it?' His words were as pointed as if he had etched them on glass.

'It was inside the wardrobe. I thought it might contain items of clothing, so I lifted it out to take a look.'

Once again he gave me a look from under his eyelids such as you might give a market-place urchin who tries to steal your bread.

'You are covered in gore, Doctor Bruno,' he remarked, his eyes flicking back to the desk.

'Yes, I tried to help a man who was bleeding to death,' I replied quietly.

'You simply cannot be helpful enough, can you?' He strode across to the doorway of the small bedchamber and glanced past me. 'Have you been up the staircase?' he asked, gesturing brusquely to the small inner door.

'That door is locked,' I said.

'Locked?' He looked puzzled. 'Curious.'

He crossed to the door and tried it himself, as if to prove

125

that he would not accept my word on anything. There was another uncomfortable silence; I knew he was waiting for me to leave and I was reluctant to abandon the room in case whatever he and the other searcher wanted was still there to be found. But I could not plausibly prolong my presence there, so I gave a terse bow.

'Well, I will leave you to your sad task, Master Slythurst.'

He only nodded, but as I reached the door, he called,

'Doctor Bruno – have you not forgotten something?'

I thought for a moment he meant the keys, and was expecting me to hand them over to him. I looked at him, uncomprehending, as a smile of satisfaction cut across his face.

'The clothes? To dress the body?'

'Of course.' Hastily I ran back to the wardrobe and gathered an armful of garments without stopping to look at them, aware that my pitiful lie had now collapsed entirely.

'I'm sure the rector will be most grateful for your assistance,' Slythurst said pleasantly, holding the door open for me as I struggled out with the unwanted clothes. As I passed, he hissed, 'I shall be watching you, Bruno.'

I offered him my most charming smile in return as I passed through. Moments later I heard the sound of a key turning smoothly in the lock.

Returning to the courtyard I caught sight of Gabriel Norris, now more soberly dressed in a suit of black and a plain gown, which made his good looks stand out all the more. He stood at the entrance to the west range stairway on the other side of the tower and appeared to be regaling a group of fellow students with tales of his heroism; one hand was held out flat at chest height, a vastly exaggerated account of the dog's size, and I could not help smiling to myself at the bravado of the young. He spotted me and broke off

126

mid-sentence, looking with some suspicion at the bundle of Mercer's clothes in my arms and then at the entrance from which I had just emerged.

'What, has the looting begun already, Doctor Bruno?' he called, a little too jovially.

'I am assisting the rector,' I repeated, since it seemed this defence could not be contradicted.

'Ah.' He nodded and, leaving his friends, sauntered over to me. At close quarters I noticed that he seemed older than the boys who now stood waiting for him; I would have guessed his age at twenty-five or more. 'That was a bit of excitement we had this morning, was it not?'

'I'm not sure that's the word I would use.'

'No – no, of course.' He assumed a solemn expression. 'I meant only – Oxford life is usually so uneventful, and now we have a royal visitation and a tragedy all at once, we hardly know which to talk about first.'

'You were very level-headed this morning,' I said. 'I don't think I would have had such a steady arm in the heat of the moment. It is lucky you are a good shot.'

Norris inclined his head, acknowledging the compliment.

'My father taught me to hunt as a boy,' he said. 'I only wish I could have been quick enough to save Doctor Mercer.' He rubbed the back of his hand across his brow; I suspected that, under all his swaggering, the experience had shaken him profoundly.

'Did you know him well?' I asked.

'He has been my tutor since Doctor Allen was deprived last year.' A strange expression crossed his face, as if he were struggling to master some emotion. 'We were close, I suppose. I respected him, in any case.'

'That was a hunting dog that killed him, was it not?' I said.

'Irish wolfhound. Very efficient hunters – always go straight

127

in to break the neck, you know,' he said in a brisker tone, pleased to display his knowledge. Then he frowned. 'But it is usually a gentle dog, too – people keep them as pets. They're not so unpredictable in temperament as, say, a mastiff – they rarely attack unless they have been trained to do so.'

'It was starving, though – did you not see the scrawny state of it?'

He nodded slowly.

'Must have been a stray – I suppose if it was desperate for meat it would savage the first living creature it found.'

'Is it not unusual that a stray wolfhound should be roaming the streets of Oxford at night?' I asked.

He looked at me curiously, as if he found my questions odd, but shrugged.

'There is hunting in the royal forest of Shotover, to the east of the city – you can hire dogs from the keeper there for a day's hunt. Some of the commoners go from time to time when we have permission. Perhaps one of their dogs got loose and wandered into the city.' He sounded as if he had lost interest in the subject, and looked around to check that his group of admirers was still waiting. 'Well, Doctor Bruno – I must collect my books and get along to lectures. I hope this morning's adventure will not mar your stay in Oxford too badly.' He bowed briefly and made to enter the staircase.

'You have a room in there?' I asked, gesturing with my thumb.

'That's right,' he said, carelessly. 'One of the best in the college. I share it with my servant, Thomas.'

'Then,' I glanced across the courtyard at the passages that led either side of the hall to the garden, calculating the distance. 'You must have exceptional hearing to have been woken by the commotion from the Grove, when these rooms are the furthest away from it.'

128

He regarded me for a moment with a closed expression, then stepped towards me, taking my elbow, and leaned in with a confidential whisper.

'There you have me, Doctor Bruno – I will confess that I was not abed when I heard the noise, but please let that be a confidence between us.'

I raised an eyebrow; he gave me a knowing nudge in the ribs, from which I was presumably supposed to infer some manly nocturnal pursuit. In such an intimate stance it was clear that he had no smell of drink on him, and a man who had been carousing all night could not have had such a steady hand as I had witnessed with the bow and arrow; I guessed, then, that he had been bedding some woman and was secretly pleased to share the triumph. That at least would account for his ridiculous garb at that hour of the morning, I thought.

'I had spent the night away from college – you understand my meaning, I'm sure,' he said, with a wink, 'and on my return I was passing along St Mildred's Lane by Jesus College when I heard the frenzied barking of that dog and those dreadful cries. I realised it was coming from the Grove and ran straightways for my bow and then to the gate, where I found you all gathered, looking on.'

The reproach stung, so I countered with one of my own.

'Did you not try the gate from Brasenose Lane? You might have arrived sooner.'

'But I don't have a key to that gate,' he said, puzzled. 'Only the senior Fellows do. I was not to know it had been left open – the Fellows treat that Grove as if it were sacred. I acted as quickly as I could, Doctor Bruno.'

'And did you see anyone near the college walls as you approached?' I asked, as lightly as I could.

Norris tilted his head, considering.

'Now that you mention it – at one point I thought I heard footsteps up ahead, running, but the sound was lost in the din from the garden and in all that followed I forgot all about it. Why do you ask?'

'I only wondered if many people were abroad at that time of day,' I said, turning to go. 'I should really take these to the rector.'

He eyed me curiously for some moments, before clapping me on the shoulder.

'We are all looking forward to your disputation this evening. I don't care much for cosmology either way, but I shall applaud you if you can make the rector look a fool. Although I imagine he will do that quite efficiently by himself.' He grinned and turned as if to leave, then looked back at me with a serious expression. 'I suppose you and I shall be called to give account if there is an inquest. There will be trouble for me over the bow and arrows, no doubt – no one is allowed to keep weapons in the university precincts. Perhaps you could mention that the hound could not have been subdued without my intervention, Doctor Bruno?'

'I will certainly give a true account of events to the best of my ability, if one is requested,' I replied, bowing in return.

'Thank you. *Arrivederci, il mio doctore!*' he cried, turning on his heel and striding swiftly towards the main gate. I watched him walk away, intrigued. Gabriel Norris might be an unbearable peacock, but it would be a mistake to underestimate his sharpness.

I stood in the courtyard, my arms full of Roger Mercer's clothes, wondering what I should do next. The sun was obscured behind rows of pewter clouds, stretching out in waves over the rooftops like an inverted ocean; I shivered in my thin shirt. Slythurst was sure to tell the rector that I had been found rummaging in the dead man's room and had even got as far as dragging his money chest from its hiding place; the only way I could hope to protest my innocence was to repeat my ridiculous lie about trying to help out with the clothes. I looked down at the bundle in my arms, garments which still retained the musky smell of their owner's body, and decided I must take them to the rector as soon as I could, before Slythurst could insinuate anything unpleasant in his ear I would tell him it was an old Nolan custom to show respect for the dead; he might think me absurd, but I hoped he would not suspect me for a thief. He would also wonder why I had taken the dead man's keys; these I must return as soon as possible, though I would have liked to keep them in case I had the chance to search the tower room further. But surely Slythurst would have found what he came for by now, if the first ransacker had not.

My head was swimming; I wanted nothing more than to return to bed and lie down, but I turned again towards the gatehouse and found a door set into the wall of the archway to the right of the vast wooden gate with a painted sign proclaiming the porter's lodge.

I peeked around the door; a fat, old man with a brush of wiry grey hair sat beside a wooden table, his head slumped to his chest, breathing heavily. There were beer stains on his jerkin and a tired-looking black dog lay at his feet, its muzzle all peppered with grey. It half raised its head at my footsteps, regarding me through milky eyes, then returned to its sleepy position as if that small effort was as much as it could offer. I cleared my throat and knocked at the same time; the old man's head jerked upwards in confusion and spittle glistened on his grizzled chin.

'Pardon me, sir, must have drifted for a moment there,' he muttered.

'Goodman Cobbett? My name is Giordano Bruno—'

'I know you, sir, you are our honoured guest come to cross swords with the rector tonight – I refer to the swords of words, naturally, for your actual sword is not permitted about the college, sir. And what a dreadful day for you to be here, sir, for such a misfortune as we have had this morning, it hardly bears thinking of.' He shook his head theatrically and his jowls swung from side to side.

'Yes, I am deeply sorry,' I said, taking the keys from my pocket. 'I was there in the Grove assisting the rector – he asked me to see that Doctor Mercer's keys were safely returned, I presumed he meant to you?'

The old porter's face lit up with relief at the sight of the key-ring.

'Oh, thank Heaven for that! At least we have one set back. I begin to think keys have legs round these parts.'

'Do you not keep a spare?' I asked, gently easing the door closed behind me.

'We do, sir, but the spare disappeared from my key cupboard a couple of days ago, which seemed curious at the time, since Doctor Mercer never asked me for it and I am rarely out of the lodge. I thought perhaps the bursar had needed it to get to the strongroom in a hurry – you must go through the sub-rector's room to access the tower, you see – but he says he knows nothing of it either.' He shook his head again. 'The Fellows are worse than the students, if you ask me – forever mislaying keys. They don't seem to realise new keys cost money.'

'Do you keep spare keys to all the rooms in the college?'

'Certainly, sir – I'll show you.' The old man heaved himself to his feet, wheezing alarmingly, and lumbered across to a shallow wooden cupboard mounted on the back wall behind his desk. Proudly he flung open both doors to reveal rows of iron keys of assorted shapes and sizes hanging from hooks, each labelled with a combination of letters and numbers.

'How do you ever tell which is which?' I asked innocently.

'Ah,' Cobbett said, tapping the side of his bulbous scarlet nose. 'I have a system designed to prevent them falling into the wrong hands, see? If I were to just label them "Tower Room", "Library" and so on, be too easy for the young 'uns to sneak in and help themselves when I'm sleeping or relieving meself or whatnot. So I made up a code, oh, years ago now. If anyone loses a key they come to me and I find them the spare, but they can't steal them to get in where they don't belong to play pranks or what have you.'

'So you have a complete set of keys to all the doors and gates in the college?'

'That I do, sir, 'cept when people lose 'em,' he said darkly. 'The only ones I don't have are to the college strongroom. You can only get to it through the sub-rector's room, as I say, up the tower staircase, and only the rector and the bursar have a key. It is designed that way so that no one person can get into the strongroom without at least one other person present,' he added.

'And only you have keys to the other rooms?'

'No, sir – the rector also keeps a complete set to all the rooms in his lodgings, but he doesn't hand those out. Students and Fellows alike must come to me, and only me.' He shuffled back to his chair and regarded me with curiosity.

'Does the bursar have a key to the sub-rector's room?'

'The bursar?' Cobbett looked surprised. 'No, sir – he has his key to the strongroom, but the sub-rector must be present to let him up to the tower. It's supposed to guard against theft, you see.'

'But if the sub-rector should be away, and the bursar needs the strongroom?'

'Well, then, he would need to come to me or ask the rector to let him up. Why you so interested in keys, anyways?'

'Oh – I have only been wondering how a stray dog might have got into the Grove,' I replied, though I was now also wondering how Slythurst had obtained a key to Roger Mercer's private chamber. Had he somehow contrived to steal the spare key from Cobbett's cupboard? And if that was the case, how had the person who first turned over Mercer's room let himself in? Who had a third key, except the rector?

'Ah.' The old porter rubbed his stubbly chin. 'Well, now – I dare say that was my fault, sir – it must be that I didn't check the Brasenose Lane gate carefully enough last night.'

A silence followed; it was clear that the old man was uncomfortable telling a lie that reflected poorly on his competence, and that he was doing so dutifully but reluctantly.

'I find that hard to believe,' I said, encouragement in my voice. 'For everyone tells me you have served the college man and boy and have never neglected your duty.'

A look of gratitude spread across the porter's face; he beckoned me closer. I leaned in; his breath was heavy with stale beer.

'I thank you, sir – I told the rector, I said, "Sir, you know I will do as you wish, but I hope no one will ever believe old Cobbett left any cranny of this college unchecked on his rounds." People here know I do my job well, sir.' He puffed out his great barrel chest and fell to a fit of coughing.

'Well, I hope you will not be punished for what is not your fault,' I said.

'Thank you, sir, you are kind.'

'Tell me, Goodman Cobbett,' I said casually, turning to go, 'if a man ever wanted to go into the town and return after you lock the main gates, might that be possible?'

The porter's face creased into a broad, gummy smile.

'All things are possible, Doctor Bruno,' he said, with a wink. 'Perhaps you have heard I sometimes come to certain agreements with the undergraduates regarding the locking of the gates. But you should not need any such arrangements – Fellows and guests may have a key to the main gate.'

'Really?' I asked, surprised. 'So the Fellows may leave the

college by the main gate and enter at whatever hour they please?'

'It is not exactly encouraged,' Cobbett said, warily, 'but yes, they may. Not many of 'em do, mind – they are all too serious-minded for gadding about the town. It's the students who want to get out and are denied the liberty. But I was a young man once, and I say it does more harm than good to deny young men their pleasures. All work and no play makes Jack a dull boy, sir.'

I bent slightly and peered through the little window that opened on to the tower archway. Two students in black gowns passed, leather satchels clutched to their chests.

'Can you see from here everyone who comes in and out at night, then?' I asked.

'As long as I'm awake,' said Cobbett, with a husky laugh that quickly turned into another round of coughing.

There was more I wanted to ask, but I sensed my questions were making him suspicious, so I turned to the door.

'Thank you for your help, Cobbett – I must be getting along.'

'Doctor Bruno,' he called, as I opened the door. I turned back. 'Please do not repeat what I said about the Grove, will you? As much as it pains me, I must do as the rector instructs and say the blame was mine.'

I assured him that I would not mention our conversation. His face slumped with relief.

'I will gladly tell you more of locks and keys another time if you care to know,' he added, casually twirling Mercer's keys in his stubby fingers. Then he reached beneath the table and pulled out an earthenware flagon, waving it meaningfully in my direction. 'But it is thirsty work, all this jawing. Conversation flows all the better for a bit of refreshment, if you catch my meaning.'

I smiled

'I will see what refreshment I can find for you when we next converse, Cobbett,' I said. 'I shall look forward to it.'

'And I, Doctor Bruno, and I. Leave the door open, if you'd be so kind.'

He reached down and ruffled the dog's fur between its ears; I could hear him chuckling to himself as I left the lodge and stood in front of the high main gate, wondering.

I returned to my chamber, glad to rid myself of the shirt now stiff with Roger Mercer's blood, and to take the book out of my breeches, where its corners were digging uncomfortably into my stomach. Clad only in my underhose, oblivious to the chill of the room, I took a tinderbox from the mantelpiece and lit one of the cheap tallow candles with which the room had been provided; the chamber quickly filled with its acrid smoke as I took Mercer's almanac and opened it, this time at the back. There were several blank pages bound into the covers, and one of these was oddly stiff, the paper slightly warped as if it had got wet and then dried out. I sniffed it closely; here the smell of oranges was most insistent. Carefully, so as not to scorch it, I held the page up close to the candle's flame and watched as, slowly, a series of marks in dark brown began to grow visible. Moving the paper up and down past the flame, it gradually revealed its secret writing: a sequence of letters and symbols, with no logical pattern I could discern. Below this was a shorter series of the same symbols, though in a different order: grouped in two lots of three different symbols, then a group of five. It was evidently some kind of cipher, though I knew little of cryptography and had no idea how to begin decoding it. I wondered if Sidney might have a better idea, given that he had had more contact than I with such work, so I took a piece of paper and a quill and made a copy of the symbols exactly as they appeared on the page, thinking I would give this to him to work on. But as I copied the first three lines, it became clear that the symbols were arranged in a sequence of twenty-four, and that this sequence was repeated three times.

I paused. There were twenty-four letters in the English alphabet, but surely no cipher could be that obvious? None the less, I thought it worth a try, and on my copy I wrote out the alphabet underneath the first sequence of twenty-four symbols. If this was a basic substitution cipher, then according to this system the groups of letters underneath might mean something. I copied out the first group of three symbols according to the alphabetical substitution, and as I saw the result, O-R-A, I felt my pulse quicken. Hurriedly I translated the remaining letters of the short phrase, and drew my breath in sharply. I had written the words *Ora pro nobis*. Pray for us.

Folding the copy carefully and hiding it under my pillow, I laid my head down gratefully, trying to imagine why Roger Mercer had written those words – the refrain from the Catholic Litany of the Saints – invisibly in the back of his almanac. But I had to put the puzzle from my mind; there were more pressing matters for my attention. I had intended only to close my eyes for a few moments before gathering my thoughts and setting them to concentrate on the evening's disputation, which was supposed to be the crowning glory of my first visit to Oxford, but I was awakened all of a sudden by a furious hammering on the door and sat upright, confused and bleary.

'Open up, for Christ's sake!' a man's voice bellowed, and for a moment my bowels clenched: had there been another violent death? The door handle rattled urgently as I struggled out of my sheets and into a clean shirt, and when finally I wrenched it open, there stood Sidney, quiffed and impatient, dressed head to foot in green velvet, with a neck ruff that made his head look as if it were perched on a platter.

'Christ alive, Bruno, I came as soon as I heard!' He strode past me into the room, stripping off his gloves with a businesslike air. 'I had barely breakfasted this morning when what should I hear from the servants but that all of Christ Church cloister is aflame with the news that a savage beast stalks Lincoln College, dragging innocent men to their doom.' He looked me up and down, eyes wide in mock terror. 'Well – at least you still have all your limbs, God be praised.'

'Philip – a man died in front of me this morning,' I said wearily.

'I know – I want to hear all about it,' he said. 'Come on, dress yourself, man – I have come to take you out to dinner.'

'What time is it?' I said, suddenly panicked; clearly I had slept much longer than I intended, and my stomach was crying out with hunger, but I had not yet even begun my preparation for the disputation at five.

'Just past one.' Sidney sauntered around the room, picking up books and considering them idly while I rummaged for clean hose and a plain doublet. 'One lad at Christ Church said a wolf had got into the college – I thought that seemed unlikely. Did you see what happened?'

'By tomorrow they'll be saying it was a lion,' I said. 'These students seem starved of incident here, they will make legends out of any matter. But I will be glad to tell you all, for there is much that troubles me, and I have something to show you. Let us find some food first, though.' I took the almanac from under my pillow and tucked it inside my doublet before fastening the buttons, Sidney watching me curiously as I did so.

The air was still damp though the sky was lighter as we passed under the tower gate into St Mildred's Lane, then south past the tall spire of All Hallows Church. At the High Street we paused to let two riders on horseback pass, then crossed between piles of dung and straw that littered the muddy thoroughfare, churned up after all the rain. I was glad I had put on my riding boots. Young men in short black gowns hurried past us in groups, all chattering over one another. At the corner of a narrow lane edged by low timber-framed houses, Sidney turned and led me towards a two-storey building with gabled roofs which bore a painted sign creaking above its door: Peckwater Inn.

The cobbled yard was busy as we passed under the gate; men led horses across towards a stable block at the back as others unloaded heavy-looking barrels from a high cart. The building occupied three sides of a quadrangle, with two levels of balconies on each side overlooking the yard.

Inside, the tap-room was dim and a fire burned in a stone hearth at one end. Long, rough-hewn tables and benches were set around the edges of the room, many of them occupied already by busy diners talking and eating at once; a serving hatch was built into the wall opposite the fireplace, and a red-faced woman in an apron scuttled between it and the tables ferrying wooden platters and pewter tankards, pausing occasionally to brush a strand of damp hair from her face with the back of her hand. When she noticed us, her harried expression changed to one of delight and she rushed over, wiping her hands on her apron.

'Sir Philip! What a pleasure – we heard you were back in town,' she said with a wink. 'They said there was a great procession in your honour.'

'It was a very wet procession, and the honour was not mine, Lizzy,' Sidney said, removing his hat and making a solemn bow. 'May I present my dear friend from Italy, Doctor Giordano Bruno?'

'*Buongiorno, signorina,*' I said, playing up to Sidney's exaggerated courtliness.

'Pleasure, I'm sure,' the tavern-mistress giggled, her considerable bosom quivering.

'Now then, Lizzy – we'd like a quiet table, a jug of beer when you have a moment, your best game pie and some fresh bread, if you please.'

She beamed up at him.

'You best take the corner table, you won't be disturbed there,' she said, and bustled off towards the kitchen.

'I used to come here all the time,' Sidney explained. 'The inn is hard by Christ Church and there was more varied company to be had here than inside the college when I was a student, if you know what I mean. We will be well treated in any case, they know I tip generously. Now then, Bruno – tell your tale.'

He sat back and folded his hands together with the air of one who expects to be entertained. I could not help feeling he was taking a man's death rather lightly, treating it as material for an exciting anecdote; in that he reminded me of Gabriel Norris. Perhaps it is a trait of rich boys, I thought: craving adventure in a life made dull by the absence of daily cares. I was about to launch into my account when Lizzy arrived with a jug of beer, two tankards and a loaf of bread that Sidney ripped into immediately, handing me the first piece.

With my mouth half-full, I told him of all that had happened since I was first awakened by the dog's fearsome noise at dawn. When I came to the part about the locked gates, his complacent expression vanished and he leaned forward eagerly, his eyes alert.

'You suspect foul play?' he asked, as the tavern-mistress arrived again with a platter of thick game pie.

When she had gone, I told him of my visit to Roger Mercer's room, the interruption by Slythurst and my subsequent conversation with the old porter. When I had finished, Sidney whistled through his teeth.

'Extraordinary business,' he said, shaking his head in

disbelief. 'So you surmise someone set that dog on him on purpose, then ransacked his room looking for something valuable?'

'That is the mystery,' I said. 'It can't be valuable in the usual sense, because whoever did it had no interest in the ten pounds he was carrying, or the chest of gold in his room. But that is what I can't fathom – someone lured him to the garden on the pretext of a meeting, clearly someone to whom he owed money. So why didn't they take the money and then kill him?'

'Not necessarily a debt,' Sidney said, his mouth full. 'Might it not have been someone who had something to sell?'

I frowned.

'But what would he be buying at that hour, in the Grove? Something contraband, you think?'

Sidney was regarding me with amusement, a knowing smile playing about his lips.

'Think, Bruno – what might a man want to buy under cover of darkness?'

I looked back at him blankly, then caught his meaning.

'Whores, you mean? But in that case, how much simpler – and warmer – just to find a whorehouse in town.' I shook my head. 'Even if he *was* whoring – someone else knew to find him there at that time, someone who had a key to the Grove. And it still doesn't explain who went through his room, or why. Whatever they were looking for must have been of value to the person who wanted it – the place was torn to shreds, as if they sought it with utmost urgency.'

'But you say at least two people wanted whatever it might have been – the bursar and the other fellow who got there before you.' Sidney's brow creased for a moment and he took a long draught of beer. 'One thing is strange, though. It's such a cowardly way to kill a man, and so imprecise, too. If you want a man dead, why not just run him through with a sword? Especially if you know where to find him alone and unarmed. A dog is so unpredictable.'

'You know about hunting,' I said, cutting myself another brick of the pie. 'Could a hound like that be trained to attack a particular person, follow a scent?'

Sidney considered.

'I suppose – if it can be trained to follow the scent of a boar or a wolf, why not a man? If it was given one of his garments, perhaps. The Irish used to use them in battle – apparently they could pull an armoured knight off his horse. And you say it had been kept hungry, so its instincts would be all the keener.' He leaned his elbows on the table and rested his chin on cupped hands. 'It's as if the dog were part of some kind of show, as if it were done to create a spectacle. And what a way to die – locked in with a bloodthirsty animal. Makes me think,' he said, putting another hunk of bread into his mouth, 'of how the Romans used to execute the early saints, by throwing them into an arena with wild beasts. The way John Foxe describes it in that grisly *Book of Martyrs*.'

I stopped, a piece of meat halfway to my mouth, and stared at him, slack-jawed.

'What?' Sidney stopped chewing.

'Foxe's *Book of Martyrs*. The rector of Lincoln has a great interest in him – he has been preaching sermons in chapel with Foxe as his text.'

Sidney frowned.

'You think someone wanted to get rid of this Mercer and took inspiration from Foxe for his method?'

His expression betrayed his scepticism.

'It does seem far-fetched. Perhaps I am reading too much into it.' I passed my hands over my face. 'You are right – it was probably just a bad debt or trouble over a whore. No wonder the rector wants it covered up while a royal visitation is in town.'

Sidney was silent for a moment. Then he banged a palm down on the table.

'No, Bruno – I think you are right to be suspicious. The dog was loosed into the garden by someone who had a key, which suggests one of the Fellows or someone with access to the college keys. And at least two people wanted something from his room, but not money. Perhaps something that might be dangerous to them. And if everyone in the college has recently heard stories of the saints' gruesome deaths from Foxe's book, thanks to the rector – perhaps in some way it was staged as a deliberate copy. The question is, why? Did you find nothing in his room?'

'Only this. Take a look,' I said, extracting the slim almanac. 'What do you notice first?'

Sidney turned a couple of pages, then looked up at me, his face serious.

'Gregorian calendar. Was our man a secret papist after all, like his friend Allen?'

'I wondered. I heard him cry out to Mary before he died.'

'I'd cry to Mary if a dog that size was snapping at my arse,' said Sidney bluntly, turning the book over in his hands. 'That signifies nothing. But this calendar – you would only need this if you were corresponding with anyone in the Catholic countries. Especially if you needed to co-ordinate movements. Edmund Allen went to Rheims, did he not? Wasn't he related to William Allen, who founded the English College there?'

'A cousin, they said. Mercer could still have been in touch with him, you mean?'

Sidney glanced to either side and lowered his voice.

'Remember why we are here, Bruno. These seminaries in Rheims and Rome are Walsingham's greatest headache at the moment – they have vast funds from the Vatican and are in the business of training dozens of priests for the English mission, many of them former Oxford men.' He pulled his beard into a point as he thought, then picked up the book again. 'What is this little circle here?' he asked, pointing to the wheel symbol that marked the previous day's entry in Mercer's calendar.

'I don't know. It appears often. I wondered if it might be a code.'

Sidney peered closer, then shook his head.

'I recognise it, but I can't think from where. Looks like one of your magical symbols, Bruno.'

I had not liked to say so, but the thought had crossed my mind; Mercer had secretly confided an interest in magic. Even so, the symbol was not one I recognised, and so it intrigued me.

'It's not an astrological symbol, that is certain,' I said. 'But that is not the most important thing. Smell the book.'

Sidney frowned indulgently, but brought the book close to his face.

'Oranges?'

'Yes. Look to the back.'

He flicked through the pages, then looked up at me, nodding with something like admiration.

'Good work, Bruno. That is an old trick, the invisible writing in orange juice. Have you found some secret message?'

'A cipher. I made a copy – here.' I pushed my piece of paper across the table at him. 'You see what he has written at the bottom?'

'*Ora pro nobis*. Well, well.' Sidney folded the paper carefully and handed it back to me. 'Could be some sort of password or secret sign.'

'That's what I thought. Should we inform Walsingham?'

Sidney thought for a moment, then shook his head.

'We have nothing to tell him yet, except that we suspect a man of Catholic affiliations who is already dead. He would not thank us for wasting his time, and I cannot spare the expense of a messenger to London until we have something better. No – I think you should pursue this as discreetly as you may,' he continued, closing the book and handing it back. 'Especially if you say Rector Underhill seems keen to have it hushed up – he may know more than he lets on. Just because he was appointed by my uncle it does not follow that he can be trusted – the earl has made mistakes in his judgement before now.' He set his lips in a tight line. 'And who is this J – have you any thoughts?'

'I have met three men whose names begin with J,' I said. 'John Florio, James Coverdale and John Underhill, the rector. But it may not signify a name. Perhaps it is another coded symbol.'

Sidney nodded grimly.

'Perhaps. There is much to think about. But for now, my dear Bruno,' he said, suddenly smiling, 'you must think only about this evening's disputation. You must dazzle all Oxford with the new cosmology, and put this business from your mind. Lizzy – let me settle this account!' he called, as the serving-woman glanced in our direction. 'And I will take a large bottle of your strongest ale for the road,' he added genially, counting coins from his purse. When she had gone to fetch one, he leaned in and winked. 'A little gift for you to take your new friend the porter. I'll tell you this about Oxford – the porters guard more secrets than anyone in the university. Befriend your porter and he will quite literally open doors for you. And now, Bruno,' he said, clapping me on the back, 'you must go and settle this small matter of whether or not the Earth moves around the Sun.'

I was about to rise and take my leave when a great gale of laughter and chatter erupted from behind us as the taproom door opened to admit a group of four tall young men dressed expensively in jerkins of buff leather, silk peasecod doublets and short slashed breeches to show off their legs in fine silk stockings, all sporting bright starched ruffs above their collars and short velvet cloaks over one shoulder. They carried themselves with an identical swagger, talking loudly in cultured voices, making crude jokes to the serving-girl, and when they turned around I realised that the tallest of them was Gabriel Norris. He recognised me and raised a hand in greeting.

'Ah, *il gentil doctore*!' he cried, beckoning his friends over to our table. 'Come, boys, meet my new friend, the renowned Italian philosopher Doctor Giordano Bruno, and –' he stopped suddenly as he looked at Sidney for the first time and smartly executed a low bow, then turned to me expectantly and I realised I was supposed to effect the introductions.

'This is Master Gabriel Norris,' I announced, as Norris bowed again, 'who so expertly despatched the mad dog in the garden this morning. This is my friend Sir Philip Sidney.'

'You are the brave huntsman, then?' Sidney said, arching an eyebrow in amusement.

'I cannot claim too much praise for that feat, sir – the dog was barely yards from me. I prefer more of a challenge when I draw my bow,' Norris replied, with a self-deprecating laugh. 'There is good hunting to be had at Shotover Forest, though, Sir Philip, if you are looking for some sport during your stay.'

'I'd welcome the chance, if this weather clears,' Sidney said. 'Norris, you say? Who is your father?'

'George Norris, gentleman, of Buckinghamshire,' Norris said, effecting another bow. 'But he lived most of his later life in France and Flanders.'

Sidney appeared to be consulting some kind of mental register to see if the name meant something. Eventually he shook his head politely.

'Don't know him. France, eh? Exile, was he?'

'Oh, no, Sir Philip.' Norris laughed again. 'He was a

merchant. Cloth and luxury goods. He was exceptionally good at his business.' He gave Sidney a broad wink and rubbed his fingers together in the international sign for money. His manner was beginning to grate on me.

'Will you stay and drink with us?' he continued eagerly, already reaching into his purse for coins. 'Hie, girl – over here!' he called, gesturing imperiously at Lizzy. 'My friends plan to try and wrest some of that money from me over a few hands of bone-ace, but I am unbeaten yet this term. Are you a gambling man, Sir Philip? How about you, Doctor Bruno?'

I held up my hands in apology, but I saw the light of adventure spark in Sidney's eyes, and he rubbed his hands together, shunting over on the bench to make room for Norris.

'Philosophers are notoriously bad at cards,' Sidney said, waving a hand at me to move over and make room for Norris's friends beside me.

'All the more reason for Doctor Bruno to stay and join our game,' Norris said, smiling widely at me. He reached into his doublet and drew out a pack of cards, which he proceeded to shuffle expertly with the ease of long practice. I realised with a prickle of discomfort why he bothered me: it was not so much that I resented the hearty backslapping bonhomie of English upper-class gentlemen, for I could tolerate it well enough in Sidney on his own. It was the way Sidney fell so easily into this strutting group of young men, where I could not, and the fear that he might in some ways prefer their company to mine. Once again, I felt that peculiar stab of loneliness that only an exile truly knows: the sense that I did not belong, and never would again.

Norris snapped the pack against the flat of his hand and began swiftly to deal three cards to each player, two face down and one face up.

'Shall we put in a shilling each to begin? If you hope to

hold on to any of your money, Tobie,' he remarked to the dark-haired young man seated opposite, 'you had better start praying to St Bernardino of Siena, the patron saint of gamblers, for I am feeling lucky today.'

'Praying to saints, Gabe?' said the young man named Tobie with a sly grin, picking up his cards and considering them. 'Do not let anyone overhear you encouraging that, or they will think you gone over to Rome.'

Norris snorted.

'I speak in jest, you dull-wit. Gentlemen should never debate theology at the card table. But am I not right, Doctor Bruno – your countryman is said to intercede for gamblers? By those who believe in that kind of folly,' he added, throwing a handful of coins into the middle of the table.

'Actually, in Italy, he is more renowned for his tirades against sodomites,' I replied, getting up from the table. Norris looked up sharply from his hand and regarded me with interest.

'Is that so?'

'He lamented that in the last century the Italians were famed throughout Europe as the greatest nation of sodomites.'

'And are you?' he asked, a smile twitching at the edge of his mouth.

'We are the greatest nation at everything, my friend,' I said, returning the half-smile.

'Bruno spent most of his life inside a monastery,' Sidney said, leaning over to dig Norris in the ribs. 'He should know.'

The group fell into raucous laughter then as Lizzy slapped two large pitchers of ale down on the table. I decided it was time to leave.

'Well, I will leave you to rob one another with the blessing of St Bernardino,' I said, attempting to sound light-hearted. 'I have more pressing business.'

'Bruno must reorder the cosmos before five o'clock,' Sidney said, though he was intent on the cards he held.

'We are all most eager to hear it,' Norris said, his head still bent to his hand, then he flung down an ace of diamonds with a great cry of triumph and swept all the coins from the table as the others exploded in a riot of cursing. None of them looked up as I left.

# SIX

The Divinity School was the most breathtaking building I had yet seen in Oxford; inside its high wooden doors a magnificent fan-vaulted ceiling of blond stone arched over a plainly furnished room perhaps ninety feet long, bathed in natural light from the ten great arched windows that reached from floor to ceiling the full length of the room, so that the north and south walls seemed almost entirely of glass. These windows were surmounted by elegant tracery and their panes decorated with designs of coloured shields and heraldic devices of benefactors and university dignitaries, according to the custom. From the supporting arches at the top of the windows the ribs of the vault fanned out in symmetrical patterns across the ceiling before dovetailing again in points decorated with elaborately carved bosses and pendants inset with statues, drawing the eye constantly upward and inward to the centre. There was a pungent smell of warm wax from the plentiful candles, lamps and torches that had been set blazing along the walls, and their light was welcome despite the grand windows, for the sky was still overcast and the day already fading.

At the west end of the hall a stage had been erected and

high-backed chairs set with plump velvet cushions placed there for the most eminent persons – the palatine sat in the centre, with Sidney on his left side and the vice-chancellor in his ermine-trimmed robes on his right, their chairs surrounded by the other university dignitaries in their crimson and black gowns and the velvet caps of professors, ranged according to their degree. Below this, tiered seating had been built facing the length of the hall towards the east doorway, and was now filled with the figures of senior men in Fellows' gowns, while in the second of the five grand bays from the west end, two carved wooden pulpits were set opposite one another on the north and south walls, where Doctor Underhill and I now prepared to take up our positions for the confrontation.

Further towards the eastern end, rows of low benches had been set out for the undergraduates, who were even now still pouring into the hall, jostling and shoving one another to take their places amid a great murmur of animated conversation. For a moment my stomach tightened as I mounted the steps to the lectern that was to be my platform for the next hour, but as I cast my eyes over the expectant rows of faces I was buoyed up again by the old thrill of public performance, my first in England, and found I was anticipating the coming debate just as a sportsman might relish the challenge of a good fencing match.

I glanced at the stage to my left and caught Sidney's eye; he winked encouragement. The palatine slumped next to him, legs akimbo, picking his teeth with his thumbnail and examining whatever he extracted with more interest than he seemed prepared to devote to the coming argument. I noticed Coverdale, Slythurst and William Bernard sitting in the centre of the second row; Coverdale cast only a brief glance at me with complete composure, while Slythurst allowed his cold gaze to slide over me before pointedly turning away. Bernard cracked his bony hands together and nodded to me once; I chose to interpret this as encouragement. Doctor Underhill climbed his podium opposite and leaned forward over his lectern, fixing me with a combative stare. A stillness fell over the assembled crowd. I cleared my throat.

Earlier that afternoon, at a quarter to five, a student had been sent to escort me to the Divinity School from my chamber, a stocky and sensible-looking undergraduate with dark hair who introduced himself as Lawrence Weston and explained that the rector had sent him to show me the way to the place of our disputation, as he, the rector, had gone on ahead. This seemed a courteous gesture, and I followed young Weston across the quadrangle to the tower gatehouse. As we drew nearer, I noticed two servants coming from the tower-room staircase hefting a large wooden chest between them; behind them followed another, his arms laden with books.

'They are clearing Doctor Mercer's belongings already?' I asked Weston, trying not to reveal the alarm in my voice. The boy shrugged, as if the matter were not for the likes of him to question.

Outside, in St Mildred's Lane, we came upon Cobbett the porter, who stood looking on as his old dog pissed copiously against the wall of the college.

'Afternoon, Doctor Bruno!' he called cheerfully, raising a hand in salute. 'Off to bandy words with the rector?'

'*Buona sera*, Cobbett.' I gestured casually to the gatehouse behind us. 'I see they are clearing the tower room.'

Cobbett chuckled.

'They don't hang about with these matters, the senior rooms are great prizes here. Doctor Coverdale wants to move in as soon as possible.'

'He is to take over as sub-rector, then?'

'It's not official yet, but that won't stop him. Come on, now, Bessie, home again.' The old dog had finished her business and was hobbling painfully towards the gate, Cobbett ushering her gently along. 'Oh, by the bye, Doctor Bruno – here is another mystery for you . . .' He grinned, showing decayed gums.

'What is that?' I turned back, eager for information.

'That spare key to Doctor Mercer's room I said had been taken from my lodge – well, Master Slythurst brought it to me this morning. Found it on the north-west staircase just outside the tower room, he says. Whoever took it must have let it fall there the day before and not noticed – it is gloomy on those stairs at the best of times. Well, at least I have the full complement back again ready for our new sub-rector.'

'On the staircase? But how did the bursar come to find it there?' I asked, wondering how Slythurst had covered this lie.

'I suppose he was on his way to the strongroom.' He shuffled to the gate and pushed it open, then turned back to me. 'Good luck with your disputation, sir,' he added. 'And may the best man win.'

'Thank you,' I said, but I was distracted by this new information. It now seemed almost certain that Slythurst had taken that missing key and used it to let himself into Mercer's room: if he had truly been there on official business he would have had no need to confect such a story for the porter.

'Sir, we – ah – do need to hasten our steps, you are expected at five,' Weston said awkwardly. I nodded and ran my hands through my hair as if to untangle my thoughts; it would not do to have my brains running on locks and keys while I was supposed to be disputing the laws of the cosmos in front of all Oxford.

'Yes – I am sorry. Let us make haste – you lead the way,' I said.

'They were saying you were right there this morning, sir, when Gabe Norris shot the dog. Did you see the whole thing?'

Weston spoke with a boyish excitement, looking at me eagerly as he showed the way into Brasenose Lane, a narrow alley running along the north side of the college. Here the ground was muddy underfoot and the alley smelled as if it were a favourite place to piss. I took a deep breath and followed him.

'I was there, yes. But we were all too late – something for which I cannot forgive myself. Young Norris is a true shot – if we had been just a few moments earlier, poor Doctor Mercer might have stood a chance.'

Weston pursed his lips.

'Aye, well – the likes of Gabe Norris have nothing else to do with their time except practise their sports. It won't matter a jot to him whether he even takes his degree – Oxford is just one more amusement to his sort, strutting about in his London finery. Not so for we poor scholars obliged to go into the Church, alas.' He laughed bitterly.

'You don't like him, I deduce?' I said, smiling.

Weston appeared to relent.

'Oh, he's all right. I resent the commoners in principle – in a community of scholars one should feel oneself among equals, and their presence reinforces the notion of degree. And it is galling the way most of them don't care for their studies at all. But Gabe Norris is not the worst – he is quite generous with his fortune really, and not as stupid as some. Do you know, he has his own horse, sir?' Weston paused, shaking his head with a young man's envy. 'A roan gelding, the finest creature you ever saw. He stables it outside the city walls, for students are not supposed to keep their own mounts. But he does what he likes, for who would punish him?'

'He does seem very sure of himself,' I agreed. 'I imagine he gets more than his fair share of women, too, with that face.'

Weston only turned his head to glance at me, a sly grin curling at the corners of his mouth.

'You might *imagine* so, aye,' he said, and his peculiar emphasis, together with the mischievous smile, caught my attention.

'Ah,' I said, guessing at his meaning. 'You mean to say that women are not Master Norris's principal area of interest?'

'I would speak no slander against him, sir. I have no idea what he does in private, it is only what is said.'

'Much may be said in envy,' I observed as we walked. 'Why is it said of him, do you know?'

Weston looked down, embarrassed.

'Well, for one, he does not like to visit the bawdy-houses, sir.'

'It does not follow that he is therefore a sodomite.' Privately, though, it would not surprise me to learn that it was true of Norris, with his dandyish ways. I remembered the curious look he had given me when I mentioned St Bernardino's tirade against sodomites. 'And you should be careful with such gossip – sodomy is a hanging offence in this country, is it not?'

'Yes, sir. You are right, of course.' Weston looked chastened. 'But we have all noticed it. If a beautiful girl makes eyes at you like a calf, while you show yourself so entirely indifferent, it cannot be that you have a man's blood, would you not say, sir?' His cheeks were flushed crimson, and I guessed from this outburst that he was speaking of matters close to home. Since there was only one female in the immediate orbit of the young scholars, it was not hard to fathom who he meant.

'You are talking of the rector's daughter?' It should not have surprised me; as the only young woman in the college, why should she not set her fancy at the handsomest of the rich young men there? Yet I felt somehow disappointed by

155

the revelation, as if I had imagined a girl with Sophia's quick mind would not be blinded by such superficial qualities. 'She has confided in you?'

'Oh no, sir – and I have said too much already.'

He tried to change the subject but at that moment I stopped abruptly, realising that we were now at the end of Brasenose Lane and the wall running to our right was the wall of Lincoln Grove. The thick wooden door set into the wall was firmly shut. This must have been where the dog was released into the garden.

'Wait a moment,' I said, crouching down to examine the mud around the base of the door. It was undoubtedly churned up, but the passage of feet in the wet ground since the morning had obliterated any clear trace of prints and I cursed myself for not having had the wit to go and look for evidence straight away. I stood up and tried the handle to the door; it was locked. I was about to turn away when something caught my eye among the tufts of grass growing at the foot of the gate. I crouched again and drew out a thin leather strap, torn at one end – the kind of strap one might use for muzzling a dog. I did not know what use it might be, but I slipped it into my pocket just in case.

'Sir, we shall be late.' Weston seemed agitated, but I had noticed him watching me with curiosity as I pocketed the strap. 'Just at the end of the lane, and we are almost there.'

We passed into a wide square bordered by St Mary's Church to the right and, just visible to the left, above the wall of Exeter College garden, the pinnacles of the Divinity School. Ahead I could see the bulk of the city wall, its crenellated battlements outlined against the sky. Rounding the corner, we were dwarfed by the spectacular façade of the Divinity School and I paused to admire it, craning my neck up to the turrets above the grand arched window. Usually only ecclesiastical buildings were designed in such splendour,

156

but here was a secular edifice built like a cathedral, consecrated to the pursuit of knowledge, quite equal to the grand church of San Domenico Maggiore in Naples where I had first learned the art of disputation. To think that my ideas would join the echoes in its magnificent vaults was almost humbling, and I was about to make a remark to that effect to my guide, when I prickled with the discomfiting sense that I was being watched. I turned, and saw, leaning up against the blackened stone of the city wall, a tall man with folded arms, staring at me quite blatantly. He was dressed in an old leather jerkin and breeches of worn brown cloth, his hair was severely receded on top but long at the back, leaving his large forehead bare, and his face was pitted with the marks of pox; he might have been my own age or he might have been fifty, but the most striking aspect of his appearance was that he had no ears. Ugly welts of scar tissue surrounded the holes where they would once have been, betraying the fact that he had at one time been brought to justice as a petty criminal. He continued to watch me with a cool, level gaze in which I could discern no malice, rather a kind of mocking curiosity. I wondered if he was staring at me in particular, or if he were an opportunist pickpocket or some such, on the lookout for opportunity among the crowds gathering for the disputation. I had noted on my travels through Europe how petty thieves always seem to assume that men of education are necessarily also men of wealth; in my experience the two are rarely found together. If so, the man was bold; a further arrest for theft and he would risk the rope.

On another occasion I might have challenged his insolent stare, but there was no time to spare, so I turned towards the great porch of the Divinity School and was about to mount the stairs when I saw Doctor James Coverdale hurrying down them, pushing his way against the tide of young men in black gowns crowding to get in. He noticed me and stopped, a look of relief on his face; from the corner of my eye, I saw the figure in brown against the wall stir himself and take a step forwards. Coverdale also noticed; he froze for a moment and stared at the man with no ears, who looked directly at him and appeared to nod. It was clear that they recognised one another; Coverdale glared at him for a moment, his expression divided, it seemed to me, between irritation and concern, then he pasted on a smile for my benefit and guided me gently by the elbow to the right of the doorway, away from the man's inquisitive gaze.

'Thank you, Weston, for delivering our guest safely – you may join your friends inside,' Coverdale said pleasantly to my young guide, though his face had turned pale. Weston bowed to me before galloping up the steps and into the throng.

'Doctor Bruno, I wondered if I might have a brief word before we go in?' Coverdale murmured. 'Don't worry, we have time – our royal visitor is not yet arrived and it cannot go ahead without him.'

I nodded; it would be typical of the palatine not to bother arriving on time on my account. I adopted an air of polite attention; Coverdale seemed uncomfortable with what he needed to say.

'There is to be an inquest into the death of poor Doctor Mercer, you understand, and those who were first to arrive on the scene will be required to give evidence,' he began, his hand still clutching my elbow; I could not tell if this was supposed to be reassuring or menacing. 'I understand you were there early, together with the rector and Master Norris.'

'Yes, and I will gladly recount what I saw for the inquest, though I hope it will be before my party has to return to London,' I said expectantly, for I was sure there was more to come.

'It is only that – ah . . .' Here he faltered, and produced a little nervous laugh. 'The rector mentioned that you believed the garden gate into Brasenose Lane was locked when you all found poor Roger.'

'Yes, I tried it and it was locked fast. As were both the other gates.'

'Well, when I heard that, it occurred to me that of course you are not familiar with our college, so you would not have known that the gate to the lane has a very stiff handle on the inside.'

I raised an eyebrow to indicate my scepticism.

'Yes,' he went on, not quite looking me in the eye, 'it is very hard indeed to turn and requires a particular knack of twisting it to the right, just so. I only mention it because if you were to suggest at the inquest that the gate had been locked – well, you can see it would add all manner of complication to what is really a very simple and tragic explanation. The porter forgot to lock the gate, a feral stray got in, poor Roger paid the price for someone else's carelessness. It is dreadful, quite dreadful –' here he pressed his palm to his breast, his fat face worked up into a mask of sorrow – 'but all this talk of locked gates will, I fear, create alarm of some conspiracy where none exists.'

I could not quite believe what I was hearing. I removed my arm from his grip and moved to face him; students were still pressing up the stairs around us and I lowered my voice accordingly.

'Doctor Coverdale, the gate was locked – I cannot be in any doubt about that fact. I tried it myself. And even if it were only closed, the dog did not close it after it strayed in.'

'The wind could have blown it shut,' Coverdale said dismissively.

For a moment I was incredulous; did he really imagine I could so easily be persuaded to doubt the evidence of my own eyes?

'A heavy wooden gate like that? I was *there*, Doctor Coverdale – I went through all the possibilities with the rector,' I protested, *sotto voce*.

'The rector has had time now to reflect on this morning's events with sober judgement,' said Coverdale smoothly, 'and he has concluded that in the mist and panic it was hard to discern anything for certain. It was he who remembered how stiff the handle can be from the inside, and how that might confuse a foreigner. Any coroner conducting an inquest would certainly take into account that you could not be expected to know your way around the college. I mention it because for you to insist that there is some mystery will only prolong and complicate a process which will already be most distressing to Doctor Mercer's friends and colleagues. There is nothing to be gained by adding spurious fancies and suspicions to a tragic accident.'

I looked at him for a moment. So they had decided to rewrite the circumstances of Mercer's death in a way that would avoid any scandal to the college – and a murderer would go free. Were they protecting someone in particular, or was it for them simply a matter of collectively saving face? I wondered if the rector would keep to his promise to investigate the matter privately, but I doubted it; he was the most anxious of all about the college's public standing.

'I feel that I must report to the inquest what I believe I saw this morning,' I said. 'If I was mistaken, you are right – I will look a fool, but I will have to take that chance. I would not sleep easily knowing I had not given all the evidence.'

Coverdale narrowed his eyes, then appeared to accept my statement.

'Very well, Doctor Bruno, you must act according to your conscience. Shall we go in?' He motioned to the steps up to the porch of the Divinity School, where the crowd had begun to thin to a trickle; most of the audience were now inside.

'Oh, but – there is one rather curious thing,' he added breezily over his shoulder as he climbed the first step. 'Master Slythurst told me he was on his way up to the strongroom this morning when he heard noises from inside Doctor Mercer's chamber – and when he looked in, he found the place turned upside down and who should be there, going through Mercer's belongings, but our esteemed Italian guest? Trying to open his strongbox, no less. And the porter said you brought back a set of keys you had removed from the body.'

I cursed my stupidity in falling asleep that morning; I had forgotten to take the clothes to the rector with my poor excuse and now, as I feared, Slythurst had covered his own tracks by suggesting I was no more than a common thief. I noticed his version omitted the detail of his having a key to Mercer's room.

'There is an explanation,' I began, but Coverdale held up his hand to forestall me.

'Oh, no doubt, Doctor Bruno, no doubt. But it might be that to a magistrate such behaviour would look extremely odd – not to say suspicious – and here among the towns-people there is such dislike of *foreigners*, you understand, especially of the *Romish* sort,' he said, affecting an apologetic tone, 'that judgement can often be clouded by blind prejudice. And if the inquest is made more complicated than it need be, these are just the kind of difficult details that might come to light.'

We were now on the threshold of the Divinity School; I glanced inside and saw that the auditorium was full and students were finding themselves places along the window-ledges and standing at the back. Coverdale was smiling expectantly up at me after delivering this direct threat. I studied his face for a moment and then nodded.

'I understand your meaning, Doctor Coverdale, and will certainly give some thought to the matter.'

'Good man,' Coverdale said agreeably. 'I'm sure you will see the sense in it. Shall we go in?'

I paused at the doorway and glanced over my shoulder in the direction of the city wall; the man with no ears was still lounging there, still casually watching us. I touched Coverdale's elbow.

'Who is that man?' I gestured with my head in his direction. Coverdale looked, blinked, then shook his head.

'No one of significance,' he said abruptly, and held the door for me to pass through.

I tried to put this conversation from my mind as I prepared to speak; a great hush descended upon the hall, broken only by the usual shuffling, coughing and rustling of gowns from the audience. I cleared my throat, and leaned forward over my lectern to begin my address.

'I, Giordano Bruno the Nolan, doctor of a more sophisticated theology, professor of a more pure and innocent wisdom, known to the best academies of Europe, a proven and honoured philosopher, a stranger only among barbarians and knaves, the awakener of sleeping spirits, the tamer of presumptuous and stubborn ignorance, who professes a general love of humanity in all his actions, who prefers as company neither Briton nor Italian, male nor female, bishop nor king, robe nor armour, friar nor layman, but only those whose conversation is more peaceable, more civil, more faithful, and more valuable, who respects not the anointed head, the signed forehead, the washed hands, or the circumcised penis, but rather the spirit and culture of mind which can be read in the face of a real person; whom the propagators of stupidity and the small-time hypocrites detest, whom the sober and studious love, and whom the most noble minds acclaim – to the most excellent and illustrious vice-chancellor of the University of Oxford, many greetings.'

I bowed low towards the stage where the vice-chancellor sat, anticipating the volume of applause such an opening would invite in the European academies, and was taken aback when finally I realised that the susurration reaching my ears was that of mocking laughter. Out of the corner of my eye I saw Sidney; he grimaced and made a chopping motion across his throat as if to imply that my speech had been too much. I could not understand this; in Paris, a disputation was hardly considered worth the name unless the rhetoric reached absurd heights of grandiosity, but it seemed that in this, as in so much else, the English preferred to hide behind a plain and self-effacing style. I could hear them sniggering quite openly now – and I mean the Fellows, not the students, though they were beginning to pick up the cue from their elders; I heard a number of them mimicking my accent like schoolboys. Across the hall, Rector Underhill was leaning on his podium with a smile that suggested he was enjoying the spectacle; evidently he seemed to think he had already won. The palatine yawned loudly and ostentatiously.

'I reject absolutely,' I cried, banging a fist on the lectern and then raising my hand for emphasis as the laughter died away to a startled silence, 'the notion that the stars are fixed on the tapestry of the heavens! The stars are no more nor differently fixed in the universe than this star the Sun, and the region of the Bear's tail no more deserves to be called the Eighth Sphere than does that of the Earth, on which we live. Those with sufficient wisdom will recognise that the apparent motion of the universe derives from the rotation of the Earth, for there is much less reason why the Sun and the whole universe of innumerable stars should turn around this globe than it, on the contrary, should turn with respect to the universe. Let our reason no longer be fettered by the eight or nine imaginary spheres, for there is but one sky, immense and infinite, with infinite capacity for innumerable worlds similar to this one, rounding their orbits as the Earth rounds its own.'

I paused for breath, better pleased with this opening salvo, and Underhill took the opportunity to jump in.

'Do you say so, sir?' he countered, that self-satisfied smile playing at his lips. 'It seems to me that, rather than the Sun standing still and the Earth running around it, it is your head which runs around and your brains which do not stand still!'

He turned to the audience of Fellows for congratulation and was not disappointed; a chorus of guffaws erupted and it was some moments before I could make myself heard in response.

The disputation, I am sorry to say, was not a success, and I will not trouble my reader with any more of its substance. It continued in much the same manner; Rector Underhill advanced nothing but the old, tired arguments in favour of Aristotle – claiming no more scientific proof than the weight of scholastic authority in placing the Earth at the fixed centre of the universe, as if authority has never been mistaken, and at one point suggesting that Copernicus had never meant his theory to be taken literally but had only developed it as a metaphor to aid mathematical calculation. All these arguments I had heard and rebutted many times before, in better society than this, but I was barely given the chance that afternoon, since Underhill's main concern was not to persuade the audience by his own skill in debate (most of them were already squarely of his opinion and had not the courtesy even to listen to my arguments) but to ridicule me and expose me as often as possible to the mockery of his peers. This, it seemed, was their idea of entertainment, and the manners of the crowd were so poor that for the most part they chattered and commented throughout both our speeches. I was part way through an impassioned argument involving complex mathematical propositions when I was interrupted by an alarming noise that sounded like the low growl of a dog; overly sensitive to such sounds since the morning's events, I started visibly and turned, only to discover it was in fact the palatine noisily snoring, but by then, the thread of my argument was badly frayed. A few moments later, we were disturbed by a great scuffle as an undergraduate pushed his way through the ranks of the seated Fellows to attract the attention of one of them; it turned out that he sought Doctor Coverdale who, apparently responding to a summons, immediately left his place in the middle of a row, apologising in a theatrical whisper to all those between him and the door who were obliged to rise in their seats to allow him through. I would not have expected Coverdale to show any restraint on my behalf, but I was surprised that he would behave with so little courtesy to his own rector as to leave in the middle of the debate.

We proceeded laboriously towards an ending that was nothing like a conclusion; I put forward my own complex calculations to account for the relative diameter of the Moon, the Earth and the Sun in terms even an idiot could understand, and in response Underhill merely repeated the old scholastic misconceptions common to all those who conflate science and theology and believe the Holy Scripture to be the last word in scientific enquiry. He also made frequent pointed references to my status as a foreigner, implying that it necessarily bestowed inferior intelligence, and more than once noted that Copernicus too was foreign and therefore could not be expected to display the robust reasoning of an Englishman – apparently forgetting that the whole occasion for this sorry pretence at debate was to honour Copernicus's royal countryman. I was glad to be done with it; I bowed tersely to the smattering of insincere applause and climbed down from my pulpit feeling bruised and belittled.

Afterwards, as the hall cleared, none of the departing

Fellows would meet my eye. I remained seated morosely beneath the window, thinking that I would wait for them all to leave so as to avoid any further mockery – or, worse, commiseration – when I saw Sidney fighting his way down from the dais. He pushed through to me, shaking his head.

'This evening I was ashamed of my university, Bruno,' he exploded, two spots of crimson flaming with indignation on his cheeks. 'Underhill is a weasel – he didn't once engage with the substance of your argument! I call it shameful – it was a display of pure blind arrogance.' He shook his head, his lips pressed together as if he were reprimanding himself. 'It is our least attractive trait as a nation, this belief in our own superiority.'

'I have been too fortunate in counting you and Walsingham among my acquaintance,' I said, shaking my head. 'I imagined all Englishmen to be as liberal-minded and curious about the world. I see I was badly mistaken.'

'Mind you,' he said, philosophically, 'you don't help yourself, Bruno – what was that opening speech all about?'

'It served me well in Paris.'

'No doubt. But it's not really how we do things here. We tend not to warm to those who sing their own praises too fulsomely – I think that was when you lost your audience. And perhaps leave out the circumcised penises next time.'

'I will bear that in mind,' I said stiffly. 'Though I doubt there will be a next time.'

'It has not been much of a visit for you thus far, old friend, has it?' he said, with an affectionate cuff on the shoulder. 'First the company of that Polish oaf, then a man is brutally done to death outside your window, and now you suffer this indignity from fools who could not begin to comprehend your vision. I am sorry for it, truly. But perhaps from hereon we can concentrate on our real task,' he added, dropping his voice. 'In any case, we are all invited to dine at Christ Church

166

tonight, so let us empty their wine cellars, forget all about this dreary business, and make a night of it – what do you say?'

I looked up at him, grateful for his efforts but thinking that his buoyant company was the last thing I wanted that evening.

'Thank you, Philip, but I fear I would not be much of an addition to the table this evening. Let me retire to lick my wounds and I promise by tomorrow I will be ready for any adventure you propose.'

He looked disappointed, but nodded in understanding.

'I will hold you to that. In fact, the palatine has a fancy for hunting or hawking in the Forest of Shotover if this rain breaks, and of course I must bend to his whim. But I do not think I can bear it if you are not one of the party.'

'I will see how I feel. Why don't you take your new friend Gabriel Norris?'

'Oh, I did invite him, but he has another commitment tomorrow,' Sidney said breezily, missing the barb in my tone. 'Not that I'm too sorry – that young braggart is going home with half my purse. Remind me never to play cards with him again.'

'Well, I will join you if I feel rested,' I said.

Norris had suggested the wolfhound could have strayed from Shotover Forest; I was no huntsman, but it would be a chance to see if there was some connection. Sidney shook my hand, gave me another resounding thump between the shoulder blades – the English way of displaying manly friendship – and left me to wander the short distance back to the college alone.

'*Dio fulmini questi inglesi*!' I burst out as I rounded the corner into Brasenose Lane, kicking in fury at a stone in my path. '*Si comportano come cani di strada* – no, they are worse than dogs! Was ever a race so arrogant, small-minded and self-congratulating as the men of this miserable island? They could no more contemplate new philosophies or science than they could imagine eating food with flavour! It must be the endless rain that has turned their brains to pulp. To sneer at a man, not for the meat of what he says but because he had the good fortune to be born beyond these dismal shores! And how dare they presume to laugh at my pronunciation – where in God's name do they imagine the Latin tongue came from in the first place? *Asini pedanti*!' I cursed freely in this vein, in Italian, all the way to Lincoln gatehouse until my anger was partly vented; it was fortunate that there were no passers-by to take fright.

It was with a heavy heart that I pushed open the main gate and stopped by the porter's lodge to ask Cobbett if I might borrow a lantern for my chamber. The old porter was dozing gently in his chair, a pot of ale on the table, the dog resting her head on his knee. I coughed and he spluttered awake, brushing himself down.

'Oh, pardon me, Doctor Bruno, I didn't hear you come in. I was deep in thought there.' He winked and I mustered a smile.

'Good evening, Cobbett. Might I trouble you for a spare lantern?'

'Of course, sir.' Cobbett heaved his great bulk effortfully upright and shuffled off towards one of the wooden cupboards that lined the walls. 'You're back early, sir, if I may remark – I thought there was to be a great entertainment at Christ Church tonight for the royal visitation?'

'I was tired,' I said, hoping to avoid any questions about the disputation.

Cobbett nodded in sympathy.

'Not surprised, all the goings-on this morning. Let's hope we can all sleep sound in our beds tonight, eh? Funny,' he remarked, opening the lantern's glass casing to light the candle from his own, 'Doctor Coverdale come back early tonight as well. In a great tearing hurry, he was. I saw him rushing through the gate there and I said to myself, they must have finished proceedings in a rare haste tonight. Generally there's no stopping them at these debates once they get a taste for the sound of their own voice – with the greatest of respect, sir. But then as no one else followed, I concluded he must have had business of his own.' He finished with a throaty chuckle.

'I fear Doctor Coverdale had more important matters to attend to than my poor speech,' I said, unable to disguise the resentment in my voice.

'Well, I hope God sends you good rest tonight, sir,' Cobbett said, handing me the lantern, its flame jerking with the motion. 'I suppose you will be staying with us until the enquiry now? You will be feeling quite at home here before long.'

'I'm sure I will,' I replied flatly, and bade Cobbett a good night, realising the import of his words. How long would I be detained here? I wondered, and would I be obliged by law to stay behind and testify even if Sidney and the palatine left on the appointed day?

All around the small quadrangle the umber light of candles burned in various windows, giving out a friendly glow, but I could not shake the sense of unease that had followed me from London. Something cruel was at work here, and I had a horrible intimation that it was not yet over. As I paused to look around me at the blank windows, I prickled with the sense of being watched.

My staircase was silent and so dark that without Cobbett's lantern I would have had to feel my way as a blind man; so dark that I would have missed the paper that had been slipped under my door, had I not stepped on it and heard an unexpected rustle as I entered the room. I bent to retrieve it;

169

one leaf, folded neatly in half, and when I opened it another, smaller slip of paper no wider than a ribbon fluttered out and fell to the floor. By the dim light of the lantern, I made out a series of concentric circles on the larger sheet of paper; intrigued, I impatiently set about lighting the candles in the sconces around the room to give me more light by which to examine this strange missive. Once I could see it clearly, my puzzlement only grew: the substance of the diagram was clear enough, but not its meaning. For this was unmistakeably a drawing of the Copernican universe, made by a skilled hand, with the seven planets tracing their orbits around the Sun; at least, so it seemed at first, but there, in the centre, where the figure of Sol should have been, was a representation not of the Sun but of a small circle with spokes, the exact symbol I had found dotted through Roger Mercer's almanac.

Utterly perplexed, I reached for the second slip of paper, which had almost become lost between the floorboards, and saw that there was writing printed on it; on closer inspection, it was clear that it had been very neatly cut from a book, and the sentence that had been so carefully excised made me gasp aloud:

*I am the wheate or grayne of Christ, I shall be grounde with the teethe of wilde beastes, that I may be found pure bread.*

# SEVEN

My hammering on the door of the rector's lodgings was so frantic as to bring the servant running to open it with an expression of expectant dread, as if he feared news of another tragedy.

'I must speak with the rector immediately,' I gasped, brandishing my papers in his face.

'He dines at Christ Church tonight, sir, with all the senior men.' He regarded me anxiously, his hand trembling slightly as he held up a candle to see my face, sending shadows skittering up the walls. 'Has something happened?'

Of course – I had forgotten how early it still was; Underhill would be celebrating his triumph this evening and may not return for some hours yet.

'It is a matter of great urgency,' I said, trying to catch my breath. 'I can wait for him, but I must speak to him tonight.'

The servant, a severe man perhaps in his late fifties, eyed me with some suspicion.

'You may call back at a later hour, sir, but it would not be proper for me to allow you to wait in the rector's lodgings with the ladies here alone.'

'I intend them no harm – I wish only to be sure not to miss him.'

'Who is it, Adam?' called Sophia's voice within, and then she appeared behind the servant, her slender figure illuminated by the candles, a book in her hand.

''Tis the *foreign* gentleman, Mistress Sophia, come to see your father. I have told him to call again later.'

'Nonsense – let him wait in the warm, I am sure Father will not stay out long. Conviviality is not his strong suit,' she said, smiling to me over the servant's shoulder. 'Doctor Bruno, good evening – please do come in.'

The servant glanced from me to her with consternation.

'I do not think your father would approve, Mistress—' he began, but Sophia waved a hand to interrupt.

'Doctor Bruno is my father's guest, Adam, and a philosopher of most prestigious reputation – I'm sure Father would be appalled if I did not extend to him the proper hospitality. Perhaps you would be kind enough to take Doctor Bruno's cloak and fetch some wine?'

Adam seemed extremely put out, but allowed himself to be commanded, bowing curtly to me and standing aside to let me enter with a further look of distaste. Sophia smiled again, and gestured for me to follow her through the high dining room we had occupied the previous evening to a door on the other side. She was wearing a plain green gown and her dark hair fell in ripples down her back as she walked, with the kind of self-possession that comes from natural beauty. My spirits greatly cheered by the unexpected prospect of her company, I followed her into a dark-panelled room, warmed by a low fire and dominated by a great oak desk under the window, piled high with books and papers.

'This is my father's study – you may wait for him here,' she said politely, ushering me to one of the tapestried chairs that bordered the hearth. She watched me for a moment. 'You did not wish to celebrate with the Fellows at Christ Church this evening then, Bruno?'

'I was not in the mood for a feast. I'm afraid to say your father carried the audience with him tonight.' I eased into my seat and leaned nearer to the twisting flames. 'In that, at least, he may consider himself the victor.'

'Did he ride roughshod over your every point without taking the trouble to actually listen?' she asked, smiling with a bitter sympathy. 'My father has no skill in debate, Bruno,' she went on, without waiting for me to respond, 'he has only the unshakeable conviction of his own rightness, yet it is surprising how effective that can be in rebutting argument. I used to think it was a mark of arrogance, but as I grow older I begin to suspect it may be fear.'

I raised a questioning eyebrow, thinking how perceptive she was for such a young woman.

'He has been so dependent all his life on the favour of great men like the Earl of Leicester, as academics and clergymen are,' she continued, a note of pity in her voice, 'and he knows well how capricious such preferment can be. So he lives in constant fear of losing his position – and there have been so many factions in the university these past few years, so many people denounced for being seen in the wrong company, reading the wrong books, making a chance remark that could be maliciously interpreted.' She sighed. 'Poor Edmund Allen's fall shook him badly.'

'Why – does he secretly favour Rome too?'

'Oh no! God, no, he is the last person . . .' She shook her head fiercely, as if to underline how preposterous the idea was. 'But to see how the Fellows rushed to close ranks against Allen, against all ties of friendship, in case they should be tainted by association. An accusation need not be true to stick, you know, in these times. My father craves stability more than anything, and believes that change is always for the worse. He is not a bad man, but he is constantly glancing over his shoulder, and that makes him defend his certainties like a mother bear defends her cubs. This, I think, is why he appears so pompous.'

She grinned, and leaned forward to poke the fire. There was a soft knock on the door and the servant Adam came in with a pitcher of wine and two cups, which he set on a low wooden footstool near the fire.

'Thank you, Adam. Would you send to the kitchens for some bread and cheese and any cold pie they might have – I suspect our guest may be hungry.'

I nodded my grateful agreement, only now realising that my affronted withdrawal from the dinner at Christ Church meant that I had missed supper, and my stomach was beginning to complain.

Adam bowed, shot me another look to signify his disapproval, and pointedly left the door open when he left. Sophia rose to close it, brushing down her dress. I poured us both a cup of wine.

'You were banging on the door fit to wake the dead there, Bruno,' she said, settling herself again in the chair opposite, tucking her feet neatly under her like a cat, 'and your face was pale as the grave – I feared you brought us news of more horror.'

'Nothing so terrible, I assure you,' I said, taking a long drink.

'Then what brings you here with such urgency? Have you thought of some brilliant riposte that you forgot to make during the disputation and brought it round so my father can hear it late rather than never?' She smiled mischievously, indicating the paper I still clutched.

'No – that will come to me during the night,' I said, only half joking, as I passed it to her. 'What do you make of this?'

She skimmed her eyes briefly over it and looked up at me, puzzled.

'But this is a map of the heavens according to your Copernicus, is it not?'

I nodded.

'But why bring it to him now in such haste, after the debate is over?'

'Nothing strikes you as odd about it?'

She frowned at the paper again, and then her eyes widened, just for a moment, before she raised her head again.

'That is a strange way to represent the Sun,' she said lightly.

'Yes.'

'Like a wheel. But it is very elegantly drawn,' she added, handing the paper back.

'It is, but I cannot claim the credit for that – it is not my work.'

'Then – whose?' Her voice faltered for a moment. 'Where did you get it?'

'It was sent to me. By whom, I don't know, but it may have a hidden meaning. I thought I would ask your father's advice.'

A strange laugh tumbled from her, as if in relief.

'You came haring round here, pounding on the door as if the world were ending, just to show him this? If you would take *my* advice, Bruno, I would guess that someone is playing a joke at your expense, making fun of Copernicus. My father may not like you wasting his time with such trifles.'

'Perhaps you are right,' I said neutrally, folding the paper and smoothing it between my hands. 'All the same, I will wait for him, if I may?'

She nodded briefly. What, I wondered, was the expression that had flitted so briefly across her face a moment ago when she looked a second time at the diagram? Had it been recognition, or even fear? It seemed improbable that she could know anything of the hidden meaning of the little symbol but then, I reflected, the life of the college was so close-knit that perhaps there were no secrets here. If the symbol meant something to Roger Mercer and to my unknown correspondent, why should it not be known to others, Sophia among them?

'Tell me,' I leaned back on my chair and indicated the large chests against the wall, 'does your father have an edition of Foxe?'

Sophia rolled her eyes.

'That, my dear Bruno, is like asking if the pope owns a crucifix. My father has copies of all three of Master Day's editions, the latter two running to twelve books apiece, and I believe there is a new edition to be printed this year, so I'm sure he will soon add that to his collection. Foxe is one thing we do not lack in this house. Which edition did you particularly seek?'

'I don't know.' I paused, running my eye over the books on the desk before turning back to face her. '"I am the wheat or grain of Christ, I shall be ground with the teeth of wild beasts, that I may be found pure bread."'

She looked at me with an expression of polite confusion. 'Pardon?'

'Is that Foxe, do you know?'

'Oh. A quotation. Truly, I wouldn't know – my father is the martyrologist, not me. To tell the truth, Bruno, I have only briefly looked into Master Foxe's book and I detested what I found there – what kind of man devotes his life to recording endless lists of tortures and brutalities done to other human beings? And in such lavish detail? I got the sense he thoroughly enjoyed his own descriptions. Some of those woodcuts gave me nightmares.' She shuddered and screwed up her face.

'He meant to encourage the faithful, I suppose, and looked for the strongest images with which to do so.'

'It is nothing but propaganda, for no purpose but to inspire hatred of Catholics!' Sophia spat, and I was amazed at the vehemence in her voice. Catching my look of surprise, she blushed, and added, in a more moderate tone, 'as if there were not enough discord and division between Christians already, without books like that to fan the flames of hate.'

I regarded her with renewed curiosity as, perhaps embarrassed by her outburst, she turned her attention back to the fire. She was so unusually outspoken and unpredictable in her opinions that I did not wonder her father despaired of marrying her well; such independence of mind went against everything that was expected of a modest wife, yet it was this spirited refusal to keep her proper place that I most admired about her. What could she have meant by this last protest, for instance? While I was contemplating pressing her further on the subject of Foxe, the door was again opened and Adam the servant laid out, with pointed slowness, a platter of bread and cold cuts beside the jug of wine.

'I do not think your father would like food to be taken in his study,' he began primly, but Sophia was already ripping into the bread.

'He has his supper in here all the time,' she said. 'Thank you, Adam, that will be all now.'

He hesitated.

'Mistress Sophia, I wonder if your mother—'

'My mother took to her bed yesterday evening at dinner and has not stirred from it since. When her nerves are bad she wishes to be left alone. Thank you, Adam.' She smiled pleasantly, but there was steel in her voice.

Adam, clearly believing himself the appointed defender of Sophia's honour, seemed about to find some other objection to our continued presence together in the rector's study, but after a moment's pause he dipped his head and retreated, this time closing the door behind him with a soft click.

'Help yourself,' Sophia said, indicating the food. 'We can search through Foxe after, if you like.'

I took my place on the chair by the fire and gratefully tore off a hunk of the rough-grained bread.

'Now then, Bruno,' she began, lowering her voice and leaning forward purposefully, as if it were she who had summoned me, 'you promised to teach me more of the magic book of Agrippa and here we are with an unexpected opportunity for a lesson.'

'So I did,' I replied, my mouth full, 'but first you must tell me why you wish so fervently to know of spells and love talismans? These books are forbidden here and merely to possess such knowledge is considered dangerous.'

'I never said I wished to learn love spells,' she said, affecting hauteur, 'that was *your* assumption.' But the sudden colour in her cheeks gave the lie to her protest.

'I only wondered why a well-born young lady would occupy herself with the idea of practical magic.'

'I am fascinated by the idea that a person could master forces beyond our understanding and turn them to her own purpose. Isn't everyone? Because I have always thought magic must be immensely powerful, mustn't it – I mean, it must work, or the Church would not be so anxious to keep it out of the hands of ordinary people?'

I hesitated.

'There are undoubtedly forces of great power in the universe, but to draw them down demands long and profound study. The Hermetic magic of which Agrippa writes is not a matter of mixing a few herbs and muttering incantations like a village wise woman – it requires knowledge of astronomy, mathematics, music, metaphysics, philosophy, optics, geometry – I could go on. Becoming an adept is the work of a lifetime.'

'I see.' Her mouth set tight, and she clasped her hands together on her knees. 'And you mean to say that I have not the wit for it, being only a woman?'

'I mean nothing of the kind.' I held up a hand in protest; how quick she was to take offence on this subject! Then I remembered the impotent anger I had felt in the Divinity School at her father's repeated insinuations that my nationality was synonymous with stupidity; at least I could find parts of Europe where such prejudice would not be current, but to my knowledge there was nowhere in Christendom where a woman like Sophia would be suffered to learn or converse with men as an equal, no matter how sharp her mind or how widely she read. Only in a queen was such an intelligence tolerated. 'I meant only that to devote one's life to the study of Hermetic magic requires enormous sacrifice, and I would not lightly recommend it. For a start, it could likely see you burned as a witch.'

She appeared to consider this for a moment, then lifted her head suddenly to look at me, her eyes lit with a vivid anguish.

'Then is there no way of learning any magic that might work?' she burst out.

'Work for what?' I said, taken aback at the force of her expression. 'You seem to have something very specific in mind, but if you will not say what, I cannot advise you.'

She turned her face back to the fire and sat without speaking for a while. I cut a lump of cheese and waited to see if she decided to trust me.

'Did you never love anyone who could not return your love?'

'No,' I said, frankly. 'But I have loved someone I could not have, so perhaps I understand a little.'

She nodded, still staring into the weaving flames, then raised her head and fixed me with those clear, tawny eyes.

'Who was she?'

'A French noblewoman, when I lived in Toulouse. She also scorned the pursuits of ladies and hungered after books. In

179

fact, she was a lot like you in spirit and beauty,' I added gently.

She ventured a shy smile.

'Did you want to marry her?'

I hesitated.

'I wanted to go on loving her, certainly. I wanted to be able to talk to her, and hold her. But marriage – it was so far from possibility. Her father intended her to make a match that would suit his ambitions, not hers.'

'Like my father,' she said, nodding again, her hair tumbling around her face as she rested her chin on her hand and continued to look intently at me. 'So you were forced to part?'

'Her father wanted to separate us. On top of that, Toulouse was then in the grip of religious conflict between the Catholics and the Huguenot Protestants and it was safer for me to leave. That has been my life for the past few years, I'm afraid. I have had to move around so much and shift for myself, perhaps it has made me unfit for a settled life with a wife and family.'

'That is sad. But I'm sure you would not be short of admirers here, Bruno. No Englishman has eyes like yours.'

I was so surprised by this compliment that I could not think of an immediate reply. Sophia looked embarrassed and hastily turned her attention back to the fire.

'You have travelled so much, you cannot imagine how envious I am. You must have had many adventures. I have not left Oxford in six years. Sometimes I feel so restless,' she poked the fire vigorously, 'I fear I shall never see anything of the world, unless I can make some dramatic change happen. Oh, sometimes I just want to shake this life I have into pieces! Do you ever feel like that?' She looked at me earnestly, her eyes full of feeling.

'Certainly. I spent thirteen years of my youth in a monastery

– I knew more about restlessness and that desire for new horizons than anyone. But be careful what you wish for, Sophia. I have also learned that adventure is not always something to seek for its own sake. You don't realise the value of a home until you no longer have one,' I added quietly.

'My father said you lived at the court of King Henri in Paris – you must have met many beautiful ladies of fashion there, I suppose?'

'There were beautiful faces, certainly, and many beautiful costumes, but I never found much beauty of mind at court.'

'Still, I expect you dazzled them all with your ideas,' Sophia said, her eyes reflecting the crackling flames.

'I don't know that my ideas were of much interest to the ladies at court.' I gave her a rueful smile. 'Few women there cared to read or trouble themselves with ideas. Most of them had little grasp even of the politics of their own city, and I'm afraid I could never feign interest in a woman whose conversation is limited to court gossip and fashions. I am too intolerant of stupidity.'

She sat up then, looking at me with curiosity.

'Then you would value in a woman the capacity to form her own opinions and express them?'

'Of course, if they are well informed. Otherwise she is no more than an ornament, however lovely. Better to buy a painting if you just want something beautiful in a corner of your parlour. And a painting's value increases with age.'

Sophia smiled and shook her head.

'You are not like most Englishmen, Bruno. But then I saw that when I first met you. My father assures me that no man values a strong mind in a woman, and that if I want a husband I would do well to smile prettily and keep my thoughts to myself.'

'Then his understanding of his fellow men is as wrong-headed as his cosmology.'

She laughed then, but it was not reflected in her eyes.

'And your *inamorato*?' I prompted. 'What does he value?' When she did not answer, I continued, 'because I cannot believe that a young woman so favoured by nature should even need to consider magical arts to secure any man's affection. With the greatest respect, I can only imagine that your *inamorato* is either blind or an idiot.'

'There is no *inamorato*,' she snapped, folding her arms across her chest and turning pointedly away from me. 'Don't make fun of me, Bruno. I had thought you were different.'

'Forgive me.' I poured another glass of wine and sat back, stifling a smile. If she wanted to confide in me, I reasoned, she would do so in her own time. We sat in silence for a while, with only the spitting of the logs and the lulling rhythm of the flames for company.

'To answer your question, Agrippa had his knowledge of practical magic from an ancient manuscript known in Europe by the name of *Picatrix*,' I began, to break the silence when it appeared that she was not going to speak. 'Its true name is the *Ghayat al Hakim*, the Goal of the Wise, and it was transcribed by the Arabs of Harran about four hundred years ago. In fact, it is a translation of a much older work, from before the destruction of Egypt, thought to be inspired by Hermes Trismegistus himself.' I paused to take a sip of wine, confident that I had now won back her attention; she was staring at me, rapt, her chin cupped in her hands. 'This book is forbidden by the Church of Rome and has never been printed – it would be too dangerous to do so – but it was translated into Spanish at the order of King Alfonso the Wise and then into Latin, so for some years there have been a small number of manuscript copies in circulation. One of these was imported in secret to Paris by King Henri ten years ago. He has a fancy for collecting obscure books of esoterica, but he does not know how to use them once he has them.'

'And you have read it?' she asked, also in a whisper, leaning in eagerly.

'His Majesty eventually allowed me to see the manuscript, after I solemnly swore that I would not copy any part of it. He apparently forgot that I am one of the foremost practitioners of the art of memory in all of Europe.' I allowed myself a modest smile; Sophia ignored it.

'So what is in this *Picatrix*?' she demanded.

'It is a manual of astral magic, a treatise on the art of drawing down the powers that animate the stars and planets by means of talismans and images.' I lowered my voice even further and glanced round to check that the door was closed. 'It works on the principle that the infinite diversity of matter in the universe is all interconnected, part of One Unity, animated by the Divinity, so the adept with the requisite knowledge can create links between the elements of the natural world and the celestial powers to which they correspond.'

Sophia frowned.

'But how does it *work*?' she insisted.

'You are determined to know,' I said, smiling. 'Well, for example – suppose you wanted, for the sake of argument, to secure the love of another person.' I watched her reaction; her cheeks were flushed and her lips slightly parted in anticipation, but she held my gaze almost defiantly. 'Then you need to capture the power of the planet Venus, so you must know what plants, stones and metals belong to the influence of Venus. You would also need to learn the most powerful images of Venus, and inscribe these on a talisman made from the appropriate materials, on a day and hour most conducive to the astrological influence of Venus, with the correct invocations, names and numbers – you see it is immensely complex.'

'Can you teach me?' she whispered.

'Do you know what you are asking?' I responded, dropping my voice even further. 'For me to teach you what many consider diabolical sorcery – do you know what the risk would be? Besides, I must confess that I have never attempted to use this practical magic – my interest has always been in the hieratic, intellectual element. But Sophia,' I spread my palms out wide, an advocate of common sense, 'if the object of your affection does not return it, would it not be simpler just to set your sights elsewhere?'

She reached across and laid her hand on mine for a moment, a sad smile hovering at her lips.

'Yes, it would be simpler,' she agreed, in a soft voice. 'But the heart does not always listen to reason, does it? You should know, Bruno.'

I looked at her for a long time then as my own heart lurched unexpectedly and I realised that I was in serious danger of growing attached to this thoughtful, spirited young woman with the fiery eyes. I could not tell whether she was attracted to me or saw me only as someone who would listen and take her seriously; in the same moment I felt a sudden unreasonable jealousy that all this depth of feeling on her part might be wasted on a peacock like Gabriel Norris.

I was wondering whether to question her on that scrap of hearsay, and how to broach the subject, when an unmistakable thud was heard outside the door on the other side of the study, as if someone on the other side had lost his footing and stumbled into the jamb. Sophia snatched her hand away, threw her chair back and leapt to her feet, glaring angrily at the door, but as she took a step towards it her legs suddenly buckled under her and she gave a little cry, grasping at the chair to keep her balance. Alarmed, I jumped up and held out an arm to steady her; she gripped my shoulder gratefully and leaned on me for a moment, breathing heavily.

'Are you unwell?' I asked – unnecessarily, as her face had turned pale as ash.

'I – I don't know what happened, I'm sorry,' she faltered. 'I must have stood up too fast, I felt suddenly very faint. Perhaps this wine is stronger than I thought. Damn that old busybody Adam – I should have guessed he'd be listening at the keyhole.'

'We spoke very softly – he may not have heard the substance of the conversation,' I whispered, though I could not dampen the fear that crept up my spine.

'I'm sure he heard enough to tell my father,' she muttered through clenched teeth.

For what seemed like a long while, neither of us moved. She continued to clutch the fabric of my doublet with her left hand, while I gently supported her right arm; her hair was almost touching my cheek and smelled warmly of woodsmoke and chamomile. I could hear the blood pounding in my ears and at my throat, hardly daring to catch my breath, until eventually she raised her head with a great sigh.

'Forgive me, Bruno – I need to sit.' Her voice was subdued; she was still very white.

I helped her back to her chair, and from the corridor beyond there came the sound of a door slamming firmly and two male voices in conversation.

Sophia lifted her head.

'That is my father returned. I had better go and explain your presence, before Adam fills his head with suspicions.' She took a deep breath and pushed herself up again, pausing to steady herself.

'Are you still faint?' I asked, reaching out a hand. She passed me without taking it, turning back only at the door

'I will be fine. Good night, Bruno, and thank you for listening to my foolishness. We will speak again soon.' She smiled, and slipped out into the passageway, closing the door behind her.

185

I picked up the Copernican map and studied it again. Sophia had seen something in that mysterious symbol, I was certain, and instinctively I folded the paper away; perhaps it would be wiser not to alert her father until I could win her confidence enough to draw out whatever she knew. From the passageway beyond I heard voices – Sophia's and the rector's – raised in heated discussion, though I could make out only the odd word: 'improper' and 'papist' on his part, 'absurd' and 'hospitality' on hers. Then Sophia burst out in a tone of fierce exasperation:

'And how should I not conduct myself as mistress of this house when you are never here and the true mistress will not leave her bedchamber? Who else is going to take care of the household?'

'Take yourself to your room, daughter, and reflect on your place and your duty – or do you wish that I should send you to your aunt in Kent? Or perhaps I should engage another governess to fill your hours of idleness and teach you proper womanly obedience?' the rector spluttered, as he flung open the door to the study and strode in, turning a face purple with fury (and, I suspected, the good wine of Christ Church hall) in my direction. Immediately his manner changed; he clasped his hands together and half-bowed, not quite meeting my eye.

'Ah – Doctor Bruno – you have rather taken me by surprise at this hour.' All trace of his earlier superiority seemed to have vanished and he would not quite meet my eye, which gave me some satisfaction; it is one thing to sneer at a man in front of five hundred people certain to take your part, I thought, and quite another when you must stand three feet away from him alone. He seemed defensive, perhaps fearing that I had come to reopen the debate. 'I assure you that this evening—'

'Rector Underhill –' I barely knew where to begin – 'I

186

must seek your advice on another matter altogether – the death of Roger Mercer.'

Immediately the colour drained from his face and his eyes became watchful. He wiped his brow with his sleeve.

'Yes. The talk at Christ Church was of little else, but I am confident that we have put all malicious rumour to rest.' He grew thoughtful. 'Perhaps tomorrow the morning service in chapel should be a service of remembrance, especially since the funeral will have to wait until after the inquest – which I learned at dinner cannot be for a few days, as the coroner is away. You will be able to stay in Oxford to testify, Doctor Bruno, I presume?'

I did not answer. Instead I passed him the slip of paper with the quotation that had been cut from a book.

'Do you recognise this?'

He peered closely at the small type, then slowly raised his head to fix me with an expression of uncomprehending fear.

'The wheat of Christ,' he said softly. 'Ignatius. What is this?'

'It is from Foxe, then?'

He nodded slowly.

'The martyrdom of St Ignatius – or, rather, Bishop Ignatius of Antioch, we should call him, martyred under the Emperor Trajan. Foxe quotes these as his last words as he is thrown to the wild beasts.' He handed the paper back to me with an expression that might almost have been anger, although his hand was trembling.

'This paper was pushed under my door while I was at the disputation. It seems that someone wanted to draw my attention to the manner of Doctor Mercer's death.'

'By cutting up a book? Who would do such a thing? I'm afraid I don't follow your reasoning at all, Doctor Bruno.'

'Not for the first time today,' I muttered, but forced myself to be polite. 'You and I both saw this morning that Roger

187

Mercer had been locked into that garden with a savage dog. I have wondered, Rector Underhill, if his death was intended by someone who lured him there on the pretext of a meeting, and then set the beast on him in some kind of perverse parody of martyrdom. And it seems this message has been sent to me as a clear indication that someone here knows why he was killed, perhaps by whom.'

Underhill gestured frantically for me to lower my voice, glancing fearfully at the study door. He was undoubtedly shocked, but after a moment he composed his features and produced a choked, nervous little laugh.

'Dear God, what a fevered imagination you Italians do have, Bruno!' He shook his head dismissively. 'I fear that in the confusion and horror of this morning's tragedy we allowed ourselves to rush to somewhat hysterical conclusions. We must not permit our natural shock and grief to spin improbable fancies out of a terrible accident. As for this paper, it rather looks as if someone is toying with you, feeding these wild fancies of yours with the intention of making a fool of you. Better not to give them the satisfaction of rising to the bait.'

I turned to leave, furiously trying to quell my boiling blood. When I spoke, it was with all the self-control I could muster, my nails biting into the palms of my hands with the effort.

'I was an eye-witness, Rector Underhill. I was examining Roger Mercer's body and the scene of his violent death while you were vomiting over your shoes like a woman. My testimony will be of more value to any inquest than yours.'

At this he bristled and his tone was of open hostility.

'Oh, you imagine so? The word of a foreigner? A Catholic? A man reported to practise magic, who openly believes the Earth goes around the Sun?'

I took a deep breath and waited until the urge to hit him had passed, before opening the study door back to the dining room.

'Thank you for your time, Rector. I will not impose upon you any longer.'

'One thing more, Bruno. I don't know what customs you keep in Italy, but in England it is not considered proper for an unmarried woman of good reputation to converse alone with a man, even a gentleman. Therefore I forbid you any further private conversation with my daughter.' He folded his arms pompously. I paused in the doorway.

'With the greatest respect, Rector, do not presume to command me as if I were one of your undergraduates. But if you wish, you may send for a governess to teach me obedience. I might benefit from that,' I added, with a wink, and closed the door behind me, my heart pounding hard with indignation. The servant, Adam, handed me my cloak and bade me good night with a condescending sneer; I snatched the garment up quickly without thanking him and hastened for the door, thinking that if I stayed another moment among those insufferable people there might well be another murder committed that day.

# EIGHT

I woke before dawn and lay on the narrow wooden bed watching the patterns of pale light gradually spread across the ceiling from the chink in the window drapes. I had slept fitfully, knotted up with anger at the way I had been treated by Underhill and his colleagues. During the many hours of wakefulness I had determined that it was fruitless for me to stay in Oxford, regardless of the inquest or the royal visitation; I would seek out my horse from the rector's stables at first light and find my way to London by any means possible. I was conscious that I had found out little of use to Walsingham yet, and he would surely not appreciate the explanation that I had left in a fit of pique because I had been publicly humiliated, but I was so clearly unwelcome here that it seemed unlikely I could ever carry out his plan of gaining the Fellows' confidence and thereby learning anything useful.

I sighed and turned on my side, wrapping myself tightly in the sheet against the draught, and allowed my thoughts to drift back to Sophia. I had lain awake the previous night, my thoughts full of her. She was a compelling enough reason to stay in Oxford and an equally compelling one to leave. I realised that it had been some time since I had been as close to a woman as I had come the evening before when she had almost fainted into my arms, and the jolt of longing that shook me at that moment had left me profoundly disconcerted. I wondered if she had felt it too; there were moments while we talked when her frank gaze had locked with mine and it seemed she wanted me to read something there, but I knew that as a guest of her father's I must take great care how I approached her. Besides, I reminded myself, had she not spoken with a kind of pitying regret of the way her father had spent his life dependent on the patronage of great men, and was I not in the same position? I had no means to marry, no money or property of my own, nothing to offer a young gentlewoman except my affection, and I knew from experience that a father places little value on such things in his daughter's suitors. So I could not court her respectably, and although that fleeting touch the night before had powerfully awoken my desire, I already knew that I liked her too much to think of a casual seduction. I wanted urgently to see her again, yet had no idea what I hoped might happen between us. My mind kept running back to the expression on her face when I showed her the Copernican diagram; the fleeting light of recognition in her eyes at the symbol of the wheel. What did Sophia know, and how could I persuade her to confide in me?

The chorus of birdsong became more insistent. I pulled back the sheet and crossed the room to draw the drapes and look out over the courtyard of Lincoln as the pink early light streaked across the sky in gaps between jagged clouds. The rain had given Oxford a temporary reprieve, though there was no guarantee the road to London would be passable after the weather of the past two days. The flagstones of the quadrangle gleamed under the night's rain, puddles reflecting slashes of pale rosy sky. I could not make out the hands of the clock from my window, but thought I may as well dress anyway;

as soon as the college was up and stirring I could ask Cobbett how I might go about recovering my horse. I wondered if I should say a formal goodbye to the rector, claiming I had pressing business to return to, but then I might learn that I had a legal obligation to stay and testify at the inquest; better to leave first and plead ignorance later, I thought, and I did not want to give Underhill the satisfaction of seeing that he had driven me away. Perhaps I could leave a message for Sidney on my way out of the city.

I was about to turn away from the window when a sudden movement in the courtyard caught my eye; a figure wearing a black cloak with the hood pulled up scurried from the south-west corner of the quadrangle and disappeared into the tower archway. Immediately I felt my muscles tense; I had not been able to make out who it was, but if I was quick to follow I might see who could be dashing about so furtively at such an hour. I grabbed for my shirt, and then paused, berating myself. Had I not already decided that whatever undercover comings and goings went on in this place were not my business? I would leave today, and if there was a murderer in the college they would just have to deal with it themselves; my attempts at finding the truth had been met with contempt and threats, and I wanted nothing more to do with any of it.

As I pulled on my shirt and breeches, a single bell began the doleful call to Matins and I recalled with a sinking heart that it was Sunday. The servants would probably have a day off; I would be unlikely to find anyone able to help me locate the horse and, in any case, I would have to return it to the stables at Windsor and how I might make my way back from there to London alone on a Sunday, I had no idea. In the unsparing daylight, my planned flight began to look as ill judged as it was cowardly.

I poured some water from the pitcher left on the small

table and washed my face slowly; if I had to stay for one more day, I could at least try to put it to some profitable use and I would start by attending chapel. I had no wish to hear the English service for its own sake – while I found no spiritual nourishment in the Roman Mass, at least it put some effort into its theatrics, and I found the English prayer book as bland as uncooked dough beside it – but it would be a useful opportunity to observe the whole college community gathered in one place. If one of them had sent me the strange message last night, as seemed likely, it was possible that he might give himself away by looks or gestures. I thought of him now, as I splashed my face, with irritation; if he had any useful information to impart, why not make himself clearer?

James Coverdale had mentioned at the first night's dinner that the rector was preaching a series of sermons based on Foxe's book; if Roger Mercer's killing was some twisted parody of martyrdom, as someone clearly wanted me to believe, it was possible that the killer had taken inspiration from the rector's sermons. It was even possible that he would be among the congregation that morning. I shivered, pulled on my boots and, as the bell continued its solemn clang, I hurried to join the black-gowned figures heading for the central archway of the north range, under the clock, which showed the hour to be almost six.

The chapel occupied the larger portion of the first floor of the north range, to the right of the archway, and I filed dutifully up the dim stairs among the students and Fellows, the only light offered by a candle lantern suspended from the landing above. By the door I noticed a holy water stoup, long dry, as we passed into a modest, lime-washed room with a wooden-beamed roof, the floor strewn with rushes. A small altar stood at the furthest end, opposite the door, with a lectern to the right of it; candles burned on each side of the chapel and on the altar, and the men arranged themselves along the rows of hard oak benches apparently designed for maximum discomfort, to prevent anyone from drowsing during sermons. Narrow arched windows of plain glass on both sides of the small chapel filled it with early morning light that gleamed from the white walls and on the long dark hair of Sophia Underhill, who was seated on the front pew by the lectern, where she would be under her father's watchful eye. I wondered that he allowed her to attend chapel with the scholars; her presence seemed guaranteed to distract young men from pious prayer. Then I noticed that her mother was seated beside her, her thin shoulders hunched beneath the white coif which bound her hair. Around her the senior Fellows were ranked along the front benches, with the older students – those proceeding to masters or doctors degrees – seated in the rows behind them, and the undergraduates at the back. As I hovered by the door, wondering where I should properly take my place, I had a chance to see just how small the college community was. There could not have been more than thirty men, including the senior Fellows; with lives spent in such close proximity, surely one among them had some knowledge of what had really taken place in the Grove the previous morning. Taking in the room in a swift glance, I spotted Thomas Allen and Lawrence Weston among the undergraduates, though there was no sign of Norris or the loud commoner friends he had brought to the tavern; I presumed that Matins was yet another college rule they were able to buy their way out of. William Bernard and Richard Godwyn, the librarian, sat on the front bench, and I noticed John Florio in the middle, whispering animatedly to his neighbour. These were the only men I had met personally in the college, yet there was every possibility that my mysterious correspondent was someone who had yet to introduce himself.

194

But he must have been a member of the college, to have known where to find my chamber. I turned to glance again at the young men seated behind me and those in my line of sight returned my stare with mild curiosity; these English boys all looked the same – pale, underfed and anxious. One among them knew something he wanted to impart to me and was afraid to say outright – but which one?

I had intended to find a seat that would give me a vantage point over all those gathered, but Godwyn, seeing me hesitating at the door, smiled and gestured to a place next to him on the front bench. I could hardly refuse; conscious of all the eyes on me, including Sophia's, I walked down the short central aisle and sat down beside Godwyn, who welcomed me in a whisper as we bent our heads to pray. I could not help noticing that both Walter Slythurst and James Coverdale were absent. When the men were all seated, they rose again as one, as the rector processed the short distance from the door to the altar followed by four young men in the white surplices of choirboys.

Looking up, I caught the rector's eye; if he was surprised to see me among his congregants or repented of his hard words the night before, his face gave no sign of it. Instead he merely bowed his head and intoned the Our Father.

'O Lord, open Thou my lips,' he began, and the congregation dutifully responded,

'And my mouth shall show forth thy praise.'

I was not familiar enough with the order of the responses to follow them fluently, and kept my voice to a whisper to avoid drawing unwelcome attention to my mistakes. Godwyn rose to read the first lesson from the Gospel of Matthew, and after he was seated again, the small choir sang a four-voice version of the *Te Deum Laudamus* in English, which was remarkably sweet for all its plainness.

'Yesterday, gentlemen,' the rector went on, staring

resolutely over the heads of his congregation, apparently excluding his wife and daughter from his address, 'sudden violent death intruded most horribly into our little community. I know that the tragic attack on our dear friend Roger Mercer as he walked at prayer in the Grove has shaken all of us to the core, and I know too that when such a dreadful accident occurs, we can all too easily allow our brains to grow heated with the shock and indulge in all manner of wild speculation.' Here he flashed a pointed glance at me, so quickly as to go almost unnoticed. Doctor Bernard cracked his bony knuckles together; the snap was startling in the still room.

'It would be more profitable,' the rector continued over-loudly, as if he were speaking to a much larger gathering, 'if, instead of unhelpful rumour, we allowed some good to come from this tragedy by concentrating our minds on the brevity of our lives in contrast to the vastness of eternity, and looked to our own standing before God. Let us mourn Roger, as is right and proper, but let us also learn from his death and ask ourselves, would we face death assured of our own salvation, if it should come upon us as suddenly?'

'It almost sounds as if he expects another tragedy,' I whispered to Godwyn; Underhill glanced up and frowned angrily from behind his lectern, though he could not have heard my words.

'Let us return, then, as we have in recent weeks, to Master Foxe's account of the persecutions of the early believers, our forefathers in faith in the days when the Church was pure. Not so that we may pay them idolatrous reverence as saints, as the Roman Church does, for they were only men and women like us, but so that we might emulate their faith and better understand the long and venerable history of suffering for Christ and of standing firm, as those martyrs of Reform have done in this troubled century of ours. Let us ask ourselves, as we consider today the story of Alban, the first English martyr, if we truly believe that the preservation of the faith is the highest good. For these are turbulent days, my friends,' he continued, his voice rising slightly as he leaned over the lectern to fix his listeners with a stern eye. 'Our English Church is besieged on all sides by those who would drag us back to Rome. You young men sitting before me today are the future leaders of Church and State, and you do not know how you may be called upon to fight for both in the years to come. Will you be resolute, even in the face of death? Will you defend our liberties from the idolaters and tyrants who would tear them from us? I pray it may be so.'

From the benches behind me, a collective movement could be heard; the sound of several rows of young men drawing themselves up proudly in response to this rallying cry. I found something disturbing in Underhill's tone; there was a barely suppressed fanaticism to it, but his words reminded me of Walsingham's.

The rector's homily was more of a lecture than a sermon, though it was a relief to find that his talent for expounding on a text was greater than his talent for debating ideas. But as he spoke, I became so lost in my own speculation that I barely noticed when he pronounced the final collect, and was only dislodged from my reverie by Godwyn nudging me apologetically as the men around me all stood. The rector and his choir filed out and the congregation shuffled and stretched as they made ready to leave. One young man with violently red hair and a face peppered with freckles, who looked barely old enough to be away from his mother, busied himself at the front of the chapel, tidying away the accoutrements of the service, closing the large bible on the lectern and snuffing out the candles around us. As she drew towards me, Sophia smiled and seemed about to speak, but her mother, noticing

197

the look that passed between us, pinned her daughter firmly by the elbow and led her towards the door. Sophia glanced once over her shoulder and there seemed to be something imploring in her expression, but I might have imagined that.

'I am sorry to have poked you so unceremoniously, Doctor Bruno,' Godwyn whispered, as the red-haired young man clearing the chapel approached us and handed Godwyn the last remaining flickering candle, 'but I feared you were having some trouble following our Book of Common Prayer – the manner of our service must seem very strange to you.'

'Not so strange,' I replied, watching as Sophia passed out of sight before turning back to him with a smile, 'you have borrowed a great deal of it from us, after all.'

He gave a small, polite laugh.

'But tell me, did you not think our little choir sings well?' he asked brightly as we walked towards the door, making a shield of his hand to protect the candle as the draught from the stairs assaulted it.

'I have heard choirs twice their number make a poorer job of the psalms,' I said truthfully.

'The arrangement is by Master Byrd, Her Majesty's own composer,' he said, looking pleased at the praise.

'A Catholic himself, is he not?'

Godwyn looked aghast.

'Well – yes, he is, but that is not why I admire him,' he said quickly. 'If the queen can tolerate his faith for the sake of his music, I do not see why we should not do the same.'

'Quite. And of course, your own reading of the gospel was given with true poetic expression,' I added, in a devout tone.

'Thank you. That duty should fall to the sub-rector, but Doctor Coverdale did not arrive for Matins this morning, so the rector asked me to step in at the last moment.'

Instead of following the crowd of undergraduates down the stairs, he crossed the landing to a low wooden door

198

opposite the chapel's entrance, one hand still cupped around his candle, and gestured to me to follow.

'I remember you expressed an interest in our library, Doctor Bruno – would you like to take a look, now you are here? Unless you are impatient to break your fast, of course,' he added. 'Perhaps you would not mind holding this for a moment?'

He handed me the candle and took a ring of keys from his belt, selecting the largest.

'I should be delighted,' I said, following him, though I was more interested by his news about Coverdale. 'Is Doctor Coverdale away, then?'

'Well, if he is, he gave no one any warning,' Godwyn said, sounding piqued as he turned the key stiffly in the lock and pushed open the heavy door, which groaned as if in complaint at being disturbed.

I remembered the boy who had come to summon Coverdale in the middle of the disputation the previous evening, and Cobbett's report that Coverdale had returned to college as if in an almighty haste. It was curious, then, that Cobbett had not mentioned his leaving again – unless he had somehow slipped away in the night, or early in the morning. I wondered if his disappearance could have anything to do with the inquest into Roger Mercer's death and his threats to me over my testimony.

'Strange. I noticed the bursar, Master Slythurst, was also absent,' I added lightly.

Godwyn made a dismissive gesture as he closed the door behind me,

'Slythurst is often away, it's part of his duties – he has to check the college's estates regularly, and they are scattered about the country, some several days' ride. I believe he left for Buckinghamshire this morning as he has some business there, but we expect him back tomorrow. Now then – here we are.' He spread his arms expansively to encompass his domain, and smiled encouragement, as if urging me to admire it as much as he did.

The library took up the first floor of the north range on the west side of the central staircase, directly opposite the chapel but slightly smaller in proportion. Like the chapel, it had a rush-covered floor and wooden beams in the roof, and was laid out in the style of the last century, with long wooden lecterns at which readers would stand to study the large manuscript books secured by brass chains to a brass rod running beneath the desks. There were four of these lecterns on each side of the chapel, secured to the wall between the arched windows. At each end of the room, wooden benches stood against the wall and at the far end, a small writing desk was placed under the last window overlooking the courtyard; Godwyn strode towards it and carefully placed his keys beside an inkwell before turning to me to retrieve his candle.

'Which books are of particular interest to you, Doctor Bruno, or shall I just begin by showing you our most valuable manuscripts?' he asked over his shoulder, as he made his way methodically down the length of the room, lighting candles in the holders at the end of each lectern and in the wall niches between the windows.

'This is not your whole collection, surely?' I asked, gesturing to the books that lay chained to the reading desks.

'Oh, goodness, no – these are only the older books that must be chained up, I regret to say, for fear of theft, and the ones the students use most frequently. They are largely works of scholastic theology and are extremely valuable, many of them part of our original benefactor's gift.'

'Dean Flemyng, from his travels in Italy,' I said thoughtfully, nodding. 'And where do you keep the prohibited books?'

Godwyn blanched and stared at me, a puzzled frown creasing his high forehead. He looked almost frightened.

'But we keep no prohibited books here, Doctor Bruno. What can you mean?'

'Come now, Master Godwyn,' I said, holding out my palms to show I meant no offence. 'Every university library I have known keeps some books away from the inquisitive eyes of the students. Books that only the senior members are judged able to understand?'

Godwyn's relief was visible.

'Oh! Yes, of course – we have a number of books available only to the junior and senior Fellows, which they may borrow and take away to read in their own rooms. We keep them in the chests in this room here.' He crossed to a door in the wall behind his desk and opened it, revealing a small chamber annexed to the library. Though it was shadowy inside, by the faint light of his candle I could make out several large trunks lining the walls. 'I thought for a moment you referred to heretical books,' he added, with a self-conscious laugh.

'No, no – I understood those had been rooted out by the queen's commissioners some time ago.'

He nodded, a little sadly.

'There was a great purge of the university libraries in '69. Anything that had survived the previous purges under Her Majesty's father, and then her brother and sister, was taken away. Books that, between you and me, Doctor Bruno, were no more heretical than any other, but there was great suspicion cast over the university after the Catholic resurgence in Bloody Mary's time and the colleges must all be seen to expel anything with so much as a taint of unorthodoxy. The collection here was badly depleted, I'm sorry to say.'

'The notion of heresy changes with reliable frequency according to who happens to be in charge,' I agreed. 'But what happened to the books that were deemed dangerous?'

He looked at me blankly, as if he had not considered the question before.

'I presume they were burned, though if they were, it was not publicly. I doubt they could have been sold openly once they were on the forbidden list. I was an undergraduate then, so I was only dimly aware of the commission – too busy sweating over my Greek and trying not to think about girls – but I would have remembered if there had been a book-burning.' He smiled fondly at the image of his younger self. 'You would need to ask William Bernard – he was librarian at the time.'

'Really?' This was indeed valuable news, and I thought it curious that Bernard had not mentioned it during our discussion about books at the rector's table on my first night. My blood quickened; could that irascible old man have squirrelled away somewhere a cache of books judged too dangerous for the minds of young men destined to shape the future of England? And was there the ghost of a chance that among his acquisitions from a certain Florentine bookseller more than a hundred years earlier, Dean Flemyng might have picked up a manuscript whose value he did not recognise, but whose existence William Bernard had seemed unusually eager to deny?

I breathed deeply, trying not to betray my agitation. It was almost certainly too much to hope that the manuscript I sought was here, but it was not beyond the bounds of possibility. If anyone knew whether an uncatalogued Greek book had been part of the Dean's original bequest, it would be William Bernard, who had been in the college longer than anyone, who read Greek and would know exactly what he had in his hands, should he have unearthed it. The challenge would be persuading him to confide in a stranger; the old man was wily as a stoat and already suspicious of me for my apparent disobedience to all religions.

Godwyn had finished lighting his candles and turned to me, clasping his hands like an anxious host.

'Perhaps you would like to see our copy of Cicero's *De Officiis*, which Dean Flemyng copied in his own hand?' he ventured, gesturing to one of the lecterns at the far end. 'I light the candles because, although it is Sunday, many of the scholars like to spend it here in quiet study. The undergraduates may not take books to their rooms, you see.'

'Do you, by any chance, keep a copy of Master Foxe's book among your loan collection?' I asked as I followed, in as off-hand a manner as I could.

'The *Actes and Monuments*?' He looked surprised. 'Yes, I have the 1570 edition, the second printing, though it may be out with someone at the moment – did you want to see it?'

'May I? I was interested in reading further after the rector's sermon this morning.'

'You are welcome to read it,' he said, doubtfully, 'though I'm afraid you will not find Foxe very generous to those of your faith. But I must ask you to look at it here in the library – only the Fellows are permitted to sign the books out, you see. That way we have some surety if they come back the worse for wear.'

'The books, or the Fellows?' I said.

Godwyn laughed politely, and led the way to one of the large wooden trunks in the small back room. As he crouched to lift out a pile of books, I noticed a smaller chest, tucked away into the corner and fastened with a padlock. Godwyn stacked the volumes carefully on the floor, then reached again into the chest and handed me a fat volume, plainly bound in cloth.

'I have seen a copy in the library in Paris,' I said, turning the book over in my hands, 'but I have not read it in detail. The rector's sermon whetted my appetite. And the story of Ignatius – that too is among the tales of the early martyrs?'

'Yes, indeed – the ten primitive persecutions under the

Romans,' he said, tilting his head slightly as if he found my question strange. 'All in Book One.'

Just then, the door opened and all the candles wavered along the lecterns as the red-haired young man who had been tidying the chapel earlier leaned in and coughed nervously.

'Master Godwyn, sir? Rector Underhill wants to speak with you about a private matter, if you have a moment.'

Godwyn looked anxiously at me, then back to the boy.

'You would not mind if I step out for a minute, Doctor Bruno? I am sure I may trust you not to steal the books.' He laughed nervously.

I waved a hand, eager to examine the Foxe.

'Your books will be safe with me, Master Godwyn.'

'Might I ask you to wait until I return, then? The library must not be left open and unattended, you see.' He looked apprehensive. I assured him that I would guard the place with my life and he followed the red-haired boy out with an anxious backwards glance, closing the door softly behind him.

I settled myself at Godwyn's large desk and opened the volume of Foxe at Book One, but as I did so, I realised that the librarian had left his bunch of keys behind. A thought struck me; glancing briefly at the door, I grabbed the keys and found among them a small iron key of the size to open a padlock. In the back room, I knelt by the locked chest and fitted it to the lock; to my surprise, it sprung open smoothly to reveal a pile of black cloth. As I lifted this out, I saw that it was an academic gown, placed there to conceal the books beneath. I picked up the topmost volume; it was bound in aged calfskin and felt fragile to the touch, its corners frayed, but it was the title page that caused me to draw a sharp breath and check instinctively once more to make sure I was alone.

It was a copy of the executed Jesuit Edmund Campion's

*Ten Reasons*, and the printer's mark showed it had come from Rheims. There was no doubt that this book, Campion's staunch defence of the Catholic faith, was prohibited in England, and certainly in Oxford; beneath it I found other texts and pamphlets equally distasteful to the English authorities, by Robert Persons, William Allen and other Catholic writers out of Europe. I leafed through them for a moment, my pulse quickening, until I was startled by a creaking timber from the library behind me and remembered that Godwyn would soon be returning. I searched quickly to the bottom of the chest but there were no books in Greek; these were forbidden books of a different sort. Replacing them quickly and recovering them with the gown, I locked the chest in haste and returned the keys, then seated myself quickly at Godwyn's desk in case he should return.

I concentrated my attention on the Foxe, flicking hastily through the pages in search of the story of Ignatius. The task was not difficult; there, on page forty-six, I found what I had anticipated – a gap in the paper the length of two lines of print, cut so neatly as to leave the surrounding text intact. Only the text that had been pushed under my door was missing, the incision as precise as only a bookbinder's knife or similar instrument could make. Or a pen knife, I thought suddenly, catching sight of Godwyn's quill and inkwell on the desk in front of me. But that could hardly narrow the search; every scholar in the college must own one of those.

The latch clicked and Godwyn reappeared, pulling the door shut behind him and shaking his head to himself.

'I am sorry to abandon you, Doctor Bruno – Rector Underhill wanted to discuss which of poor Roger Mercer's books should be given to the library's collection. Did you find what you wanted?' he asked pleasantly.

'I fear the rats have been at your books, Master Godwyn,' I replied, beckoning him closer and turning to the ravaged page forty-six, which I held open in front of him. He looked from me to the book with incomprehension for a moment, before a flush of outrage spread over his sagging features.

'But whoever would do such a thing?' he exclaimed, then glanced over his shoulder as if someone might have overheard. 'How did you know . . .?'

'I found the missing lines pushed under my door last night.'

'But – *why*?' Godwyn continued to stare at me as if he feared my wits had fled.

'Look at the passage,' I whispered.

He raised the book closer to his face and skimmed the page. When he looked up at me again his expression was one of severe shock.

'Ignatius,' he whispered. 'I am the wheat of Christ – I forget the exact words, but that is the missing part, is it not? Something about the teeth of wild beasts.'

I nodded. He looked at the book again and exhaled carefully, as if trying to control his response.

'Ah. You think this is a reference to Roger's death?'

'I think that is what whoever sent me those lines wishes me to conclude, yes.'

He closed the book and frowned, so that the lines in his brow formed deep runnels.

'Why you, Doctor Bruno, if that does not seem rude?'

I hesitated again, unsure again how much to reveal.

'I was among the first to arrive in the Grove yesterday morning after Doctor Mercer was attacked by the dog.' I dropped my voice even further until it was barely audible. 'On the evidence of what I saw, I suggested that his death may not have been an accident.'

Godwyn's eyes widened until his eyebrows threatened to disappear.

'But – they said the gate was unlocked – the wild dog strayed in—'

'My hypothesis was not widely taken up by your colleagues. But it seems that someone else wants to strengthen my conviction that his death was by design.' I gestured to the book in his hands. Godwyn scrutinised its cover with as much disbelief as if it had spoken aloud, then turned his keen eyes back to me.

'You think someone is trying to imply that Roger was *martyred*?'

'I don't know,' I said. 'Someone certainly wants me to notice a similarity in the manner of his death, but why should Doctor Mercer be considered a martyr?'

Godwyn looked at me in silence for a long while as my whispered question hung in the air.

He shook his head sharply. 'I cannot think.'

'Who would have access to the books in that back room?' I asked.

'Well, all the Fellows have a key to the library, but they are not supposed to take any books on loan without first checking with me and signing the ledger. The students may only use the library when I am present to keep an eye on them, but – well, I am not always as scrupulous as I might be in that regard.' He looked guilty for a moment. 'If I need to pop out and there are a few students here deep in their work, it seems harsh to lock them out if only for a short while. It's not as if they can easily steal a book, and I would trust them to take care of the library.'

'Well, it seems your trust in someone was misplaced,' I said.

Godwyn's face clouded, as if he was only now registering the gravity of the assault on library property.

'But I was here in the library until about quarter to five yesterday afternoon, when I locked up and left for the disputation, along with the students who were here.'

'And you did not leave the library unattended before a quarter to five?'

'Anyone would think you were a magistrate, Doctor Bruno, with all these questions,' he said, forcing a smile, but his eyes were guarded. 'I may have had to go and use the privy during that time, I really can't remember, but I'm sure I would not have been gone long enough for anyone to achieve *this*.' He banged the cover of the Foxe with his palm. 'It has been very carefully done, I do not think it was a rushed job by someone looking over his shoulder all the while.'

'No,' I agreed. 'And no one could have come in while you were out at the disputation?'

'Well, as I say, the Fellows all have keys, but they were out at the disputation too,' he said, though his eyes swerved away from mine as he said it.

All except James Coverdale, I thought, but I had already dismissed him as the person most eager to persuade me away from the theory of murder.

'No one else at all has a key?'

'Only the rector. Oh – and, of course . . .' Here he hesitated and his demeanour became awkward.

'Who?' I pressed.

'Mistress Sophia has the use of her father's key sometimes,' he said, cupping a fist against his mouth as if he were about to cough. 'She has a fancy that she can be as good a scholar as any and he indulges her in it. I suspect it comes of the loss of his son – though, of course, that is his business.' He shook his head. 'Mind you, I would not allow any daughter of mine such freedom, if I had one, for women's minds are not made for learning and I confess I fear for her health – but I must be thankful that he only permits her to visit at times when the scholars are unlikely to be present. Otherwise she has them all panting after her like dogs in season, Doctor Bruno, and I don't want my library used for that sort of thing – at least with her own key, she can come in when the young men are out at public lectures.'

'Does she use the library when you are not here to supervise?'

'Oh, I expect so,' Godwyn said, as if the matter were out of his hands. 'If she has her father's permission I can hardly gainsay him – besides, she is not going to steal the books, is she?'

No, I thought, but might she have used her key to gain access last night, knowing the whole college would be at the Divinity School for over an hour? She had not betrayed a flicker of recognition when I mentioned the quotation, but that was not in itself proof of ignorance. But why on earth would Sophia write to me anonymously and then feign ignorance when she had a chance to discuss the matter with me alone? The person who had written to me was clearly anxious not to be identified as the source of the information, scant as it was – could it be that Sophia knew something about someone in the college, but could not be seen overtly to denounce him? Could that someone be her own father?

'Thank you, Master Godwyn,' I said, rising from his chair to take my leave.

'Oh, but I have not yet shown you our illustrated manuscript of St Cyprian's letters which Dean Flemyng also brought out of Florence,' he began, his eyes clouding with disappointment. I studied his face as I apologised for leaving, reflecting that those large, melancholy eyes lent his face an air of disarming frankness. But I now knew that Godwyn was also a man hiding his own secrets, and I reminded myself that I must not trust the face that any of them presented to me or to the world. As William Bernard had so pointedly told me that first night, no man in Oxford was what he seemed.

# NINE

Trying to marshal my thoughts, I emerged into the quad-rangle, now lit by the first tentative glimmers of sun I had seen since leaving London. Streaks of cloud still lingered over-head, but the determined rain of the past three days seemed temporarily to have abated. The clock above the archway to the chapel and library staircase showed it to be just gone half past eight; the college seemed ominously quiet.

I paused to look up at the windows of the rector's lodg-ings, wondering which room might be Sophia's and how I might find a way to see her again today, despite her father's explicit ban, when I remembered with a sudden curse that I had half-promised to go hunting with Sidney and the Palatine Laski at Shotover Forest. I decided that I would walk over to Christ Church and excuse myself to Sidney in person. He would be angry, I knew, and I had every sympathy for him, being saddled with the Pole from dawn till night, but I could hardly be considered an asset to any hunting party even when my attention was not so distracted by trying to catch a killer; I had no talent for gentlemen's sports and no opportunity to learn them in my youth, as he had. Sidney could make the necessary enquiries about hunting dogs while he was there;

reasoned I could make more useful progress by staying in the town. The two people whose confidence I most wanted to gain were Thomas Allen and Doctor William Bernard; both, I suspected, would have at least some knowledge of the underground Catholic network, which in turn may have a connection with Mercer's death, though I knew very well that if they had any such contacts they would not admit them to me easily.

Reluctantly I returned to my own chamber, where I washed thoroughly in cold water, since the scholars of Oxford seemed to possess nothing so civilised as a bath house, reflecting that I must ask Cobbett about seeing the college barber to have my beard trimmed and the laundress to wash my shirts, as it seemed we were destined to stay at least three more days. My stomach rumbled loudly as I dressed; hunger had crept up on me while I was at my ablutions, and I took Walsingham's purse from my travelling bag and hung it at my belt, deciding that I would venture out into the town to see if I could find any place that would sell me something to eat at this hour on a Sunday.

The courtyard was empty when I stepped out from my staircase, and seemed unnaturally quiet; apparently the students kept to themselves on Sundays. I was about to cross to the gatehouse when Gabriel Norris emerged from his staircase in the west range carrying a leather bag slung over one shoulder; instinctively I took a step back into the shadows, wishing to avoid further speculation with him about what may or may not be said at the inquest. He was dressed all in black, but it was clear even from a distance that his doublet and breeches were satin and expensively cut, and he wore a short cloak around his shoulders that gleamed with the sheen of velvet. He glanced briefly around the courtyard but appeared not to notice me, still half-hidden, before setting off with a quick tread towards the gate. Something about

211

his haste struck me as curious; I recalled that he had turned down his invitation to hunt with Sidney today, and wondered what prior commitment could be more attractive to a young man than that? I decided then that it might be amusing to follow him, since I had planned to go into the town anyway; after his own confession about his nocturnal expeditions, and Lawrence Weston's report of the rumours about his preferences, I half-hoped I might catch him out in some illicit tryst and prove Weston's theory true. Then, if the right moment arose, I could make use of any such proof to dissuade Sophia away from him for good – if, indeed, he was the indifferent object of her affections.

I allowed him a few moments to gain some distance so that he would not notice me trailing behind. Waving to Cobbett through his small window, I leaned tentatively out of the main gate into St Mildred's Lane to see Norris already some way ahead, walking at a brisk pace northwards in the direction of Jesus College. I had to half-skip to keep up with his long strides, staying close to the wall of Exeter College as we passed it, but not so much that I would seem to be doing anything other than taking a casual stroll if he happened to turn around and spot me.

The lane was clogged with mud after the past days' rain, and Norris fastidiously sidestepped the worst of the ruts and puddles, stopping at one point to wipe a splatter of dirt from his fine leather boots with a gesture of irritation. Where St Mildred's Lane met Sommer Lane he turned right without hesitation and after a moment's pause I followed, keeping in the shadow of the old city wall which rose up solidly on my left like a fortress. There were few souls abroad in the street, only one or two couples in their best clothes, no doubt heading for one of the city's many parish churches. Bells pealed from somewhere up ahead, announcing a service.

My quarry walked purposefully, as if he had an appointment,

but there was nothing shifty about his demeanour, nothing to suggest his destination was at all out of the ordinary or that he would prefer not to be seen, and he did not walk as if the bag he carried was heavy, large as it was. I suppressed a shudder as we passed the wall of the Divinity School on our right, and just ahead, opposite the mouth of a street whose sign read Catte Street, he turned towards a small postern set into the city wall beside a little chapel. Hovering in the shadows of the houses opposite, I began to feel somewhat foolish for my sneaking pursuit.

Outside the city wall stretched a broad avenue with few houses, those that stood by the road low and shabby, each surrounded by scrubby plots of land and orchards that extended back further than I could see. The ground was rutted by the wheels of carts and horses' hooves, and I watched as Norris crossed the lane and set off to his right, his bag swung over his shoulder, past a row of poor-looking dwellings towards open farmland. It was harder here to find any cover, so I dropped back and allowed a greater distance to open between us, keeping myself in tight to the shadow of the city wall; even so, had he turned I would not have been able to conceal my presence. After perhaps ten minutes Norris turned again to his left, down a wide road flanked on each side by orchards and fields, and here I thought of turning back, as I was obliged to leave the shelter of the wall, but my curiosity was piqued. The road was almost bare of buildings; ahead the only masonry visible was the squat tower of a little church that, as I drew closer, I saw was very ancient. Norris passed around the side of the church; beyond it rose the pale stone wall of an impressive farmhouse, three storeys high with gabled windows set into the roof, its grounds encircled by a high wall of that same golden stone. From the corner of the church I watched as Norris approached a gate set into this wall at the side of the house, and after a short while was admitted, though I did not see by whom.

I had no choice then but to turn around and retrace my steps back to the city, reproaching myself for a wasted journey. I confess I would have been delighted to see Norris meeting with some young swain, but there was nothing eventful in the trip he had made; it was to be expected that a rich young man should have acquaintance among Oxford's grander families, and the farmhouse looked as if it belonged to people of wealth. I had learned nothing of any use, and it was only as I walked back past the fields, taking my time now and savouring the scent of wet earth and fresh leaves that drifted to me from the orchards, that I remembered what Lawrence Weston had said about Norris keeping his own horse outside the city wall. No doubt he had been on his way off for a ride, and I felt particularly thankful that I had not been caught stalking him and been obliged to explain my own foolishness.

But I was enjoying the air after the rain and the sensation of freedom that the open countryside outside the city brought after the oppressive closeness of Lincoln College, with all its intrigues and undercurrents of malice that had somehow led to the death of poor Roger Mercer. I was not eager to return too soon to that walled-in quadrangle, with all those windows like so many hostile eyes, watching my every move, so I decided to walk back the long way around the outside of the great city wall and see what more I could discover of my surroundings while looking out for an inn that might serve me some hot food.

I was almost level with the old church of St Mary Magdalen, at the side of a crooked building that looked as if it might once have been a tavern but was now fallen into disrepair, when a sudden gust of wind ripped along the street, scattering the last few scraps of blossom from the nearby trees. I started at a violent creak from above and looked up o see an old painted sign swinging violently on its rusty hinges, groaning as if it might come loose at any moment; it was then that I jolted backwards with a cry of shock, because the sign over my head, though its paint was faded and flaking so badly that the picture was barely visible, depicted a spoked wheel, identical to the symbol in Roger Mercer's calendar and the astronomical diagram slipped under my door.

I had not expected the door even to open, the place looked so derelict from the front, but when I turned the handle it groaned open to allow me a glimpse of one low-ceilinged room smelling of must and damp and furnished with a few rickety tables and benches. A pervasive chill hung in the air; the hearth that filled one wall was piled with cold ashes and the handful of customers conversed in muted tones, hunched over their pots of beer as if they were half-ashamed to be found in such a place. It was not an inn to welcome passersby. I closed the door gently behind me and took a seat at a table in a dingy corner next to the serving-hatch, blood pounding in my chest, aware that my entrance had attracted the attention of the other guests. With a stab of surprise, I recognised, in a group of four men across the room who were staring and whispering behind their hands, the pock-faced man with no ears I had seen outside the Divinity School before the disputation – the man I was certain James Coverdale had also recognised. 'No one of significance,' Coverdale had said. The earless man did not join in with the muttering of his companions but merely regarded me, unblinking, over their heads with that same cool, insolent gaze, as if he knew me. I met his look for a moment before looking quickly away, noticing that his eyes were as striking as his face; a blue so pale and translucent they seemed almost lit from within, the way sunlight shines through water in the Bay of Naples.

His stare was so disconcerting that I lowered my own eyes anxious not to provoke any confrontation, but it was clear that this was not a place where a stranger could take a quiet drink without his presence arousing an unspoken but palpable reaction. When I looked up again, a sturdy-looking woman of perhaps forty in a stained apron was standing in front of me, her arms folded. She had stringy greying hair scraped back from her square-jawed face and her brown eyes were sceptical.

'What'll you have, sir?'

'A pot of ale?'

She nodded curtly, but continued to stand there appraising me.

'You are not a familiar face, sir, what brings you to the Catherine Wheel?'

'I was hungry, I saw your sign and thought to stop for food.'

Her eyes narrowed further.

'You are not from hereabouts, I think.'

'I was born in Italy,' I said, meeting her stare as frankly as I could. She pursed her lips and nodded.

'Friend to the pope?'

'Not personally,' I said, and finally her face softened a little and she almost smiled.

'You understand my meaning, sir.'

'Will my answer determine whether or not you bring me the beer?'

'Just like to be sure we have the right kind of people here, sir.'

I looked around the tap-room; a less salubrious crowd it would be hard to picture. I was reminded of the roadside inns I had been forced to make use of during my flight from San Domenico.

'I was raised in the Church of Rome,' I said evenly. 'I don't

216

know if that makes me the right kind of person, but I promise it does not affect the coins in my purse.'

She seemed to concede then, and half-turned as if to go.

'What do you call yourself?' she asked, as an afterthought.

'Filippo,' I said, surprised at the ease with which the name slipped out; it had come almost as a reflex. Perhaps it was the memory of those years as a fugitive, when I had travelled under my birth name, knowing that to own my identity could be fatal. Here, in this gloomy tavern among the sidelong glances and murmurs, instinct had prompted the same need for caution. 'Filippo il Nolano.'

The landlady seemed satisfied. She nodded, unfolded her arms and made a slight dipping movement which might almost have been a curtsey.

'Joan Kenney, widow, at your service. Will you eat, sir?'

'What have you?'

'Pottage,' she said firmly.

I had by that time been in England long enough to know that pottage was a sludgy concoction produced by mixing oatmeal with the juice left over from stewing meat, something that should rightly be served to livestock but which the English seemed to find an indispensable addition to any table.

'No meat?' I asked hopefully. 'It is Sunday.'

'We have pottage, sir. You may take it or leave it.'

Reluctantly, I said that I would take it.

'Humphrey!' she called, and a door opened beside the serving-hatch to admit a young man with fair curly hair holding a dirty dishcloth in his hands. Though he was at least six feet tall and probably in his twenties, he looked first at the landlady and then at me with the blank, open face of a child eager to please, and I guessed he was probably slow-witted.

'Fetch Master Nerlarno some pottage and a pot of ale quick as you can, and don't even think of imposing on him with your idle chatter,' she snapped, and Humphrey nodded furiously, with exaggerated up and down movements of his head as a child might, twisting the cloth in his hands as he looked at her. 'He's Welsh,' the landlady added darkly, as if this explained much.

While the boy disappeared to the kitchen, the woman crossed the room and leaned over the table to whisper something to the earless man, who inclined his head and nodded sagely without taking his eyes off me.

The boy, Humphrey, returned promptly with a bowl of tepid grey slurry which he slopped half across the table, and a wooden cup of beer topped with a film of grease, and stood by the table smiling energetically down at me.

'Thank you,' I said eventually, and when he still didn't leave, I wondered if I was supposed to tip him.

'Are you from Italy?' he asked, in a lilting voice, crouching so that he was at my eye level and considering me with his head on one side.

'That's right,' I said, poking the contents of my bowl with a piece of bread. They seemed to have congealed already.

'Say something in Italian then,' Humphrey said, as if challenging me to impress him, the way a child might challenge a street conjuror. I thought for a moment.

'*Non darei questo cibo nemmeno al mio cane*,' I said, smiling pleasantly but keeping my voice low, just in case. His eyes lit up with as much wonder as if I had produced a coin from the air and his broad face creased into a smile.

'What does it mean?'

'Oh – it is hard to translate directly. It was a compliment on your delicious food.'

He leaned in very close, so that his breath was tickling my ear. He smelled overwhelmingly of onions.

'I don't know Italian,' he whispered, 'but I do know Latin.'

'Good for you,' I said indulgently, expecting a string of

218

onsense, for it was impossible that a simple-minded pot-boy could truly have been educated in Latin. He nodded hard, his face serious.

'*Ora pro nobis*,' he hissed into my ear, then drew back to look at me expectantly, proud of himself, awaiting my approval.

I felt my own eyes widen then, and fought to keep my face steady; a faint light of understanding was beginning to spread over the questions that jostled in my mind.

'That is very good, Humphrey – do you know any more?' I whispered back. He beamed and leaned in again, but at that moment the landlady's shrill voice broke in.

'Humphrey Pritchard! Did I not tell you to leave the poor gentleman alone? Ha'n't you got work to do? He don't want to listen to your foolishness – let him enjoy his meal in peace.' With this misplaced optimism, she appeared suddenly at Humphrey's shoulder, cuffed him lightly around the back of the head and shoved him towards the kitchen. Though he was twice her size, his face crumpled with guilt and he scurried away, his big body hunched miserably.

The landlady wiped her hands on her apron and forced a smile.

'He wasn't saying anything, ah – offensive, I hope?' she asked, but I thought I caught a note of anxiety in her voice.

'Not at all,' I said. 'He was only asking if the food was all right.'

Her eyes narrowed.

'And is it?'

'Mm. Thank you.'

She looked at me for a moment as if she wanted to add something, then nodded curtly and disappeared into the kitchen, where I heard the sound of muffled voices, hers berating poor Humphrey and his raised in protest.

Dinner was an uncomfortable affair; I forced as little of

the grim stew as possible through my clenched teeth, consciou.
all the while of the level stare of the earless man and his
cronies in the corner. I half-hoped he would at least come
across and confront me, perhaps explain why he looked at
me with such interest or familiarity, but he remained in his
seat, stirring only occasionally to lean across and murmur
something to one of his companions.

I kept my eyes on my plate, my mind chasing after frag-
ments of conversation. *Ora pro nobis*. Pray for us. The words
written in code in the back of Roger Mercer's almanac. A
prayer of intercession, a fragment of the Ave Maria or the
Litania Sanctorum, for where else would an uneducated man
like Humphrey learn Latin except from the responses of the
Mass? So young Humphrey Pritchard had either overheard
or taken part in Catholic liturgies. Had he heard those words
through association with people he knew from the tavern?
That would explain why his employer was so keen to keep
him from talking to strangers. And why had Mercer written
out that same phrase in code? A password, perhaps, or a
sign to be recognised among co-conspirators. Was the
Catherine Wheel some kind of meeting place or safe house
for secret Catholics – was that what my enigmatic correspondent at Lincoln College was trying to steer me towards?

I realised that I had been staring at the earless man as I
contemplated this; almost as if he had been stirred into life
by my thoughts, at that moment he rose to his feet, brushed
down his doublet and called to the landlady to settle his bill.

'Alas, Widow Kenney, I must leave you for now – though
it is the Sabbath, business presses as always,' he announced,
and I was surprised to hear that he had an educated accent.
It made a disconcerting contrast with his appearance, which
gave him the look of a common criminal. Once again, I had
to reprimand myself for making hasty judgements on a man's
manner or looks. I waited until the door had swung shut

behind him before following suit; if Widow Kenney saw anything suspicious in my haste to leave, it was indistinguishable from her habitual expression, and she thanked me flatly as I threw some coins on the table and hurried out of the door, craning my neck in both directions along the street in the hope that I would still have the earless man in sight.

I was in luck; he had almost reached the top of the street by the church. Keeping again to the shadow of the buildings on my left, I told myself that this pursuit was far more worthy of one of Walsingham's agents, and I found I was relishing the drama of the moment and the rush of adrenalin in my veins.

The earless man crossed the broad street and passed under the North Gate, by the church of St Michael and the Bocado prison. I followed him at a safe distance along Sommer Lane, past the front of Exeter College and the rear wall of the Divinity School; at one point, I had the sense that someone was following me and turned sharply, but there were only a handful of people in the street, all going about their business without apparently taking any notice of me, so I put it down to heightened nerves and kept my eyes fixed on the earless man.

At the corner of the University Schools, he turned right into the narrow lane called Catte Street, where the houses stood closer together, the timber-framed upper storeys overhanging the road so that it stood in shadow, keeping the ground still wet underfoot. From the abundance of painted signs jutting out from the buildings, groaning gently in the wind, it was clear that this was a commercial street; closer inspection revealed businesses catering to the needs of an academic community: printers, stationers, makers of robes and regalia and a number of book dealers and binders, all shuttered and closed.

The earless man slowed his pace and I followed suit, just

as I noticed a figure coming towards us from the other direction, dressed in a black academic gown and velvet cap. He
carried himself stiffly, like an old man, and his steps were
halting, as if he found walking effortful. The earless man
stopped in front of a narrow shop front with grimy windows
and raised a hand in greeting; the figure in the cap made a
small gesture of acknowledgement in return. I ducked into
a doorway just as he drew level with the shop and removed
his cap, checking the street as if anxious not to be seen, and
I realised then that it was Doctor William Bernard. Without
speaking, the earless man removed a ring of keys from his
belt and unlocked the dingy shop; I shrank back further out
of sight as, with a last glance in both directions up the street,
he held the door open for Doctor Bernard and followed him
in through the low doorway. The door closed and I heard
the lock click behind them. The shop had no sign above, but
as I stepped out from the doorway and drew as close as I
dared, though it was unlikely that much of the street could
be seen through the thick film of dirt encrusting the diamond
panes of the only window, I saw that painted above the
doorway, in small but carefully wrought letters, were the
words *R. Jenkes. Bookbinder and Stationer.*

Turning from the shop, I slammed straight into a tall man
with a hat pulled down low over his face, almost causing
him to fall over.

'*Scusi,*' I said instinctively, as he too muttered an apology
and hurried away up the street. The sight of his retreating
back left me oddly unsettled; I wondered that I had not
noticed him in the street before. Could he have stepped out
from one of the shops? It seemed unlikely; all were closed,
and I remembered the moment before I turned into Catte
Street, when I had sensed I was being followed. The man
turned down a side alley without looking back. I had seen
almost nothing of his face except that he had a dark beard;

222

I could not recall if any of the earless man's companions from the Catherine Wheel had had a dark beard, but I had not observed them closely and they had been sitting with their backs to me. Why would I have been followed from the tavern, I wondered, unless it was because my presence there alone had aroused their suspicions, or because I had made it so obvious that I was in turn eager to follow the earless man?

I made my way back down Catte Street towards the city wall, my thoughts spinning. Who was that earless man, who had associates among the tavern low-lifes and the doctors of Lincoln College? If he was Jenkes the bookbinder himself, that might explain his connection with the academics, but it was curious that Bernard should choose a Sunday to do business with a stationer; indeed, the old doctor had looked very much as if he hoped not to be seen. Were I to seek the most obvious explanation, I might reason that if the Catherine Wheel was a known meeting place for recusants, and since Bernard was a sympathiser with the old faith, and the one man who linked the two dealt in books, was it not highly likely that I had stumbled upon some connection to the city's underground trade in banned books, of which Walsingham had spoken with such fury? Except that I had not stumbled upon it, I reflected; someone had deliberately and cryptically pointed me to this discovery, someone who had also made sure I linked it with Roger Mercer's death, and I must find out the source of this information, and what he feared from making himself known.

I walked back past the Divinity School and turned left into St Mildred's Lane; the gatehouse tower of Lincoln College loomed up on my left, squat and pale against the sky. As I passed through the main gate and under the tower arch, I heard a knocking on the window of the porter's lodge and looked around to see Cobbett waving for me to come in.

'Feller come looking for you just now, Doctor Bruno,' he said, wheezing furiously, as if he had been the one carrying the urgent message. 'Servant from Christ Church, wanted to know if you're going hunting at Shotover this afternoon.'

I cursed quietly; in all the excitement of my discovery of the Catherine Wheel, I had completely forgotten my promise to Sidney and my intention of excusing myself in person. At least now, with any luck, I would be too late to join them.

'I can't,' I said, half to myself. 'I suppose I had better go and leave a message for my friend.'

'No,' said Cobbett, sympathetically. 'I didn't think you looked the hunting sort. Bit short for a longbow, if you don't mind my saying.'

I only nodded and turned to leave. Then I suddenly remembered Sidney's advice about the college porters and their storehouse of information, and the bottle of ale we had bought to encourage Cobbett to talk freely, which was still sitting in my room.

'Would you like a drink, Cobbett?' I asked.

'Why, it's almost as if you read my own thoughts, Doctor Bruno.' He flashed his knowing, gummy grin. 'I was just thinking I'm parched near to the death. Almost witchcraft, that is.'

'No witchcraft, I assure you. I know a thirsty man when I see one. Wait for me here a moment,' I said, smiling, and he sat back heavily on his chair.

'Oh, I won't go nowhere, don't you worry. Might even see if I have a clean cup. Not used to guests, are we, Bess?' he said, gently scratching the old dog behind her ears. She made a small gurgling noise from the back of her throat.

When I returned with the bottle, Cobbett pulled out the stopper eagerly and poured a generous amount into two wooden cups placed on his table for the occasion. I tried not to look too closely at the state of the cup he passed me, his round face creased into a smile of satisfaction as he indicated to me to pull up a low stool tucked into the corner of his small room.

'Good ale and good company,' he said, when he had taken a long draught from his cup and swilled it around his mouth before swallowing noisily. 'Now then. I sense you have a question. I can read minds too, you know.' He winked.

With Cobbett, I had decided, my best course would be to match his frankness; he would see straight through any pretence.

'Have you ever come across a bookbinder in Catte Street by the name of Jenkes?' I asked.

Cobbett threw back his head and launched into one of those fits of guffaws that made me fear for his health. When he had recovered from the wheezing he turned an incredulous look on me and wiped his mouth with the back of his hand.

'Holy God and all his saints, Doctor Bruno, what have we done to you?' He shook his head, still laughing. 'You arrive in Oxford in the company of the highest men in the land, and in a matter of days you're consorting with the most notorious rogue in the city! Stay well away from Rowland Jenkes, that's all I have to tell you.'

'How, notorious? A mere bookbinder?'

'Not a mere anything, Rowland Jenkes. A papist and a sorcerer.'

'Really?' My interest was piqued now; Cobbett knew an eager audience when he saw one.

'Have you never heard of the Black Assize?' he said, adopting a portentous tone.

I shook my head.

Cobbett leaned forward with all the relish of a grandfather preparing a tale to frighten small children.

'Well, now,' he said, and a frustrating extended pause

225

followed while he drained his cup and generously poured himself another. 'Six years ago, summer of 1577 it was, and cursedly hot, Rowland Jenkes was arrested for sedition and imprisoned in Oxford castle, where they keep prisoners until the local Assizes are held.'

'What manner of sedition?'

'I'm coming to that, hold your horses,' Cobbett grumbled. 'Well, on this occasion he'd been found to be distributing seditious books, you know – papist books, ones they don't allow to be printed here. Shipping them in illegally from France and the Low Countries – they say he has some Flemish blood, but that might just be gossip and I never pay any mind to gossip.'

'No,' I said, nodding sincerely.

'No. Well, he was arrested for the books and some witnesses popped up to say they'd heard him speak treasonable words against the queen. But it was during his trial the terrible business happened. He was brought to the Shire Hall, just outside the prison wall, with all the other prisoners to be tried before the Lord High Sheriff and the Lord Chief Baron. Naturally, he was found guilty and just at the moment his sentence was pronounced, the courtroom was filled by the most foul stench you could imagine, such that everyone in the room thought as how they might choke or faint with it.'

He paused again for refreshment, and I found myself jigging impatiently on the edge of my stool.

'And then?'

'Well, now, you will hardly credit this but I know folk who saw it with their own eyes, Doctor Bruno,' Cobbett whispered, his own eyes growing wide with the momentum of his story. 'Every man on that jury died within a few days. Not only them, but every man jack in that courtroom, all of them, stone dead before a week was out. The sheriff, the baron, the sarjeants – all of them. Three hundred men died in Oxford over the course of a month. Then it was all over as quick as it come. But, here's the thing . . .' He leaned in even closer, so that his chin was almost in his beer. 'Not a one of the prisoners who was in the Assize that day died, nor any woman nor child. Now, you can't tell me that was any natural plague.'

'A curse, then?'

'The curse of Rowland Jenkes,' Cobbett said reverently. 'While he was locked up, awaiting the Assize, he was permitted to walk out with a keeper, you understand. Well, the story goes Jenkes visited an apothecary with a list of ingredients. The apothecary noted they were all mightily poisonous, and asked why he had need of them – Jenkes replied it was on account of the rats gnawing at his books in the shop while he was incarcerated, see? Anyhow, he procured these ingredients and it's thought he made a wick covered in this filthy potion, and fired it up the moment he was condemned.'

'Where would a condemned prisoner hide a tinderbox and flint about his person in a courtroom?' I asked. 'Is it not more likely it was some gaol fever brought in by the prisoners?'

Cobbett looked disappointed that I had not entered into the spirit of the legend.

'Well, I don't know about that, sir. All I know is good Christian folk cross the road if they see Rowland Jenkes in this town, and if you know what's good for you, you'll do the same.'

'What about the seditious books? Is he still in that trade?'

'Who knows what he does, sir – I told you, everyone leaves him alone now. I dare say he gets up to all sorts, but what jury would dare bring him to trial now?'

He refilled his cup and made a show of offering to pour some for me, but was clearly pleased at my refusal.

'What was his punishment?' I asked.

'Nailed by the ears to the pillory,' Cobbett said with relish. 'And you know what he did?'

I had already guessed, but didn't want to deprive him of this part of the story, so I shook my head and looked expectant.

'Stayed there an hour, he did. Then one of his acquaintance brought a knife, and calm as you like, he cut his own ears off in front of all the gathered townsfolk and walked free. They said he didn't even cry out. Left his ears still hanging on the post, if you can imagine.'

I winced; Cobbett nodded sagely.

'That's the kind of man Rowland Jenkes is. Don't get mixed up with that lot, Doctor Bruno.'

'Which lot? Do you mean the Catherine Wheel tavern?'

Cobbett stared at me as if I had cursed his entire family to his face.

'Christ alive – what *have* you been up to, Doctor Bruno? Seriously, sir – even mentioning the name of that place will bring you trouble.'

'How do you mean?' I said, thinking that to play the ignorant foreigner might serve me best here.

'Listen.' Cobbett dropped his voice to a whisper and beckoned me closer. 'Folk that go to the Catherine Wheel don't go there for the food or the beer, if you take my meaning.'

'I have learned that much for myself,' I said, with feeling. 'But do you know if any of the Fellows or students of Lincoln might ever go there?'

Cobbett narrowed his eyes, sucked in his jowly cheeks and considered me for a moment, as if weighing up how much he should reveal to this funny, nosy outsider. He seemed about to answer, when the door to the lodge was flung open and Rector Underhill strode in, his gown billowing about him. Surprise flickered briefly over his face at the sight of his guest drinking beer with the porter, but he composed himself quickly and smiled.

'Good afternoon, Doctor Bruno,' he said, warily polite. 'Cobbett, I wondered if you might have seen anything of Doctor Coverdale today? It seems he is not to be found anywhere, but he gave me no warning that he would be away.'

'I've not seen hide nor hair of him, sir, not since last night,' Cobbett said, moving the bottle and cups to the floor under his chair, rather too late to hide them from the rector's notice.

Underhill flared his nostrils in irritation.

'Well, the moment you see him pass through that gate, would you kindly tell him to come straight to my room, I wish to speak to him urgently.'

'Will do, sir,' Cobbett said dutifully.

'Might I have a brief word with you outside, Doctor Bruno?' Underhill said, turning to me with a pointed glare.

'Certainly.' I rose with some effort from the rickety stool, nodded to Cobbett, who sent me a broad wink in return, and followed the rector into the tower archway.

'I would appreciate it if you didn't encourage the servants to drink while they are at work. That one in particular needs no help.' He pursed his lips. I opened my mouth to protest, but he held up a hand to forestall me. 'I hope you will join us for supper in Hall tonight? We are all rather subdued since the death of poor Roger and your presence would certainly enliven High Table.'

'Thank you, I would be delighted,' I replied, matching his tone of polite insincerity.

'Good. We dine at six thirty, but you will hear the bell, I'm sure.'

Before he disappeared into the archway by the hall that led to his lodgings, I called him back.

'Rector Underhill? I was wondering – I went for a walk

this morning, after chapel, to get some air and admire your beautiful city better.'

He folded his hands together and watched me carefully.

'I hope you found the experience gratifying?'

'Oh, yes. But I went outside the city wall and got myself somewhat lost, I'm afraid. I passed through the gate by the Lady Chapel and took a right turn, and after a short distance of passing fields and orchards, the road turned to the left and I saw a very fine manor house beside a little church that appeared very ancient. I only wondered what the place might be?'

The rector thought for a moment, then appeared to judge this question innocent enough to merit a straight answer.

'By the Smythgate? I believe you must mean the church of St Cross, which is indeed of great antiquity. The house would be Holywell Manor, it is the only residence of any size in that direction. The well itself is supposed to be Saxon. It used to be a place of pilgrimage but obviously that papist custom is discontinued.'

'Ah. Well, thank you for satisfying a tourist's curiosity. A seat of the local gentry, I suppose?'

Underhill pursed his lips.

'Well. They are gentry of sorts, I suppose, but they are hardly well-regarded in Oxford society. It is owned by the Napper family – the father was once a Fellow of All Souls, but he is long dead, and the younger son, George, lies in prison at the Wood Street Counter in Cheapside.'

'Really? For what crime?'

He frowned, perhaps now suspicious of my interest.

'For refusing to attend church, I believe. But really, I cannot stand here gossiping like a laundress, I must prepare to take Evensong at All Saints.' At the archway to his lodgings, he turned back to me. 'Oh, and – Doctor Bruno? I shall see Magistrate Barnes this evening at church, so I hope we shall know by tomorrow when to expect the inquest into poor Doctor Mercer's accident. Let us pray it is soon,' he added, smiling thinly. 'I should not wish to detain you in Oxford any longer than is necessary.'

'Nor should I wish to impose on your hospitality,' I said, equally coldly. 'And please do convey my respects to Mistress Underhill and your daughter.'

'Indeed,' he said, touching his fingertips together for a moment as he considered whether to follow this up, but instead he turned on his heels and disappeared into the shadows of the archway.

# TEN

The bell tolled for dinner no less mournfully than it had for Matins, jolting me out of my distracted thoughts, jotted on the notes now scattered across the table in my chamber. After my exchange with the rector I had walked to Christ Church to find, with some relief, that I had indeed missed Sidney's hunting party. I left him a note apologising and explaining that I had been detained by other pressing business, then returned to Lincoln and retired to my room, where I spent an hour or so lying on the bed trying to make the new pieces fit the puzzle. If the unguarded words of Humphrey Pritchard and Cobbett's dark warning implied that the Catherine Wheel was the focal point for Oxford's secret Catholic fraternity, the obvious conclusion must be that Roger Mercer knew something about that group – the days in the almanac marked with the wheel could signify meetings at the inn. Could Mercer have been planning to expose them, just as he had testified against his former friend and colleague Edmund Allen, which meant that he had to be silenced? If that were the case, then whoever had ransacked his room could have been searching for evidence that they knew he intended to use against them. Then there was Richard Godwyn, the placid librarian;

232

he was apparently involved in receiving contraband Catholic books, but did that connect him to Rowland Jenkes and thereby to the Catherine Wheel? Could Mercer have found him out?

Determined to watch the students and Fellows closer than a hawk at dinner, I pulled on my doublet and was about to open the door when a furious knocking on it from the other side made me jump almost out of my skin. Cautiously I opened it a sliver and through the crack I saw the anxious face of Sophia Underhill, glancing fearfully over her shoulder.

'Let me in, Bruno, quickly, before anyone sees me – I need to speak to you!' she hissed, looking again down the stairwell.

'Of course,' I said, pulling the door wider to admit her. She slammed it quickly behind her and leaned against it heavily, her cheeks flushed. I saw with concern that her usual composure was in tatters; in place of her faintly cynical smile, her lip trembled though she fought hard to control it, and her eyes shone as if she might at any moment burst into tears.

'Forgive me, Bruno,' she began, her voice barely a whisper. 'My father has forbidden me to speak to you, but I must disobey – there is no one else I can tell.' She stopped, her breath coming in jagged gasps as if she had been running or weeping. 'Forgive me,' she repeated, then seemed to stumble forwards as if she might faint, as she had the night before. This time I stepped forward in time to catch her and she fell gratefully against my shoulder as a sudden sob shuddered through her thin ribcage; I held my arms around her and stroked her hair as she tried to master this outburst of emotion. I could not begin to guess what she had come to tell me but Sophia did not strike me as the sort of woman to fall prey to such distress for frivolous reasons; I could only suppose that what she wanted to say was a matter of some gravity.

When she had recovered enough to lift her head from my shoulder, she leaned back and looked me full in the face with an expression of such fearful intensity that I felt she wanted to search the depths of my soul through my eyes, and before I was even conscious of making the decision to move, almost by instinct I leaned forward and kissed her. For a brief moment, I felt her respond, her warm body softening and moulding itself to mine in my arms, her palms pressed flat against my chest, but just as suddenly she jerked back, pushing my arms away and staring at me now with a look of confused horror.

'No – oh, no, I can't – you don't understand,' she blurted, flapping her hands helplessly at her sides as if her distress had increased a hundredfold.

'I am sorry,' I began, disconcerted, but she shook her head frantically.

'No, it is I who am sorry, Bruno – I should never have – but I did not know who else I could come to.' She twisted her hands together and looked at me, her eyes pleading. 'I think I may be in danger.'

My heart froze; tentatively I reached out a hand and gestured towards the chair by the desk, quickly sweeping Roger Mercer's calendar and my notes on his death under a book.

'You must tell me everything,' I said. 'What kind of danger? Is it to do with Doctor Mercer?'

Her eyes widened at the name; she hesitated, took a deep breath, and seemed about to speak when there came another urgent knock on the door. Sophia whipped around and stared at the door in fear, a hand clasped to her mouth; I waited, afraid that perhaps her father had seen her coming to my staircase and followed. After a moment, the knocking came again.

'Doctor Bruno? Are you there?'

It was a young man's voice, not the rector's; all the same,

it would not be prudent for anyone to see Sophia in my chamber and I could not very well pretend to be out, as I would need to leave in the next few minutes for dinner in Hall.

'One moment, please, I am just dressing,' I called, ushering Sophia behind one of the floor-length window drapes. The situation was so absurd it brought a weak smile to her lips; I squeezed her arm and when she was sufficiently concealed, I crossed to the door and opened it to find John Florio on the threshold, his face alert with curiosity.

'Master Florio!' I said, forcing brightness into my voice. 'What brings you here?'

'Have I disturbed you, Doctor Bruno?' he asked, peering around me to survey what he could see of the room. 'I can come another time if you have company – I thought I heard voices.'

'That is an unfortunate habit I have of talking aloud to myself,' I said. 'It is the only way I can be sure of winning a disputation.'

He laughed warmly and shook his head.

'As for that, you were hardly given a fair fight, Bruno, and those of us who are not blinded by prejudice know that. I have come to see if you dine at High Table this evening? We have hardly had any time to talk and I should like to stake my claim to your company at dinner.'

'Oh – yes, certainly.' My eyes flickered towards the curtain and I made an effort to draw them back to Florio. 'But, I wonder if you would mind – first I must use the – ah – the pot before I leave.'

'Oh – of course. I can wait for you downstairs.'

As I pulled the door to, I could hear his feet shuffling on the landing for a few moments before descending. When I was sure he had reached the bottom of the stairs, I drew back the curtain and Sophia stepped into the light, a smile on her face despite herself.

'I feared I would be caught here all night,' she grinned.

'I could think of worse fates,' I said, and regretted it instantly when she responded with a sad, embarrassed smile.

'I am sorry,' I said, flustered, 'I thought it would not do your reputation nor mine any good if you were found here. But first you must tell me of this danger. Has someone threatened you? Is it because you know something?'

Her eyes snapped upwards.

'About what? What would I know?'

'I only thought – because there has been one violent death in the college—'

'That is nothing to do with me,' she said, with surprising sharpness. Then she sighed and brushed a loose strand of hair from her face. 'It is all too complicated, Bruno – I can't tell you now if you must rush away. I will wait and explain another time.'

'But,' I took her gently by the shoulders and looked her straight in the eye, 'do you fear someone will hurt you?'

She bit her lip and twisted away.

'Remember I said I dreamed of some great adventure that would change everything? You told me to be careful what I wished for.' She fell silent for a moment. 'How do you know if you can trust someone, Bruno? I mean, if you must trust them with your life?'

'The answer is that you cannot know until they have proved themselves. But what has happened to you, Sophia? Who is it you are afraid to trust?'

'This is all just foolishness.' She knit her fingers together and glanced up at me as if embarrassed. 'I am sorry, Bruno – I should not have troubled you.'

'It is no trouble—' I turned sharply at the sound of a creak on the landing outside, though I had not heard footsteps climbing the stairs.

'Go, then,' she said, pushing me towards the door. 'I will

leave when I am sure it is safe. I am used to sneaking about the college by now.' She forced a smile. 'And, Bruno – I am sorry about – you know.'

'It is I who should be sorry. I did not mean to impose on you.' I stopped, awkwardly rubbing my thumb along my lower lip, unsure of what best to say.

'You did not,' she whispered, shyly. 'The fault is mine. I was drawn to you from the first, but there is nothing I can do about it now. You can't understand now, Bruno. Perhaps I will have a chance to explain everything, but you had better go or my father will send someone else to find you.'

I squeezed her gently by the shoulder once more, not knowing what else to do, and she reached up and softly placed a kiss on my cheek.

'You are certain you will be all right?' I asked, pausing at the door.

She nodded.

'I will wait a few moments and then slip out. They will all be in Hall by then.'

'I meant – the danger you spoke of?'

She pressed a finger to her lips then and nodded, gesturing for me to go. I took a last look at her and closed the door behind me, silently furious with Florio for his ill-timed interruption.

Outside, the bell had stopped and the quadrangle was empty; a murmur of conversation drifted through the tall mullioned windows of the great hall, all lit with the glow of many candles as I followed Florio reluctantly towards the door, thinking of Sophia.

After the meal I returned to my chamber to consider how I might find an opportunity to speak again with Sophia. Her outburst earlier had troubled me greatly; if, as I had suspected, she knew more than she was willing to share about the

237

circumstances of Roger Mercer's death, then it was all too likely that she was in serious danger, especially if Mercer was killed to silence him. But who was this mysterious person she was being asked to trust with her life? And then there was that kiss. I stood before the fireplace and glared at the man in the glass, his unshaven chin and unruly hair, and frowned at him in disapproval. I had behaved like a boor, I told myself; she had come to me in distress because she believed I knew how to listen, and instead I had thrown myself on her like a stag. My reflection looked back with large, dark eyes that seemed to venture a counter-argument: she had wanted me to hold her, she had at first responded when I kissed her, before some pang of conscience or honour abruptly obliged her to step back. She felt drawn to me, she had said, and yet would not explain her sudden change of heart; was this obstacle that I could not understand her pre-existing affection for someone else? Was that connected to her fears? Damn Florio, I thought bitterly, though I had appreciated the young Anglo-Italian's friendly manner and his breezy conversation, as the other Fellows seemed sunk in introspection and had spent the meal throwing apprehensive glances at Mercer's empty chair.

I was still staring moodily into the mirror when the door to my chamber was flung open without ceremony and I turned with a start to see Sidney, his tall frame filling the doorway, a short green cape slung from one shoulder and a bottle of wine raised in his right hand.

'I have escaped from the Pole for one evening only!' he announced triumphantly, slamming the door behind him and pulling the cork from the bottle with his teeth while he scoured the room for drinking vessels.

Finding none, he eventually sat down on the chair beside the writing desk under the window and took a long swig from the bottle.

'Just as if we were students again, Bruno,' he smiled, brandishing the bottle at me in a mock toast. 'So.' He pointed a finger at me sternly. 'You abandoned me to Laski all day, so you had better have some worthwhile news for me, Bruno, or I shall consider it poor sport of you. What the hell have you been up to?'

He held out the bottle and I drank gratefully, before giving him a brief account of all that had happened since the previous night. I showed him the papers I had found under my door, then told him of my discovery in the library, my unexpected stumbling across the Catherine Wheel inn, Cobbett's curse of Rowland Jenkes, Coverdale's threats to me and subsequent disappearance and finally Sophia's fear that she may be in danger. I tried to convey this latter in a neutral tone, saying nothing of my interest in her nor of my badly judged attempt to kiss her, but still a smile curved across Sidney's face and his eyes took on that old lascivious gleam.

'No wonder you have shunned my company, Bruno, you sly fox,' he said, cuffing me on the shoulder as he rose to reclaim the bottle. 'So the rector has a daughter, eh? No such luck for me at Christ Church – all I have to look at are jowly old men and spotty boys. Are you practising the old Italian magic on her?'

I smiled, but looked away.

'The fact that she thinks she may be in danger is my only concern,' I said, ignoring his snort of derision. 'She would not say, but I suspect it may be connected to the murder of Roger Mercer, and if that in turn is connected to this nest of Catholic conspirators at the Catherine Wheel—'

'Then you must investigate the Catherine Wheel at the first opportunity,' Sidney said, passing the bottle back, considerably lighter. 'That is a job I cannot do – my face is too well-known. It was for this that Walsingham wanted you, Bruno – you can pretend to be one of them. Gain their trust,

239

work your way in among them. You have some excellent leads, I must say. The books, that boy parroting the Litany of the Saints. They may simply meet to say Mass, or they may be plotting against the government with the backing of France or Spain. Find out what you can.'

I nodded, though the thought of trying to dupe Jenkes and his hard-faced cohorts at the Catherine Wheel was not one to take lightly.

'And now,' Sidney continued, standing and stretching his long arms above his head, 'I have some news for you. The Keeper of Shotover Forest is indeed missing a hunting dog. One of five Irish wolfhounds hired for a hunting party a week ago – the gentleman in question reported that the dog had been startled by a noise and taken flight. Apparently they searched the forest for it but to no avail.'

'Did he tell you the gentleman's name?' I asked eagerly.

'He certainly did,' Sidney said, leaning casually on the mantelpiece, proud of his information. 'It was a Master William Napper of Holywell Manor, Oxford. But any huntsman will tell you that a trained wolfhound wouldn't just bolt like that – they have better discipline than most of the queen's soldiers.'

'Napper?' I jerked my head up, surprised. 'That is strange.'

'Why so?'

'Your new friend Master Norris – I think he stables his horse at Holywell Manor. I saw him heading there this morning.'

Sidney put his head on one side to consider this, and at the same moment I noticed something that made my heart drop like a stone.

'That is a coincidence. The family are well known, of course,' he continued, ambling back to the window to peer across the courtyard, 'but William Napper has always been what we call a church papist – he toes the line, attends service

240

like a good citizen, even if everyone knows he holds a different faith in his heart. It is the younger brother, George, who has gone looking for trouble. He studied in Rheims and is currently detained at the Wood Street Counter in Cheapside. Curious that young Norris should associate with them. I suppose we must keep an eye on him as well.' He turned to face me. 'Bruno, are you even listening to me?'

'One moment, Philip.' I was not the neatest of men, but I was certain I had not left the books and papers on the desk in the state of disarray that I now observed. Rising quickly from the bed, I lifted a few sheets to confirm my suspicion, then began frantically rifling through the papers that remained. Someone had already searched my desk; Roger Mercer's almanac and all the theories I had jotted down about his death were gone.

'Sophia,' I whispered, disbelieving.

# ELEVEN

The rain's steady rhythm against my window panes woke me early on Monday morning even before the chapel bell had summoned the men of Lincoln to Matins. A thick cover of cloud had returned in the night and the sky was the colour of slate, the quadrangle slick with puddles; again I had been too preoccupied to sleep well. Sidney and I had sat up late into the night exchanging theories, but we had only a cat's cradle of speculation and nothing conclusive to untangle one thread from another. I needed to find a means of speaking to Sophia Underhill before the day was much older; either she had taken Mercer's almanac and my notes from my desk, or someone had seen her leave my room and taken his chance, surmising that the door would be unlocked.

As I swung my legs over the side of the bed, I glimpsed something white on the floor beneath it and reached down to retrieve a piece of paper. Turning it over, I saw that the writing on it was my own; it was the copy I had made of the strange code at the back of Mercer's calendar, and my efforts to write some basic sentences using it, a task I had set myself before falling asleep the night before last. The paper must have slipped under the bed and escaped the attention of whoever – I was reluctant to believe it could have been Sophia – had taken all the other notes from my desk while I was at dinner. At least, then, I still had a copy of the code – but I was no closer to tracking down any letters Roger Mercer might have written or received using it. I was now certain that the person who searched Mercer's room before me, and perhaps Slythurst after me, had been looking for just such letters or documents; what I did not know was whether either searcher had found them.

Sidney was burdened for the day with the entertainment of the palatine, but had promised to look into Gabriel Norris's connection with the Napper family and see what he could discover about William Napper's hunting party when the dog went missing. My task was to visit Jenkes's shop in Catte Street on the pretext of purchasing some books, to see what I could learn about his illicit business there, and then to brace myself for another meal at the Catherine Wheel in the hope of further conversation with Humphrey Pritchard. I suffered a slight twinge of conscience at the thought of manipulating the trust of a simple-minded pot-boy – but I had a job to do, and I tried to concentrate on the long view, as Walsingham had instructed. Unlike my employer, however, I was not a natural politician, and the idea of sacrificing individuals to the hazy concept of the greater good did not sit easily with me. Before I could turn my attention to any of this, however, I needed to find a way to speak to Sophia.

I had decided not to attend Matins – one show of piety during my visit was enough, I felt – and instead spent the early part of the morning trying to read by my window in the hope that I might see Sophia if she crossed the quadrangle on one of her regular visits to the college library. I knew that the rector would never admit me if I asked to speak to her directly, so my best hope was to wait and see if she would venture out when the students were all at public

243

lectures – assuming that her father would still allow her that privilege. My stomach moaned at the lack of breakfast, but I dared not go in search of food in case I missed Sophia.

It was shortly before nine that I saw her emerge from the rector's lodgings; my heart gave an involuntary leap and I quickly gathered my cloak to catch up with her, but she did not cross the courtyard towards the library. She was dressed more formally than usual, in an ivory gown with embroidered sleeves, the hood of her short cape drawn up around her face against the rain, and she walked with a determined step towards the gatehouse. Hastily I locked the door to my chamber, though I had left nothing there of value, just to be sure, and had folded the paper with the code inside my doublet. Walsingham's purse hung heavy at my belt. If I should be attacked in the street, I would lose everything, I thought grimly, but at least it wouldn't matter if the room was searched in my absence. I scrambled down the stairs and charged across towards the tower archway, slipping on the wet flagstones, but when I reached the main gate and stepped out into St Mildred's Lane, there was no sign of her in either direction. She could not have moved fast enough to have disappeared from the street, I reasoned; concluding that I must have mistaken her destination, I returned to the college, closing the gate behind me, when I head the low murmur of a woman's voice coming from the porter's lodge.

Knocking gently, I opened the door to see Sophia in all her fine clothes crouched on the damp floor with the old dog's head cradled in her lap; as I entered she raised her head and smiled politely at me as if we had only a passing acquaintance, before returning all her attention to fondly mussing the dog's ears. A low growl of contentment emanated from Bess's throat as she nuzzled her head deep into Sophia's skirts. Oh to be a dog, I thought, and immediately reprimanded myself.

'Morning, Doctor Bruno,' Cobbett said affably from his position of authority behind his table. 'You seem in a rush today.'

'Oh – no, I – good morning, Mistress Underhill,' I said, bowing slightly.

Sophia looked up briefly, but this time her expression was preoccupied and she did not smile.

'Doctor Bruno. I think poor Bess is growing blind, Cobbett,' she said, barely looking at me. I guessed she must be ashamed of what had happened the night before.

'Aye, she's not long for this world,' Cobbett agreed, as if he had long been resigned to the idea. 'Sophia loves that dog,' he added, for my benefit. I blinked, surprised at the familiarity with which he, as a servant, referred to the rector's daughter in her presence. Sophia noticed my look and laughed.

'You are shocked that Cobbett does not call me Mistress, Doctor Bruno? When I first arrived at Lincoln College, I was thirteen years old and my brother fourteen. We had no company of our own age and the Fellows of the college were not used to having children around, they made it very clear they disliked our presence. Cobbett and his wife were the only ones who were kind to us. We spent half our time in here chatting and playing with Bess, didn't we, Cobbett?'

'Aye – distracting me from my post,' the old porter said gruffly, with obvious affection.

'I didn't know you had a wife, Cobbett,' I said.

'Not any more, sir. The good Lord saw fit to take her these five years back. She was the college laundress for years, and a damned fine one. Still, this is how the world turns. And soon my old Bess will be gone, too.' He sniffed heartily and turned his face away to the window.

'Don't say that, Cobbett, she'll hear you,' Sophia said, pretending to cover the dog's ears.

'You are dressed very finely this morning, Mistress Underhill,' I ventured.

She made a face.

'My mother has roused herself sufficiently to go *visiting*,' she said, in a tone that conveyed exactly what she thought of that idea. 'We are to call upon an acquaintance of hers in the town whose own daughter, though two years younger than me, is recently betrothed to be married. So she and I will no doubt entertain one another on the lute and virginals, while our mothers extol the many blessings and virtues of marriage and we all revel in her success. As you may imagine, I can hardly contain my excitement.' She said this with a perfectly straight face, though Cobbett misunderstood her sarcasm.

'Why, Sophia, you have no need to feel hard done by – you know you may have any husband you wished if you would only put your mind to it,' he said. He meant to be reassuring, but I did not miss the shadow that passed across her face then, as if his words caused her some secret pain.

I had no chance to speculate further, however, as at that moment there was a great thundering of footsteps on the flagstones outside and the door to the porter's lodge crashed open with such force that it hit the wall behind and juddered so hard I feared it might splinter. In the doorway stood Walter Slythurst, the bursar, shaking like an aspen leaf, his face so deathly white and his eyes protruding with such terror that you would have thought someone had a knife at his back. He looked thoroughly drenched and dishevelled, and was wearing a thick cloak and riding boots all spattered with mud; I remembered that he had been away overnight and wondered if he had been attacked on the road.

'Fetch . . .' he choked, and the effort of speech made the veins in his neck stand out like knotted cords under the sallow skin. 'Fetch the rector. The strongroom – he must see this –

246

horror.' Suddenly he leaned forwards and vomited on the stone floor, one hand grasping the wall to keep himself upright.

Cobbett and I exchanged a glance, then the old porter began ponderously to heave himself out of the chair. I stepped forward; it was clear that the situation required more urgency than Cobbett could give it.

'I will go for the rector,' I said, 'but what should I tell him has happened?'

Slythurst shook his head frantically, his lips pressed into a white line as if he feared his stomach might rise again. He jerked his head towards Sophia.

'A monstrous crime – one I cannot speak of before a lady. Rector Underhill must see . . .' he broke off again, his breath suddenly coming in jagged gasps as his knees buckled beneath him and he began shivering wildly as if it were the depths of winter. I had seen these effects of a severe shock before, and knew he must be calmed down.

'Sit him down, get him a strong drink,' I said to Cobbett. 'I'll find the rector.'

'I can go for him if you like, he is at work in his study this morning,' Sophia offered, rising quickly to her feet; as she stood, she clapped a hand to her brow and stumbled just as she had before. I caught her arm and she clutched my shoulder gratefully, then quickly withdrew her hand as a glance briefly passed between us acknowledging our moment of intimacy last night. She leaned against the wall, but her face had turned almost as pale as Slythurst's; the rank stench of his vomit was rising in the small room, and, perhaps prompted by the smell, Sophia tried to reach the door, but had only partly opened it before she too leaned forward and vomited in the doorway.

Cobbett rolled his eyes mildly, as if this were all part of the job.

'Will you take your turn too, Doctor Bruno, before I go for a pail of water?' he said wearily.

In truth, I could feel my own stomach rising with the smell, and I was glad to get out.

'Do not move – I will be back with the rector in a moment,' I said, from the doorway.

'No one must go near the tower,' Slythurst croaked. His violent shaking was beginning to subside; Cobbett had produced one of his bottles of ale and poured the bursar a good measure in one of his wooden cups.

My frantic hammering on the rector's door brought Adam the old servant running to open it; when he saw it was me, his face twisted into a sneer of open dislike.

'Back *again*, Doctor Bruno?'

'I need to see the rector urgently,' I panted, ignoring his tone.

'Rector Underhill cannot see you this morning, he is extremely busy. And the ladies are out,' he added, with an emphasis that implied he knew just what I was after.

'Christ's blood, man, did you not hear me? The matter is urgent – I will fetch him myself if I must.' I shouldered my way past him through the dining room and thumped on the door of the study.

'What is the meaning of this?' the rector blustered, throwing it open. 'Doctor Bruno?'

'He forced his way in, sir,' Adam whined, waving his hands ineffectually behind me.

'You must come immediately,' I said. 'Master Slythurst has discovered something in the strongroom – he called it a monstrous crime. He was too much affected by what he saw – I was sent to bring you as a matter of urgency.'

The rector's eyes widened in fear and his jowls trembled. 'A theft, you mean?'

'I don't think so,' I said quietly. 'A theft does not generally

248

make a grown man heave up his breakfast. I guess Slythurst has seen something more – disturbing – to make his stomach turn like that.'

The rector stared at me.

'Not another . . . ?'

'We will not know, sir, until you come to investigate.'

Underhill nodded mutely, then gestured for me to lead the way.

When we reached the west range, Slythurst was already waiting by the door to the sub-rector's staircase; some of the colour seemed to have returned to his cheeks but he had not yet regained his composure.

'You must steel yourself, Rector,' he said, his voice still hoarse. 'I returned this morning from my business in Buckinghamshire – I left at first light and had only just now returned to college. I thought to take the revenues I had brought from our estates straight up to the strongroom before I changed. I knocked for James but there was no reply, so I went to Cobbett for the spare key to his room. The inner door to the strongroom was locked, as usual, but when I opened it, I found . . .' His eyes bulged again and he shook his head, his teeth firmly clenched.

'Found what?' the rector asked, as if he did not want to be told the answer.

Slythurst only shook his head and pointed to the stair-well. The rector turned to me awkwardly.

'Doctor Bruno, perhaps you would . . . ? You have shown us a clear head in such situations before.'

I nodded; the rector was a coward at heart, comfortable ruling his little domain of books, where men snipe at their enemies with rhetoric, but out of his depth when the violence became real. He clearly feared what he was about to witness; suddenly the funny Italian was not so laughable, and he wanted me at his side. Slythurst gave me a sideways glance through narrowed eyes; it seemed that, despite his shock, he had not forgotten his dislike of me and would have preferred me not to be included, but he was in no state to argue with the rector.

The stairs creaked unexpectedly under my feet, making the rector jump; though there was hardly any light in the stairwell, I could make out marks on the threshold of Doctor Coverdale's room as I entered the door Slythurst had left open. Holding a hand out behind me, I bent to take a closer look and saw that the stains were smudged footprints leading from the tower room. I touched a finger to one of the marks and it came away with a sticky, rust-coloured coating which, when I sniffed it, could only be blood, though it was not fresh. I turned to look at my companions with a grim expression; below me, the rector's round white face, pale as the moon in the shadowy stairwell, flinched but nodded me onwards.

The low door at the back of the tower room was also swinging open; inside it, I found a narrow spiral staircase barely wide enough for a man to pass, curving upwards to the top of the tower. Halfway up there was a small arched doorway, whose studded oak door had been left ajar by Slythurst in his flight from the sight within. The smell of death was unmistakeable now, stinging my nostrils as I approached the threshold; the rector gave a strangled cry as he cowered behind me. Taking a deep breath, I pushed the door open and stepped into the college strongroom; immediately I gagged and cried out at what I saw, and felt the rector's hand grasp at the back of my jerkin as he jostled to see through the doorway. Here, then, was the answer to the mystery of what had happened to Doctor James Coverdale.

The strongroom seemed more claustrophobic than the sub-rector's room below it, though much of that had to do with the smell; the dimensions of the walls were almost the same, but the wooden-beamed ceiling was lower and the two windows, one facing into the quadrangle and the other towards St Mildred's Lane, were smaller and narrower, a single perpendicular arch letting in little light on this overcast day. Along each wall stood a number of heavy wooden chests of varying sizes, all painted with heraldic devices, girded with iron bands and fastened with formidable padlocks – the coffers containing the college revenues. To the left of the window that faced into the college was James Coverdale. His wrists had been bound together and tied over his head to an iron bracket fixed into the wall for candles. He was naked except for his linen undershirt, and his head slumped downwards so that his chin rested on his chest, which was drenched with blood, now matted and dried – he had not died in the past few hours, it seemed. But the most extraordinary aspect, the sight that had made me cry out in shock, was that he had been shot numerous times with arrows from a close range. Nine or ten stuck out from his torso at various points, giving him the appearance of a pincushion – or an icon. I knew immediately what I was witnessing; so, it seemed, did the rector, who tightened his grip on my sleeve so that I could feel his hand trembling. I glanced sideways at him as he stared in unblinking horror at the corpse of a second colleague in two days; his lips were working rapidly and I thought at first that he was uttering a silent prayer, until I realised that he was trying to speak but could not make his voice obey him. When eventually he managed to pronounce the word, it was the one that had leapt instantly to my own mind:

'*Sebastian.*'

'Sebastian who?' said Slythurst impatiently. He was still lingering behind us on the stairs, his eyes averted, as if reluctant to enter the room a second time.

'St Sebastian,' I said quietly.

The rector nodded absently, as if in a trance.

'"He was commanded to be apprehended, and that he should be brought into the open field where, by his own soldiers, he was shot through the body with innumerable arrows",' he recited hoarsely; I had no doubt that the words belonged to Foxe. 'And look.' He lifted a trembling hand and pointed. On the wall beside the window, raggedly traced with a finger dipped in the dead man's blood, was the symbol of a spoked wheel.

'And there is the weapon,' Slythurst said decisively, entering the room and pointing at the wall beneath the window, where a handsome carved English longbow, inlaid with green-and-scarlet tracery, had been left leaning beside an empty quiver decorated in similar fashion, as if the killer had placed it there calmly and carefully when his work was done.

'But that is Gabriel Norris's longbow,' the rector croaked in disbelief. 'I told him to have it locked away here the other morning, after he shot the dog.'

'Then we have our killer,' Slythurst asserted, nodding a full stop to his pronouncement.

I took a couple of paces towards the body, crouching to peer up at the face.

'These arrows did not kill him,' I said.

'Oh? You think he died of a fever?' Slythurst seemed to have regained his old manner remarkably quickly; I sensed his impatience with my presence in what he regarded as his domain.

'Quiet, Walter,' said Underhill sharply, and for once I was grateful to him. 'Go on, Doctor Bruno.'

'His throat has been cut,' I said, and clenching my teeth I grasped Coverdale's abundant hair and lifted the head so that the dreadful face was visible. The rector gave a little squeal into his handkerchief; Slythurst winced and turned away. The dead man's eyes were half closed, a rag stuffed into his mouth as a gag, and his throat had been sliced straight across. The wound pulled open as I lifted the head, and from its sticky edges I could see that the incision was a botched job, though it had, in the end, achieved its aim; his neck was scored with the nicks and scratches of aborted cuts, as if the killer had taken several attempts to hold his knife steady and in the right place, suggesting that he was not a practised assassin.

'Who would have such a weapon?' the rector asked tremulously. 'All the university men are forbidden to carry daggers in the city precincts.'

'A razor could have done it,' I said grimly. 'Or a small knife, if it was sharp enough.'

'Then why shoot him like a boar afterwards?' asked Slythurst, daring to step slightly nearer. 'And the picture – is that a message?'

'The rector has already told you,' I said. 'For show. This is a parody of the martyrdom of St Sebastian, just as Roger Mercer's death was supposed to mimic the martyrdom of St Ignatius. I do not think you can pass this one off as an accident, Rector,' I added, turning to Underhill, who had sat down heavily on one of the sturdy chests, his face in his hands.

'What arrant nonsense!' Slythurst exclaimed, now fully over his initial shock, it seemed. 'Roger is attacked by a dog and you read into that the mimicry of a martyrdom? What murderer would go to such lengths? I rather think your brain is fevered, Doctor Bruno. *This*, I grant you –' he gestured at the punctured corpse of James Coverdale hanging from the candle bracket – 'is clearly some horrific violence against poor James by a madman, but these fanciful patterns will not help us catch a dangerous intruder! I can only guess that someone tried to break into the strongroom, James tried to stop him, and this was the result.'

He paused, breathless, hands on his hips as if daring me to challenge this hypothesis.

'A thief who stopped to paint pictures in a dying man's blood?' I said, returning his insolent stare. 'And none of the doors have been forced, nor have these chests been tampered with. You said yourself that both the strongroom and the door to the outer room were locked when you returned this morning,' I reminded Slythurst. 'Who would have had a key to the strongroom?'

'The three of us,' Slythurst said, indicating the rector and the bloody corpse in the corner of the room. 'Each of us has a key to open the strongroom door, but the principal coffers here have three padlocks apiece, so that the rector, the bursar and the sub-rector must all be present to open them. We call them the chests of the three keys. The bulk of the college funds are kept in these. The trunks containing account books and deeds I can open alone.'

'A safeguard against embezzlement,' the rector added.

'So Doctor Coverdale must have unlocked the door himself and let the killer in,' I mused, 'and his killer could have locked it afterwards using Coverdale's own key.'

'He must have been forced to open it at knifepoint by a robber,' Slythurst speculated.

'But that would have been fruitless if he could not then open the coffers on his own,' I said.

'A robber would not know that. Perhaps that's why he was killed,' Slythurst said. 'The thief flew into a rage because he did not believe James couldn't open the chest. That must be it!'

He seemed remarkably keen to discount my theory that Coverdale's death was connected to Roger Mercer's, I thought, and wondered if that was just because he could not stand to concede that I might be right in anything, or because it suited him to throw up a false trail. After all, he was one of the two people alive with a key to the strongroom.

'When were either of you last here?' I asked.

Slythurst glanced anxiously at the rector, who appeared lost in his own thoughts and was making every effort to avoid looking at the body.

'With respect, Doctor Bruno, have you been appointed to investigate this crime, that you should start questioning us as if you were the magistrate?'

'Oh, just answer him, Walter, he is trying to help us,' said the rector wearily, to my surprise. 'For myself, I have not been up here since last Tuesday, when we took out the monies and papers for the college attorney. Is that right, Walter, was it Tuesday?'

'That was the last time we were all here together,' Slythurst agreed, shooting me a look of distaste. 'I was last here on the evening of Saturday, just before the disputation, when James let me in to collect the papers I needed relating to the management of our estates in Aylesbury, together with some money for the journey and sundry expenses when I arrived. I left for Buckinghamshire first thing on Sunday morning and have not been near the strongroom until my return just now, which you witnessed. There – am I in the clear?' he added, his eyes flashing sarcasm.

'That is not for me to say.' I shrugged. 'What time did you collect the papers on Saturday evening?'

'Just before the disputation, I told you, so I suppose some time around half past four. I wanted to have everything in order for my journey the next day because I knew the dinner at Christ Church would end late and I did not want to have to disturb James when I returned.' He flicked a brief glance then at Coverdale's bizarre corpse and lowered his head.

I crossed the room back to the body with its protruding arrows and considered it again from various angles, touching my finger to the bloodstains on the shirt, which left a thick residue.

'This body could well have been here since Saturday night,'

I said. 'The blood is dry and the stiffness that sets in after death has already passed – he is beginning to rot. If the weather had been warmer the decay would be more advanced, we would not be able to breathe in this room. But I have remembered something – Doctor Coverdale was summoned early from the disputation, one of the students brought him an urgent message. I wonder then if he was lured back to his death.'

'I do recall that he did not attend the dinner for the palatine that night,' the rector murmured, 'and I thought it strange because he had been looking forward to it – he likes to make an impression on men of state. *Liked.*' He corrected himself quickly, shaking his head. 'Oh, God in heaven!' It was a cry of genuine anguish, though not, I felt, of grief for his colleague, and his voice rose to a frantic pitch. 'You are right, Doctor Bruno, we shall not be able to keep the manner of this death secret. There will be a full investigation, the coroner and the magistrate will be called – the college will be ruined! I can think of several of our benefactors who will not want their names associated with a place of such iniquity – they will withdraw funds and give them to other foundations less blighted by evil deeds. This is truly the work of the Devil! To make a mockery of the Christian martyrs in such monstrous fashion.' He buried his face in his hands and I thought for a moment he was sobbing, but he was only trying to master his breathing.

'Well, it is the work of someone who can wield a longbow,' I said pragmatically. 'Though I think at this distance even I could hit a target that was tied to the wall and already dead, so we are not necessarily looking for someone with any great skill in archery. Whoever it was has staged this murder very carefully so that we would link it to the other.'

'So that *you* would link it,' said the rector. 'Foxe, the false martyrdoms – this is your theory, Doctor Bruno.'

'It was suggested to me by someone unknown,' I reminded him.

'Yes, don't you see? That paper you showed me, cut from Foxe. *This* –' he gestured wildly at the corpse in the corner – 'has been done for your benefit, knowing that you would understand the reference.' He stared at me incredulously, as if it were my theory that had delivered Coverdale to his fate.

'But the killer could not have known that I would be around at this precise moment to witness the discovery,' I objected. 'Yet – it does seem that he wanted to make sure you would not miss the martyrdom reference this time and fail to make the connection with Roger Mercer's death.'

'So it must be the same person?' The rector looked up at me, his eyes filled with anxiety.

'Norris owns a razor, you know,' Slythurst spoke up suddenly. 'Shaves himself every day, if you please.'

I considered, rubbing my own beard.

'A razor and a longbow. Someone is keen for the evidence to point to Norris, that seems clear.'

'You think it could not be him?' the rector asked, still looking up at me like a child craving reassurance.

'From the little I know of Norris, I cannot believe he would commit so showy a murder and then leave behind a weapon that points directly to himself. Besides, what could be his motive?'

'James hated the commoners, he was always railing against them. You heard him yourself at the rector's supper,' Slythurst said.

'Hardly a reason for one of them to kill him,' I retorted. 'On the other hand, someone who bitterly resented the presence of commoners might think to kill two birds with one stone, as you English say – to despatch Doctor Coverdale for some reason yet unknown, and leave evidence incriminating

257

Norris at the same time. There were marks on the staircase, footprints – if we had more light I could examine them, but I fear the rain will have washed away the trail outside by now.'

'Walter – could you go down and ask Cobbett for a lantern? Doctor Bruno is right – we must look at the room carefully before we jump to any conclusions, and it is too dim. And a basin of water,' the rector added. 'We must wash that mark from the wall before the coroner is called.'

Slythurst's eyes widened.

'Surely, Rector, that mark is part of the evidence? It may have some significance – we should not tamper—'

'Those are my instructions, Walter. Now please do as I ask.'

Slythurst looked from me to the rector with momentary outrage at being ordered like a servant, but unable to think of any reason for defiance, he turned on his heel and a moment later we heard his footsteps thundering down the stairs.

'Doctor Bruno?' With a great effort, Rector Underhill heaved himself to his feet and grasped me by both wrists. His bombast was all deflated and he looked old and frightened; I found I pitied him the scandal that would break in the wake of this second death. 'You foresaw this, and I did not. I dismissed your theory about Foxe – it seemed to me preposterous, and it suited me to avoid damage to the college by allowing myself to be guided by others, James chief among them, in presenting Roger's death as an accident. But I must humble myself and acknowledge that you were right – it seems a madman is targeting the Fellows in these horrible travesties of Christian martyrdom. Perhaps if James and I had not scoffed at your idea, he would not be dead.'

'If it's any consolation, Rector,' I said, patting his hand

gently, 'I think Doctor Coverdale was already dead by the time you were ridiculing my theory on Saturday night. But I will say it again – someone in Lincoln College knows who did this. He is very likely one of your number.'

'You are determined that it is the same killer?' He was still grasping my sleeve.

'It seems so.'

'Then there may be more victims to come, unless he is stopped?'

'I don't know, Rector. Until we know why these two were made martyrs, we cannot predict this murderer's intent, or what he hopes to gain by making his handiwork so ostentatious.'

'Doctor Bruno . . .' The rector's voice cracked, and he hesitated, trying to breathe evenly. 'I know the college cannot hope to keep this hidden from the world. But these murders will be the end of my rectorship – perhaps of the college. We are not as wealthy as some and if the benefactions dry up, the rich students will look elsewhere. And it is not just for myself that I fear, Doctor Bruno – what are the prospects for my daughter if I no longer have Leicester's favour? Hm?'

He shook my arm with some force, as if this might extract a quicker answer.

'Your daughter has her own qualities to recommend her, with or without the earl's patronage.'

Underhill shook his head.

'That is not how it works in society, as you must know. Among the good families of Oxford she is spoken of as ungovernable. It is only my standing with the earl that makes her any kind of prospect – without that, no respectable man will take her to wife. She should not be in such a place as this if her mother will not chaperone her, but I am a foolish, indulgent father and I cannot bear to send her away. Yet every day she spends in this college damages her reputation further.' He took a deep breath and I saw that shock had forced all his emotions to the surface; I half expected him to break down weeping, but he gathered himself and continued, 'The Earl of Leicester must hear this dreadful news, of course, but how much better it would go for us if he were not to learn of it until we could also present him with a murderer apprehended. Do you see?'

'You must hope your coroner and magistrate work quickly then,' I said, pretending not to guess at his meaning.

'That is the thing – they do not. And they lack the subtlety to comprehend a crime of this nature. I fear they would blunder into corners of college life that would seem curious to all except men of learning, like ourselves. Whereas *you . . .*' He let his implication hang in the air, regarding me with an expression of wary hope.

'*I*, sir?' I raised my eyebrows with exaggerated surprise. 'A foreigner? A Catholic? A man reported to practise magic, who openly believes the Earth goes around the Sun?'

Underhill lowered his eyes, and released his grip on my arms.

'I beg your forgiveness for my hasty words, Doctor Bruno. Fear breeds such prejudices, and we are a fearful nation in these times. And now fear visits us even in this sanctum of learning . . .' His voice died away and he looked helplessly towards the far window, away from Coverdale's corpse.

'Are you asking my help in finding this killer?' I said briskly.

He turned to me, a faint hope in his small watery eyes.

'In ordinary circumstances, I would not think of imposing on a guest – but it seems this killer wants you involved. The paper you showed me – I thought someone was making sport with you, but with *this* –' he raised a hand again behind him towards the body – 'perhaps you can draw him out before there is any more blood spilled.'

'Then *you* believe he will find more victims?' I said, perhaps too sharply.

He turned to me and blinked rapidly, shaking his head.

'I only meant – because it seems clear we are dealing with a fiend who is either possessed or mad—'

Just at that moment, there was a scrape and a dull thud from behind us; from the corner of my eye I glimpsed a sudden movement and whipped around to see Coverdale jerk and shift position. The rector shrieked and grabbed my arm again; I heard myself gasp, and for one hideous moment a cold dread washed through me as I wondered if he was not yet dead and had been hanging there in mortal agony all this time. But as I steadied my breathing and took a hesitant step forward, I realised that the knot in the rope holding him to the sconce had begun to slip.

'It's all right, Rector Underhill,' I said gently. From the juddering of his clasped hands around my arm I could tell that he was experiencing his own delayed shock and could do with some of Cobbett's strong ale himself. 'It was only the rope. But we must take the body down.'

'Why did he come here in only his underclothes?' the rector wondered softly, still shaking his head as I helped him to sit again on the largest chest.

'Well, it seems clear that he came up here under duress – perhaps his killer surprised him as he was changing,' I offered, as something caught my eye by the window. Next to the longbow, a pile of black material had been neatly folded and placed on the floor. I walked over and picked it up; it was a long academic gown, its cut and trim indicating the degree of Doctor of Divinity, and it was stiff with dried blood, especially on the front and sleeves.

'That is James's own gown,' Underhill said, turning away.

'I think our killer must have put this on over his own clothes while he carried out the act,' I mused. 'I had wondered how someone could have walked away through the college with his clothes bespattered with such a quantity of blood as this killing must have made.'

Footsteps echoed on the stairs below and a moment later Slythurst appeared carrying a lantern. He glared at me briefly before handing it to the rector, who was still trembling and wringing his hands. I took the lantern before he had a chance to drop it and a brief smile flickered across his dry lips. The bursar appeared to interpret Underhill's inertia as an invitation to assume responsibility for the situation.

'We must, in the first instance, send for the coroner to remove this body so that the strongroom may be cleaned and returned to its proper purpose and the inquest can be carried out so that poor James may have a Christian burial. His family must be notified – I believe he has a brother in the Fens somewhere, is that not so, Rector?' On receiving no answer, he continued as if he had not expected one: 'And I think it would be politic when we announce the death to give out that he was attacked by an unknown thief trying to break into the strongroom – we do not want the students indulging in any more idle speculation.' He shot me a warning glance.

'That is wise, Walter,' said the rector, turning his attention back to Slythurst with a distant, puzzled expression, as if he barely recognised him. 'That will give you a little time in hand, won't it, Bruno?' He turned to me with the same look of vague anxiety.

Slythurst snapped his head around.

'Time for what?'

'Rector Underhill has asked me to look into the circumstances of the two deaths and see if I can find any connection,' I said, returning his stare with a level gaze.

Slythurst's face blanched with fury and his lips almost disappeared.

262

'With the greatest respect, Rector,' he stuttered, choked with indignation, 'is that prudent? Doctor Bruno may have a lively imagination, but it can hardly be sensible to involve an *outsider* –' he pronounced the word with icy scorn – 'in a matter which so intimately affects the life of the college. What may come to light ..' He paused, eyeing me as a muscle twitched in his cheek, then changed tack. 'Besides, he will be gone in a few days.'

'He is already involved, Walter,' the rector said sorrowfully. 'Doctor Bruno received a communication relating to Roger Mercer's death from someone who appears to know something – perhaps even the killer himself.'

'Students playing pranks, surely,' Slythurst snapped, his eyes darting from the rector to me with undisguised anger. 'I would speak to you further about the wisdom of this, Rector – in private.'

Underhill nodded wearily.

'We will speak, Walter, but first there is much to do and we must work together. Fetch the water – I will clean the wall myself. I want no trace of that left, and I trust that neither of you will mention it? Perhaps you could find a suitable messenger to take a letter to the coroner,' he said to Slythurst. 'I will go to my library now and write it. Doctor Bruno, how do you wish to proceed?'

I wished the rector had not mentioned my mysterious letter; I still did not trust Slythurst. We had only his word that he had collected his papers from the strongroom on Saturday evening *before* the disputation, and I was not sure how much his word was worth, after his deliberate lies over the searching of Roger Mercer's room. If anyone had easy access to the sub-rector's room and the tower strongroom, it was the bursar. Whatever my correspondent knew, the fewer people who learned that he – or she – had tried to share it with me, the better. And now the killer himself wanted this murder explicitly linked to the Catherine Wheel – and the rector wanted that link washed away. I was beginning to feel overwhelmed. The one element that seemed clear was that Coverdale's early exit from the disputation was a key to his murder.

'I would like to find the student who delivered the message to Doctor Coverdale during the disputation, to find out what drew him back to college so urgently.'

Underhill nodded.

'I will make enquiries. But I beg both of you – say nothing of this to the students until I have the chance to make an announcement at dinner. By then I will try to find a way to explain it with the least alarm – if that is possible.'

'Before that, Rector Underhill,' I added, 'I think I should call on Gabriel Norris. If he delivered his bow and arrows to the strongroom as you commanded, we need to learn when, and whether Doctor Coverdale let him in. And I think you should go to your study, take a large glass of your strongest drink and gather your thoughts for a moment before you decide what to do next.'

'It is a fine day when the rector of an Oxford college is told how he may proceed by an Italian papist,' muttered Slythurst, but the rector coughed and looked embarrassed and grateful at the same time.

We descended the stairs gingerly, I leading the way with the lantern and pausing to examine the traces of bloody footprints still visible on the stone steps. Faint traces also remained on the floor of Coverdale's rooms below, but otherwise both the main room and the adjoining bedchamber in the tower were neat and orderly. I crossed and examined the door that led out to the courtyard staircase.

'The room was locked this morning when you arrived?' I asked Slythurst again.

He snorted impatiently.

'I have already told you that three times. I assumed James had gone out and I wanted to deposit the monies and deeds I had brought from Aylesbury so I borrowed the spare key from Cobbett and let myself in. What is it you are trying to imply, Doctor Bruno?'

'Only that there is no sign of the door to the tower staircase or this main door to Doctor Coverdale's room being forced,' I said. 'So he must have willingly admitted his killer – or been killed by someone already in possession of a key.'

Slythurst aimed at me a look of such venom then that I could easily believe him capable of murder. I turned to Underhill, his face painted in eerie shadows from the flickering light of the lantern.

'The tower will need to be sealed until the body is removed in any case,' I said. 'If you post one of the college servants at the foot of the staircase, we will soon learn if anyone tries to go near it. The killer may try to come back, perhaps to look for something in the room. But I would like to have a look around myself, to see if the killer left any trace behind him.'

'Yes. Yes, that seems sensible.' The rector's face was drawn and flustered. 'I must send for the coroner. Walter – you are now the most senior official here under me, I will need your help in deciding what we tell the college community. Perhaps you could come with me to my lodgings? And tell Cobbett to set one of the kitchen men by the tower stairs.'

Slythurst nodded and scuttled off down the stairs to the porter's lodge. Underhill turned back and I sensed something unspoken in the long look he gave me.

'The arrows were shot after he died, you say?'

'It is hard to tell, but I think the blood came mostly from the throat wound. If he was not yet dead, he was near it – I think he would not have been sensible of what was happening, if that is what you mean to ask.'

265

'So it would have been quick?' the rector asked, almost hopefully.

I hesitated, but decided it would be kinder not to dwell on the hacking I had seen at Coverdale's neck. The coroner would find it out soon enough.

'It was a terrible death, I will not pretend otherwise. But I have seen men with their throats cut before – they do not linger in this world.'

Underhill regarded me with his head on one side. The candle in the lantern was dying and the room enfolded in shadows again despite the early hour; it seemed to me that the smell of decay was rising from the tower stairs behind us.

'You have lived a strange life for a philosopher, Doctor Bruno,' he said softly. 'Ours must seem a soft and sheltered life to you. I thought it was so, until this week. I have hidden here from the world, thinking an Oxford college a place of sanctuary. Now I have turned a blind eye for too long, and it will be the destruction of me and my family.'

'Rector Underhill,' I said, leaning in towards him, 'if there is anything you know or suspect, anything at all that may have a bearing on these deaths, do not hide it. To what have you turned a blind eye?'

He glanced nervously over his shoulder to the door, a quick, rodent movement, then leaned in closer, his round face lit from beneath by the lantern.

'Your friend, Sir Philip . . .'

'What of him?'

'He must not learn of this. You will promise me, Doctor Bruno, that you will not speak to him of what is happening within these walls? He is Leicester's nephew, he would feel compelled to tell him all.'

At that moment footsteps echoed from below and Slythurst reappeared. Underhill shook his head at me tightly to warn me not to say anything further, then looked from me to the bursar apprehensively before turning to the door.

'Walter?'

'It occurs to me, Rector,' Slythurst began, folding his hands together unctuously, 'that if Doctor Bruno is to examine this room, it might be best if I help him. Two pairs of eyes are better than one, after all.'

'Very well. But I have need of you, Walter – come to my lodgings as quickly as you can afterwards.'

He gave me a last, imploring look, before closing the door behind him. His footsteps echoed on the stairs as he descended to the courtyard with a heavy tread.

Slythurst crooked his head back and gave the room a cursory glance.

'What is it you think you will find here, then?'

'I had thought, Master Slythurst, that you would have a better idea than I of what a man might hope to find in this room,' I said smoothly.

He turned to me then, his lips curled with undisguised contempt.

'And I might well ask what *you* took from this room, Bruno, the last time you and I found ourselves here among a dead man's things? What souvenir did you carry away then?'

'I took nothing,' I said mildly, but I turned my face away all the same and stepped towards the window. Rain drove hard against the pane, washing in rivulets down the glass, blurring the view.

'Is that so?' He spoke through his teeth now, and I heard him close at my shoulder. 'You may have duped the rector into giving you his trust, Bruno, but I see you for what you are.'

'And what is that?' I asked, folding my arms across my chest as if I did not care one way or another.

'You are one of those men who thinks himself gifted enough to live by charm and wit alone rather than by hard work. You seek to ingratiate yourself with men of high position so that you may live in the gilded shadow of their favours. You arrive here flaunting your fame and your patronage from courtiers and kings, but this is the University of Oxford, sir – we are not impressed with such baubles. And you will get no position here, no matter how much you seek to involve yourself in matters that are not your business.' Spume had gathered at the corners of his lips by the end of this address and he paused to collect himself, his eyes still blazing with a hatred that surprised me with its force.

'You think I am angling for a position here?' I repeated, incredulous.

'I do not see why else you would be seeking to make yourself indispensable to the rector by meddling in these deaths,' he snapped back.

'No – you would not see, because you could not imagine exerting yourself for any reason than your own immediate profit.' Unfolding my arms, I stepped right across to him until I stood only a few inches from his face, daring him to look me straight in the eye. 'Let me tell you something, Master Bursar. I was a fugitive in my own country for three years. I saw men murdered as casually as boys throw stones at birds, cut down for the shoes they wore or the few coins they carried, and I saw the law look the other way because it was too much effort to bring anyone to justice – because to the law, the dead men were as worthless as those who killed them, who would probably be killed tomorrow in their turn. And I believe that no man's life is worth so little that, if it is ended by violence, the crime should be shrugged away and a murderer left unpunished. *That* is why I involve myself, Master Slythurst – it is called justice.' The vehemence of my reply was at least equal to his, but although he took

268

a step back, the look he fixed on me was subtly mocking and it was I who looked away first, conscious that all my high-minded words were so much hot air. My interest in finding this killer was above all to prove myself to Walsingham and the Earl of Leicester, because this was my first mission, and there would be reward and preferment if I were successful. 'Let us return to the matter in hand,' I said brusquely. 'We are supposed to be holding one another accountable, after all.'

Though the room was neater than the last time I had been there, it had been left in a state of transition, and I felt a sudden pang of loss for James Coverdale, who had barely enjoyed one day as sub-rector before he met as grisly a fate as his predecessor. I had found little to like about the man, but it was a horrific death to have come knocking on the door of the room that he had coveted for so long, just as he was in the process of unpacking his belongings. Slythurst occupied himself straight away with the bundles of paper on Coverdale's desk; I did not like this, as I guessed that any clue as to what had happened to Coverdale on Saturday night would probably be found among his documents, and I was about to suggest that we divide the work of looking through the desk, when I noticed a smudged bloodstain almost in the hearth.

Crouching to look closer, I saw that one brick in the fireplace, to the right of the hearth, was slightly out of alignment, protruding from the wall as if it were not joined by mortar. I was just able to grip its sides by my finger-tips, though I did not have quite enough purchase to ease it from its place, and as my fingers slipped and I grazed my knuckles, I gave a small cry.

'What have you there?' Slythurst jerked his head up, dropping the book he had been perusing, and rushed to crouch at my side. I licked the blood from my scraped fingers and tried again. With some patience, I gently worked the brick from one side to the other, feeling it give a little more each time as it crunched against the bricks either side.

'Come on, man!' Slythurst muttered. 'Shall I try?'

'I have it,' I snapped, and in a few moments the brick was free, revealing a dark cavity built into the side of the fireplace. I thrust in my hand and rummaged as far as I could, but all I felt was the brickwork at the back of the hole. 'Nothing,' I said, bitterly, sitting back on my heels.

'Out of the way,' Slythurst barked, elbowing me roughly to one side. His skinny arm seemed to disappear further into the recess, but though he seemed determined to prove me wrong, he too withdrew his hand empty. 'Devil take him, that whoreson!' he cursed, rubbing his knuckles.

'Well, whoever came this time knew where to look,' I said grimly, my knees cracking as I stood. 'And it seems he found what he came for.'

'To hell with it!' Slythurst spat. He seemed to be taking the discovery of the empty hiding place as a personal injury. I wondered if the cavity in the fireplace had contained whatever Slythurst had been searching for after Roger Mercer's death – it was not a large space but it could easily have concealed a bundle of letters or documents – and if his anger was therefore directed at himself for not having found it on his previous search. But this time there was no sign of a frenzied rummage through Coverdale's belongings; whoever killed Coverdale had evidently known of the loose brick and moved straight to take whatever was hidden there, after first washing Coverdale's blood from his hands. But this could only mean that whoever had searched the tower room before I arrived on Saturday morning, while Mercer was still in the garden being savaged by the dog, had *not* known of the hiding place, and was therefore not the same person who had killed Coverdale. Neither, by this reckoning, could it be Slythurst,

270

unless he was a supremely skilled actor; he was, after all, the only other person who could legitimately demand a key to the sub-rector's room and no one would be able to confirm or deny the precise time of his departure for Buckinghamshire, or his return.

Slythurst appeared impatient to leave; plainly he had decided that there was nothing more of use to be found.

'I do not see what further purpose we achieve here,' he muttered, moving towards the door and clinking the keys as if this were a signal that my time was up. 'I am needed by the rector, and I must lock this room, so if you have done—'

'Tell me, Master Slythurst,' I said, 'do you believe our killer has found whatever you yourself were hoping to find here after Roger Mercer's death?'

The look he gave me dripped with contempt.

'I don't know what you are talking about. I did not take a key from a man's pocket as he breathed his death rattle, like some,' Slythurst said, his face very close to mine so that I could smell the sourness of his breath.

'I only ask, because it would seem that two men have died for whatever was hidden in that hole, and I'm assuming you know what it was,' I said.

'One might think that would be warning enough to the over-curious,' he replied, with a smile that cut through his thin face like wire. 'I must go to the rector. You might do well to get on with finding the owner of the murder weapon. That would seem a useful place to start your enquiries, Doctor Bruno, since you have been good enough to offer the college your services.'

As I passed him in the doorway with a last look of disdain, I found myself fervently wishing that Slythurst would prove to be the killer so that I could have the enormous pleasure of seeing that sarcastic sneer wiped from his sallow face, and

271

immediately tried to shake myself free of such dangerous prejudice.

At the foot of the staircase, a large stocky man with almost no neck stood blocking the archway through to the quadrangle; he started when he heard the noise behind him and his hand moved swiftly to his belt. I could not help smiling when I saw he carried some kind of kitchen fork there as a makeshift weapon; this, then, was the guard appointed to keep the tower sealed.

'Peace, Dick,' Slythurst said, holding up a hand. The man lowered his head deferentially and moved aside to let us pass into the rain that still fell in steady sheets, splashing from spreading puddles between the flagstones of the courtyard; I pulled my jerkin up around my ears and made to step out into the deluge when three students came running and laughing out of the adjacent staircase, holding their leather satchels over the heads against the weather. I recognised one of them as Lawrence Weston, the boy who had escorted me to the disputation on Saturday evening, and I reached out to accost him.

'Master Weston, I wonder if I may ask your assistance?' I began urgently. He looked somewhat taken aback, and I realised that in my haste I had grabbed hard on to the sleeve of his gown.

'I will help if I can, Doctor Bruno,' he said uneasily, for my manner clearly struck him as out of sorts. 'Let us step out of the rain, though.' He motioned me back into the shelter of the staircase he had just left. I noticed Slythurst watching our exchange with suspicion; when I caught his eye, he quickly pulled his gown around him and scuttled off towards the rector's lodgings opposite.

'There was a boy, a student,' I said to Weston, once we were under shelter, 'who delivered a message to Doctor Coverdale during the disputation on Saturday night, that

272

caused him to leave immediately after he read it. Do you know who the boy was?'

'How should I know, sir?' he replied, perhaps sounding more ungracious than he had intended, for he then said, 'I mean, I could ask around, if it is important.'

'Thank you,' I said, turning to leave. 'There will be a shilling for you if you find him.'

Weston looked briefly impressed, and nodded before rejoining his friends. I braced myself to run into the courtyard.

# TWELVE

Gabriel Norris's room was on the ground floor in the west range, tucked behind the staircase, his door marked with a painted name sign; I knocked hard and was certain I heard some movement within, but a few moments passed and no one answered. I knocked again and called out Norris's name; there was a hasty scuffling of feet and the door swung open to reveal Thomas Allen. He had evidently been engaged in some of his servant's duties, as his shirtsleeves were rolled up to the elbow and he clutched a dirty cloth between his hands.

'Oh – Doctor Bruno,' he exclaimed, and his face reddened violently as he bunched the cloth into a ball, looking flustered.

'Sorry to disturb you, Thomas – I see you are at work. I was looking for Master Norris.'

'He is not here,' Thomas said, still looking perturbed, then glanced over his shoulder as if to check the truth of his own assertion. Through the open door I glimpsed a comfortable chamber, furnished as a parlour with a high-backed wooden settle in front of the fire. Compared to the austerity of most scholars' rooms the chamber offered a distinct sense of luxury. Windows on both sides opened on to the lane and the quadrangle and filled the room with light even on this bleak day. Beneath the outer window was a heavy trunk, iron-bound and secured with a solid padlock.

'He is out at the public lectures, I expect. I was just cleaning his shoes,' Thomas added, defensively.

'Do you not attend the public lectures too?'

'Not when there is work to be done,' he snapped. I was surprised at his manner, but I supposed he did not like to be seen at his menial tasks.

'His shoes needed cleaning urgently today, then?' I asked, as a thought struck me. Thomas must have caught something in my tone because he frowned and his shoulders seemed to tense.

'I clean his shoes every day,' he said, a wary note in his voice. 'Why did you want to see Gabriel?'

'I wanted to ask when he took his longbow to the strong-room.'

Thomas looked mildly surprised at the question, but shrugged carelessly before wiping his hands on his shirt front.

'I took it, on Saturday morning. Gabriel was furious – he said the rector had commanded him to give it up, after he'd done them a service, too, shooting that mad dog.'

'So you took it there yourself?'

He blinked at my tone, then shook his head.

'I went to do so, but as I was crossing the quadrangle I was seen by Doctor Coverdale and Doctor Bernard, who were standing by the stairs to chapel. They stopped me and asked what I was doing with such a weapon in college. When I explained, Doctor Coverdale told me that I could leave it outside his door on the landing and he would see that it was safely locked away.'

'Did Doctor Bernard hear this exchange?'

'He was standing right beside Doctor Coverdale, so I presume so.' Thomas looked puzzled.

'Could anyone else have overheard?'

'I don't know. There were a few people in the courtyard coming and going, but I don't recall anyone stopping by us. What is the problem, Doctor Bruno, if I might ask?' He was twisting the dirty cloth now between his hands, his face searching mine keenly.

'Oh – there is no problem,' I said airily. We looked at one another in awkward silence for a moment.

'Doctor Bruno,' Thomas said, stepping closer and lowering his voice, 'I hope this will not sound presumptuous, but there is something I would speak to you about urgently. It is a matter of some importance, and I do not know who else I may confide in here.'

The hairs on my neck prickled; could it be that Thomas knew something of the murder?

'Please – speak freely.'

'I meant – somewhere private.'

'Are we not alone here?' I asked, looking around the empty room.

He shook his head and pressed his lips into a tight line, twisting the cloth between his hands.

'Away from college, sir. I would not have us overheard.'

I hesitated. I did not really have time to spare – my priority was to find the boy who had called Coverdale out of the disputation – but the expression of pained urgency on Thomas's face convinced me that whatever he needed to unburden must be serious.

'Very well, then. Have you broken your fast this morning? Perhaps we could find ourselves a tavern where we might eat and talk at more leisure.' I realised that I had not eaten in all the consternation over Coverdale's murder.

His face slackened.

'Sir – I'm afraid I do not have the means for visiting taverns.'

276

'But I do,' I said, 'and surely you may eat with me if I invite you?'

'I'm afraid it would not do your standing in Oxford any good to be seen with me, sir,' he said dolefully.

'To be honest, Master Allen, my standing in Oxford is not worth a horse's shit at the moment,' I said. 'But to hell with them – let us enjoy a good breakfast, if we can find one, and take the consequences afterwards, and you may tell me what is on your mind.'

'You are kind, sir,' he said, following me through the door, which he stopped to lock behind him.

As we drew near to the tower archway, I stretched up to look at James Coverdale's blank window, though it was too high to see anything.

'Are you all right, Doctor Bruno?' Thomas asked, following my gaze, his angular face politely solicitous. 'You seem disturbed this morning. Has something happened?'

I looked at him, gathering my scattered thoughts. Thomas had not yet heard the news of Coverdale's murder, but by the time we returned the college would be abuzz with rumour and speculation. If he knew anything of value, I would need to take advantage of these few unguarded moments.

'No. No, I am fine. Let us go.'

We walked in silence down St Mildred's Lane towards the High Street. Though Thomas was a good five inches taller than I, he walked with such a hunched posture, as if hoping to make himself less noticeable, that we appeared almost the same height. His worn air of defeat made it impossible not to feel pity for the boy. As if reading my thoughts, he turned his face briefly to me, his hands wrapped deep in the sleeves of his frayed gown.

'It is good of you to take time to listen to me, sir. With the difference in our positions, I mean.'

'If we are to talk of positions, Thomas, let us not forget

277

that you are the son of an Oxford Fellow and I am the son of a soldier. But I have little interest in such distinctions – I still dare to hope for a day when a person is judged by his character and his achievements rather than for his father's name.'

'That is a bold hope,' he agreed. 'But to most people in this town, sir, I will always be the son of an exiled heretic.'

'Well, I *am* an exiled heretic, so I win.'

He looked me in the eye then, and smiled properly for the first time since I had met him, before his face turned sombre again.

'All the same, you are a friend of kings and courtiers, sir,' he reminded me.

'Well, after a fashion, Thomas. If you mean King Henri of France, he likes to surround himself with philosophers, it flatters his intellectual vanity. Kings do not have friends in the same way as you or I.'

'I have no friends at all, sir,' he responded, his voice subdued. There was a long pause while we both looked for something to say. 'In any case, you are friends with Sir Philip Sidney, and that is something.'

'Yes,' I agreed, 'I am fortunate to count Sidney a friend. Is that why you wished to speak to me – so that I might petition him for your father's sake?'

Thomas was silent for a moment, then he stopped walking and fixed me with a serious expression.

'Not for my father's sake, sir. For my own. There is something I must tell you, if you will promise me your discretion?'

I nodded, intrigued. At the place where St Mildred's Lane met the High Street, we paused and looked to left and right along the rows of uneven timber-framed houses and the pale stone fronts of the college buildings; at this hour the street was almost deserted, the sky reflected undisturbed in the still water pooled in cart ruts.

'The Flower de Luce is just along the street,' Thomas said, gesturing to our left, 'but it is expensive, sir.' He pulled anxiously at the hem of his gown.

'Well, no matter,' I said brightly, reaching to my belt to cup the reassuring weight of Walsingham's purse against my palm as we began to walk in the direction he had indicated. 'But I do not know the taverns of Oxford. Tell me, do you know anything of an inn called the Catherine Wheel?'

I glanced innocently at Thomas as I said this; the fear that flickered over his face was unmistakeable, but he quickly assumed a neutral countenance.

'I believe it is a bad sort of place, sir. In any case, we students are not allowed to pass beyond the city walls. We would be severely disciplined if we were caught.'

'Really? But that is strange – I took a walk yesterday and I was sure I saw a young man in a scholar's gown passing through one of the gates.'

Thomas shrugged.

'Probably one of the gentlemen commoners, then.' His voice was not bitter, merely resigned, as if he had long ago accepted that the rich lived by different laws and it was fruitless to hope for change.

'Like your master Gabriel Norris?' I asked.

'I wish you would not call him my master, sir. I mean, he *is,* I suppose, but it is a humiliation to be reminded of it.'

He had stopped outside a whitewashed, two-storey building that fronted the High Street, its exterior obviously well cared for and clean. Inside, the tap-room was just as neat and cheerful, everything that the Catherine Wheel was not, and a sharp savoury smell of roasting meat pricked our nostrils the moment we closed the door behind us. A smiling landlord, apron stretched tight over a belly so vast he looked as if he were near to giving birth, bustled over and ushered us to a table, at the same time reeling off a list of dishes so varied that I had forgotten the first by the time he had finished. We ended by ordering some cheese and barley bread, with a pot of beer each. Thomas looked about him with as much disbelief and delight as if he had been suddenly given the freedom of the city.

'Well, then, Thomas,' I said, gently, 'what is it you wish to confide?'

Finally he raised his head and regarded me with a weary expression.

'Three nights ago, the day I so shamefully accosted you in the quadrangle on your arrival, sir, I learned something about my father.' He stopped with a heavy sigh just as a young pot-boy appeared with the tankards of beer and bread. I thought of Humphrey Pritchard and his snatches of Latin, and remembered I must also find a way to speak with him again. Thomas had buried his face in his beer mug as if he had not had a drink in days. I waited for him to put it down before continuing as casually as I could with my questions.

'You are in touch with your father, then?'

'We write to one another,' Thomas said, 'though of course you may imagine our letters are all monitored, at the earl's request. My father resides at the English College of Rheims, where all the seminary priests are trained for the English mission, so any letters that come out of that place are deemed to be of great interest. And since I am assumed to share his views, they are waiting for me to betray myself in one of my letters to him. They watch me at every turn – everyone I meet or speak to. They will probably interrogate me about this –' he gestured to the table between us – 'when they find out.'

'Who are "they"?' I prompted, pausing to take a drink from my own cup. 'Who intercepts your letters?'

'The rector. And Doctor Coverdale. He wanted me sent down from the college after my father was exiled – he argued fiercely that allowing me to stay would imply that the college tolerated papists.'

His tone was resentful, but I watched his face carefully and could detect no sign that he knew the man he spoke of was recently dead.

'But you are not a papist?' I prompted.

'I am the son of one, so they assume my loyalty to England is compromised. Eventually the rector decided I could keep my place, but Coverdale argued that I should not continue at the expense of the college, so I lost my scholarship. I do not fool myself that the rector felt sorry for me – I suppose he thought my correspondence with my father would be useful.' He gave a bitter little laugh. 'It must be a terrible disappointment to them – he writes to me only of the weather and his health, and I write of my studies. We dare not say anything beyond that. And then it is rumoured that the Earl of Leicester has placed a spy in the college already, so fearful are they of the secret influence of papists.'

'A spy? Is there any truth in that?' I asked, leaning in more keenly.

'I do not know, sir. But then, if he were any good as a spy, I should not know him, should I?'

'So you do not share your father's faith?'

Thomas met my eye with a level stare as if challenging me to contradict him.

'No, sir, I do not. I spit on the pope and the Church of Rome. But I have sworn so until I am hoarse with saying it, and still I am suspected, so what is the point?'

I waited for a moment until he had finished chewing, watching him with my elbows propped on the table and my chin resting on my clasped hands.

'What was it you learned of your father three days ago?' I asked. 'Is he ill?'

Thomas shook his head, his mouth bulging.

'Worse than that,' he said bitterly, when he could speak again. 'He is—' He broke off, a piece of bread halfway to his mouth, looking at me then as if he had only just realised who I was. His anxious eyes flicked keenly over my face as he calculated whether or not I could be trusted. 'You swear you will not repeat this to a soul?'

'I swear it,' I said, nodding sincerely and holding his gaze as steadily as I could manage.

He considered for a moment, still searching my eyes, then nodded tightly.

'My father will not return to England now or ever, even if Queen Bess herself were to write assuring him of his pardon.'

'But why not?'

'Because he is *happy*,' Thomas said, pronouncing the last word with undisguised anger. 'He is happy, Doctor Bruno, because he has found his vocation. Sometimes I think he chose to be found out at Lincoln, so that he could finally confess his faith openly. When he writes to me now, he has to dictate the letters to a scribe – do you know why?'

I briefly shook my head and he continued, without waiting for an answer,

'Because he was interrogated by the Privy Council. They had him hung by the hands from metal gauntlets so his feet could not touch the ground for eight hours at a time, until he passed out, and still he told them nothing. He has more or less lost the use of his right hand. But I think he would gladly have gone to his death at the time, believing himself a martyr. Three days ago, I learned that my father is to take vows as a Jesuit priest,' he said, in a tone that sounded almost like wry amusement. 'The Church will have him completely, and he will forget he ever had a wife or a son.'

'I am sure no father could do that,' I said.

'You do not know him,' he said, setting his mouth in a

282

grim line. 'Ours is an old Catholic family, sir. But I ask you – how can a religion that talks of love at the same time urge men so cruelly to cast aside the natural ties of love and friendship? To martyr themselves for the promise of an unseen world, and leave their families grieving! I want no part of any God that demands those sacrifices.'

He had shredded what remained of his bread into tiny pieces with his agitated fingers as he spoke. He reached forward to take another hunk of bread and as he did so, the frayed sleeve of his gown fell back to reveal a soiled makeshift bandage around his wrist and the lower part of his right hand, blotched with brownish stains over which a few, fresher crimson spots had blossomed more recently.

'What happened to your hand?' I asked.

Immediately he tugged his sleeve down over the bandage and rubbed his wrist self-consciously.

'It is nothing.'

'It does not look like nothing – it's bled badly. I could look at it if you like?'

'Are you a doctor?' he snapped, withdrawing his arm hastily as if afraid I might tear the bandage off without his consent.

'Only of theology,' I admitted, 'but I did learn a little of the art of making salves when I was a monk. It would be no trouble to examine it.'

'Thank you, but there is no need. It was just a foolish accident. I was sharpening Gabriel's razor for him and my hand slipped.' He looked down and gave his whole attention to the bread as if the subject was closed. I felt myself tense, but tried to give no sign that I found his words significant.

'Your friend Master Norris does not use the college barber, then?' I asked, in a neutral tone.

Thomas ventured a smile.

283

'He calls him the college barbarian. No, he prefers to do the job himself.'

'When did he ask you to sharpen his razor?'

Thomas thought for a moment.

'It must have been Saturday, because he wanted to shave before the disputation.'

'And has it been in its usual place since then?'

'I – I don't know, sir. I have not looked. Why would it not be?'

He looked at me, his brow creased with curiosity, and I thought it best not to arouse his suspicions further.

'I only wondered if Master Norris ever lent the razor to his friends.'

'Never, sir. He is careful with his possessions. Many of them are valuable, or else they came from his father.'

He didn't ask any further, but continued to regard me with curiosity. After we had sat for a while in silence, I put down my bread and wiped my fingers.

'But this news of your father – you did not learn it directly from him, if his letters are intercepted? He would surely not have written to you of his plans to take holy orders.'

'No, he had another correspondent,' Thomas said with his mouth full.

*'Had?'*

He stopped and his eyes flickered guiltily upwards towards mine as he realised his slip.

'You mean Doctor Mercer?' I persisted. If he had learned the news three days ago, there could only be one person who now required the past tense.

Thomas nodded.

'They continued to write to one another. My father always confided more in Roger Mercer; they were the closest of friends.'

'But Mercer denounced him.'

'I don't think so. My father never knew who denounced him, but he was certain it wasn't Mercer. Mercer only testified against him at the trial.'

'Surely that would be enough to end a friendship? Your father must have an exceptional capacity for forgiveness.'

Thomas laid down his knife and was looking at me impatiently.

'You don't understand, do you? This is exactly what I was saying about faith – the *cause* is always more important. The natural laws of friendship must be sacrificed. My father would not have expected Roger Mercer to do otherwise – and he would have testified against Roger if their positions had been reversed. Both had a greater loyalty. If Roger had spoken in his defence they would likely both have been imprisoned or exiled, and then who would be left to carry on the fight?'

I stared at him.

'You mean to say that Roger Mercer was also a Catholic?' I whispered.

Thomas hunched lower over the table.

'I suppose it will not hurt him now that I tell you,' he said, 'but do not repeat it to anyone, I beg you. It could only hurt his family.'

'No, no, of course. But if Roger was a Catholic,' I mused, my mind scurrying to catch up, 'and your father was writing to him from Rheims, might he have confided details of the English mission? Might Roger even have played a part?'

'I do not know the contents of their letters, sir,' Thomas said, twisting uncomfortably in his seat. 'Doctor Mercer only told me news he thought might affect me directly.'

'But was their correspondence not intercepted by the college authorities too? Did they not think it suspicious that Mercer continued to write to the man he had helped condemn?'

'Doctor Mercer did not send his letters through the college post, sir.' Thomas's voice was now barely audible. 'He paid to send them privately, through someone in the town who had the means of carrying letters overseas.'

'Ah. A book dealer, perhaps?'

'Perhaps. I did not ask – that was his business,' Thomas said evenly, but his eyes were evasive. Then he suddenly leaned forward so that he was almost lying across the table and grabbed my sleeve.

'I am not responsible for my father, sir, nor for any communications he may or may not have sent, as I have tried to tell everyone for the last year. I just want to live quietly, to leave Oxford and study the law at the Inns of Court in London, but I fear I shall never be allowed a career as a lawyer, nor any wife of good family, for as long as I am regarded as my father's son. Especially once he joins the Jesuits,' he added, with an extra dose of self-pity. 'For the Privy Council has spies even in the seminaries and will learn of it soon enough. Unless someone with influence will speak on my behalf.'

He looked at me with imploring eyes, but I looked back unseeing, my mind occupied elsewhere. If Edmund Allen was taking holy orders in Rheims, he must be in some way connected to the mission to England. That would certainly explain the ransacking of Mercer's room; Allen's letters to him, if they contained any such matter, might be evidence enough to condemn anyone associated with them. But that still did not explain why Mercer had been killed. Had he threatened to betray the cause? Had he crossed someone? Did the letters between Roger Mercer and Edmund Allen name others who wanted to protect themselves at any cost? The 'J' in his calendar on the day of his murder might very well stand for Jenkes, I reflected; anyone who could cut off his own ears without flinching surely wouldn't hesitate to remove a man who threatened his business – unless I was falling prey to Cobbett's legends. There were too many questions, while the possible answers were all frustratingly unclear. I put my head in my hands and stared at the table.

'Are you all right, Doctor Bruno?'

'I wondered if Mercer was killed by a Catholic,' I murmured, barely aware that I had thought aloud and only belatedly looking up to find Thomas regarding me with an odd expression.

'Doctor Mercer was killed by a *dog*,' he reminded me.

'Oh, come on, Thomas – do you believe that? How often have you known feral dogs to attack men in the streets of Oxford, never mind a locked garden?'

'I do not know, sir,' he said, avoiding my eye. 'I only know what the rector told us. The door was left open, the dog wandered in.'

He made a show of looking into his empty tankard as though hoping more beer might appear if he only peered in hard enough.

'Another drink, Thomas?'

He nodded eagerly, and I summoned the serving-girl to bring us another two pots of beer. When she had gone, I leaned across the table and waited for him to meet my eye.

'Was this what you wanted to confide in me, that you could tell no one else – this news about your father?'

Thomas resumed his scratching at the boards of the table.

'That first day, when I thought you were Sir Philip,' he said quietly, 'you were kind when Rector Underhill tried to shame me. I thought – perhaps it was foolish, but I thought if you had the ear of men like Sir Philip, you might intercede for me.'

'What is it you wish me to say?'

He took a deep breath and exhaled slowly, his eyes fixed on his hands.

'I want to leave Oxford, sir. I am afraid. When my father was deprived, I was questioned twice by the Chancellor's

Court. They would not believe that I knew nothing of his secret life, and the questioning was hard – they would not accept a word I said, they kept pressing me and pressing me on the same points until I found I was contradicting myself.'

I noticed his hands were shaking and his breathing had quickened; the memory was obviously difficult for him.

'Did they use force?'

'No, sir. But they argued as lawyers do, they twisted every answer I gave until it sounded like the opposite meaning, and I became so confused and afraid I found myself agreeing to statements that I knew were not true. It is strange the way that someone who wants to find you guilty can start to make you believe in your own guilt, even when you know you are innocent. I was afraid I would condemn myself by mistake, sir. It was a horrible experience.'

'I can imagine,' I said with feeling, remembering the fear that had gripped at my guts when the abbot had told me I would be questioned by the Inquisition all those years ago. 'And you are afraid you will be questioned again if it becomes known that your father is to become a Jesuit priest?'

He nodded, finally looking directly at me.

'If they refused to believe me before, how much worse will it be when they know he is part of the Jesuit mission? What if they take me to London for questioning? I have heard tales of what they do there to get the information they want. They can make you say anything.'

I remembered my conversation with Walsingham in his garden and shivered involuntarily. Thomas's narrow, pointed face was stretched tight with fear, his skin so pale that a tracery of blue veins stood out at his temples like a river delta inked on a map. There was no doubt that this fear was real and vivid.

'The authorities would believe you know enough to make hard questioning worthwhile?' I asked.

'I know nothing, sir!' he protested, his cheeks flaming again with emotion. 'But I am not brave – I do not know what I might be capable of saying if they hurt me!'

'Tell me the truth, Thomas,' I said firmly. 'I cannot help you if you do not. Are you afraid that you will betray your father's secrets, and the secrets of his confederates, if you are threatened with torture?'

'I never wanted this knowledge, sir,' he whispered, his voice cracking as he blinked back tears. 'I told my father so, but he wanted me to share in it. He was determined to bring me to the Roman faith, he wanted me to go with him to France, so he wouldn't have to choose between his son and his church. I suppose he thought if he confided in me about his meetings, I would feel some complicity, some loyalty towards his friends. Instead I am trapped by all these secrets I never asked to be told. I am suffering for a faith I don't even share!' he cried, bringing his fist down on the table.

'You have never thought of offering up these secrets voluntarily?' I ventured. 'You must know the Earl of Leicester would surely reward anyone who could give him such information about the Catholic resistance in Oxford as you must have.'

Thomas stared at me as if it was taking him some time to process the meaning of my words.

'Of course I have thought of it. Have you ever seen the execution of a Catholic in England, Doctor Bruno?'

I confessed that I had not.

'I have. My father took me to London to see the death of Edmund Campion and his fellow Jesuits, in December of 1581. I think he wanted me to understand what was at stake.' He passed a hand across his brow and squeezed his eyes hard shut, as if this might blot out the scenes he had witnessed. 'They were sliced open like pigs in the slaughterhouse and their guts torn from their living bodies, wound around a spindle to pull them out slower. You could hear them still crying out to God while their entrails were held aloft to please the crowd and their hearts thrown in the brazier. I could not bear to watch, Doctor Bruno, but I looked at my father's face and he was rapt, as if it were the most glorious spectacle he had ever witnessed. I could not willingly deliver anyone to that fate. I don't want anyone else's blood on my hands, sir, I just want to be left alone!' His voice rose to a frantic pitch and he clutched again at his bandaged wrist.

'Thomas,' I began, and broke off as the serving-girl arrived with fresh tankards of beer. When she had set them down, I leaned in, carefully lowering my voice. 'Are there other Catholics here in Oxford who know that your father told you about them? I mean, people who know you do not share their faith, and might be afraid that you would betray them if you were questioned?'

Immediately he looked away.

'Are you also afraid that those people would try to silence you before you could hurt them? Like they did with Roger Mercer?'

'I can't say any more, Doctor Bruno.' His voice was trembling now. 'I swear, you don't want that knowledge either. I only wanted to ask if you might find a time to speak on my behalf to Sir Philip, to beg his patronage and assure him that I am a true Englishman, loyal to the queen and to the English Church.'

'I thought you had stopped believing in God?' I said, with a smile.

'What has the Church to do with God?' he countered, almost smiling in return. From somewhere beyond the windows, a church bell began to peal distantly. Thomas jumped as if he had been stung. 'Doctor Bruno – I hope this won't seem ungrateful, but I should get back to college. Gabriel will be returning from lectures soon and I have work still to do.'

It seemed to me that he was suddenly anxious to end the conversation; perhaps he had not anticipated so many questions in return for the favour he wanted. I drained the last of my beer and paid the landlord, feeling a twinge of guilt as I saw the undisguised envy with which Thomas watched me take coins from Walsingham's plump purse. If he knew that I had been given this money by the very people whose attention he feared, for the exact purpose of winkling out the kind of secrets his father kept, whatever respect he professed for me would vanish like yesterday's mist.

Out of the thick warmth of the tavern, a chill wind drove the rain sideways into our faces. Thomas pulled his gown tighter around him as we walked along the High Street under the shadows of the dripping eaves in silence, sunk deep into his own thoughts while I tried to fit what I had just learned with the matter of Mercer and Coverdale's deaths. We had almost reached the turning to St Mildred's Lane when I remembered there was something else I had wanted to ask him.

'You said you have no friends here, Thomas, but do you not count Mistress Sophia Underhill?' I said, slowing my pace so that we would not arrive at the college gate before he had a chance to answer.

He looked at me with some surprise.

'There was a time, I suppose, when I considered her a friend. But I think she regards me rather as she does her dolls – something that amused her in childhood, but which she outgrew and put aside.'

'Because of your father's disgrace?'

'No.' Thomas sidestepped a puddle that had formed in the rutted lane, the sole of one of his shoes flapping open with each step he took. 'She grew out of me long before that. When my mother died and my father decided to come back to Oxford at the earl's request, I was made to lodge with a family in the town – you know only the rector may live with a wife and family in college, the other Fellows are supposed to be bachelors. But the rector's family took pity on me, and my father and I were often invited to dine at their table – I was supposed to be company for young John, the son that died, but of course I noticed Sophia.' He sighed and appeared to stoop even further, as if the memory of those days was a physical weight on his shoulders. 'Then John was killed and Sophia's father decided to rein her in. He had ambitions for her to make a grand marriage and her mother was supposed to be preparing her by taking her into society, but Mistress Underhill took ill with her nerves after John's death, and Sophia was left to herself with no company but the men in college. There were governesses, but they never lasted long.' He laughed ruefully. 'I do not blame them – I should not like to try and teach Sophia anything against her will.'

I nodded, remembering the way she had dealt with Adam, the censorious servant.

'No, indeed. You still care for her, I think?'

He glanced at me, his face suddenly guarded.

'What does it matter? She will not have me now.'

'Does she have someone else?'

His face set hard and something like anger flashed in his eyes.

'Whatever you have heard, it is a lie! She has an affectionate nature, but she is easily deceived—' He stopped abruptly, his voice thick with emotion, and I thought for a moment he might cry, but he took a deep breath and composed himself. 'But if you want to know, then yes – I will always care for her, and I would do anything to protect her. *Anything*.'

I halted abruptly at the ferocity of his last words and turned to face him.

'Protect her from what? Is she in danger?'

Thomas took a step back, apparently disconcerted by the intensity of my expression.

'I didn't mean – that is, I only meant if she were in need, she knows that she could always depend on me.'

I grabbed him by the wrist and he yelped; I had forgotten his injury. I let go and grasped his gown instead, leaning in until my face was less than a foot from his.

'Thomas, if you know of any danger to Sophia, you must tell me!'

His eyes narrowed and I saw his jaw stiffen; again he stepped back, but with more composure this time, and his voice took on a new distance.

'*Must* I, Doctor Bruno? What would you offer her – your own protection? Or something else? And when you are gone back to London with your party in a couple of days, what will she be left with then?'

'I only meant that you have a duty to report any danger to those who might be able to help her,' I said, attempting to sound detached as I released his gown from my fist, but I knew it was too late; I had betrayed my affection for Sophia and revealed myself as a rival.

Thomas straightened his gown, then turned and began walking down St Mildred's Lane towards Lincoln College gatehouse, his arms wrapped around his thin torso.

'You have no idea what you are talking about,' he said eventually, looking straight ahead as if he were not speaking to me at all, but thinking aloud.

Then he dropped his gaze apologetically, and clasped my hand between both of his. 'Thank you for listening to me, Doctor Bruno. And I'm sorry if I spoke out of turn on occasion – I am still afraid of saying the wrong thing. You will remember my request, if it's not too much trouble?'

'I will, Thomas. I am glad we have talked.'

'I need to leave Oxford,' he said, gripping my hand urgently. 'If I could get to London and begin a life there – you will tell Sir Philip that? A recommendation from him would ease my path, and I would swear my loyalty to him and the earl.'

'I will do my best for you,' I promised, and meant it, though I was certain he had not told me all he knew. 'And take care of that wound on your wrist.'

He bowed slightly and then scuttled away through the gate to his duties.

The rain continued to blow across the courtyard in endless diagonal lines, the sky now darker than when I had first ventured out. I glanced up at the small window at the top of the tower and shivered to think of Coverdale's blood-soaked body dangling from the sconce, those arrows mockingly protruding from his chest and stomach. I had once visited the basilica of San Sebastiano Fuori le Mura in Rome, in whose catacombs the saint's remains are buried; the great icon there, with his face of pious agony and his arrows sticking out like the spines of a porcupine, had struck me then as exaggerated and unreal in his torment, like a scene from a play, garishly painted, and I realised I had had the same response on seeing James Coverdale's body. The grisly tableau had appeared almost as a practical joke; I had hardly been able to believe him dead until I saw the great wound in his throat. As I pulled my jerkin up again around my face and prepared to put my head down into the rain, I remembered suddenly a phrase from the rector's Foxe quotation: *By his own soldiers*. Sebastian, a captain of the Praetorian guard, had been executed on the orders of the Emperor Diocletian by his own men. Had the murderer kept that detail in mind? Had James Coverdale also been killed by someone who was supposed to be on his side? And what side might that be, in this place of tangled loyalties?

I had barely stepped out into the courtyard from the gate-house when I saw the rector emerging from the archway opposite, followed closely by Slythurst. Both had the hoods of their gowns pulled close around their faces and were hurrying towards me; when the rector caught sight of me, he beckoned hastily for me to join them. In the shelter of the gatehouse, he huddled closer, out of earshot of a group of students taking refuge from the rain.

'You saw my daughter this morning, did you not, Bruno, in the porter's lodge?' Underhill demanded.

'Yes – she was waiting for her mother to go out,' I said, caught by the trace of urgency in his voice.

'Did you see her leave?'

'No – Master Slythurst arrived with his terrible news and I came to fetch you.'

'Then, she must have . . .' Underhill shook his head, with an expression of vague confusion. 'It is no matter. She was ever defiant. She will be back.'

'What has happened?' I pressed him.

'When my wife arrived at the gatehouse, Sophia was no longer there,' he said, looking around the courtyard as if in hope that she might appear at any moment. 'Margaret thought she must have gone on ahead to the house of her acquaintance, so she set off herself, but when she got there, they had seen no sign of Sophia either. Margaret is fretting, as she is wont to do, but I am inclined to believe Sophia has taken it upon herself to go off walking without telling anyone – she complains often of being cooped up here. She thinks she should have the liberty to go wandering the lanes and fields outside the city for the best part of the day, just as she used to with her brother. Well, that was different. She *will* learn the manners proper to a young lady, even if she will not learn them willingly.' His face clouded for a moment. Then he glanced around again, distracted, as if hoping the events of this day might have gone away of their own accord.

'Surely she would not have chosen a day such as this to

go out walking?' I said, gesturing to the relentless sky and trying to keep my own voice even. Only the night before, Sophia herself had told me she believed she was in danger, and Thomas Allen had just implied something similar. Now she had disappeared. I hoped fervently that the rector was right, but I sensed that he had told this story to persuade himself because he could not cope with any more worries on top of Coverdale's murder and all it implied for the college.

'Yes, yes – I'm sure she will be back for her dinner before we know it,' he said, waving a hand. 'And now, Master Slythurst will take my letter to the coroner, and I must prepare what I will say to the community in Hall. The hour is almost upon us.'

He looked at me and sighed. He seemed to have aged ten years in the past hour.

'I will be in my study, Doctor Bruno. We will speak later. I would ask you to be present in Hall at noon for dinner, when I shall announce this tragedy to the college. It would be prudent for you to know the exact terms in which I have informed the college community of events so that you do not repeat anything beyond that. I would like to limit gossip as far as possible.'

I bowed in acknowledgement.

'It would likewise be prudent, Rector, not to let anyone else know that you have asked me to look into this matter,' I said, in a low voice. 'There may be some who would keep information back if they thought I sought it on your behalf.'

'I understand. Go where you will, Doctor Bruno, and I will not mention your involvement. But find who did this thing – these things,' he corrected himself, 'and whatever reward the college may offer will be yours for the asking. Provided I am still in place to grant it,' he added gloomily, before turning to retrace his steps to his lodgings.

# THIRTEEN

The bell summoning the college to dinner at midday still clanged incessantly long after the Fellows and students had filed into the Great Hall, marking time over the susurration of urgent whispered conversations that betrayed the tension crackling in the atmosphere like the charge before a storm. Outside, the rain beat against the windows so hard that we had to raise our voices to make ourselves heard even to our neighbours.

I was disconcerted to find that a place had been saved for me at the High Table with the senior Fellows. Seated between Richard Godwyn, the librarian, and Slythurst, who made no effort to disguise his distaste at my presence among his colleagues, I could not help but be aware that the seat I occupied must surely have belonged to one of the two dead men.

The High Table was raised up on a low dais that gave me a vantage over the rest of the hall. It was a handsome room, its walls whitewashed and hung with tapestries in the French style of the last century that were clearly expensive work, though now grown somewhat faded with age. The hall was dominated by the open hearth that stood in the centre of the floor beneath an octagonal louvre set in the high timber roof, its beams blackened with soot, to allow the smoke to escape. Around the hearth was a wooden pale, wide enough for several people to sit on and warm themselves; either side of this, a long table had been set beneath the windows, where the undergraduates and junior Fellows now crammed themselves on to benches with frequent glances at the dais, murmuring among themselves about the rector's drawn face and the second empty place at the High Table.

A skinny young man with unkempt red hair, dressed in a gown several sizes too large for him, mounted the lectern that stood beside the High Table and in a voice surprisingly sonorous for his slight frame, began to pronounce Grace. I recognised him as the boy I had watched clearing away the appurtenances of Matins in the chapel the previous day. The solemn tolling of the bell was silenced just as he opened his mouth.

'*Benignissime Pater, qui providentia tua regis,*' he began, as the rector dutifully bowed his head and clasped his hands and the rest of the senior Fellows followed suit. From beneath lowered lids, I noticed that most of the undergraduates were still watching the High Table with a mixture of curiosity and apprehension. '*Liberalitate pascis et benedictione conservas omnia quae creaveris,*' the boy continued, and I noticed with a sudden pitch of relief that Gabriel Norris was seated at the head of one of the long tables among a clutch of other young men whose quality and cut of dress marked them out as separate from their fellow scholars. I did not take seriously Slythurst's suggestion that the instruments of murder pointed to Norris as the killer – it seemed to me rather that the use of his longbow implied his innocence, but at least now I would have the chance to speak to him after the meal. He continued to stare resolutely ahead of him, as if the deference of bowing his head in prayer would be beneath his dignity and it occurred to me that there was something altered in his appearance, though I could not quite put my finger on what it might be. On the far side of the other table, I spotted Thomas Allen, head bent so far that his nose almost touched the table, the clasped hands in front of his face gripping one another so tightly that the knuckles were bone-white.

'*Per Iesum Christum Dominum nostrum, Amen,*' finished the red-haired boy, and a muttered 'Amen' echoed in response from the tables. The rector rose heavily to his feet and a wary silence settled over the hall.

'Gentlemen,' Rector Underhill began, his voice drained of its usual bombast, 'in the life of every Christian man there come times when God, in His divine and infinite wisdom, sees fit to test our poor faith with hardships and sorrows. Just so, in the life of our little Christian community, He has chosen these days to send us painful trials, the better to anchor our faith in His Providence.' He took a deep breath and folded his hands together in front of him in an attitude of humility. 'It grieves me to inform you, gentlemen, so soon after the terrible accident that took the life of our dear sub-rector Doctor Mercer, that a second tragedy has intruded on our poor society. Doctor James Coverdale has been mortally wounded, it would seem in defending the college strongroom from violent robbers.'

He lowered his head; there was a moment's pause before a rumble of whispered speculation erupted into the stillness. The rector did not try to silence them; rather, he waited until the first wave of shock and disbelief had played itself out, then raised a hand, which he held aloft until the murmuring subsided.

'Wagers on who'll be brave enough to be sub-rector next?' Norris whispered to his friend, just loud enough for his voice to carry, and a ripple of tense laughter spread around the undergraduates' tables. The rector cleared his throat sternly.

'If anyone saw anything over the weekend that might have some bearing on this horrible act or could lead to the apprehension of these evil perpetrators, you may leave word at my lodgings,' he announced.

Norris turned back to the rector and raised a hand.

'Rector Underhill – may we know how much was taken from the strongroom?'

The well-dressed young men among whom he sat nodded urgently; I wondered if the gentlemen commoners kept their own private wealth there too under lock and key.

The rector hesitated for a moment.

'Ah – well – it seems that nothing was actually taken, as far as we can tell. It must be that the altercation with Doctor Coverdale frightened the thieves and caused them to take flight.'

'An odd sort of robbery, then,' Norris observed, his words weighted carefully. 'To take a man's life, all for nothing.'

'Indeed, indeed,' said the rector solemnly. 'A terrible waste.'

The meal passed largely in silence among those of us at the High Table, though there was no lack of fevered hypotheses being aired among the junior men seated below us. On my right, Master Godwyn kept his eyes fixed on his plate and said almost nothing, but I noticed that when he lifted his tankard to drink, his hand was trembling like a man with palsy. Slythurst, on my left, occasionally put down his knife to comment between mouthfuls on the lax security that he believed had led to the deaths of his colleagues, as if he did not know very well that in both instances the killer had gained access with a key.

'The college should have a proper watchman on the gate,' he opined loudly, through a mouthful of bread. 'Cobbett is too old and too drunk to be of any use – why, a whole company of armed militia could march straight past his window and he wouldn't notice. As for that aged mutt of his – the college needs a proper guard dog, trained to deter intruders. And the main gate should be locked at all times, so that only those with a key can be admitted.'

'I think, Walter, that a vicious dog is probably not what the college needs at this time,' Godwyn said wearily, raising his head for a moment. 'And we are a community of scholars, not a prison. We cannot lock the world out nor our young men in. Besides, think of the expense in issuing all the under-graduates with keys to the main gate.' He shook his head and seemed to retreat inwards to his own thoughts again.

'Master Slythurst, as bursar you must be frequently burdened with the task of having new keys cut for the various locks about the college?' I said pleasantly, attempting to cut into a slice of boiled mutton.

Slythurst flashed me a furious sideways glance, as if to let me know that he divined my implication, but in the hearing of the other Fellows, he merely said,

'Indeed. It is a considerable expense – people are forever losing or breaking them.'

'And must this onerous duty always fall to you, or do you sometimes charge others with the errand of visiting the lock-smith?' I continued, in the same innocent tone.

'It is a duty I undertake myself,' he replied, his voice tighter now. 'Where the security of the college is concerned, one cannot be too careful.'

'And sometimes, perhaps, it is necessary to make extra copies of keys to certain doors, to keep some in hand against future losses?' I reached out for the jug of beer.

Slythurst scraped his chair back and rose abruptly.

'If you have something you mean to ask of me, Doctor Bruno,' he said, through his teeth, 'have the courtesy to speak frankly. But at least show some discretion – or do you believe you are now made Inquisitor over us?' He turned to his left to include the rector in his furious glare, then pushed roughly behind my chair and, without looking back, strode out of the hall in majestic offence, his gown sweeping behind him. The whispering at the lower tables ceased while intrigued eyes followed Slythurst's progress to the door, before a fresh wave of huddled conversation rippled through their midst.

'What has stung him?' Richard Godwyn asked, looking up from his meat at Slythurst's brusque departure.

'Perhaps he is distressed by the tragic news,' I suggested. Godwyn blinked.

'Who can tell? Men are harder to read than books. Perhaps Walter is plagued by remorse.'

'Remorse?' I asked, concentrating on my plate so as not to betray my interest.

'He and James detested one another,' Godwyn confided, his voice low. 'So perhaps, now that James has died so terribly, Walter regrets the words he can never take back.'

'Why did they hate one another?'

Godwyn sighed and shook his head sadly.

'I never knew. I had the impression that each knew something damaging about the other, and that they were somehow unwillingly bound to one another in secrecy. But of course it is always dangerous to make such a pact with an enemy.'

'Could it be something to do with land leases?' I asked, remembering suddenly the aborted conversation at the rector's dinner on my first night, when Coverdale had insinuated that the bursar was implicated in the rector's deals with Leicester to give away valuable revenues. 'Perhaps Doctor Coverdale knew of some corrupt scheme of that kind?'

Godwyn only turned his large, sad eyes on me slowly.

'I suppose that is possible. I do know that James thought he had reason to distrust Walter – sufficiently to try and persuade the rector that he should not continue in his position.'

'Coverdale had tried to get rid of Slythurst?' I whispered, leaning as far away from the rector as I could.

302

'He told the rector he did not think Walter trustworthy – I know this only because the rector came to ask me my opinion of him. I said I had never found any warmth in the man, but I had no reason to believe he was failing in his duties.'

'And that was Coverdale's suspicion – that he should not be trusted with the college funds?'

'I presume so,' Godwyn said innocently. 'I cannot think what else it might have been.'

'Something to do with his religion, perhaps?'

Godwyn laid a warning hand on my arm then. 'Some questions are best left unspoken, Doctor Bruno. I have no reason to believe Walter Slythurst is anything other than loyal to the English Church. But in any case, he is safe now – the dead take their secrets with them.' He raised his head to the window for a moment, then turned to me, laying down his knife, and dropped his voice even further. 'But this story of robbers in the strongroom – it troubles me greatly.'

'You do not believe it?'

'With anyone else it could be believed, but James, you see – I would not wish to speak ill of a late colleague, but anyone who knew James would tell you he was the most terrible coward. He was the very last man on earth who would take it upon himself to tackle armed thieves single-handed. This is why it seems so – strange.'

'What is your explanation?' I asked, bending my head closer to his.

'I do not know,' he said warily. 'But that is two of us dead in as many days. It is enough to make one afraid.'

I was about to ask who he meant by 'us', when William Bernard leaned around from Godwyn's right and fixed me with his watery eyes.

'You ask a great many questions, Doctor Bruno.'

'Two tragedies in two days, Doctor Bernard – such coincidences provoke many questions, do you not think?' I replied.

'It is obvious. God is punishing the college for her perfidy in religion. He will not be mocked,' Bernard said, in a tone that brooked no argument.

'You mean to imply that Doctor Coverdale needed to be punished?'

Bernard's eyes lit up with anger.

'I imply no such thing, sorcerer. Only that we are all suffering the wrath of God for our disobedience. He is pouring out his judgement upon us, and who can say where His justice will fall next?'

'Where do *you* predict, Doctor Bernard?' I said, leaning closer.

'Enough questions!' Bernard said, banging his bony fist hard on the table so that ale sloshed over the rim of his cup.

'William,' Godwyn said, laying his hand over Bernard's, his tone placatory. Bernard shook him off angrily and retreated into simmering silence.

The rector leaned across on my left, his brow creased.

'Discretion is all, Bruno.' His anxious glance took in the animated talk of the young men at the lower tables. 'Speak to them away from the students. Let us give them no further cause for gossip. The worst of this must be contained for as long as possible.'

He waved a hand then to his right, and the red-haired boy once again mounted the lectern to read a passage from the great copy of the Bishop's Bible tethered there by its brass chain. The lesson was from Ezekiel, but the boy's declamation did little to dampen the conversation among the students; though I could not make out individual discussions, from the pitch of their voices and the brightness of their eyes, it was clear that a second violent death in the college had occasioned more excitement than dread.

After the meal, as the students began to file out, breaching all etiquette I leapt to my feet and pushed my way through to catch up with Gabriel Norris, who was calling out to Thomas Allen to wait for him outside. Norris had just passed through the hall door into the narrow passageway to the courtyard when I reached out and clapped him between the shoulder blades. He gave a sharp howl of pain – quite disproportionate, I thought, since I had only struck him with the flat of my hand, but when he turned I saw that his jaw was clenched tightly as if he were biting back further exclamation. I laid a hand on his arm.

'Forgive me – I did not mean to startle you.'

'Doctor Bruno!' he said, exhaling with forced calm before removing his arm and fastidiously brushing the silk of his sleeve in case I had marked it. 'What must you think of our college – it is becoming quite the charnel-house, is it not? At least you and I cannot blame ourselves for failing to save this life, eh – they have taken my bow, in any case, so I could not have played the hero again. And what *weather*!' he added, with the same inflection, as if the rain and Coverdale's murder were alike examples of everyday vexations. It was then that I realised why he looked different; he appeared to be growing a beard. At least, his handsome face bristled with the growth of a couple of days; fair as he was, his beard grew darker and would soon be thick and full.

'You are growing a beard, Master Norris?' I observed.

'Well, not on purpose,' he said with irritation, rubbing a hand over the stubble on his chin. 'But I have not been able to find my razor these past two days, and I will not trust my chin again to the college barber. He has the finesse to take off a limb on the battlefield, which I believe is where he had his training, but I allowed him to shave me once and I nearly came away without my nose. What say you, Doctor Bruno – will a beard suit me? It looks well enough on you, but you are dark—'

'It is unlucky that you have lost your razor, Master Norris, just after you had Thomas sharpen it for you,' I said evenly, cutting off his prattling. Immediately I felt him tense beside me. When he spoke, his voice was harder, as if he had dropped his dandyish air.

'*What?* Is that a crime now? And what business is it of yours?' He took a step closer so that his face was inches from mine, and there was quiet menace in his voice.

'Peace, Master Norris. I am only enquiring for the rector who might keep weapons in college.'

'A razor is not a weapon,' he said scornfully, then stared at me then for a long moment, and suddenly a light of understanding dawned on his face; he let go of my clothes, still staring but now as if he were looking beyond me, as if an explanation only he could read were inscribed on the wall over my shoulder. 'Do you mean to say Coverdale was killed with such a weapon?'

When I did not answer, he nodded, his face suddenly hard.

'I see. And you have been questioning Thomas about my razor,' he said, his eyes narrowed. 'Well, then, I must speak to Thomas. You may find me in my room later, Bruno, I do not have time to spare now,' he said, dismissing me with a terse nod before bending his head into the rain to cross the courtyard. I was about to follow him when I felt a hand on my own sleeve and turned impatiently to find Lawrence Weston behind me with an eager gleam in his eye. Beside him stood the red-haired boy who had read the lesson at dinner.

'I said I would find him for you, Doctor Bruno, and so I have,' Weston said, with a note of triumph. 'It was Ned, the bible-clerk.' He elbowed the skinny boy forward. I looked blankly from Weston to his friend.

'What was?' I asked.

'*Ned,*' Weston said again, impatiently. 'Who brought the message to Doctor Coverdale during the disputation. You promised me a shilling,' he added accusingly, as if I had already tried to cheat him.

'So I did,' I said, reaching for the purse at my belt. Ned's freckled face stretched in indignation.

'Why should you have a shilling, Weston,' he protested, 'when you don't know a thing about the business?'

'You shall have a shilling too,' I said, to soothe him, wishing I had learned more about the value of these English coins before I started handing them out so freely; I had a feeling I may have set my price too high. 'Well, then? Who asked you to take the message to Doctor Coverdale on Saturday night, to draw him out of the disputation early?'

I realised that in my anticipation I had grasped the boy's shoulders and was half shaking him. He regarded me with a puzzled frown.

'Well – *he* did, sir. Doctor Coverdale, I mean.'

'What? That makes no sense.'

Ned shrugged.

'That's all I know, sir. Before we left college on Saturday night, he cornered me and gave me a groat – he is not so generous as you, sir . . . I mean, *was* not – to call him out of the disputation halfway through, on the pretence of an urgent message.'

'Did he say why?'

Ned shook his head.

'Only that he had to return to college early but he needed an excuse to walk out.'

'He did not say if he was meeting someone?'

Ned wriggled impatiently under my hands.

'He said nothing else, sir. I took my groat and did as I was bid, and that was all I knew of it until just now.' Suddenly his eyes grew large with the drama of the event. 'Do you think that's when they got him, sir, when he came back to college early?'

307

'You didn't see if he met anyone outside the Divinity School after you gave him the message? A man with no ears, perhaps?'

'No, sir, but I know the man you mean,' Ned said, his freckled face lighting up as if he had answered a difficult examination question. 'But it was Master Godwyn was meeting *him* outside the Divinity School, not Doctor Coverdale.'

'Godwyn?' I repeated, uncomprehending.

'Yes, I saw him meet the man you mean, the bookseller Jenkes, outside the Divinity School while I was waiting to give the false message to Doctor Coverdale. But then I followed Doctor Coverdale all the way back to college after that. I thought I'd take the chance to skip off early myself – no offence, sir,' he added, looking suddenly guilty; I shook my head briefly.

'You missed nothing, I assure you. But Coverdale – you saw him go straight to his room?'

'Yes, sir. That's to say, I saw him going into his staircase.'

'And you saw nothing else unusual? No one abroad in the college?'

'No, sir. Only—'

'What?' I asked, my voice rising higher as I shook him urgently.

'Well – I have a room above the library, as I have serving duties there and in the chapel. It's how I pay for my studies, sir,' he explained, a little sheepishly. 'Well, as I was climbing the stairs to my room, I heard voices from behind the door.'

'In the library? Whose voices?'

'I don't know, but I heard a man's voice raised as if he was angry. I couldn't catch the words, though. I just crept past the landing up to my attic as quiet as I could, but they must have heard my tread on the stairs because they fell silent for a moment. Then when I heard the library door close a few minutes later, I tried to look down from my window into the quad to see who it was so I could report them to Master Godwyn.'

'Could it have been Master Godwyn himself, returned early?' I asked.

'I don't know. They both had cloaks on with hoods up, so I couldn't tell.' He shrugged, as if it was of no great interest.

'Thank you, Ned.'

Defeated, I let go of his shoulders and rummaged again in my purse for another shilling. Next time I needed information, I thought, I would remember to make it a groat. Ned snatched it gladly and grinned; as his fist closed around it, I glanced across the courtyard to see Slythurst emerging from the stairway that led to the library and chapel. He shot me a look of pure loathing and hurried through the curtain of rain in the direction of the rector's lodgings. So Godwyn had also left the disputation early, in order to meet Jenkes. Could they have returned to the college together in search of Coverdale? Or might they have had other business in the library, perhaps involving those illegal books?

People continued to shove and press around us as they peered out into the courtyard, trying to decide whether to wait for the rain to ease. I braced myself and skittered across the courtyard into the downpour, weaving around the dispersing crowd of students. Under the tower archway, a small crowd had gathered to watch with interest the arrival of three men in long cloaks and tricorn hats, shaking the water from their shoulders. One carried an official looking staff with a brass carved head, and I supposed these must be the constables and the coroner, come to retrieve the body. Rector Underhill stood behind them, twisting his hands fretfully while Slythurst tried to keep the undergraduates at bay. I wondered if the rector would tell the coroner about the

309

martyrdom of St Sebastian, or leave him to draw his own conclusions.

'*Dio buono, amico mio* – what a day!' exclaimed a voice behind me. I turned to see John Florio pulling a cloak tightly around his shoulders as if preparing to brave the weather. 'You never saw rain like this in Naples, I'll wager?'

'Not even Noah saw rain like this,' I replied grimly, casting a glance heavenwards.

'Are you going out?' he said, taking my arm and fixing me with an oddly expectant look as I followed him through the gate into St Mildred's Lane. 'Perhaps we could walk together,' he went on eagerly, without waiting for an answer, 'I am headed for Catte Street to enquire after some French books I have ordered from a dealer there, and I must say, I will be glad to get away from the college even for an hour, despite this weather. This dreadful attack has left us all quite shaken. Why don't you come with me? His shop would interest you, I think – his real trade is bookbinding, but he has good contacts with printers in France and the Low Countries and there are often interesting imports to be found, obscure texts that you won't find elsewhere, if you can tolerate the man himself.'

We fell into step through the filthy streets, Florio speculating wildly in Italian about the assault on Coverdale, gesticulating with his hands as he talked, while I nodded and murmured agreement in the few pauses he left to draw breath. At the corner of St John Street and Catte Street, I suddenly heard shouting and peals of coarse laughter rang out across the street; we both turned to see a gang of apprentice boys by the Smythgate jostling one another and pointing in delight, jeering and calling out insults. Florio steered me by the elbow away from them as they yelled, 'Papist whoresons! Get out of England!'

'Ignore them,' Florio muttered, quickening his pace as one

of the boys reached down to throw a stone and another spat in our direction. They followed us for a few paces but did not have the nerve for more than shouting and eventually grew bored with their baiting.

'They are not over-fond of foreigners here,' I observed as we ducked gratefully into the scant shelter of the overhanging upper storeys of the houses in Catte Street. Florio gave me a rueful glance.

'It is an excuse to make trouble. To the ignorant, all foreigners are Catholics who want to slaughter them in their beds. I live with this all the time, and I was born here. Forget about it, *amico mio*. Look, we are almost here.'

'What is this book dealer's name?' I asked, though I had already guessed.

'Rowland Jenkes,' Florio called over his shoulder, since there was not room for us to walk two abreast and still have the meagre respite offered by the caves. 'You will hear of him before long, I'm sure. He is greatly reviled in the town – they call him a necromancer – but you know how people gossip. Jenkes will find you books that could not be had without travelling to France yourself – and that is of particular value to me. There are those who would not step foot in his shop and will spread malicious talk about any Fellow who does, but I try to close my ears to all that. I have enough trouble here already as *un inglese italianato,* as you have seen. Here we are,' he finished, pointing to the low shop front where I had seen William Bernard and Jenkes enter the day before. The shutters were open now, but the windows looked no less dark and forbidding.

Florio hesitated, then laid a hand on my arm.

'Forgive me, but before we go in, I must ask you, Doctor Bruno, if you read my note?' he whispered, his eyes bright with urgency and apprehension.

I stared at him, speechless.

'*Your* note?'

'Yes. I left you a note. Did you not receive it?'

'Well – yes, but – I did not realise it came from you.' I was still looking at him with incredulity; if the mysterious letter had come from Florio after all, it could only mean that he had vital information about the killings. Why, then, had he not told someone in authority what he knew? Then I remembered what Thomas Allen had said about the rumours of a government spy in the college; Florio, with his languages and his high-born contacts, would be just the sort of man Walsingham might make use of. Perhaps, then, he was afraid to reveal his cover and had been waiting until he could make contact with Sidney and me. I continued to stare at him, waiting for some further clarification. He looked slightly perplexed.

'Oh. I had thought it would be clear, for obvious reasons. I am sorry for any confusion.'

'But, Florio,' I said, clutching his arm and drawing him in closer; the water from the overhanging timbers above cascaded in sheets to the sodden ground and I had to raise my voice to be heard. 'Why did you not come and speak to me about this in person?'

He lowered his eyes as if abashed.

'It is a delicate matter, Doctor Bruno – I thought it best that I approach it in a more formal manner. One must observe propriety in such things.'

'Propriety be damned, Florio – two men have died and there may be more to follow!'

He looked at first startled, then his expression turned quickly to fear.

'But, Bruno – you think there will be more deaths? What makes you say so?'

'We cannot know, until we learn what links these two victims and discover the killer's motive – do you not agree?

And there I think you have something to tell that could illuminate the matter, am I right?'

Florio stared at me then with a look of utter incomprehension, but before he could reply, the door beside us opened and Rowland Jenkes stood on the threshold of his shop, surveying us with his habitual expression of amused detachment.

'*Buongiorno, signori,*' he said, in that sly, educated accent that so belied his ravaged face, while effecting a little bow that I took to be sarcastic. 'Not the weather to be standing out of doors, Master Florio. Please, come in, and bring your friend.' He moved backwards and made a grandiose gesture with his arm to usher us in. Florio looked at me for a moment longer, then lowered his dripping cloak and stepped inside.

# FOURTEEN

The room we now entered was built below street level, so that we had to descend three stone steps on to flagstones strewn with rushes, which quickly soaked up the rainwater that streamed from our clothes. A low ceiling, ribbed with dark timbers, made the shop feel close and intimate; Florio and I, being short of stature, could stand upright but Jenkes had to hunch his shoulders so as not to clip his head, a posture that gave him a slightly obsequious air, as if he were permanently half-bowing. There was little light in the room, the grimy diamond-paned windows either side of the door admitting scant daylight in this gloomy weather, though a pair of candles burned in a wall-sconce behind the ware-bench opposite the door. They were of good wax, too, as they did not give off the filthy smell of the cheap tallow kind that lit my chamber at Lincoln. In fact, the narrow shop smelled more like home than any place I had been since my arrival in Oxford, for it smelled of books; a warm scent of new leather and paper, and the mustier traces of old vellum and ink, a heady mixture that brought on a sudden pang of nostalgia for the scriptorium at San Domenico Maggiore where I had spent so many hours of my youth.

314

Carved wooden book stacks lined each side of the shop showing the bookbinder's art: each was filled from floor to ceiling with volumes bound in coloured leather and organised according to size, placed with their fore-edge outwards so that the brass clasps glinted under the darting flames of the candles. Along the bench where Jenkes now stood, rubbing his hands and looking from me to Florio with an expression of greedy anticipation, examples of different types of binding and format were ranged, from the old-fashioned wooden boards encased in calfskin that would keep a parchment manuscript from cockling, to the newer Paris bindings of double paste-board for lighter books of paper, that needed no brass clasps but were tied together with leather thongs or ribbons. All were secured, like the books in Lincoln library, by a brass chain attached to a rod running beneath the bench. Behind this bench, opposite the street door, was another door which gave on to a larger interior room, no better lit than this one, which, from the little I could see within, appeared to be the workshop. I thought I glimpsed the shadow of someone moving, out of sight, and supposed that Jenkes must have apprentices at work.

'And this is Signor Filippo Nolano, is it not?' Jenkes greeted me with a feline smile, holding out a surprisingly delicate hand, which I shook with some reluctance, feeling Florio's curious eyes on the side of my face. 'I wondered when we would be seeing you here, after you followed me from the Catherine Wheel the other day.'

'I – that is . . .' I was unsure how to meet this accusation, especially with Florio's amazed stare burning into me.

Jenkes waved his hand as if to dismiss my small offence.

'No matter. But Signor Nolano, I cannot help noticing that our friend here, Signor Florio, seems surprised to hear me address you so. Perhaps he knows you by a different name?' He raised one eyebrow theatrically, steepling his fingertips together. He had a habit of speaking almost without moving his lips, so that every sentence had the air of a confidence that could not quite be spoken aloud.

I looked him in the eye, feeling myself at a disadvantage; not only was I in his shop, soaked to the skin, but he had clearly made it his business to find out about me even as I had thought myself to be tailing him.

'For many years I travelled in places where it was not safe to give one's own name,' I said, setting my shoulders back and attempting to hold myself with some dignity. 'It has become a habit when among strangers, that is all.'

Jenkes smiled.

'A man would go to any lengths to avoid the Inquisition, I am sure, Doctor Bruno.'

I nodded carefully, trying not to betray any surprise. Florio continued to frown, bemused.

'I hope you will not long think of us as strangers. But there are places even in our glorious free realm where a man would do well to watch his words. What drew you to the Catherine Wheel, I wonder?'

I shrugged.

'I was hungry. I saw the sign and went to look for hot food.'

At this, Jenkes threw his head back and guffawed, revealing his crooked teeth.

'You soon learned your lesson there, I think. Though it was mischievous of you to tell young Humphrey that you would not give that food even to your dog.' He stopped laughing just as abruptly as he had begun, leaving a sudden silence hanging in the air.

'You speak Italian?'

'I speak seven languages, Doctor Bruno, though you would not think it to look at me, would you? I do not have the visage of a scholar, I know. But then you know better than

316

to judge a man by his looks. I fancy you are another who is more than he seems. Do you know what they say of me in Oxford?'

'I do not,' I said bluntly. He clearly took pride in his notoriety and I had no wish to flatter his vanity further. I was gratified to see that he looked somewhat disappointed.

'They call me a disciple of the Devil, Bruno,' he informed me, a half smile playing about his thin lips. 'Folk songs are made about me to frighten children. They say I killed three hundred men with a single curse. What do you say to that?'

'I say that gaol fever spreads rapidly in certain conditions,' I replied evenly.

'You are right, of course. But how, then, was I not touched?'

'Evidently you have the constitution of an ox,' I said, glancing at the whorls and knots of scarred skin where his ears had once been. 'You are no more a sorcerer than I am, or Florio here.'

'No more a sorcerer than you?' Jenkes watched me for a moment, then burst into another of his sudden gales of laughter. 'I like your friend, Signor Florio, he is quite the comedian,' he said, with an air of indulgence. Poor Florio seemed uncomfortable with the undercurrent of antagonism between me and Jenkes, and continued to glance nervously between us.

'Have you my Montaigne, Master Jenkes?' he asked mildly. 'I do hope so, for I have come out in this treacherous weather for it.'

'Treacherous indeed,' Jenkes said, sending me the briefest flash of his cryptic smile. 'Two volumes arrived with a cargo at the end of last week, my dear Florio, and despite this apocalyptic weather, the cart made its way through from Plymouth on Saturday. Let it never be said that I disappoint those who place their faith in my abilities. If you will bear with me a moment, I will find them.' He gave another brief

317

bow, and keeping his head low, ducked through the doorway into the workshop behind him.

Florio turned to me.

'I must beg from you an oath of secrecy, Bruno,' he whispered, laying a hand on my arm, his eyes wide and earnest. I nodded breathlessly, thinking he was still referring to the matter of his note, in which we had been interrupted.

'I have decided to take upon myself a great and solemn task, which will commit my name to posterity as well as that of the great humanist genius I serve – a far greater work, I may say, than my own silly collections of proverbs could ever be.' He clutched my sleeve tighter, his eyes shining. 'I am going to bring the essays of Michel de Montaigne to English readers!'

'Does he know?' I asked.

He lowered his gaze, somewhat subdued.

'I have written to the great man proposing my humble services as his translator, but as yet I do not have his imprimatur, it is true,' he said. 'I have asked Master Jenkes to order the French editions for me so that I could send Monsieur de Montaigne a sample, in the hope of winning his approval. But as I'm sure you can imagine, until it is complete, this is a labour of love that will be both time-consuming and expensive, and so you understand now why I had to write to you as I did—'

'Any book you desire, from any country – just ask Rowland Jenkes, and if I cannot find it, it does not exist,' Jenkes announced, springing from the shadows like a showman and holding up a slim volume in each hand, each bound in dun calfskin and tied with leather strings. He fixed me with a conspiratorial eye. '*Any* book, Doctor Bruno, for the right price.' His eyes wandered pointedly to my belt, where Walsingham's purse was hidden beneath my jerkin. I made no move to acknowledge the look, but I felt suddenly exposed;

he already seemed to know more about me than I would have credited, and I wondered if his source was Bernard.

He handed the volumes to Florio, who cradled one in the crook of each arm and looked down at them as lovingly as if they were newborn twins.

'You bring in a good many books from the Low Countries, then?' I asked, as casually as I could.

'France, the Low Countries – Spain and Italy sometimes, if there is demand. There are many in Oxford who crave certain material that cannot be got except from abroad. And occasionally the opportunity to traffic the other way arises too.' He continued to level at me the same half-meaningful, half-mocking stare, as if appraising me for some employment. 'But I expect you have heard that already, Bruno. Perhaps that explains why you followed me?'

I did not reply; Florio had begun hopping from one foot to the other in agitation, his face pent-up as if he might burst into tears at any moment.

'Whatever is the matter, my dear Florio?' Jenkes asked.

'I – it is only that I did not expect two volumes at once, Master Jenkes, and I fear I cannot – that is, I may need to leave one in your care for a month or two, though I beg you not to sell it, for I will have the money eventually, but—'

Jenkes waved the apology aside.

'I have not the space for unclaimed books, Florio – better you take both now and pay me when you can.'

Florio's face lit up with the surprise of a child given sweetmeats.

'Thank you, Master Jenkes – I assure you that you will not have to wait long for your payment, especially if certain developments unfold as I hope.' Here he threw me an encouraging glance, as if to imply that I understood his meaning; he was mistaken, however, for I remained in the dark. If this was a reference to his enigmatic note, did he mean to imply that he hoped to profit from the deaths at Lincoln? I could only stare blankly at him in response as he fumbled at his belt for the coins he had brought.

'Well, then, Bruno – our business is done,' he said, when the payment had been made and his new purchases wrapped carefully in oilskin against the weather. 'Shall we brave the flood once more?'

'A moment, please,' Jenkes intervened, as I turned to look at the torrents still sluicing down the window panes. The sky seemed to have grown even darker. 'I would not wish to detain you longer, Master Florio, but there are matters of business I would discuss with Doctor Bruno, if he could spare me a moment of his time?' He raised the snaking eyebrow again to convey that he meant more than he was willing to say in front of Florio, who hesitated briefly, then appeared to remember the generous credit Jenkes had just extended and decided to take the hint.

'Of course – I must be back at college in any case. Doctor Bruno – if we do not drown on the journey, shall we speak further this evening?'

I nodded; Florio clutched his parcel closer to his chest, pulled up the hood of his cloak and, with a final meaningful glance at me, stepped out into the downpour.

Left alone in the small shop with Jenkes, I shuddered involuntarily as the door banged shut behind Florio; the draught had chilled me in my wet clothes, but not as much as the intense stare the bookbinder now turned on me in the wavering shadows of the candles.

'Come – you will catch a fever standing there and the world will say I cursed you,' he said with a dry smile, gesturing for me to pass through the door behind the ware-bench. 'In here we may speak freely, Doctor Bruno, and you may warm yourself. I will heat some sweet wine.' He crossed to the street door, took a ring of keys from his belt, and locked it.

Seeing me hesitate, he turned back, one hand on the door jamb. 'You may watch me drink it first, if you prefer. But I thought you did not believe in my diabolical powers?'

The watchful glint in his eye was momentarily displaced by self-mockery; despite myself, I returned his smile and followed him as he ducked through the doorway into the back room. Perhaps I should have been more apprehensive, but though I did not believe the superstitious gossip about the Black Assizes, I found something mesmerising about Rowland Jenkes; so much so that I was willing to be locked into a room alone with him in the hope of learning more about him. But we were not alone. As I crossed the threshold, from the corner of my eye, I caught the movement of a shadow; there, by a fire that blazed in a hearth on the left-hand wall, stood Doctor William Bernard, his thin arms folded across his chest.

'My workshop – and you are acquainted with Doctor Bernard, of course,' Jenkes said, taking in the room with a sweeping gesture and paying Bernard no more heed than if he were one of the fittings. Along three walls, long benches lay covered with quires and manuscripts in various states of disrepair; portions of leather, calfskin and cloth were spread out with patterns marked for cutting. Some books were being fitted for linen chemises, outer covers to keep the calfskin bindings clean, while others were halfway through having new brass bosses and cornerpieces fitted to cover frayed or damaged edges. Some of the manuscripts that caught my eye appeared to be of great antiquity, the bookbinder's skill now preserving and renewing them, ready to continue their journey through the world for the coming generations. In the corner opposite the hearth, two large iron-bound chests stood at right angles to one another, both heavily padlocked.

'You have business with a number of the Lincoln College Fellows, I see,' I remarked, nodding a greeting to Bernard.

'I am a bookbinder and stationer, Doctor Bruno, of course I have business with the doctors of the university. How else should I make my living?'

'Master Godwyn, the librarian of Lincoln – he is a customer of yours too?'

'Of course,' Jenkes replied smoothly, his strange translucent eyes never leaving mine. 'I am often charged with repairing the books of his collection when need arises.'

'And James Coverdale?'

Jenkes exchanged a glance with Bernard.

'Ah, yes. Poor Doctor Coverdale. William was just telling me he had been the victim of a violent assault. To think of such things happening in Oxford.' He pressed a hand to his chest and shook his head ruefully; there was something in his manner that suggested he was mocking me. I wanted to ask further about his connections with Godwyn and Coverdale but Bernard's hawk-like glare made me hesitate.

'Here is a sight to make your heart bleed, Doctor Bruno,' Jenkes said, turning aside and lifting a small volume from one of the benches, which he placed into my hands. It was a little Book of Hours in the French style from the beginning of the century, and had clearly once been an expensive piece; gingerly I turned over a few pages to reveal richly coloured illuminations in cobalts and crimsons and golds, the borders of each page of text decorated with intricate tracings of leaves, flowers and butterflies against a background of primrose yellow.

'Here.' Jenkes took the book from my hand and opened it at a page where both the text and the facing picture had been attacked with a sharp implement, perhaps a knife or a stone, in an attempt to erase them from the vellum. The illumination remained almost intact, showing a kneeling St Thomas Becket being stabbed at the altar with only his face blanked out; the accompanying prayer had been scrubbed to a ghostly trace. 'Criminal, isn't it?' Jenkes remarked. 'The edict was King Henry's, near fifty years ago now, but these come into my hands quite often, with all the saints and indulgences obediently cut or rubbed away. If I can restore it, this will fetch a good price in France. Good French workmanship, you see? God's death, I hate to see a book violated like that, at the whim of a heretic prince! Father to another heretic bastard.' His lip curled back as he said this, revealing his brown teeth, but his long white fingers stroked the page as if comforting it. This display of sentiment towards his books did nothing to make Jenkes more appealing.

'Will you report me now for seditious words, Doctor Bruno?' He smiled his thin smile, his eyes never leaving mine. 'I have no more ears to lose, as you see.'

'I will not report any man for his words,' I said evenly, meeting his gaze to show him I was unafraid. 'I came to your country to think and speak and write freely – I assume every citizen here wishes the same.'

'But to write freely about what?' Bernard unpeeled himself from the wall by the fire, unfolding his arms and peering at me with his faded eyes.

'About anything I choose,' I replied, turning to face him. 'That is what freedom means, does it not?'

Jenkes was carefully replacing the Book of Hours on the work bench beside the small knives and implements he would need for its restoration. It occurred to me, watching the neat, almost obsessive way that he laid out his tools, that a bookbinder's knife would certainly be sharp enough to cut a man's throat.

'Do you send many books to sell in Europe?' I asked, indicating the Book of Hours and trying to keep my voice casual. Jenkes missed nothing; he looked up sharply, then exchanged a glance with Bernard.

'It sometimes happens that books fall into my hands which

could see a man condemned to prison or worse in this country,' he said, rubbing the edge of his thumb along his lower lip. 'Then I can find a ready market overseas. But in truth there is no shortage of customers in Oxfordshire and London. Men like yourself, who do not accept the prohibition of books, who believe God gave us reason and judgement to weigh what we read, and who are willing to run the risk for the sake of knowledge.' He gave a soft laugh and raised his head again to look across at Bernard. 'You were right, William. Doctor Bernard told me you had a special interest in rare books. Especially those believed lost.'

Bernard had resumed his stance by the fire and remained motionless, merely offering the briefest of tight-lipped smiles. Of course: Bernard had been the Lincoln College librarian during the great purge of the Oxford libraries, when the authorities had tried to banish all heretical texts from the reach of impressionable young men, just as my abbot had at San Domenico.

'I sense there is something you wish to ask, Doctor Bruno?' Jenkes said, cocking his head.

'The books purged from the college libraries – did they pass through your hands?'

'Many of them, yes.' Jenkes glanced at Bernard briefly, then leaned back against his work bench and folded his hands together. 'Some of the more zealous librarians burned the offending material to please the Visitors, but those with more regard for the value of books brought them to me to redistribute.'

I looked across to Bernard, who remained motionless.

'And the books culled from Lincoln in the great purge – did those volumes come to you?'

'I remember every book that passes through my hands, Doctor Bruno. You look sceptical, but I assure you that I do not make idle boasts. When you heard me tell Signor Florio

324

I could procure any book for the right price, that was also the truth.' His eyes darted hungrily again to the purse at my belt, and this time my hand moved instinctively to cover it, as if I were naked and covering my privates. 'Tell me, then, is there a particular book you have in mind?'

He was toying with me, and his repeated allusions to the money I carried made me suddenly uncomfortable; I cursed myself for not having been more discreet with Walsingham's purse about the college. Well – I had allowed him to lock me inside his shop, so if he meant to rob me, there was little I could do except stand and fight; I checked the work bench beside me to see how quickly I could grab for one of the knives if the need arose. As if reading my thoughts, Jenkes casually reached out and picked up a silver-handled blade and began picking the dirt from under his fingernails with its point.

'You need have no fear of speaking here, Bruno – whatever the title, however dangerous the civil authorities or the Church, whichever Church, deem it to be, you cannot shock me.'

'You do not believe in the idea of heresy, then?' I asked, keeping my eyes on the knife in his hand.

'Oh, you mistake me,' he said, taking a step towards me so suddenly that I involuntarily stepped back, alarmed at the flash of menace in those strange luminous eyes. 'I believe in it without question. There is absolute truth, and all else is heresy. There is the true Church, founded by God's Son upon the apostle Peter, and then there is the blasphemous abomination founded by a fat, crippled fornicator who could not keep his cock in his breeches, and which is now ruled by his heretic bastard. I do not believe that any book should be denied to the man who possesses the wisdom to understand it, Bruno, but that does not mean I am confused about where truth lies. The question is – are you?'

'I do not understand your meaning,' I said, but my shoulders tensed.

325

'I think you do,' he said, his voice light and pleasant but his eyes still steely, and he moved slowly to position himself between me and the door to the shop. Sweat prickled in my armpits despite the chill of my clothes; I glanced across at Bernard, who stood impervious by the fire as if he were not a part of the scene playing out before him. Draped in his long, black gown, with his thin neck and loose skin, he had the air of a great bird of prey, waiting to see what he might scavenge once the dust had settled.

'I wish only to know whose side you are on, Bruno,' Jenkes continued.

'I was not aware that I was required to choose a side,' I replied, turning to face him. 'Perhaps I find the idea altogether too simplistic.'

He barked out that sudden laugh again; the sound echoed from the walls.

'Is that what you will tell the recording angel on the Day of Judgement? When the Son of Man returns to divide the sheep from the goats, will you protest that you did not care to be either, that you found the choice *too simplistic?*' Abruptly he cast the knife away from him; it landed with a clatter among the paraphernalia laid out on the bench, and he stepped closer, laying a hand gently on my shoulder. I braced myself, but did not move. 'You are a conundrum, Doctor Bruno, do you know that?' His limpid eyes raked over my face repeatedly, as though by this he might decode the puzzle. 'You are excommunicate, yet you have the patronage of a Catholic monarch. You reject the supreme authority of the pope and preach the heretical theories of the Pole Copernicus, yet I am told you publicly declare yourself a Catholic. What *is* your faith, Bruno?'

I looked him in the eye. 'I am a son of the Roman Church, Master Jenkes. You must be the only man in Oxford who doubts my religion – your fellow townsmen cross the street for the chance to spit upon me.'

'Do you attend Mass and confession?'

'Am I on trial here? Are you my Inquisitor?'

He merely continued his stony gaze, though his mouth twisted slightly with contempt. I sighed.

'Yes, I attend Mass.'

'Yet you travel in the company of Sir Philip Sidney, a lapdog to the bastard Elizabeth and an agitator against the Catholic cause.'

'As does the Palatine Laski. Do you also question his religion?'

'Laski is a prince,' Jenkes said impatiently. 'You are a runaway monk, a philosopher-for-hire – though evidently a successful one, given the amount of money I am told you flaunt around the town,' he added, his eyes again straying to my purse. 'How did you find your way into the company of men like Sidney? Did he or his friends seek you out?'

'I met him in Padua. He is a fellow writer. What is it you accuse me of, Jenkes?' I was growing tired of this game; only the possibility that Jenkes knew something about Dean Flemyng's books and might have seen the lost treatise of the Greek Hermetic manuscript, the book Ficino would not translate, kept me from forcing my way out.

'I accuse you of nothing,' he said, patting my shoulder reassuringly, his manner immediately changed. 'But I thought you more than anyone would understand that a man must know to whom he speaks before he speaks too freely. My friends and I are not used to seeing strangers at the Catherine Wheel inn, particularly not those who travel with a royal visitation and offer up false names – naturally, it makes us curious. So I will ask you again: what brought you there?'

I hesitated; if I could persuade Jenkes of my sincerity, it

was possible that he would open to me the secret world of the Oxford Catholics, whose contacts with the seminaries in Europe and knowledge of the English mission would be worth more than gold to Walsingham. Yet I sensed that if Jenkes even suspected that I had deceived him, he would despatch me with far less artistry than the Lincoln College killer had displayed.

'I was told it was a place one might go to meet – like-minded people,' I said quietly.

Jenkes nodded encouragingly.

'Told by whom?'

'A contact.'

'In London or Oxford? Or abroad?'

'Oxford,' I said, without a pause.

'His name? Or hers,' he added, as an afterthought.

'I prefer not to say.'

'Then how am I to know you are not lying to me, Bruno?' he asked, his face now inches from mine, so that all his pox scars seemed magnified.

'He grew quickly intimate with young Allen, as I told you – they were seen together this morning at the Flower de Luce,' Bernard interjected from the other side of the room. Jenkes narrowed his eyes; I could almost see his calculations as he weighed this news.

'So Thomas Allen has been sharing his confidences with you, has he? I fear he may give you a bad impression of our little group, Bruno – was it he who directed you to us?'

Realising that Thomas could be in danger if Jenkes believed he had been telling me Edmund Allen's secrets, I knew I had to deny his involvement, even though I had no idea what effect my next words would have on the two men now watching me.

'It was not Thomas who suggested I visit the Catherine Wheel,' I said. 'It was Roger Mercer.'

Jenkes frowned, letting go of my shoulder. He seemed genuinely wrong-footed.

'Mercer?'

'It is true that I saw deep him in conversation with Mercer in the courtyard, the night before Roger died,' Bernard confirmed. 'I was watching from my window.'

'How did the Catherine Wheel enter your conversation?' Jenkes asked, pointing a long finger into my face.

I raised a hand and gently moved his finger aside before speaking.

'I asked if he knew of any place in Oxford where I might hear Mass said.'

'You just asked? And he sent you to the Catherine Wheel, just like that?' Jenkes looked as though he could not decide whether to be incredulous or furious; he twisted his hands together until the knuckles cracked.

'He suggested I would find friends there, but that I should exercise discretion,' I said.

'Discretion – as if he knew the meaning of the word! He was ever a damnable fool. His loose tongue would have seen us all dead eventually. To tell a stranger, William, and one who travels with a royal party – can you credit it?' Jenkes wiped his brow with the back of his hand. 'Though I was sorry to hear of his cruel death, of course.'

'It hardly matters now,' Bernard said, before piously adding, 'God have mercy on his soul.'

Jenkes gave me another long, hard look, then appeared to decide in my favour.

'Well, then, Doctor Bruno – let poor Mercer be proved right. You have found yourself among friends. Come tonight – be there at half-past midnight. Use the rear door, through the inn yard, not the street door. Humphrey will be there – say the password and he will admit you. Wear a cloak with a hood, keep it drawn over your face and take care you are not followed.'

'Will there not be watchmen at the North Gate? Surely they will want to know my business at that hour.'

'Give them a groat and they will not give two shits for your business,' he said, his eyes flicking again to my belt. 'But have a care for your purse walking the streets so late. Have you a weapon?'

I replied that I did not carry one. He picked up the little silver-handled knife from the work bench and held it out to me.

'Take it for tonight. It is only small but it cuts through leather well enough, I am sure it could do some damage if you were set upon. Better than an empty scabbard, anyway.'

'Thank you – but in any case I will not need my purse for such a meeting, will I?' I replied.

'Oh, but you must bring your purse tonight,' Jenkes said, his expression suddenly concerned; seeing my look of suspicion, he leaned in with a sly smile. 'For I do not give away my books for nothing, Doctor Bruno, not even to my brother Catholics.'

My heart quickened.

'Books?'

'You are interested in a book, are you not? A Greek book, brought out of Florence by Dean Flemyng a century ago, bequeathed to the library of Lincoln College, removed by our friend Doctor Bernard here during the purge by the Royal Commission of '69. Am I correct?'

'Do you have this book?' I whispered, hardly daring to breathe.

He replied with the same slow, infuriating smile.

'I do not have it here. But I have held it in my hands, and I can direct you to it. I'm sure we can work out an arrangement that will suit us both, Doctor Bruno. Be sure to bring your purse.'

'You said the book did not exist,' I said, turning to Bernard with a note of triumph.

'I said so for the sake of those fools gathered around the rector's table that night,' he said dismissively. 'It would have raised too many questions. Underhill is a puppet of the chancellor and the Privy Council – he would not know the value of such a book, but I did not wish to awaken his old anxieties. If he had his way, he would purge the library until there was nothing left upon the lecterns but the Bishop's Bible and the volumes of Master Foxe.' For a moment I thought Bernard might spit on the floor, so bitter was the contempt in his voice as he spoke the name, but he restrained himself. I wondered what Jenkes had meant when he said that Mercer's loose tongue would have had them all killed?

'We must not detain you any longer, Doctor Bruno,' Jenkes said, turning back towards the shop and reaching for the keys at his belt. 'You will be wanting to catch up with your friend Florio. By the way – it goes without saying that you do not breathe a word of our conversation to anyone. I am the only one who can tell you who to trust in this town where matters of religion are concerned. You understand the dangers, I'm sure.'

I nodded, as he unlocked the door to the street and I saw with some relief that the rain had finally begun to thin.

I turned back to see him standing in the doorway, arms folded across his chest, with an air of satisfaction.

'And the book?'

'I will tell you all about the book when we next meet.'

'You have forgotten one thing,' I said, in a low voice. 'The password.'

Jenkes's pitted face creased into a lop-sided smile.

'Why, you have already been told, Doctor Bruno,' he whispered, before mouthing the words, '*Ora pro nobis.*'

# FIFTEEN

A chill wind chivvied the dark rain-clouds in drifts across the sky, revealing a higher layer of pearl-grey cloud as the rain thinned and finally ceased altogether. I walked through the muddy lanes back to Lincoln barely aware any longer of my damp clothes chafing at my skin, my head caught up in whirling thoughts. As I passed under the tower archway I heard the bell tolling its melancholy summons to Evensong, but I was unprepared for the sight that greeted me as I emerged into the quadrangle. Groups of students and Fellows stood huddled together around the entrance to the staircase that led to the library and the chapel, staring up at the windows, all seemingly transfixed by something. An eerie silence hung over the quadrangle, the men gathered there exchanging only muted whispers and frozen glances. The air was taut with unspoken fear. I slowed my steps and approached the nearest knot of students to find out the reason for this sombre congregation, when Richard Godwyn pushed his way through to greet me unsmiling, relief etched on his face.

'Doctor Bruno, the rector has been asking for you,' he said in a low voice. 'Come.'

Taking me by the elbow, he guided me through the staring crowd to the entrance that led up to the library and chapel. At the foot of the stairs stood the stocky kitchen servant who had been set to guard the stairway to Coverdale's room earlier; he glanced at us and nodded brusquely. Godwyn led the way up to the chapel and tapped gently on the door with his knuckles; it was opened immediately by Slythurst, who scowled at me, but stepped aside to let me pass through. Instantly, I recognised the smell of blood. Rector Underhill rose from one of the wooden benches nearest the door and clasped my wrists with both hands, staring into my eyes with desperation, his own red-rimmed above sunken cheeks.

'God is punishing us, Bruno,' he whispered, his voice cracked. 'He is heaping burning coals on my head for my sins of omission. Even here, in our consecrated chapel.' He stepped aside, his grip still tight around my wrist, and I witnessed the cause of the rector's latest distress. At the foot of the small altar a body lay slumped. I stepped slowly closer; blood was spattered across the rushes on the floor and up the white altar cloth and even from the other end of the chapel I could see that the body had a shock of red hair.

'Nothing has been touched,' the rector croaked. 'I wanted you to see. I came into the chapel just before five to prepare for Evensong and found . . .' his voice trembled and he sat back down heavily on a nearby bench.

I knelt by the body, my teeth tightly clenched. Ned, the young bible-clerk, lay on his back in his shirt and breeches, his eyes bulging unnaturally wide and protruding towards the ceiling in a fixed expression of terror. It took a moment before I realised why his stare was so hideous: his eyelids had been cut off. I bent closer, holding my breath in disbelief. This was not the only mutilation of the boy's face; a wide gash had been cut down both cheeks, so deeply that the blade appeared to have pierced right through his face, and his mouth was swollen and bloodied, thick rivulets of blood coating his downy chin. The boy had barely been old enough to shave.

'The altar,' Underhill whispered, nodding me towards it.

I looked up and recoiled instantly; a dark red fleshy lump sat in the centre of the altar, blood seeping from it to form an ugly stain on the white cloth.

'Oh, God,' I breathed, for I knew what I was looking at. Gingerly I prised Ned's lower jaw downwards to reveal the stump of his tongue. The movement unleashed a fresh flow of blood down his chin and I jumped back instinctively, though I knew he could not possibly be alive.

'This happened very recently,' I observed, turning to the rector. He nodded, passing his hands over his face.

'Ned came every day at around four to make the chapel ready for Evensong at five,' he said, his voice still barely audible. 'That is the bible-clerk's principle duty. Anyone would have known to find him here. The chapel is not kept locked. They must have hidden and waited for him. Poor boy.' He shook his head. 'But you see what they have done to him, Bruno?'

He looked up at me expectantly.

'Foxe again?'

He gave a brief nod.

'I believe it is meant to be Romanus. His martyrdom comes in Book One of Foxe, just after the story of St Alban that I recounted in chapel yesterday. Romanus's torturers mutilated him to stop him singing hymns, but when they cut wounds in his face, he thanked them for opening many more mouths with which to praise God.'

'They always had a ready wit, these saints,' I said grimly.

'So they cut out his tongue. Eventually they strangled him.' Underhill made a strange noise like a hiccup, and clamped a hand over his mouth.

I loosened the cloth of Ned's shirt that had bunched up around his neck; sure enough, his pale flesh was marked with dark bruises where fingers had gripped his throat.

'They cut out his tongue to silence him,' I mused, half to myself. Only a few hours earlier, Ned had told me what he had seen on Saturday evening. Had he died for that? I cast my mind back to our encounter after dinner on the way out of the Great Hall. Who could have overheard our conversation? Lawrence Weston? But the passageway had been thronged with students and Fellows sheltering from the rain; any one of them might have seen me handing Ned the shilling he never even got to spend. The idea that I might unwittingly have called down this vengeance on the poor boy seized me with horror for a moment, but my thoughts were interrupted by an impatient cough.

'Now that Doctor Bruno has been good enough to give us his expert verdict,' Slythurst said, his voice chilly with disdain, 'perhaps I should alert the constables, Rector? Whoever did this cannot have got far in so short a time – if they put out the hue and cry now—'

'He is most likely still here in the college,' I said, turning to the rector. 'If he is, he will barely have had time to wash the blood from his hands – you must gather the whole community in the Great Hall at once. Someone must have seen something.'

The rector nodded and turned to Slythurst.

'Walter – go down and call all the students and Fellows together as Doctor Bruno suggests,' he instructed. 'Make sure everyone is present and comes just as he is – knock on every door, drag men from their rooms if you have to.'

Slythurst gave me one of his furious glares, but turned on his heel and left the chapel.

'What did you do after you found the body?' I asked.

'I – I cried out for help – I could not think clearly,' he

stammered. 'Richard was in the library and came running across. Then I stayed with the body and he went to find Walter.'

'You were in the library all the time?' I asked, turning to Godwyn, who was still standing by the door in a state of some agitation.

'Well, yes,' he said, somewhat defensively, 'I was working there all afternoon.'

I stared at him in disbelief.

'And you heard nothing? While a boy was murdered just across the landing?'

'The doors of the library and the chapel are both solid oak, Doctor Bruno,' Godwyn said, his voice rising in protest. 'I heard footsteps on the stairs earlier but I did not think that unusual. But I didn't hear a voice until Rector Underhill opened the chapel door and called out.'

I looked back at the body.

'I suppose if someone lay in wait and surprised him, they could have strangled him before he had much of a chance to fight back or cry out.' The thought offered a degree of comfort, but still I regarded Godwyn with suspicion. Did he know Ned had seen him meeting Jenkes outside the Divinity School?

'Then he would have been dead before all this . . . ?' the rector gestured to the boy's mutilated face.

'Let us hope so,' I muttered, rising to my feet.

'But *Ned*,' Godwyn said, looking down at the battered corpse, his brow crumpled as if the scene somehow did not make sense to him. 'Why *Ned*?' He shook his head as if that might rid him of his confusion. I suddenly recalled something that Ned had told me in our fateful conversation earlier.

'Did Ned undertake duties in the library as well as the chapel?' I asked.

Godwyn turned and looked at me sharply.

'Sometimes he helped me out with small tasks,' he said, his eyes guarded. 'Matters of tidying and upkeep, generally – he did not handle the books. Why do you ask?'

'Master Godwyn,' I said, 'someone was in the library on Saturday evening, while most of the college was out at the disputation, the evening James Coverdale was murdered. Ned heard them, but he didn't know who it was.'

Godwyn bit the knuckle of his thumb and regarded me anxiously.

'Well, as I have told you, the Fellows all have their own keys. I suppose it is possible that someone came back early, but I have no idea. Or else . . .' he shot a furtive glance at the rector and allowed his sentence to tail away. I recalled what he had told me about Sophia using her father's key to access the library. Ned said he had heard a man's voice raised in anger, but who was that man speaking to? Godwyn's composure was clearly affected; I could not help wondering if Ned, in the course of his library duties, might have stumbled across Godwyn's cache of illegal Catholic books.

'And you?' I asked, looking him directly in the eye. 'You did not see anyone when you returned early?'

'I?' Godwyn looked away, his large drooping eyes assuming a hurt expression. 'I was at the disputation, Doctor Bruno.' He shifted uncomfortably and folded his arms across his chest.

'But you left early to meet someone, I understand.'

The rector looked up, mild surprise displacing the expression of weary despair on his face for a moment. Godwyn coloured violently and did not try to maintain his lie.

'It's true – I slipped out at the beginning on a matter of personal business,' he added, his voice growing strained. 'Nothing to do with the college. But I did not return until

337

just before six, when I found the library locked and empty, just as I had left it. That is the truth, before God, I swear it.'

I looked at Godwyn's hands as he twisted them together, folding and unfolding his fingers. Broad hands, stained at the fingertips with ink, though not, as far as I could see, with blood. The rector looked from me to Godwyn as if he didn't know what to believe any more.

'Wait – what is that?' A heap of something dark had caught my eye by the foot of the altar. I bent to examine it; on closer inspection it appeared to be a pile of folded black cloth. Lifting it gingerly by one corner between my finger and thumb, I saw that it was a scholar's gown, frayed in the sleeves and sticky with fresh blood.

'This trick again,' I said, holding the gown up to show the rector. 'This must be Ned's gown. He puts his victims' gowns on over his own clothes so that he can walk away without any noticeable trace of blood on him.'

The door creaked open and the three of us jumped, made skittish by our proximity to murder. Slythurst's face appeared in the gap.

'The college is assembled in Hall, Rector, whenever you are ready, though I'm afraid not everyone is accounted for.' He glanced at me. 'I cannot find William Bernard. Gabriel Norris and Thomas Allen do not appear to be in their room either. And John Florio has not been seen since this afternoon.'

The rector nodded and rose heavily to his feet.

'Go on ahead, Walter, and you, Richard,' he said. 'I will be with you in a few moments. After I have spoken to the men I am going to impose a curfew. Everyone to remain in his rooms this evening, until we have had a chance to search the college.'

'Guests included, I presume?' Slythurst said, wrapping his arms around his torso.

'Everyone,' said the rector firmly. 'Now, I would have a word with Doctor Bruno alone.'

Reluctantly, Slythurst followed Godwyn through the door. Underhill turned to face me, slowly, as if the effort cost him dearly, and I saw utter desolation inscribed in the lines of his face.

'My daughter has not yet come home, Bruno.'

There was such finality in his voice that I too felt momentarily as though I would buckle under his despair, but I shook my head.

'Perhaps she has gone to the house of a friend. Is there no one you can think of?'

He passed both hands over his face very slowly, then raised his eyes to mine.

'Sophia did not have friends in the usual way. She refused the company of other young ladies of her age. If you had asked me a few days ago about her friends, I would have answered that she had none I could name. But now . . .' He broke off and turned back to the window, as if something were luring him through the glass.

'Now what? You have discovered something?'

'I have been blind, Bruno. I failed both my children, just as I have failed the college.'

Though I could not help feeling that this was probably true, the sight of the man's distress moved me to cross the room and lay a hand on his shoulder.

'You cannot blame yourself for these deaths. And Sophia will be found safe and well, you will see – even if I have to ride all night myself to find her.'

I had not meant to speak with quite so much passion; Underhill looked up at me with mild curiosity before the expression of misery returned.

'It is kind of you to say so,' he said, patting the hand I had placed on his shoulder as if to thank me for the gesture.

'But you are wrong. When she did not return this afternoon I made a search of her room. Sewn into her mattress, I found this.'

He reached inside his doublet and retrieved a small book with a worn leather cover, which he handed to me. I flicked through a few pages and saw at once that it was a little·Book of Hours, similar to the one I had seen in Jenkes's workshop, of a comparable age and workmanship though smaller and plainer. The pages were in good condition, and I could not see that any of the images of the saints or indulgences had been defaced. My heart grew heavier. For Sophia to have such an obviously Catholic book in her possession, guarded closely from her parents, could only signify one thing.

'Look at the flyleaf,' Underhill said, nodding towards the book.

I turned to the inside front cover. On the flyleaf was a handwritten dedication of a verse from the Bible: *For wisdom is more precious than rubies, and nothing you desire can compare with her.* Beneath this, the inscription read, in an elaborate, curlicued hand, *Ora pro nobis. Yours in Christ, J.*

Underhill watched me expectantly.

'The verse is from Proverbs, is it not?' I said.

'Do you not see?' he burst out, impatiently. 'What is the Greek for wisdom? *Sophia!* A papist prayer book, with a dedication written for her. They have converted her, right under my nose, while I buried myself in my Foxe and strove to keep the peace here for Leicester!' He shook his head again and looked at the floor.

'Rector Underhill – *who* has converted her?' I said sharply. 'Who is this J – do you know? Who are you protecting?'

'No one but myself,' he said sorrowfully, in a voice barely audible. 'And my family – or so I thought. I could not have believed it would come to this.'

Jenkes, I thought grimly. Only he could have got his hands

on such a beautiful French Book of Hours, and he had all but given himself away with his initial. I felt my hands clench around the book as I read the dedication again; the biblical verse was innocent enough, but there was something unpleasantly lascivious in the implication, if you substituted Sophia's name for the word 'wisdom'. The thought of Jenkes, with his pitted face and his scarred, earless head, giving Sophia such a private, intimate gift – which did indeed imply that she shared some sympathy for his faith – made my teeth clench. Then another thought struck me, freezing my heart for a moment: what if Jenkes was the danger of which she had spoken? What if she had been involved with him in some way and he had ended up threatening her? And was any of this connected to the mutilated corpse lying at the foot of the altar? My hand strayed to my belt, where I had tucked the little silver-handled knife he had given me. That night, I determined, I would have the truth from Jenkes, even if it meant he had to find himself on the wrong end of his own weapon. Underhill was looking up at me with sad, expectant eyes, as if waiting for me to prescribe a course of action.

'Was James Coverdale a Catholic?' I asked abruptly.

Underhill squeezed his hands together and nodded.

'And you knew? Was that why you could not leave the sign of the Catherine Wheel there for the coroner to see?'

The rector struggled with a sigh so great it threatened to burst his ribs, then looked at me with something like resignation.

'I have always believed that if a man can hold his faith privately without it touching his politics or his work, that is a matter between him and God. I fear that is not a view held by many on the Privy Council, but I flatter myself it is closer to Her Majesty's own feelings.' He leaned in towards me and lowered his voice. 'But the rules are changing. Lord Burghley every day introduces new legislation regarding Catholics, so that it is now an offence to withhold information about known papists. A man can lose his property or find himself in gaol simply for failing to tell the authorities what he knows about his neighbours or colleagues, and everyone lives in fear of his friends.' He shivered, and folded his hands together between his knees.

'So,' I said slowly, trying to piece together his reasoning, 'you do not want the truth about these murders to be made public because you are afraid someone is targeting the known Catholics in Lincoln College, and if this is discovered, Leicester may ask how so many could have remained here unmolested on your watch?' I said, my sympathy for him fast ebbing away. 'You preferred to send the magistrate and the coroner chasing after stories of robbers and stray dogs so that the real killer was free to strike again.' I gestured at Ned's body. 'Perhaps you are secretly hoping he will finish the job and rid Lincoln of its stubborn Catholics without your losing face?'

'God, no, Bruno – how could you think such a thing?' he cried, looking genuinely appalled. 'You cannot think I would wish for any man's death? Why do you think I have not simply reported those Catholics within the college long before now? Of course I know who they are,' he hissed, dropping his voice, 'and for the most part they are good men who work well here. To my knowledge they are not plotting to overthrow Her Majesty or her government, and I knew what I would be handing them over to. But by not doing so I have risked losing everything.'

'And now someone is killing them off, one by one, according to the martyrdoms of the early church described by Foxe,' I said, almost to myself, as I crossed the room to the fireplace. 'But who – someone opposed to them, or one of their own? And why so elaborately, except to draw all

342

eyes to Lincoln College and the punishment of its unrepent-ant Catholics? If we could only understand his motives, everything might become clear.'

'I did not want to credit your Foxe theory at first,' Underhill said softly, raising his head. 'I could not believe that anyone could contemplate something so barbaric and blasphemous, and neither did I want to acknowledge that my sermons on Foxe could in any way have inspired such diabolical acts. But you are right – it cannot be ignored any longer.'

'And this poor boy?' I looked back at Ned's ravaged face. 'Was he one of them?'

'Not to my knowledge,' Underhill whimpered, allowing himself the most fleeting glance at the corpse on the floor. 'He had no family of note, but he was the most dedicated student. I cannot imagine who would want to hurt Ned – it is truly evil.' His shoulders convulsed.

'I think Ned saw or heard something he should not,' I said grimly. 'Have you informed the constables or the officer of the watch that Sophia is missing?'

'No,' he said, and hung his head again. 'It is not dark yet – I suppose I have been hoping that she would return before supper, or at least before nightfall. My wife has taken to her bed – she is of course convinced that Sophia is dead or dying somewhere. She does not know about Ned yet. I am trying to take a more rational view, but it is not easy.' He took a deep, steady breath, as if to demonstrate the struggle to master his weaker feelings.

'If she has not come home by tomorrow morning, I will do everything in my power to help you find her, I swear,' I said solemnly. The rector seemed about to reply, but I suddenly held up my hand for silence; from outside in the corridor I had caught a noise so slight it might only have been a rafter creaking, but to my taut nerves it sounded very like the tread of a foot on a floorboard. We waited for several moments, our breath held tight in our throats, but there was only the muted buzzing of an insect against the window pane.

'I must go to the hall and declare this latest tragedy to the community,' Underhill said, taking the Book of Hours from my hand and replacing it inside his doublet. He ushered me through the door and bent to lock it behind us. 'I think we cannot avoid calling in the constables now, since it seems the killer is indeed among us. But if you are questioned, Doctor Bruno, perhaps it would be prudent if we keep Foxe to ourselves,' he added in a whisper.

I nodded, and watched him descend the stairs, his shoulders bowed under a burden I suspected he would never shake off.

Cobbett had left the door to his lodge open and stood with his back to it, arranging his keys in the little wall cupboard. The room still smelled strongly of vomit. He glanced over his shoulder as I entered.

'Another death, they're saying,' he grunted. 'In the chapel itself, this time. I've been instructed to keep the gates locked now. He was a good boy, that Ned, proper hard-working. Who would do such a thing? I begin to wonder if this isn't the Devil's work after all, Doctor Bruno.'

'Sophia Underhill –' I said, pressing the door shut behind me – 'did you see her leave college this morning, Cobbett?'

'Aye,' Cobbett said noncommittally, turning back to his key cupboard. 'Slipped out in all the commotion, right after Master Slythurst went back up to the tower. When her mother come down a few minutes later, I just told her Mistress Sophia must have gone on ahead.'

'And you haven't seen her return at any time?'

'No. Is she not back?'

'She hasn't been seen all day,' I said. 'Did she tell you where she was going?'

'No,' he said shortly. 'But she'll not have got far.'

'Not in this weather,' I agreed.

'Not in her condition.'

He shuffled back painfully to his chair behind the desk and looked at me expectantly. I stared at him in disbelief, feeling as if time itself had slowed almost to a standstill.

'What condition? Do you mean that she is ill?'

Cobbett raised an eyebrow to indicate what he thought of my naiveté.

'Come on, Doctor Bruno, you haven't been in the cloisters that long.'

'You mean, she . . .? No.' I shook my head; surely this was some malicious gossip the old porter had picked up from the servants. 'How can you be sure?'

'My wife had ten, sir, God rest her, and the last one took her up to Heaven with him. Do you think I can't spot the signs? A good three months in, I'd say, poor girl.'

My head was reeling with the magnitude of this revelation. If Sophia was indeed with child, the fear she had confided to me seemed all the more urgent. But then who was it that she feared – her father or the child's father? Was that the danger she had mentioned?

'But who? Did she confide in you whose child it was?' I heard the note of panic rising in my voice.

'She confided nothing, Doctor Bruno, I just use the eyes God gave me, unlike most round here. I seen her meeting someone in the library Saturday evening, while all the college was out at the disputation. Least, I seen her going up there and some feller following not long behind.'

'Who, though?' I cried, exasperated.

Cobbett shrugged, his expression ruminative.

'He had a cloak on with a hood up. Could have been anyone. I do know I didn't see him come through the gateway, so whoever it was must have been in college already.'

345

I paused, pinching the bridge of my nose between my thumb and forefinger as I struggled to make this latest information fit. So Sophia had been one of the people in the library whom Ned had overheard. But who had she met there, while the college was almost empty?

'Does her father know?' I asked Cobbett.

'You are joking, aren't you? Her father would barely notice if she gave birth to it right in front of him, and Mistress Underhill's no better. If you ask me, they've only themselves to blame – both behaving like the world ended when young John was killed, as if his sister was of no matter to them. Mind you,' he said, leaning in, 'I was wondering how she was going to keep it from the rest of the world once she couldn't do up her corset, and that day wasn't so far off. Perhaps that's why she's chosen to run away now.'

'I didn't know you had ten children, Cobbett,' I said, pausing at the door and looking at the old man with renewed respect.

'Well, I haven't now,' he said philosophically. 'Good Lord saw fit to take most of 'em back. Got two daughters left, one married a farmer out Abingdon way, the other's a laundress.'

'I'm sorry,' I said, redundantly.

'Nothing to be sorry about, it's the way of things. Anyhow, listen to me prattling, I almost forgot – I have a letter for you.' He pulled open a drawer from his table and rummaged around until he came up with a folded piece of paper, which he held out to me.

Intrigued, I turned it over; my name was written in an elegant, unfamiliar hand and I quickly opened the letter to see that it was written in flawless Italian.

'He left it with me this morning,' Cobbett said, 'and in all the upheaval over poor Doctor Coverdale and now this latest, I clean forgot to hand it over. I do apologise.'

My heart plummeted as I skimmed the letter; in a very elaborate style, it begged my assistance in recommending its author to the service of the French ambassador as a tutor of languages to his children, as he wished to marry soon and his tenuous university post would not allow him to keep a wife.

'This is from Master Florio?' I asked with a sigh, glancing at the foot of the letter where it was signed with only an initial so curlicued and ornate that it could have been anything.

'Course. Does it not say?'

So this was the letter he had mentioned so furtively; Florio was not, then, the mysterious correspondent who had first set me on the trail of the Catherine Wheel. Another blind alley, and I was no closer to finding the one person in the college who had known about the Foxe connection before any of us.

'Damn him,' I muttered, crushing the letter in my fist, though I was not sure if I was damning Florio for his innocence or the anonymous letter-writer for being so cryptic. 'Cobbett – might I ask you a favour?'

'I shall do my best to oblige, sir.'

'I need to leave college late tonight. I have an – errand that I must see to. Would you leave the gate open for me, say at half an hour to midnight?'

The old porter's brow creased in consternation.

'I would like to help you out, sir, but the rector has given strict instructions for the gate to remain locked now with these latest deaths, and no one to be allowed in or out after dark. I dare not go against his word – if there is another attack I will be out on my ear for neglecting my duty.'

'I understand,' I said quickly. 'Perhaps, then, I could knock for you, and you could let me out and lock the gate again behind me?'

He looked doubtful.

'Well, I could, sir – and would I have to keep awake until you returned?'

'I don't know how long it will take – but I could knock on the window for you to let me back in?'

'We can try that if you like, sir,' he said, sounding unconvinced. 'But you must swear no one in Lincoln will hear of it, or I will be for the chop.'

'I swear it. I will vanish like a thief in the night.' I thanked him and stepped out, into the damp quadrangle, still shadowed by a heavy grey sky, my head aching with these new revelations.

# SIXTEEN

A damp chill hung over the courtyard as I peered out from the mouth of my staircase at twenty minutes to midnight, though the heavy clouds that had brought the day's punishing rain had broken at last to allow the merest glimmer of moonlight to illuminate the slick flagstones. I was grateful for the pale light, since it had allowed me to read the clock on the north range from my window – I had been pacing my room in a state of pent-up anticipation since the end of supper – but I was now anxious that I should not also find myself lit up like a spectacle as I tried to leave the college unobserved. Keeping close in to the shadows, I crept the length of the south range wall and then along the west towards the tower, praying that Cobbett would be awake. Twice I started at a noise, thinking I had heard something stirring in the opposite corner, pressing myself tight against the damp stone, but eventually convinced myself that I had heard nothing but the nocturnal antics of a fox or owl outside the walls, a noise now dulled by the thudding of my own blood in my ears. All the windows facing the courtyard were dark, save for a flickering light in the upper storey of the rector's lodgings; if Sophia had still not come home, I thought, no wonder the poor man could not sleep. As I passed the west range, I wondered if Gabriel Norris and Thomas Allen had returned; neither had been present at supper and it seemed strange that both should have disappeared after the discovery of Ned's body. William Bernard was also missing, an absence more noticeable for the fact that none of his colleagues had mentioned it at High Table, despite the frequent glances at his empty place.

Under the tower archway, I tapped gently on Cobbett's little arched window; I was pleased to see that candlelight burned within and to my surprise, the door opened almost immediately. Pressing a grimy finger to his lips, the old porter shuffled with painful slowness towards the gate, a small lantern in his right hand, glancing fearfully out at the shadowy courtyard as he did so. He handed me the lantern and I watched as his arthritic fingers sorted expertly through the enormous bunch of keys hanging from his belt, selecting one with barely a sound. The gate creaked in complaint as it opened, the sound like nothing so much as the trunk of an ancient tree bending in a storm, and we both froze for a moment until we were satisfied that there was no movement from the buildings behind us.

Cobbett motioned to me to keep the lantern.

'Tap on the street window when you come back,' he reminded me in a hoarse whisper. 'Never fear, I shall hear you. And take care abroad in the streets, sir. Have your wits about you.' His face in the candlelight was unusually serious, so I nodded with equal solemnity as I stepped through the gate into the mire of St Mildred's Lane. The hinges groaned mightily again as Cobbett heaved the gate closed behind me and a moment later I heard his key turning in the lock with an ominous finality.

I had barely passed the walls of Jesus College and was almost upon the place where St Mildred's Lane meets Sommer

Lane when I whipped around sharply on my heels, my hand on the knife, convinced now that I had heard the unmistakeable sound of a footstep in a puddle somewhere at my back. I held the lantern up, peering frantically into the blackness of the lane I had just walked along, but its circle of light barely reached beyond the length of my arm and only made the darkness seem more impenetrable. I almost called out for whoever was there to show himself but stopped myself at the last moment, thinking it best not to draw more attention to myself.

I trudged on through the muddy street, staying close to the solid blackness of the city wall on my right as I followed its line down Sommer Lane towards the North Gate. Again, the quiet splash of a footfall behind me, like the ones my own boots were making in the brimming ruts left in the road from the day's rain; again I spun around, this time drawing the knife, hissing 'Who's there?' in so low a voice as to be barely audible. This time I was sure I detected something in the deep shadows; not so much a movement as a stirring of the air, the chill mist reassembling itself into the space where a man had been moments earlier. I had no doubt now that someone was following me, but only a few yards ahead I saw the reassuring bulk of St Michael's church hard against the city wall, and beside it the lights on the watchtower over the gate. I took a deep breath and, replacing the knife at my belt, reached inside the pocket of my breeches for the few coins I had earlier taken out as bribes for the watchmen, thinking it best not to let them see the full purse I carried.

Two young men carrying pikes and smelling strongly of ale stepped forward half-heartedly as I neared the gate.

'State your business,' the taller one said, as if he did not care either way. He ostentatiously bit the groat I handed him, while I anxiously glanced over my shoulder for any sign of my pursuer, but I could see nothing beyond the spheres of lamplight. When my bribe was judged authentic, I was ushered through the gate and found myself alone outside the city wall.

The inn yard was shrouded in shadow, overhung by a muffled silence which seemed taut with anticipation. I could see no light in any of the windows, and the only illumination came from my lantern. From somewhere in the dense dark to my right came the soft whinny of a horse, the shifting of its weight in slumber, close by. I held up the light to see where I should go.

'Put that out, you fool. Would you have the watchmen on us?' hissed a man's voice at my ear, his breath warm against my cheek. My heart leapt and I almost dropped the lantern with the shock, but managed to reach inside the glass and snuff out the candle. The figure who had spoken overtook me and crossed the yard without hesitation, his cloak swishing around his legs as he walked. A sliver of moonlight penetrated the clouds and in its thin gleam I saw other shadows come to life, more figures gliding silently through the still air to the back of the inn building, all cloaked and hooded. For a moment the sight reminded me of rising for Matins in the early hours at San Domenico, the hooded figures looking like nothing so much as the monks among whom I had spent my youth. I followed the shapes I could make out to a small door, which closed just as I reached it. I could just make out the shape of a grille at head height, so I leaned towards it and whispered '*Ora pro nobis*.' For a moment there was only silence, but then the door opened a crack and out of the shadows a pale hand beckoned me inside.

I slipped through the gap into a narrow passageway which, from the smell of stale food, appeared to run alongside the inn's kitchen. From his sheer size, I guessed that the person who had admitted me was young Humphrey Pritchard, the pot-boy; whether he had recognised me, I did not know. He ushered me along the passage, which ended in a rickety-looking staircase that curved around to the next floor. One tallow candle burned low in a sconce halfway up, filling the narrow stairwell with its bitter smoke. Footsteps creaked on the stairs behind me and I hastened my climb, emerging on to a landing with a low, beamed ceiling and uneven floor. I noticed that the windows had been hung with black cloth to prevent the candlelight from showing to the world outside. Still unsure of where to go, I followed the landing to its end, where a low door stood ajar; tentatively pushing this open, I found myself in a small room crowded with hooded figures who stood expectantly, heads bowed, all facing towards a makeshift altar at one end, where three wax candles burned cleanly in tall wrought silver holders before a dark wooden crucifix bearing a silver figure of Christ crucified.

From the anonymous depths of our hoods, my fellow congregants and I furtively regarded one another, though in the dim candlelight all the faces I glimpsed wore the same mask-like effects of the dancing flames, features elongated, eyes submerged in pools of shadow. Then suddenly, a tall figure across the room turned towards me, the light caught his face for a moment as his eyes met mine and I recognised with a jolt Master Richard Godwyn, the librarian of Lincoln College. Surprise and fear registered on his face in the instant before he dropped his eyes to the floor, folding his hands prayerfully in front of him. I wondered how many of these others, if I could only see them clearly, would turn out to be men I already knew, creeping through the sleeping city under cover of darkness to live their secret forbidden life. I could not help but admire their courage, though I no longer shared their faith; after all, had I not also once risked my life in defying the beliefs the authorities prescribed for me? Was I not, in a sense, still doing so? In that moment, glancing around the little congregation of fourteen souls, I was seized by the enormity of my own task there. I was the wolf among the flock, the one who wore the same uniform and would speak the same responses, but beneath my right arm I felt the weight of Sir Francis Walsingham's purse – money I carried to betray these defiant faithful people to prison or perhaps to death. It was all very well for Walsingham to talk in the abstract about the threat to the realm, but could this Mass really be considered treason? I found it hard to believe that any of the ordinary people gathered here in the night to celebrate a rite denied them on pain of death were secretly plotting to assassinate the queen or tip off French forces. Was their faith alone sufficient reason to deliver them up to the Privy Council's version of justice, I asked myself, and could I justify that to my own conscience? I remembered Thomas Allen's palpable fear of the interrogation methods the queen's ministers used against those they accused of treason. I felt suddenly horribly exposed, as if my treacherous intent could be visible to those around me; at that moment a hand closed tightly around my wrist and I raised my eyes to find myself staring into the luminous blue eyes of Rowland Jenkes. He gave me a hard look, then nodded at me once in what I took to be affirmation, an almost-smile flickered over his lips and he let go of my arm, turning expectantly towards the door through which we had entered.

A stillness descended on us, an audible intake of breath as the door began to open and I felt in that small room, as I had not for many years, a tiny shiver along my spine at the old magic of the Mass. These people among whom I stood, disguised, truly believed that they were in the presence of a holy mystery; believed it with a pure faith that I had long forgotten, and it was this, I thought, that a man like Walsingham could not hope to understand. It was the belief in this miracle that would draw them back time after time, despite the threats of death and punishment, defiantly to keep this flame alive, and the honesty of their faith was a little humbling.

The priest who had entered wore a white garment like an alb that reached to his feet, though it was hooded and the hood drawn up, obscuring his face. A green stole hung around his neck. He took his few steps to the altar with solemn dignity, eyes downcast but his bearing erect, holding out the veiled chalice before him. Upon reaching the altar, he made a deep bow, and I saw from the manner of it that he was not a young man, and the physical gesture cost him. But I could not prevent myself from gasping when he straightened and drew back his hood; the celebrant priest was Doctor William Bernard.

He laid the chalice reverently on the left side of the altar, lifted a green velvet burse from on top and, with a forefinger and thumb, removed the delicate corporal from the burse, unfolded and laid the white linen square in the centre of the altar. Then he placed the veiled chalice carefully on top. The server who accompanied him shuffled nervously; he could not have been more than nineteen, a student, I guessed, and cast nervous glances around him as he stood, bareheaded, at Bernard's shoulder, as exposed in all this hooded company as if he had been naked.

Facing the altar, Bernard made the sign of the cross from forehead to breastbone and from left shoulder to right with his right hand.

'*In nomine Patris, et Filii, et Spiritus Sancti. Amen.*'

The air in the small room seemed charged, all of us poised there as if on a knife edge, our nerves taut with the danger involved in this rite unfolding before us, of which we were all part – even I, who also stood outside it, I too was implicated. Every sudden unfamiliar noise – the cry of an owl, the creak of the inn's old timbers – caused a stiffening among the congregation, an invisible wave of fear that caught and held us for a moment, before the soft hush of breath cautiously released.

'*Introibo ad altare Dei*,' pronounced Bernard, quiet authority in his voice.

The wind gusted suddenly through the wooden shutters, billowing out the black cloths over the windows and making the candles gutter wildly; the young server swivelled his head around in panic, as if someone might have entered, but Bernard proceeded, solemn and imperturbable, with the ceremony he performed as if its every word and gesture were ingrained in his very nature.

There was no music, and the responses of the congregation were muted, barely whispered, as if someone might be listening at the door. We knelt as one as the Mass progressed according to its prescribed rhythms and I remembered again, with a stab of nostalgia, how those words and gestures had framed my own life for so many years; now, as I repeated the phrases, it was as if they no longer had life in them. Bernard took the Host from a small brass pyx and after he had elevated it and drunk from the chalice, he turned to face the congregation.

'*Ecce Agnus Dei, ecce qui tollit peccata mundi*,' he intoned, and I raised my head to find his eyes boring directly into me. My breath caught in my throat; in that moment it seemed he had penetrated my disguise and seen straight through to the very secrets of my soul. In case I had mistaken the look, beside me Jenkes laid a warning hand on my arm. I understood his meaning; though I had been admitted among the faithful that night, Jenkes and Bernard had not forgotten that I was excommunicate. I was not to think of taking the Host with the rest. They need not have feared; I had not taken communion since I left the monastery, out of some vestige of respect or superstition, or both. But as the small congregation rushed forward, dropping to their knees with mouths hungrily gaping open like baby birds, I shrank back towards the wall, afraid that my non-participation would mark me out clearly as a spy; this was, after all, the heart of the rite and abstinence would immediately provoke suspicion. But perhaps Jenkes had warned them beforehand, because although my withdrawal attracted a few curious glances, these were fleeting, and I blended back into the group, muttering '*Deo gratias*' to Bernard's '*Benedicamus Domino*.'

With the Mass said, the atmosphere of charged anticipation seemed to dissolve, and the congregation appeared restless and anxious to be gone. I kept my place by the door as they began to file out, peering as closely as I could into hooded faces as they passed me, dropping my eyes if they returned my gaze. Jenkes's long fingers closed around my wrist, signalling me to stay while the others left. One of the last to leave, a short figure with his hands tucked beneath his cloak in a monkish posture, paused and looked directly at me; at that moment the candles guttered again and I gasped as the sudden surge of light showed me his face. Adam, the rector's servant, stared back at me, mirroring my own expression of disbelief. He hesitated a moment, as if unsure whether to speak, but Jenkes gave him a hard look and he hurried through the door with the rest.

At last I was left alone with Jenkes, who removed his hood, and the tall, solid figure of Humphrey Pritchard, who began to busy himself tidying the room and putting away the trappings of the ceremony. He left the altar candles, now burning lower and with feeble light. Jenkes looked at me appraisingly.

'So, to business,' he said softly. 'Please, take off your cloak. You are among friends now. Did you bring your purse, Doctor Bruno?'

I lowered my hood and held his gaze steadily

'Did you bring the book, Master Jenkes?'

His ruined face cracked slowly into a smile.

'The book. First tell me what you are willing to pay for this manuscript?'

'I would need to see it first,' I said evenly. 'What do you ask for it?'

'That is a difficult question, Bruno. For the worth of an object – any object – depends wholly on another's desire for it, does it not? This book, for instance. I have only met one other man who wanted it as much as you appear to, and he was willing to pay me a great deal. More, perhaps, than you carry in your bulging purse.' He eyed my doublet, a hungry glint in his eye.

'Who?' I asked, a cold fear spreading through my stomach. 'You didn't sell it?'

At that moment, the door opened; I started, but it was only William Bernard, no longer wearing his vestments but dressed again in his shabby academic's gown and a thin cloak, his hands clasped behind his back.

'I was just telling Doctor Bruno of the man who wanted to buy the Greek manuscript from Dean Flemyng's collection – the one you saved from the purge of '69,' Jenkes informed him. Bernard nodded slowly.

'I discovered the manuscript buried in an old chest when I first became librarian of Lincoln,' he explained. 'My predecessor had been either unable to read it or unaware of what it was, but I recognised it immediately and understood that in the right hands it could be extremely valuable – and extremely dangerous.'

'So you stole it?' I asked.

Bernard frowned.

'I did no such thing. The college took an annual inventory of the library's collection – any disappearance would have been noticed. But the Lord provides to those who keep the faith – in 1569 the Queen's Visitors carried out a purge of the college libraries, as you know, and in their haste to remove offending items it was a simple matter to spirit away some of the unwanted manuscripts. I had already told Rowland that I had found the lost writings of Hermes Trismegistus, the book Ficino refused to translate because he would not be responsible for the consequences to Christendom. I am not sure he believed me until I was able to place it into his hands, though.'

Jenkes held up a hand as if to absolve himself.

'As soon as I read the book, I did not doubt it could be genuine,' he said. 'This was the book Cosimo de' Medici had paid a fortune to have fetched from the ruins of Byzantium, yet he never got to read it. I knew there was one man who would pay me whatever I demanded to have this book in his library.'

'You may know him,' Bernard said slyly, 'for he was tutor to your great friend Philip Sidney. I speak of the sorcerer John Dee, astrologer to the heretic bastard Elizabeth.'

'Then –' I looked from one to the other, my hopes collapsing as I spoke – 'then John Dee has the book? You sold it to him?'

'No, and yes,' Jenkes said, stepping forward with his palms spread wide to demonstrate his helplessness in the matter. 'I sold him the book for a very large sum – we had exchanged letters and Dee travelled to Oxford personally to make the transaction. But there was an unfortunate intervention – either by Providence or some other power.'

'What do you mean?' I was impatient now, and tiring of this game of cat and mouse. From the corner of my eye I could see Humphrey Pritchard lolling against the wall by the blacked-out window, picking bits of communion wafer from his teeth. I wondered, with a sense of apprehension, why he was still there, watching us with detached curiosity, and why Jenkes and Bernard did not object to his presence.

'On the road back to London, Dee was set upon by high-waymen and most brutally assaulted. He was fortunate to escape with his life, but his possessions were all stolen, including the manuscript he carried.'

Jenkes related this with perfect unconcern; at the same time he gave an almost imperceptible flick of his fingers and Humphrey moved away from the window towards us.

'And this was your doing?' I asked, turning to keep Humphrey in my sight. 'Did you have the manuscript recovered?'

'*I?*' Jenkes affected affront. 'You think me capable of such underhanded dealings, Bruno? I assure you, I am nothing but honest in my business affairs, nor am I such a fool as to make an enemy of one so close to the queen's favourites.' He gave me an odd look as he said this, then exchanged a glance with Bernard. 'No – it appeared that Doctor Dee was not the only person with an interest in the subject, who was prepared to obtain the manuscript at any cost.'

'Then where is it now?' I demanded, snapping around to face him. 'If you do not have it, why this charade of asking me to bring my purse?' But even as I spoke, the knowledge of what was to come spread through my veins like icy water; I whipped around towards Humphrey but I was not fast enough and he had both my arms pinioned behind me before I could duck away from his grasp. In the same instant, it seemed, Jenkes had lunged forward and snatched the silver-handed knife from my belt; with its tip pressed to the base of my throat, he reached inside my doublet, first one side and then the other, until he found Walsingham's purse. Bringing it into the light, he threw it casually in the air and caught it again with his free hand, testing its weight. Bernard simply stood and watched with his arms hidden behind his back and his face impassive.

'Cry out and I will slit your gizzard like a pig before the

sound has left your throat,' Jenkes hissed, pressing the knife in closer.

'It was all a lie, then?' I asked through gritted teeth, as I struggled uselessly against Humphrey Pritchard's iron embrace. 'The story about the book?'

'Oh, no.' Jenkes looked almost hurt. 'The story is true in every particular, Bruno. The book was stolen from Dee by one who must have known he was carrying it – but whoever attacked him was not in my employ, and I do not believe Dee ever found out where it was taken, or why. That is no longer my concern. No, I have not lied to you, Doctor Bruno. But I do not think you can say the same.'

'I don't know what you mean,' I said, panic rising in my voice as the tip of Jenkes's knife pricked against my skin. 'In what do you think I have lied?'

'Where did you get this money?' he hissed, holding up the purse and shaking it, all traces of his unctuous politeness vanished. 'How does an exiled, itinerant writer come to Oxford with a purse this full, I ask myself? Who pays you?'

'I have a stipend from King Henri of France,' I spat, trying to wrest my arms free; Humphrey only pulled them tighter behind me, and I realised that all I would achieve in struggling would be to dislocate my own shoulders. I stopped moving and slumped forwards, still holding Jenkes's stare. 'I travel under his patronage – anyone will tell you that.'

'You travel with Sir Philip Sidney, who has the patronage of his uncle, Robert Dudley, Earl of Leicester, lover of the whore Elizabeth. And Dudley's whole interest, like that of all the Privy Council, lies in ridding Oxford of those who remain loyal to the pope, whom you are charged with rooting out for him like a pig after truffles. Is it not so?' He stepped closer to me and raised his elbow, so that I had to force my head as far back as I could to keep the knife from piercing my throat.

361

'I know nothing of the earl's interests – I have never laid eyes on him!' I croaked, a sharp pain shooting down the side of my neck from the strain.

'You dissemble well, Bruno – I expected as much. It must be an exceptional man who can keep ahead of the Inquisition for seven years. But you do not fool me. You are a schismatic and a heretic and you seek to prosper and revenge yourself on the Catholic Church by betraying those who keep the faith you scorned.'

'You have no reason to think so,' I protested, genuinely alarmed now by the fierce light in Jenkes's eyes. 'On what grounds do you accuse me?'

'On what grounds?' He gave a short, hacking laugh and took a step back, relaxing his arm, though he did not lower the knife from my throat. 'What – apart from your intimacy with Sidney and the money you use to bribe your informers? Explain for me, then, your interest in the deaths at Lincoln College. For whose sake do you concern yourself so diligently with finding the killer?'

'What informers?' I lurched forward again unintentionally and felt something pull sharply in my shoulder as Humphrey wrenched my arm back tighter. 'I was not convinced by the account of Doctor Mercer's death, that is all – I thought others might be in danger if the killer was not found. Which proved to be the case,' I added pointedly.

'What touching charity,' Jenkes said, almost without opening his lips. 'Well, then, let us try another question – why did you invite Thomas Allen to eat with you?'

My face must have betrayed my surprise, because he smiled thinly and tilted his head to one side.

'Have you never observed, Bruno, how a blind man can develop the hearing of a dog, to compensate for his lost faculty? Just so I, who have no ears, make up for my loss by having many eyes, that see into every corner.' He laughed drily at this, as if he had rehearsed it earlier and found it pleasing. When I failed to show my appreciation, he lunged again, needling the knife tip in closer. 'What were you asking Allen? What did he tell you?'

'He told me nothing of any worth,' I panted, trying to twist my neck away from the point of the blade. 'He talked of his studies, his worries about girls – the trivia of a young man's mind only.'

'Do not lie to me again, Bruno,' Jenkes said through his teeth, his voice calm and cold. 'You deliberately sought out the one man in Oxford who wants to see us all destroyed.' Then he jerked the knife swiftly to one side and there was a moment's pause before a searing pain shot up my neck and he held up the blade to my eye level, its blade stained crimson. 'Look how you tremble to see your own blood. It's but a nick,' he said dismissively, 'you've had worse shaving. But see how you bleed, even from a little cut. Think how your blood will stain the ground when I cut your neck right across.'

I closed my eyes, my mind spinning wildly as I tried to think of ways I might try to escape. None came obviously to mind.

'If Thomas Allen wishes to destroy your group, why would he not report what he knows?'

'Ah.' Jenkes studied me for a moment. 'I see there is much you do not yet know, Bruno. It is not that simple. He cannot do it himself. But I cannot let you pass on whatever he has told you about us.'

'If you mean to kill me, then,' I said, keeping my voice as even as I could manage, 'at least tell me why you killed those men at Lincoln. Satisfy that curiosity for me.'

Jenkes frowned, then looked over at Bernard as if for approval.

'What a strange last request, Bruno. And one I cannot satisfy, for I did not kill Mercer or Coverdale, nor the boy, and I do not know for certain who did. I am as curious to find the answer as you are.'

'Then why do you wish to prevent anyone finding out? They came here for Mass, did they not? Coverdale and Mercer – they were part of your group. Do you not care that they have been violently killed, and more of you may be in danger?' I asked, looking from one to the other in confusion, the cut in my throat now stinging fiercely.

'Their deaths have provoked too many questions,' Bernard said, in the same clear, solemn tone with which he had pronounced the Mass. 'Oxford men would know well enough to leave those questions unanswered, but you are not an Oxford man and your insistence on ferreting out the truth would expose us all in the end. I'm sorry to say that your curiosity has been the undoing of you.'

He sounded genuinely sorrowful as he said this. For a moment I felt the room spin; my heart seemed to have stopped beating and I lost all sensation in my arms and legs as I realised without any doubt that they did mean to kill me and that it was quite possible I would not be able to talk my way out of it. My bowel gave a spasm at the same time, but I tensed every muscle and brought it under control. I would at least not shame myself that way.

'But,' I gasped, battling to catch my ragged breaths, 'then this killer is *your* enemy – it is he who is causing these questions to be asked! He scrawled the sign of the Catherine Wheel on the wall in Coverdale's blood – it is as if he wants to point the finger at you and your group, while it is your people he is killing! Surely, then, it can only help you if I try to find him?'

A sharp look passed between them at the mention of the symbol; Bernard's face hardened into knowing anger and Jenkes seemed rattled for the first time since he had turned on me.

'Say that again,' he hissed, forcing the knife into the tender skin of the cut he had made so that I yelped in pain and bit my lip to stop myself crying out. Bernard took a step closer and shook his head almost imperceptibly; Jenkes withdrew the knife a fraction. 'On the wall, you say? How many people saw this?'

'Apart from me, only Rector Underhill and the bursar, Slythurst,' I said, almost in a whisper. 'The rector had it removed before the coroner arrived.'

'Good.' Bernard nodded almost to himself. 'Well, then, Rowland, let us get this thing done and be on our way, or we shall risk being seen.'

'No, wait!' I cried, as quietly as I could. 'I can help you find him if you let me go back to college and continue my search. Come – we are on the same side.'

Jenkes laughed abruptly.

'We are not on the same side, Bruno,' he replied. 'Do you not see? You think you are hunting this killer down but all the time he is using you to betray us. He wants to lead you to us, to make you connect the deaths to us and probe into the secrets of our network, so that you can take the knowledge back to Sidney and your friends in London and think it was your own conclusion.'

'You speak as if you know who he is,' I said, feeling that if I could only keep him talking I might deter him from the course of action he had decided. But Jenkes, it seemed, was tired of talking; he nodded towards Bernard, who finally drew his hands out from behind his back to reveal a length of thin cord.

'You have seen and heard too much, Bruno,' Jenkes said matter-of-factly, his knife still quivering at my throat as Bernard disappeared behind me and my wrists were roughly pulled together and bound. 'But I will find out what Thomas Allen told you, and whether you have passed it on, before I send you to the Devil. You can tell me willingly or otherwise, it is up to you.'

'Why do you not ask Thomas Allen?'

'Because he is not here. But do not worry – I think it unlikely that Thomas Allen will see tomorrow's sunrise either.'

'You will kill him too?' I gasped.

'Not I, Bruno.' Jenkes shook his head and offered an enigmatic smile. 'Not I. I have not touched Thomas Allen for the sake of his father, who kept faith with us even under hard torture. But Thomas should not have spoken to you. Now others may not be so scrupulous.'

'I am a guest with the royal party,' I spluttered, grasping now at straws, 'my murder would be a scandal – it will lead the magistrate straight to this place.'

Jenkes shook his head slowly.

'You badly underestimate my intelligence, Bruno, I almost find it insulting. Even a member of a royal party may take a fancy to visit the stews in the dead of night – after all, that is no more than anyone would expect of a foreigner and a papist. And not knowing the bad streets in that part of town, he might easily find himself the victim of violent robbers – especially if he will go abroad carrying such a fat purse. It will be an embarrassment to the royal party, no doubt, but they will quickly dissociate themselves from you. What do you think, William?' he asked, raising his head towards Bernard, who was still tying my arms while Humphrey held them in place. 'Shall we leave his body to be found outside one of the boy-houses, or is that a humiliation too far?'

When Bernard did not answer, he merely shrugged and continued:

'I will be back before first light, when I have made the arrangements. I leave you in Humphrey's care while you consider what you are going to tell me about your conversation with Thomas Allen.'

366

'You would kill me to protect yourselves?' I asked, flailing as Humphrey lowered me with surprising gentleness to the floor and Bernard moved around to tie my ankles with another length of cord. Jenkes studied me severely.

'To protect the *faith*, Bruno,' he answered eventually, reproach in his voice. 'Everything I do is to protect and preserve our persecuted faith, therefore it is no sin in God's eyes.'

'What of the Sixth Commandment?' My voice sounded choked and unusually high. 'Thou shalt not kill?'

'I begin with the First Commandment. *Thou shalt not have strange gods before me. Thou shalt not make to thyself a graven image.*' His eyes narrowed and he brought his face very close to mine, so that I could almost count the blackened pores on his nose. 'This country – *my* country, Bruno, for I was born and remain an Englishman – *my* idolatrous country, then, has broken this commandment. The heretic bastard of the whore Anne Boleyn has set herself up as a rival to the Holy Father himself and the souls of her people are in mortal peril. To combat such heresy is holy war, not murder. But to show that I am no barbarian, Bruno, Father William will hear your confession before you die, if you choose to be reconciled to the Holy Mother Church.'

'I will not confess myself to you,' I said, through my teeth.

Jenkes did not seem put out.

'No matter – it is between your conscience and your God,' he shrugged, unwinding from around his neck a dirty linen scarf. Seizing my nose hard, he pinched it between his fingers until I was forced to open my mouth to breathe; as soon as I did so, he stuffed the scarf into my mouth until my jaw was stretched painfully wide and I was gagging on the material, unable to make any sound. For a hideous, panicked moment I thought he meant to suffocate me and began to struggle violently, but he released my nose and gave me a lingering look of distaste.

'You had better search his room in the college,' he said brusquely to Bernard, who nodded. Jenkes once again rummaged inside my jerkin and found the key attached to my belt; quickly he tore it off and threw it to Bernard. It was of little consolation now, but at least I had the sheet with the copy of the cipher from Mercer's almanac tucked inside my shirt, and there was nothing in the chamber at Lincoln that could link me to Walsingham. I cursed my own stupidity in not sending word to Sidney of my plans; only Cobbett knew that I had gone out, but he would have no idea of where to look for me, or even that I was in danger, until my body was found tomorrow morning lying in an alley outside a whorehouse. I shuddered, the ache in my jaw worsening as I struggled to swallow my own saliva without choking on the scarf.

Jenkes gave me a last analytic glance, bent to check my bonds were tight enough, then motioned to Bernard.

'I will see you soon enough, Bruno. Think carefully about what you want to tell me. This face of mine will seem the face of an angel compared to the way you'll look if I have to force it out of you. I hope that won't be necessary.'

Bernard peered down at me, his lined face steely yet clouded with regret. Then he pulled the hood of his cloak around his ears and swept out of the room, leaving me alone with Humphrey Pritchard.

# SEVENTEEN

A tense stillness settled over the room. From somewhere downstairs there came the sound of a door closing. The candles on the altar had burned low now, tall plumes of black smoke rising from the stubs, the flames elongating and flickering, making Humphrey's shadow loom enormously on the wall behind him. He made no move to replace the candles; indeed, he seemed ill at ease with his new responsibility, lowering himself heavily to sit on the floor beneath the window, his back against the wall. Here he waited uncomfortably, watching me with a brow furrowed in mixed concern and apology. The only sound was my quick, shallow breaths through my nose, as I struggled to keep my breathing even and not to panic at the mass of cloth jamming my mouth. I saw that Humphrey carried a knife at his belt; his fingers strayed to it every few moments, though I was sure that, for all his great size, the young man had a gentle nature and had only reluctantly assumed his role as Jenkes' strong arm. I wondered if he would have the nerve to use the knife on me if I made an attempt to escape and decided he probably would; his fear of Jenkes would overcome his natural compassion.

A sharp wind rattled at the shutters; Humphrey started, whipped his head around, then laughed sheepishly at his own nerves. I implored him with my eyes, in case I might appeal to his better nature before Jenkes returned, though I had little hope he would take pity; Humphrey had better reason than anyone to know what Jenkes did to those who endangered the cause.

My shoulders had begun to ache from the unnatural position of my arms; I tried moving my wrists but the cords were bound too tightly to try wriggling free and cut badly into my flesh if I did so. I thought again of the faces I had recognised at the Mass. There was Richard Godwyn, who distributed Jenkes's clandestine books, and Rector Underhill's sharp-eyed old servant, Adam, both associated with the Catherine Wheel and with Lincoln College; either of them might have reasons for silencing the Fellows who had died, if only to protect themselves. Adam in particular, as I had thought earlier, would have no lack of opportunity to spirit away keys from the rector's lodgings – but if they faithfully attended Mass here, I could see no reason why they would want to draw attention to the Catherine Wheel group. I closed my eyes and leaned my head back against the wall. I had to concentrate on finding a way to escape; all this speculation would be worthless if I was to have my throat cut in an alley before sunrise. The thought brought a fresh convulsion of fear as the reality of my present situation began fully to sink in; I had feared for my life before now, but never had I felt so helpless to fight for it.

I stretched my neck to try and ease the ache in my jaw, making the cut at the base of my throat gape and sting viciously; the pain made me catch my breath suddenly, sucking in a piece of the cloth which lodged in my throat. Half choking, I flung my head from side to side to try and dislodge it, emitting tiny strangled noises as I felt my eyes bulging alarmingly. It was only when I fell sideways with a thud and began writhing on the floor that Humphrey, realising what was happening, leapt to my side and began to claw the gag from my mouth. When finally he had extracted it altogether, I fell back limply against his shoulder, gasping for air, my eyes streaming.

'I'll leave it for now, Doctor Bruno, but you'd best not cry for help or I will be obliged to beat you,' Humphrey whispered apologetically, propping me up against the wall as if I were a doll and watching me with concern.

'Does he really mean to kill me?' I asked in a croak, when eventually I could speak.

Humphrey looked at me doubtfully, his big good-natured face pained, as if caught between duty and compassion.

'He says you will bring down the Earl of Leicester and all the queen's soldiers on our heads,' he whispered, his eyes growing wide, 'and we shall be taken to the Tower and racked, even the women. Even Widow Kenney, and I won't let you do that,' he added, suddenly determined.

'You are fond of Widow Kenney, then?' I asked softly.

Humphrey nodded emphatically.

'She took me in when I first came to Oxford,' he said earnestly, in his lilting voice. 'Six years ago. I didn't have a penny. Now I have a home and a good job, and it is as if I have a family.'

'I am sure you are of great value to her. Were your own family Catholics?' I asked, between painful coughs.

He shook his head, again with the same exaggerated move ment a child might make, his lips pressed firmly together.

'Widow Kenney and Master Jenkes taught me all I know of the true faith. That is why I know we must fight to keep it safe from the heretics.'

'You said "the women",' I prompted, after a while. 'Are there many women who come to these meetings?'

Humphrey looked at me hesitantly.

'Come now – I will be dead in a few hours, Humphrey, what harm can it do to pass the time by talking to me a little? You will be doing me a kindness.'

This seemed to sway him, because he shuffled closer on his backside and adopted a conspiratorial tone.

'There are some women from the town. Not gentlewomen, though – they hear Mass at one of the manor houses in the countryside along with their own sort, mainly. Except for one.' A kind of softness spread over his face and I sensed I was near my target.

'Sophia?'

He blinked in surprise.

'Do you know Sophia?' When I nodded, he beamed. 'She does not come so often now, but I always know it's her, even under her hood. She walks like a sort of – like a tree in a breeze, do you know what I mean? Like the willows by the river.'

'I do. And tell me – does Sophia have friends among the group here? I mean, friends she might go to if she were in trouble?'

'Why, should she be in trouble, sir?' he asked innocently, and I found it almost touching that he still called me 'sir' even though I was bound hand and foot and he was keeping guard over me with a knife. When I did not reply, he only frowned and shook his head. 'I do not know her friends. The only one she was close to was Father Jerome, but then everyone loves Father Jerome. It was he who brought her here first.'

'Who is Father Jerome?' I asked, sitting up, my interest piqued. 'I thought Father William Bernard was your priest here?'

'Oh no,' Humphrey said, proud of his superior knowledge. 'Father William hardly ever says Mass since Father Jerome came, only if Father Jerome has to be out of town. He goes quite often to Hazeley Court, you know, out in Great Hazeley on the London road, where the grand Catholic families come to hear Mass. I expect he has gone there tonight.'

My mind was working furiously, but I tried to keep my face and voice even so as not to betray my thoughts.

'And this Father Jerome – is he an Oxford man?'

Again, the exaggerated head-shake.

'He came from the college in France.' He looked stricken. 'Though that is a great secret and I should not have told you. I beg you, do not tell Master Jenkes I said it, will you?'

'Of course not. And what is he like, Father Jerome?'

Humphrey's face took on a dreamy cast.

'Like – like I imagine Our Lord Jesus would be if you met him. He makes you feel – I can't explain it – like he thinks you're the most special person he ever met, do you know what I mean? Though I don't understand a lot of the Mass – I have never had book learning, you see – I love to listen when he says it. I like it better than when Father William comes,' he added, his face creasing into a pout. 'When Father Jerome speaks, it sounds like music.' He sighed happily, one hand toying with the knife at his belt.

'Is he a young man?' I said, leaning forward and moving on to my knees to ease the stiffness in my legs. The movement startled Humphrey out of his reverie; he jerked upright, but when he was certain that I was not attempting anything, he relaxed back against the wall.

'Father Jerome has the face of an angel,' he said reverently. 'I've seen a picture of one,' he added, presumably lest I think the comparison unfounded.

'The face of an angel,' I repeated slowly, trying to keep as still as possible. I had discovered that the cords binding my ankles were not as tight as those around my wrists; sitting on my heels, I was able to work one finger slowly inside the knot that held them. If I could keep Humphrey talking, he might not notice my surreptitious movements. 'Tell me about Hazeley Court, then,' I said lightly. 'It sounds a grand place.'

'Oh, I have never seen it, but I believe it is very fine. The owner, Sir Francis Tolling, is now in Bridewell Gaol in London for attending private Mass, and his wife uses the house to shelter those who need it. That's all I know.'

'Missionary priests, you mean?'

'Any who labour in the English vineyard and need somewhere safe, out of sight.' He shifted his weight nervously. 'There is one among our number, Master Nicholas Owen, who is a master carpenter – he was here tonight, in fact, though you would not have known him under his hood. But he is employed in all the great houses of the faithful, they say, to build secret rooms.' He leaned in, looking carefully from side to side before lowering his voice further. 'In the attics, the chimneys, the sewers, the staircases, even inside the walls, so God's workers can hide from the searchers. Is it not cunning?' He rubbed his hands together and beamed with delight. 'Though I should not have said that either – you won't tell Jenkes, will you? Are you all right, sir?'

'What? Oh – yes, it is nothing. My shoulder pains me a bit, that is all.' I realised that I had been screwing my face up and clenching my jaw in concentration as I tried to poke one end of the knot through with only one finger. It was so close to coming free, it would not do for Humphrey to suspect me now. He nodded in sympathy, and glanced furtively at the door.

'I wonder if I might loosen your bonds a bit, sir,' he said, his eyes flitting again to the door as if Jenkes might burst through at any moment. 'Not altogether, I mean, just so you're not in pain. After all, it's not as if you'd get very far is it, you being so little, and me with the knife and all?' He laughed, though I detected a note of anxiety, and I joined in heartily at the absurd idea of my overpowering him. In truth, I had no idea of how I might proceed, even if I did manage to free my legs; without the use of my arms I could do nothing, and even with them I did not much rate my chances in a fight against Humphrey, with or without a knife. While he deliberated about whether to loosen my ropes and I continued my own attempt as best I could behind my back, there came the unmistakeable creak of a tread in the corridor outside and we both froze. My throat contracted; I had not expected Jenkes to return so soon, and my escape plan faded before it was even fully formed. I took a deep breath, as well as I was able with my heart thudding in the back of my mouth. So this was it, I thought. Back in Italy, at San Domenico Maggiore, I had invited a death sentence for the sake of a book; now, after running from it all these years, I faced death again, all because I was too foolishly greedy for a book. Well, I thought, I would try whatever means I could to fight, and if I must die, at least I would not die like a coward under Rowland Jenkes's mocking glare.

Humphrey gathered his wits as the footsteps drew closer, snatching up Jenkes's linen scarf and shoving it back into my mouth, though more loosely than it had been before, just as I felt the end of the rope pop through and the knot at my ankles subtly slacken under my scrabbling fingers. The footsteps halted outside the door and there was a tentative knock, followed by a woman's voice.

'Humphrey? Is that you?'

Humphrey deflated visibly with relief, and scrambled to his feet to open the door. Widow Kenney stood outside in her nightgown, holding a candle, a woollen shawl around her shoulders. She looked first at Humphrey, then at me in my sorry state, bundled into a corner on the floor, and exhaled with exasperation.

'That Jenkes,' she said, still looking at me with a reproving moue, as if Jenkes were a naughty cat and I a dead mouse he had dropped on her clean floor. 'What is he making you do now, Humphrey?'

The boy hung his head and Widow Kenney beckoned him towards the door.

'Let me speak with you a moment.' She studied me briefly as if assessing the danger of leaving me unattended, then appeared to decide I was harmless. 'I have told him, I will not have blood shed in my inn,' she hissed at Humphrey as she ushered him into the corridor, 'and you should know better, Humphrey Pritchard.' I did not catch his protest but the murmur of their urgent exchange was audible beyond the closed door.

I had to act quickly. Without the need to conceal my movements from Humphrey, I tugged at the loosened end of the knot binding my ankles and it came loose in my hand. Shaking my legs free of the cord as fast as I could, I struggled painfully to my feet and hobbled across the room to the small makeshift altar, where the candles had almost burned down to the sticks. With my back to the altar, I tried to position the knot fastening the bindings around my wrists over the flame, hoping it would burn through, but the cord was sturdier than it looked and the flame feeble; though I could smell it beginning to singe, I doubted whether the knot would break before Humphrey came back and caught me. Outside in the passageway, the voices grew louder in heated argument. Because I could not see what I was doing, I kept scorching my hands on the flame and was grateful this time for the cloth in my mouth that muffled my cries as I did so. My greatest fear was that I would knock the candle and set my clothes alight; to escape a burning at the hands of the Inquisition only to bring one on myself by accident would be beyond irony, I thought, as I twisted the cord first one way and then another over the flame, trying to arch my arms as far as I could from my body. The cord crackled suddenly and I felt a rush of fierce heat on my right hand; the knot had caught fire, and I screamed into the cloth as the flame seared my hand and sleeve, but the knot had loosened enough for me to pull my hands out. The flaming coils of cord fell to the floor and I stamped on them furiously, clutching my burned hand to my chest and catching a whiff of scorched flesh as I did so. The voices outside the door silenced abruptly and I knew I would only have one chance at getting past them. Ignoring the pain of my stretched and blistered skin, I grabbed the heavy silver candlestick from the altar, blew out the guttering flame and held it aloft just as Humphrey flung the door open and paused for just an instant, his mouth gaping at the sight.

His hesitation was just long enough; before he could raise his arms, I swung the solid base of the candlestick at his temple. My aim was good; there was a sickening crunch and he fell backwards, blood spurting from the gash, matting his fair hair. His large body crumpled to the floor; he appeared to be knocked out cold. The widow held up her hands in fright and shook her head violently, her mouth working in terrified silent protest; holding the candlestick aloft again so that she cowered into a corner, I wrested the knife from Humphrey's belt, threw the candlestick back at her feet with a last warning look and darted through the door into the corridor. All down the crooked stairs and across the inn yard I fully expected to see Jenkes at any moment and kept the knife levelled in front of me lest he appear, while glancing back over my shoulder to see if Humphrey might have revived to pursue me, but it seemed fortune was on my side at last; I emerged from the gates of the inn yard into the street without seeing a soul.

The sky was still dark, etched with streaks of moonlight

between the clouds, and I rested for a moment against the wall of a house to catch my breath, realising that in all the frenzy I had not stopped to remove the scarf gagging me. Now I extracted it and, holding one end in my teeth, wrapped it gingerly around my burned hand. The pain made me briefly dizzy, so that I feared my legs might buckle beneath me, and once the temporary exhilaration of my escape had subsided, I realised with a falling sensation that my purse had been stolen and I had no means of getting past the watchmen at the North Gate. Even worse, I thought, what if they knew Jenkes well and had been tipped by him to watch out for me? In this city, it was impossible to know who was a friend.

The square tower of St Michael's Church at the North Gate rose above the battlements of the city wall, its silhouette a landmark as I crept along under the eaves of houses until I was forced to break my cover and run across the broad street that lay parallel to the city wall. I looked wildly from side to side as I dashed over, anticipating the sight of Jenkes at any moment, but the street was empty. At the gate I paused, but could think of no other means of gaining the city again; the wall was far too high and sheer to be scaled and all the other gates would be guarded too at this hour. My only choice was to wait until first light, when the gates would be opened to traders, by which time Jenkes or Humphrey would likely have caught up with me, or to try and persuade the watchmen I had already paid to let me back. I banged with the flat of my good hand on the small door set into the high oak gates but there was no reply. I hammered harder and called out, and at last a bleary face appeared behind the square iron grille. Eventually I heard the scrape of a bolt and the door opened.

I murmured my gratitude, glancing around again for signs of movement in the dark streets, and as soon as I was out of the watchman's sight, I picked up my pace and ran the short way up St Mildred's Lane, holding tight to the handle of Humphrey's knife. Never had I been so glad to see the tower of Lincoln College looming above me. Gently I tapped on the narrow window of Cobbett's room. After a pause, I tapped again.

'Cobbett!' I hissed, as loudly as I dared. 'It is I, Bruno – open the gate!'

I was greeted only by silence. Hoisting myself up to the sill, I peered in and saw the old porter lolling in his chair, his chin slumped on his chest and his mouth gaping, a skein of spittle hanging from his lower lip.

'Cobbett!' I called again, tapping the window harder, but he did not stir. Cursing under my breath, I stepped back and looked up at the college walls; all the windows were dark and I wondered whether I dared risk waking anyone else by calling louder. I did not want to be left in the street outside the college; that would be one of the first places Jenkes would choose to look for me. Then, as the clouds shifted and a thin ray of pearly moonlight broke through, I remembered another possibility and hoped my guess was right. The very furthest window on the west range belonged to Norris's room; though it appeared closed, I managed to jam the fingers of my good hand inside the frame and found that it had indeed been left unlatched. As far as I could see into the darkness, the lane appeared to be empty in both directions. As I heaved myself up and levered myself sideways through the narrow opening, flinching as I scraped my burned hand against the frame, I prayed that neither of the room's occupants had returned during the evening.

I tumbled through the window, landing awkwardly on the large wooden chest beneath. I froze for a moment, listening for the sound of breathing or movement from the bedchamber beyond, but the stillness was that of an empty room. A faint light from the window facing into the quadrangle outlined the shapes of furniture; the floor seemed to be littered with debris and after some tripping and fumbling across the surfaces of dressers and tables, I managed to locate a tinderbox that had been left on an ornamental table under the window. Striking it, I lit a stub of candle on the desk and looked around to see the room in a state of chaos, just as Roger Mercer's room had been on the morning he was killed. Clothes had been flung from the wardrobe, books and papers scattered and all the drawers of Norris's fine writing desk pulled open and emptied.

I slumped down on the settle by the long-cold fireplace, its cushions all thrown about the hearth, and tried to make myself breathe calmly for the first time in what felt like hours as I gathered my frayed thoughts. My shoulders ached insistently, my burned hand was throbbing and the cut at my throat stung, though it was not deep, but now that I was out of immediate danger I found I was able to think more sharply and clearly. Not that the danger had passed, of course; Jenkes had already decided that I knew too much to be left alone and once he discovered my escape he would almost certainly try to track me down before I could speak to anyone. From my conversation with Humphrey, a theory had begun to take shape in the back of my mind about the murders, though as yet it was still hazy, like figures seen through fog. If my guesswork was correct, then I thought I knew where I might find the answers. And if Jenkes was to be believed, I had to get there before dawn, before Thomas Allen was silenced for good.

First, though, I needed to get word to Sidney, so that he would know where I had gone and the suspicions that had led me there; I hoped then he would be able to follow if I did not return – even though by then it might be too late.

Without wasting any more time, I began to comb through the mess of paper and books on Norris's writing desk for a quill to set down my thoughts for Sidney as briefly as I could before setting off in pursuit, but I could find no ink. Inside the first open drawer, I discovered a stick of vermilion sealing wax and several sheets of fine-quality writing paper. The candle I had lit was burning low; as I glanced quickly around the room to see if there was another to hand, my eye fell on the chest beneath the window. The solid padlock that had secured it was hanging open; it had clearly been forced. Grabbing the dying candle, I prised open the heavy lid, but the trunk appeared to contain only linen undershirts. Undeterred, I rummaged through swathes of cloth until my fingers scraped the wooden base of the trunk and probed into all four corners, yielding nothing. I cursed silently; it seemed anything of value here had already been taken. I brought the candle close and flung out all the contents, scattering them about the floor until I could bring the candle into the depths of the chest and confirm that it was truly empty.

'*Merda*!' I was about to close the lid when I noticed a small corner of the wood cut away in the floor of the chest, barely wide enough to slip in a fingernail. Setting down the candle, I pulled Humphrey's kitchen knife from my belt, leaned into the trunk and was just able to insert the tip of the blade into the gap and work it upwards, my heart pounding. There was a soft click, and I felt the wood loosen. I pushed down and the false bottom lifted up easily; reaching into the compartment beneath, my fingers brushed a sheaf of papers before closing on something sharp that pricked my skin, making me draw my hand back quickly in case it was a trap. Reaching in again, more gingerly this time, I pulled out the offending object into the dim light and gave a low whistle when I realised what I held.

It was a short-handled whip with perhaps forty or fifty cords tied to the end, each cord the length of about half a yard and studded with hard knots. Through each of these many knots was threaded a short piece of crooked wire bent into a hook, and many of these hooks bore traces of dried blood and torn flesh. I shuddered at the cruelty of the instrument, while at the same time it was as if the scales had fallen from my eyes and the suspicions that had formerly floated as if in thick fog suddenly emerged in almost total clarity.

I reached again into the secret compartment and pulled out the sheaf of papers I had felt earlier. It proved to be a package of dog-eared letters, dirty and tied with fraying ribbon. The topmost paper bore the unmistakeable imprint of a bloody thumb. One glance at the faded ink of the uppermost letter confirmed that these were written in a combination of symbols and numbers, but I did not need to decipher them to know that these were the letters for which Roger Mercer and James Coverdale's room had been searched. Tied together with the bundle of letters was another document, this one on older vellum and sealed with wax. The seal was still intact and in the fading light its mark was indistinct, but I hesitated only a moment before breaking the seal and unfolding the document, holding it next to the candle stub. The flame was so faint now that it barely illuminated the elaborate curling script, but the first line was enough to make my breath seize for a moment in my throat.

*Pius, Bishop, servant of the servants of God, in lasting memory of the matter: Regnans in excelsis,* it began, and I almost dropped it, my hands had begun to shake so hard. I knew immediately what I held. This was perhaps the most damning paper an Englishman could possess: a copy of the Papal Bull issued by Pope Pius V some thirteen years ago, declaring Queen Elizabeth of England a heretic and containing her sentence of excommunication from the Catholic Church. It ended by forbidding the queen's subjects from recognising or obeying her as monarch; in those words, Pius had all but called for her to be overthrown. This was the Bull that some of the more extreme Catholics in the European seminaries regarded as a licence to assassinate the queen in God's name. Even to bring a copy into this country was high treason and would earn the one who carried it a traitor's death. I exhaled slowly, then froze as I thought I heard a scuffling sound outside the window. Had I walked directly into another trap? Whoever had ransacked this room had undoubtedly been looking for these papers, just as he had been searching for them in Mercer's room, yet he had not found the chest's secret compartment. Perhaps he was still watching the room and had seen my candle. I held my breath and caught another distinct movement outside; then a high, unearthly scream rent the air, followed by another, a sound like nothing so much the shriek of an infant in pain, and I sank back to the floor, trembling and laughing at my own skittishness; it was only a pair of foxes fighting in the lane.

But the disturbance had brought me to my senses and reminded me that there was no time to waste. I tied the package of letters in one of the linen shirts from the chest, where I also found a travelling cloak that I hastily fastened around my shoulders, my own having been left at the Catherine Wheel. After some scrabbling I located an inkwell under the detritus on Norris's desk and wrote a hasty note to Sidney explaining where the items had been found and where I was going. This done, I reached inside my shirt and pulled out the sheet of paper with the copy of the code from Mercer's almanac, this I folded inside the note to Sidney and sealed it as best I could with the sealing wax I had found in the drawer, though I had no ring to imprint on it. Then I grabbed the package, blew out the guttering candle, lifted the latch of the door to the stairwell and found it locked fast. Whoever had turned over the room in Norris and Allen's absence must have let himself in with his own key, unless he too had climbed in the window. Cursing again, I wrestled open the window above the desk that gave on to the courtyard, struggled on to the sill, encumbered now by my bandaged hand and the package I was trying to hold secure under the other arm, and eased myself through, unfortunately catching the cloak on the window latch at the last minute and falling through sideways with a thud and a muffled cry.

I lay quietly for a moment in the hope that my movements had gone unheard, looking up at the marbled sky above the roofs, already turning from velvet black to a dark indigo behind the streaks of cloud. If the sky was growing lighter, I needed to get this business done and hurry out of the city before dawn. It was too dark to make out the hands of the clock; the quadrangle remained blanketed in the stillness of the dead hours. Nothing stirred; somewhere distant the fox cried again and I was about to pick myself up when I saw the lantern. It approached me at a quick pace from the buildings opposite, held up by a hooded figure who stopped, looming over me, and lowered the light to the level of my face.

'Well, well, Doctor Bruno. Helping yourself again? This is becoming quite a habit. What will your explanation be this time, I wonder? I can hardly wait to find out.'

I could not see Walter Slythurst's face, but his malevolent smirk was apparent in every icy word.

# EIGHTEEN

Slythurst tried to pull me up roughly by the arm, but I twisted away from him, curling my body around the package lest he try to wrench it from me.

'You will explain yourself this time, Bruno,' he said, anger replacing his usual cold sarcasm as I struggled against his grip and he tried to reach for the package. It was too much of a coincidence that he should be awake and dressed at this hour of the night; he must have been watching Norris's room. 'What is it you have taken from that room? I must see it. I demand you hand it over to me.' There was a hectic urgency in his voice and I saw genuine alarm in his eyes as he looked at the bundle in my hand; could it be that he knew the importance of what I carried?

'Demand all you like,' I gasped, lashing out with my bandaged hand, 'but I cannot give this to you.'

'I am a senior Fellow of this college,' Slythurst spluttered, trying to keep his dignity, 'and you must acknowledge my authority here. If you have taken something of value from a student's room, it must be shown to the rector.' His tone was shrill with panic, again he tried to snatch it; again I jerked away from him. I saw that he was determined to have it, and knew that it must not fall into the hands of the rector; both Slythurst and Underhill, I thought, were quite capable of destroying any evidence they thought might make things difficult for the college, and my discovery in Norris's room would be the end of Underhill if it was made public. Slythurst studied me for a moment, his mouth set in a grim line, then he put his lantern on the ground and rushed at me with both hands free. He was surprisingly strong for a thin man and almost knocked me over as he lunged for the package, but I kicked backwards while covering the bundle with both arms, my foot landing hard in his stomach. Winded, he doubled over, and before he could gather himself for his next assault, I threw a punch with my bandaged right hand, catching him on the chin and sending a bolt of pain up my arm. He stumbled backwards, then unexpectedly rallied and threw himself forward at my legs, knocking me to the ground. I heard my back crunch as I hit the flagstones and I tried to wrestle the package beneath me but he had the advantage of weight and quickly straddled me, pinning me to the ground. His face was almost in mine as he grasped the papers; I feared he would tear them as he tried to prise them from my grip and a sudden surge of anger redoubled my efforts to protect them.

'Hand those to me, Bruno – you are meddling in matters you do not understand,' he hissed through his teeth; I could smell his sour breath in my nostrils.

'You do not even know what I have here,' I spat back, clutching the papers to my chest.

'Whatever you have removed from a student's room is the property of the college in that student's absence,' he whispered, still pompous even as he scrabbled at my hands.

'Why do you want it so urgently?' I hissed back. 'Because you didn't manage to find it when you turned the room upside down yourself? Do you always help yourself to keys while Cobbett is sleeping?'

386

'The question, Bruno,' he said, his nostrils flaring, 'is how *you* knew what to look for and where to find it? It can only be that you are part of the papist conspiracy. But who would expect otherwise of an Italian? The rector is a gullible fool, but I always saw through you.'

'It is you who is out of your depth,' I grunted, bucking my back to try and throw him off balance, 'but I am no papist and those who matter know that.'

'You *will* give me those papers, Bruno,' he panted, shifting his weight so that he was bending right over me, his nose almost touching mine, 'or I will rouse the whole college. With three of our number newly dead, you will be locked up in the Castle gaol before you have a chance to fashion your latest implausible tale.'

So Slythurst was *against* the papists, I thought, as his knee dug into my chest. But then why was he so keen to cover up evidence of the murders? What did he want with the papers I was now fighting to keep out of his grasp, that he had ransacked first Mercer's and now Norris's room in search of them? Whatever his purpose, I knew no one must have those papers but Walsingham, and that I must deliver them to Sidney myself. As I felt the package begin to slide from my damaged hand, I mustered all the reserves of strength I had left. Clenching my jaw, I sat up as far as I could, my face so near to Slythurst's that it might have seemed I was about to kiss him, then drew my head back slightly and jerked it sharply upwards, so that my forehead hit him squarely in the nose with a smart crack. He let out a howl, clutching both hands to his nose, and I took the opportunity to throw him off balance and roll away. A dull pain swam across my head and my vision blurred, but it seemed he had come off the worse; when he took his hand away I saw his nose was bleeding copiously. Above my head another light approached, swaying, accompanied by a slow shuffle of footsteps.

'What in God's name...?' Cobbett began, lifting his lantern and stopping with a frown of amazement to see me and Slythurst brawling like drunkards in the middle of the quadrangle. I noticed that in his other hand he carried a sturdy stick. 'Doctor Bruno? Lord, you look a right state. How did you get in?'

'Long story, Cobbett,' I said, hobbling to my feet. 'I need your help.'

'Seize him, Cobbett!' Slythurst cried, the words muffled by the hand still clamped to his broken nose. 'He has stolen property – as a Fellow of this college, I order you to apprehend him!'

Cobbett looked from Slythurst to me with some concern. I grabbed his sleeve and wheeled him away, out of Slythurst's earshot.

'You must believe me, Cobbett – this is a matter of utmost urgency. I think I know where to find the killer, and others may die tonight if I don't act.' Seeing that he looked uncertain, I added, in a whisper, 'Sophia is in danger. I have to go this moment – tell me, where will I find my horse? He is in the rector's stable, I understand.'

'Cobbett, do not open the gate! This man must not leave the college buildings with that package, do you understand?' Slythurst sounded desperate now; lurching to his feet, he lunged unsteadily again at me and though I was still dizzy from the impact of the last blow, I hurled myself towards him, my teeth bared.

'*Ne vuoi di piu*? *Fatti sotto*,' I snarled, pulling out the kitchen knife I had removed from Humphrey Pritchard and thrusting it out before me. 'Come on then, if you want some more.'

Slythurst may not have understood my words but he could not mistake the meaning of the knife; he took a step back, stared at me defiantly for the briefest moment, then raised

388

his head and screamed out 'Murder!' with all the force of his lungs. On two sides of the quadrangle a number of windows creaked open and shadowy figures leaned out, alarmed by the disturbance.

'I must go this instant,' I whispered to Cobbett, still holding the knife out towards Slythurst, who had clearly decided his best hope was to wake the whole college and set them to apprehend me.

'He will have the watch on you,' Cobbett muttered, as Slythurst raised his cry of 'Murder!' again. 'You will need to ride fast if you hope to leave the city. The rector's stable is almost directly opposite, on Cheney Lane. Come.' And the old porter ushered me towards the main gate, moving at a pace I had never seen from him before.

'I must get these papers to Christ Church,' I hissed, as he unlocked the gate. Slythurst watched us but made no move towards us this time; he seemed to have decided to wait for reinforcements. 'Which is the best way?'

Cobbett shook his head.

'If you ride to Christ Church now, they will apprehend you before you can leave the city,' he whispered, barely audible. 'Give the papers to me – I will send a messenger I trust.'

I glanced back at Slythurst, who was now calling up to someone leaning from a first-floor window. Cobbett moved so that his broad back was blocking me from Slythurst's sight and motioned for me to hand over the papers.

'They must get to Sir Philip Sidney without delay,' I mouthed. 'No one else must see them. Men have died for these papers, Cobbett. Can you swear your messenger is trustworthy?'

'On my life,' he grunted. 'Now in God's name, be on your way, Bruno, and God speed you. Bring back Sophia.' The sound of more footsteps rang out on the flagstones; Cobbett eased open the small door just a crack and I passed him the package wrapped in Norris's shirt, which quickly disappeared inside Cobbett's capacious old coat.

'Has Master Godwyn returned?' I hissed, as I slipped across the threshold. He frowned.

'I've seen no one leave the college tonight except you. The gate has been locked all this time.'

'Then he must have left by another way, the Grove, perhaps.' So Godwyn too might still be at large, and I had a good idea of where I might find him.

Cobbett nodded, then pushed me urgently out into the lane and I heard the lock snap swiftly shut behind me.

I hardly dared look over my shoulder as I ran as hard as I could into Cheney Lane, a narrow street that ran along the side of Jesus College, almost opposite. Fortunately, buildings were sparse, and the brick stable block was not hard to find, even in the dark, by the smell and the soft noises of horses in sleep. I banged urgently on the gate, fearing that at any moment Slythurst and a gang of men from Lincoln might arrive to apprehend me for theft, while from the other direction I was still expecting Jenkes or any of his cronies, bent on killing me. After a few moments, a tousle-haired stable boy holding a candle opened the gate a crack, his eyes sleepy but scared.

'Sir?' he murmured, but I pushed roughly past him into the stable yard.

'I need my horse, son, this very instant. The one brought in last Friday, the grey – I am Doctor Bruno, of the royal party.'

The boy's eyes widened further and he bit his lip.

'I am not supposed to let anyone take the horses out when Master Clayton is not here, sir. And he is a very fine horse.'

'He is. From the queen's own stables. But I swear I am not stealing him. Now, bring him, will you?'

'I will be beaten, sir,' he said pleadingly. I could not blame

390

him for his caution; quite apart from the hour, I could not have looked less like a royal visitor with my bruised face and bleeding throat. I hated having to resort to this, but once again I lifted the knife from my belt and let him have a brief glimpse of it. The poor child looked around as if someone might come to his assistance.

'Please,' I added, in a gentler tone, as if this might improve the situation.

He hesitated for a moment, then appeared to decide that the prospective beating was the better option.

'It will take a few minutes to saddle him.'

'Then don't. A harness only – but hurry, please, I do not have time to lose.'

I wheeled around again to the door, thinking I heard footsteps, but there was only the shifting of the horses' hooves in their stalls. But my fear had communicated to the boy; he gave a silent nod and hastened off to fit the horse's halter. I stood, hopping from foot to foot and biting my lip as I watched the gate to the yard, careless of the pains in my hand, shoulders, throat and my back after my tussle with Slythurst; all that mattered now was that I should not be detained. I hoped I had done the right thing in trusting Cobbett, but knew he was right; even if I rode to Christ Church myself, I would not be able to see Sidney at this time of night and could only leave my precious package with the porter there, while Slythurst would have alerted the constable and the watchmen that a thief had escaped from Lincoln and I would never get through the city gates. I could only pray that Slythurst did not intercept the papers before Cobbett's messenger managed to despatch them.

The boy appeared, anxiously leading my horse by his elaborate velvet harness, its brass trappings jingling loudly in the still air; the horse seemed sluggish and less than pleased to have been disturbed in the dark. I led him to a mounting block in the middle of the yard, then scrambled on to his back. He did a little dance of surprise and snorted in protest, but I held the reins firmly and he submitted. The boy held the gate open, and I kicked my heels into the horse's flanks and wheeled him around, turning him to the left, in the opposite direction to Lincoln College.

At the other end, Cheney Lane opened on to the North Street, and the faint pallor gradually staining the skyline to my left guided me eastwards. Now I could just see enough to make out the covered stalls of the Cornmarket ahead, and I urged the horse into a trot, though he seemed reluctant to quicken his pace, the miry ground slippery under his hooves. At the Carfax crossroads I urged him left on to the High Street and presently saw the East Gate ahead, where we had entered the city amid such pomp only five days earlier, its small barbican guarding the road out to London. The light of a lantern flickered in the ramparts of the tower and I knew that everything depended on my passing the watchmen here without being detained. Slythurst would have roused the college servants by now and whoever had been sent in pursuit of me could not be far behind.

As I pulled the horse to a standstill a man in city livery brandishing a pikestaff stepped out from the gatehouse.

'Who goes there?' he barked, levelling it at me and taking a step forward. The horse whinnied in alarm.

'Royal messenger,' I panted. 'I carry an urgent message from Sir Philip Sidney.'

'A shilling to pass before first light.'

'I do not have a shilling. My orders are to take a message to the Privy Council in London without delay.' I drew myself up on the horse, hoping that an authoritative manner would distract from my appearance. 'And if this message does not get through, the Earl of Leicester will have your balls nailed to this gate as a warning, I swear it.'

I glanced again over my shoulder, certain I could hear noises from further up the High Street. The watchman hesitated for a moment, then laboriously began to unbolt and heave open the solid wooden gate while I reined the horse in tightly; he could sense my impatience and tension and was growing restless.

As I crossed the city boundary there came a distinct shout from behind me of 'Hie! Stop that rider!'

I kicked my heels into the horse's flanks and urged him into a canter. Though the ground was still soft beneath his hooves, the road was at least wider, this being the main highway out to London, and the darkness was thinning a little, the stars growing paler as dawn light edged the eastern horizon ahead. Wind caught the horse's mane as he obligingly thundered through the ruts of cartwheels and potholes, just as it stung my own eyes and nose as I crouched low over his neck, trying to keep my grip without a saddle, occasionally glancing behind me to see if anyone was following. He was a fast horse, and soon it seemed that we had covered enough distance to make it extremely difficult for anyone to catch us. Now that I could breathe again, I found room for doubts about the sense of my plan. It had seemed obvious, when I was talking to Humphrey, that I would find the missing pieces of the puzzle at Hazeley Court, but now that I was out of the city with no real idea of how to find the place, I wondered if I had only made a wild guess that would come to nothing, while the drama played itself out to the last by another route altogether.

I had ridden for perhaps half an hour, the sky growing lighter all the time and the birdsong more insistent with it, while a damp mist rose from the hedgerows, obscuring the distant fields. The scent of wet earth rose in my nostrils. There was no sign of any settlement and I began to grow fearful that I had made a terrible mistake; not only might I fail to find Thomas and Sophia before it was too late, but now I could not turn back. If Jenkes or Slythurst had pursued me from the city and caught up with me on this forsaken road, there would be no one to come to my aid.

I rounded a corner in the road between hedgerows, our pace now slowed to a steady trot, when the horse almost stumbled over a flock of sheep being driven in the direction of Oxford by an old man with a misshapen crook in his hand.

'Sir – could you tell me where I might find the manor house of Hazeley Court? Am I on the right road?' I called.

The drover looked up, suspicious.

'What you say?'

I took a deep breath and repeated my question, in the clearest English I could manage.

He pointed back in the direction he had come.

'Another half mile or so – you'll see two large oaks on the left and between them a cart track. Follow that to the manor house. What business have you there?' he asked, eyeing me curiously.

'Official business,' I said, since this had served me well before.

'They are all papists there, you know,' he muttered, as my horse picked his way between the sheep. I thanked him for the warning and, as soon as we were free of the flock, kicked the horse to pick up his pace. My back and legs were aching brutally now and the reins were chafing at my burned hand, but I was heartened to learn that the house was nearby. Perhaps here I would find the answers I was looking for.

# NINETEEN

The cart track sloped gently downhill and eventually widened into a long carriage drive approaching the front of the great manor house. From the crest of the hill, through the thin mist that hung above the trees, all shadowed in the grey light, I glimpsed tall redbrick chimneys, turrets and crenellations. The house was surrounded by woodland on three sides, a steep and densely wooded slope rising behind it. Under cover of the trees it would be possible to approach very near to the manor itself, but gaining access would be another matter. For now I could only go forward. Against his better judgement, I nudged the horse off the cart track and into the woodland, where I dismounted in a clearing and fastened his harness to a low-hanging branch, so that he could at least reach his head down to the grass underfoot. Patting him soundly and reassuring him that I would be back soon, I crept away as silently as I could, down the slope towards the grounds of Hazeley Court.

At the edge of the woodland where it opened out into lawn, I crouched in the shadows of the trees and gazed across at the building opposite. The mist was thinner here and I had a clear view of the house in the half-light. It had evidently been built to withstand assault, though its fortifications seemed part of its character, elegant rather than forbidding. It was constructed in a square formation around a central courtyard, the entrance guarded by a magnificent turretted gatehouse of two octagonal towers at least a hundred feet high, twice the height of the walls and topped with battlements. All these splendidly decorative fortifications had not saved their owner from prison, I reflected. If the Crown was short of revenues, then to seize the houses and lands of Catholic families who resisted the religious edicts must seem an easy source of profit. Should a missionary priest be found within these walls, all this estate would be forfeit and this beautiful house given to whichever of the queen's favourites proved most deserving on the given day; fortunes snatched away and parcelled out to others whose loyalty needed to be bought, under cover of defending the faith. I shivered and pulled the cloak tighter around me. I was risking my life here, I knew, and who would profit from it, if I was right? Would I? Would Walsingham? Some other courtier whose advancement depended on the fall of the people within those handsome walls? But I was now convinced that Sophia was in there, and that the people she was trusting to help her were the very people who would do her the most harm.

A chill had arrived with the dawn and I realised my legs were trembling from the bareback ride; I eased myself back to standing, stretched my aching limbs and crouched again by the thick trunk of an old oak. The façade was adorned with elaborate carved window bays, though the windows on the sides I could see were all shrouded in darkness. There would be no getting through that gatehouse; a manor house this size would be well staffed with servants even if the master was in prison, and the front of the house was too exposed. My best hope, I decided, was to keep to the edge of the woodland and make my way around to the rear where I

396

might find a postern or servants' entrance that would be easier to breach. I fingered Humphrey's old kitchen knife at my belt, reflecting that a judicious use of it might be my best hope of persuading the servants to answer my questions.

Crouching low, I began to stalk along the fringe of the trees, watching the house closely for any sign of movement or light in the windows, when suddenly I heard a twig snap behind me. I wheeled around, drawing the knife, but could see no movement in the depths of the wood, the trunks and undergrowth still shrouded in blueish mist. My breath quickened, gathering in small clouds around my face as I moved sideways, trying to keep my head turned in the direction from which the noise had come. The need to keep my own movements as silent as possible seemed less urgent than the need to move quickly; I strained to hear any further sounds beyond the crackling of sticks and leaves under my own feet, but though I heard nothing, I had the distinct sense that I was not alone in the wood.

At that moment I caught the soft crunch of a horse's hooves over gravel and paused in the shadow of a thick oak to peer out. Below me, a small high-sided cart pulled by a hunched pony was making its way up the carriage drive towards the gatehouse tower, a man perched at the front bent over the reins. I watched as it rounded the side of the house, when suddenly a hooded figure broke from the cover of the trees, tearing across the sloping lawn towards the cart, now on the point of disappearing around the back of the house. I moved as fast as I could through the trees, trying to keep them both in sight, careless of my own cover; as the figure in the cloak reached the cart, he hurled himself at the unsuspecting driver, pulling him from his seat and wrestling him to the ground. The pony, which looked as if it would struggle to reach the end of the carriage drive again, barely registered the activity, its head sagging towards the grass. I charged out of the trees

397

and ran towards them, my legs protesting; I reached them just as I saw the man in the cloak, who had one hand clamped over the other's mouth and was kneeling on one of his arms, pull out a blade.

I threw myself at him, knocking him sideways and gripping the hand that held the blade; with a cry of fury, the hooded figure turned to me and I saw, with a stab of shock, that it was Thomas Allen. His face also froze in an expression of bewilderment.

'*You?*' he said. 'But—'

The fallen driver tried to back away from the scrummage; he was perhaps in his fifties, plump-faced and plainly terrified, shaking his head and whimpering while he implored me with bulging eyes.

'Who is this?' I whispered urgently to Thomas. 'Why do you fly at him with a knife?'

He frowned at me; I glanced at his hand where I held him hard by the wrist and realised that it was not a knife he wielded after all, but an open razor.

'He is come for Sophia,' Thomas said, through gritted teeth. 'He is charged with helping her escape. But she must not go with him – it is a trap.'

'Then she is here?' I let go of Thomas's arm, feeling a great wash of mingled relief and fear; if I had guessed that correctly, then the danger was not over.

The fellow nodded, looking from one to the other of us, his eyes terror-struck.

'Wait – I know this man,' Thomas said, gripping his razor again and peering closely at the terrified driver. 'He serves the Napper household. He cannot be allowed to return – he will raise the alarm.'

The man spluttered and shook his head more violently. I drew Humphrey Pritchard's old kitchen knife from my belt and held it up to his face.

'Your services are no longer needed here, friend,' I said. 'Get yourself home and say you were set on by highwaymen. Now!' I added, giving him a shove as he continued to lie there, dumb with fright; that jolted him into gathering his wits, and he scrambled to his feet and ran off into the trees, casting nervous glances over his shoulder as he fled. Thomas turned to me, his eyes flashing.

'You should not have done that, Bruno. Now he will return to Oxford and they will send more men after us.'

'Peace, Thomas – it will take him at least an hour to walk back to the city, and there are more than enough men after me already. Tell me what is happening.'

Thomas breathed deeply, then nodded, rose to his feet and jerked the weary pony's head upright.

'I have come to save Sophia,' he said, his bony face taut with determination. I saw a strange, hectic glitter in his eyes and his hands moved incessantly in nervous agitation.

'From whom?'

'From those whose safety she threatens.'

'Because of the child she carries?'

He snapped his head around and stared at me.

'So you know about that? How came you to be here, Doctor Bruno?'

'Guesswork,' I said, setting my jaw. 'I think you too may be in danger, Thomas.'

He gave a short, bitter laugh.

'Did I not tell you that already?'

'I mean immediate danger. This very night.'

He opened his mouth to reply but at that moment a door opened in the rear range of the house and a voice called softly:

'Who is there?'

'Pull up your hood and put away your weapon,' Thomas hissed, drawing his own cloak over his head. 'Do not speak if you can help it, until we are inside.'

I saw no choice but to follow suit as he picked up the pony's reins and led the cart towards what looked like a servants' entrance. The door was open a fraction and a tall, stooping man with sparse hair surveyed us through the gap with doubtful eyes.

'I am come to carry a passenger to the coast, at the request of Lady Eleanor,' Thomas said, in a low voice, keeping his hood pulled low. There was a long pause, as if they were both expecting the other to speak.

'There is a sign,' the man behind the door said eventually, with an embarrassed cough.

'Oh. *Ora pro nobis*.' Thomas bit his lip.

'I did not know there were to be two,' the servant said, still regarding us with open suspicion. 'Well, then – step inside.' He opened the door a few inches wider and ushered us into a narrow passageway.

'Wait here, I will tell Lady Eleanor you are arrived.' He turned abruptly and strode away up the passage, taking his candle with him and leaving us standing in semi-darkness. I glanced at Thomas, who only shuffled anxiously from foot to foot and would not look at me. I wondered what we were walking into, and felt for the reassuring presence of Humphrey's knife under my cloak.

Presently the tall servant returned, his look still guarded, as if he was not convinced by Thomas's performance.

'Follow me,' he said curtly, gesturing towards the passageway ahead. 'They wish to see you for a moment, to go over the travel arrangements.'

I imagined, rather, that this Lady Eleanor had heard there were two men present and had grown suspicious. I glanced uneasily at Thomas; once inside this warren of passageways, we were trapped. The servant, holding his candle aloft, led us along the stone-flagged passageway, up a narrow flight of stairs and into a much grander, wood-panelled corridor where

400

the boards were covered with scented rushes and early morning light filtered through low windows. We walked for so long that I was sure the corridor must run the entire range of the house, and indeed eventually it turned sharply to the right and we reached a short flight of stairs ending in an imposing wooden door. The man knocked, and after a soft murmur from within, he pushed open the door and gestured us forward.

I found myself in a high-ceilinged room that spanned the two towers of the gatehouse; by one window stood a woman who was perhaps in her forties, tall and elegant in a dark red satin dress with a stiff embroidered bodice and wide skirt, her hair bound up in a coif. Behind her was a closed door set into the wall of the octagonal tower on the right, while the matching door into the left tower revealed a spiral staircase leading upwards. The servant crossed the room, his shoes clacking on the solid brick floor, and whispered something in her ear; she nodded briefly and leaned past him to regard us with an expression of inscrutable calm.

'You come from William Napper?' she asked softly. Thomas nodded confidently, though I was standing close enough to feel how his arm was trembling inside his cloak.

'Where is Simon?' She glanced sharply from Thomas to me.

'He was taken ill, my lady,' Thomas said, barely opening his mouth.

'Shut the door behind you, then,' she said, stepping forward. 'We wish to be sure you are clear about the instructions. Barton, you will stay,' she added, nodding to the stooping servant who moved to position himself strategically between us.

'My lady,' he murmured.

I glanced around, aware that Lady Eleanor was studying us intently.

401

'I would be grateful, my friends, if you would lower your hoods indoors,' she said softly. 'I know we must all be cautious about showing ourselves, but in this household we may trust one another. Sophia!' She half turned to call over her shoulder.

The small door in the eastern tower opened and Sophia Underhill stepped out, just as Thomas glanced once at me and drew down his hood with a flourish. Sophia gave a little scream and looked from Thomas to me, her hands flying up to her mouth. Reluctantly I lowered my own hood and her face seized in a strange rictus of disbelief.

'*Bruno?*' she whispered eventually, her eyes betraying her utter confusion. 'How came *you* here? And Thomas?' She jerked her head toward Thomas; I noticed that the tall lady had stepped forward, gesturing to the servant named Barton to stand by her, her face calm but clearly alert to the tension of the situation.

Before I could answer Sophia, she had turned to Thomas, her expression pleading.

'Thomas, I know what you think but you are mistaken. If you care for me at all, you will let me go. *Please*,' she added, seeing the implacable look on his face, her voice cracking slightly.

'Who are these people, Sophia?' asked the older woman with a hint of sharpness. 'Do you know them? Are they here to hinder you?'

Thomas turned to her and executed a brief, insincere bow.

'Lady Tolling, we have only come to return Sophia safely to her family, who are sorely distressed by her absence. If she comes quietly with us now, nothing more will be said of this business.'

'The same family who have threatened her life for her faith?' Lady Tolling replied evenly, giving Thomas an appraising glance from head to foot. 'We are not so easily taken in, young man.'

'But I fear you may have been, Lady Tolling,' Thomas said, with impeccable politeness, a dangerous glint in his eye. 'I fear Mistress Underhill may not have told you the whole truth about her urgent wish to leave England.'

'Thomas, no!' Sophia cried, lurching towards him, her hand outstretched. 'You do not know what you do! Do not stand in our way now, it will do no good. You will not get what you want, and all will be lost.'

The tall servant named Barton took a step closer to Thomas, who glanced at him for a moment before turning back to Sophia and laughing, his head thrown back, a wild, manic sound that echoed around the wooden timbers of the ceiling.

'Sophia, Sophia,' he said, gently chiding as if speaking to a naughty child. 'What lies have you been telling these good people? Have you persuaded Lady Tolling to help you escape so that you can join a French convent, because your family would persecute you for your conversion?'

Sophia blanched; her face stiffened and I saw real fear in her eyes. She looked frantically at Lady Tolling and then I saw her legs tremble slightly, so that she stumbled; instinctively I moved to help her but the servant, Barton, was between us in an instant, glaring at me, and I saw now that he carried an instrument that looked like a poker at his belt.

'Come with us,' Thomas said, in a softer tone. 'This will not end the way you hope, Sophia, you know in your heart it will not. He means to kill you.'

Sophia shook her head furiously, her lips pressed tightly together.

'You are blind and stubborn, Thomas, and you have ever been so!' she cried, taking a step towards him. 'You have always acted impetuously, always convinced that you are right! But you are badly mistaken this time, as I have already tried to tell you.'

Lady Tolling folded her arms impatiently and her glance flickered from Sophia to Thomas, but her voice remained steady.

'What is this about? Who are these men, Sophia? Who means to kill her?'

'He is deluded, my lady, his wits are troubled, he knows not what he says,' Sophia interrupted quickly, her throat tight with emotion.

Thomas turned to face Lady Tolling with defiant eyes, apparently undaunted by her rank, the defeated manner I had seen in Oxford entirely vanished.

'Your visiting priest,' he said, enunciating the words precisely. 'Father Jerome Gilbert.'

If Lady Tolling was perturbed either by the accusation that she harboured a priest or that this same priest was bent on murder, she gave no sign of it, save for a small twitch of her mouth.

'Well, then, let us ask him,' she said, her voice calm as ever, and she crossed the room in a rustling of satin and stepped into the small antechamber on the right-hand side, from which Sophia had entered. We caught a brief exchange of voices from within and almost immediately she returned, followed by the young man I had known as Gabriel Norris.

He was dressed as usual in a well-cut doublet and breeches of sombre black, though evidently of costly fabric, and wearing good leather boots with a silver buckle, his blond hair swept back from his face. Handsome and self-possessed, he looked every inch the country gentleman's son; no one passing him in the town or the colleges would have taken him for a secret missionary. He looked from Thomas to Sophia to me with a steady, careful gaze, then nodded slowly.

'Well, then,' he said, spreading out his hands, palms upward. 'Let us say what needs to be said. Lady Eleanor – with the greatest respect, I would ask that you leave us. There are matters that must be resolved between old friends before any of us can go on.'

Lady Tolling seemed unwilling to relinquish control of any drama to be played out under her roof.

'Your safety, Father,' she murmured, glancing at me and Thomas. 'These men have not even been searched.'

'I know them,' Norris said reassuringly. 'All will be well.'

When the door had closed behind her, Norris – or Jerome, as I supposed I must now call him – turned and fixed me with his clear green eyes.

'Doctor Bruno,' he said, a puzzled frown etched in the space between his brows. 'I had thought—'

'You had thought Rowland Jenkes would have killed me tonight?' I offered.

'Well – yes. Though I am not altogether surprised you shook him off – I told him you should not be underestimated. You are, after all, the man who escaped the Inquisition.' His mouth curved into the barest hint of a smile, showing his white teeth. 'Have you and Thomas formed your own anti-Catholic League?' He paused briefly to laugh at his own joke. His manner was oddly relaxed and easy, given the circumstances, and now that he was not playing up to his flamboyant alias, he spoke in a more measured, mature tone. When he turned again to look me directly in the eye I was reminded of Humphrey Pritchard's words: that Father Jerome made you feel you were the only person in the world that mattered. 'Well, then,' he continued, softly, 'so you know the truth. Are you come to arrest me?'

'I came because I believed Sophia was in danger,' I said, trying to return his look evenly, though there was something disconcerting about the intensity of his gaze. I determined I would not look away first.

'From me?' he asked, as if the idea were absurd. 'Why should I wish to hurt Sophia, who has so recently been

405

received through my ministry into the one true Catholic Church?'

'Your *ministry*? Is that what you call it?' Thomas burst out.

'Because she carries your child,' I said simply.

'Slander,' Jerome said, his eyes suddenly flashing with anger as he took a step towards me.

'Did Thomas tell you that?' Sophia cried, her cheeks blazing. 'You know that everything he says is a lie?'

'No one told me,' I said, now lying myself to spare Cobbett. 'I may have been a monk but I grew up in a small village – I know how to recognise such things.'

Sophia said nothing, but pressed a hand over her mouth; Thomas smirked; Jerome sucked in his cheeks and appeared to be thinking.

'You will understand better than anyone, I think, Bruno,' he said seriously, at length, 'how a man may feel trapped by the strictures of his order. Yes, I sinned, but I would not commit a greater sin to cover it. Sophia will be conveyed in safety to Rouen, where she will be looked after until such time as I can join her.' His eyes flicked towards Sophia as he spoke and she looked up gratefully, but there was something evasive about the look that convinced me he was lying for her benefit.

'I also know from experience, Father,' I said, 'that the religious orders do not let go of their own so easily. Especially the Jesuits.'

Jerome nodded as if he were reluctantly impressed.

'Very good, Bruno, you have done your work thoroughly. Yes, I was ordained a Jesuit in Rome and joined the English mission through the seminary in Rheims. Thomas's father brought me to Oxford – it was his role to co-ordinate the arrival of priests into Oxfordshire, find us safe houses, manage our provisions and disguises. The role Roger Mercer took over after Edmund's exile. But you already know this, I presume.'

'I have only recently begun to understand the connections,' I admitted. 'Yours was a very good disguise.'

'*Disguise*,' Thomas spat the word, his eyes cold. 'It was no disguise at all. He carried himself as what he always was – the son of a wealthy family who expects others to dance to his tune. Joining the Jesuits was just another means of adventuring, for him. His *disguise*, as you call it, was so natural a part of him that in the end it became all too easy for him to forget his mission.'

Thomas glared pointedly at Sophia; Jerome at least had the grace to look sheepish.

'And fall into temptation,' I mused, looking from Jerome to Sophia and remembering the Book of Hours the rector had found sewn into her mattress, with its suggestive, intimate dedication. '*J*'. Not Jenkes, then, but Jerome. So it must have been Jerome, too, that Roger Mercer had expected to meet in the garden on Saturday morning, when he met his violent death instead.

'But Roger Mercer found you out,' I said, meeting the Jesuit's level gaze as my chest suddenly tightened at the thought that I was standing mere feet from the killer. 'And I had thought he was killed for those papers.'

Jerome's eyes widened instantly and he stepped forward, his air of amused complacency vanished.

'How do you know about the papers?' he demanded, looking genuinely shaken for the first time since our arrival.

'I have seen them,' I said, managing to sound calmer than I felt.

'Where?'

'In the chest in your chamber. Where you hid them.'

'In *my* . . . ?' He swung around and stared at Thomas now in disbelief. 'But you said—'

407

'Roger Mercer caught them in the Grove one night,' Thomas cut in, a note of spite in his voice. I noticed that his right hand was tucked inside his cloak. 'Sophia used to steal the key from her father's study at night. Mercer was appalled, as you may imagine. He came to our room the next day, exploding with rage. Reminded Father Jerome here how many Catholics in Oxford were risking their lives for his sake, and how he would not take the sacrament any longer from a priest living in mortal sin, and could not allow the others in their circle to do so unwittingly. Said he had no choice but to report Jerome to the Jesuit Superior.'

'I have heard the Jesuits deal ruthlessly with those who stand in the way of their mission,' I said, taking a step back, but Jerome had turned his green eyes on Thomas. 'They are as ready to kill for their faith as to die for it – as you have already shown.'

'As *I* have shown?' Jerome looked back at me for a moment, then let out a sharp laugh of disbelief. 'I see – you have weighed up your evidence, Bruno, and concluded that I must be the Lincoln killer, because I have the most to protect. Am I right?'

'Roger Mercer threatened to expose your breach of chastity,' I said, grasping at facts that had seemed so self-evident a moment ago and now threatened to slip away from me. 'You wanted him silenced.'

'I do not deny that. I mentioned to Jenkes that Roger had been fed ill reports of me and his doubts threatened my safety – I expected Jenkes to have a quiet word in his usual way. But I made a mistake.' He paused to rake his smooth hair out of his face. 'Perhaps you know the story of our St Thomas Becket, Bruno – our greatest Archbishop of Canterbury. It is said that King Henry the Second, in a moment of frustration, cried in the presence of his nobles, "Who will rid me of this turbulent priest?" He meant it as a rhetorical question only, but they chose to understand it as an order – consequently Becket was run through with a sword while at prayer, to the king's horror. That was my mistake. I muttered something similar over poor Roger Mercer, and my faithful servant here' – he cast a look at Thomas every bit as loaded with scorn as his voice – 'chose to interpret that in his own way.'

'I did not hear you object, *Father*,' Thomas said quietly. 'You were pleased to have my help then.'

Jerome shrugged, unabashed.

'I do not deny that the thought of sparing myself – and Sophia – the disgrace Roger Mercer had threatened was attractive.' He turned back to me. 'But since you seem to have appointed yourself constable and magistrate in this case, Bruno, you should look more closely at your evidence. Thomas is every bit as good a player as I am, Bruno – it seems he had you cozened, at any rate. He may appear hare-brained and nervous as a coney, but he is shrewd as the Devil himself.'

Thomas merely returned his stare, his face inscrutable.

'He proposed that he would conjure a solution to our difficulty,' Jerome continued. 'Those were his words. I accepted his offer and said I wished to know nothing more until it was done. So I had no idea he had persuaded the Nappers to help him steal a dog. I was on my way back from Mass that night when I heard the commotion in the Grove and ran for my longbow. Only then did I learn what an elaborate display he had created.' He twisted his mouth in distaste.

'But why?' I asked, turning to Thomas as I tried to revise all the conclusions I thought I had made. 'What made you kill a man in such a manner, when you could not even be certain of the outcome?'

'*Martyrs*,' Thomas spat, as though the very word disgusted him. 'It is become their obsession. They all wanted to be martyrs for their faith, or at least they claimed they did. The highest glory.' His voice was rising to a manic pitch; he shook his head in fury. 'Even my father seeks a martyr's crown, it seems. What kind of a religion is it, Doctor Bruno, that makes men fall in love with death over life? Where is love, then? Where is human kindness?'

I could have pointed out that a man who would set a starving hunting dog on his father's closest friend may not be the best placed to talk of human kindness, but I kept silent. Thomas gestured at Sophia. 'To have the love of a woman like Sophia, the prospect of new life in her womb –'

'Thomas!' Sophia cried, stepping forward, but Jerome held out a hand to restrain her.

'But this – *creature* –' Thomas exploded, stabbing a finger at Jerome – 'throws it all aside, he saves all his desire for the executioner's blade!' His pointing finger trembled with pent-up passion. 'Well then, let them try martyrdom, I thought, see how they like it. The rector had just given a sermon on the death of St Ignatius. The teeth of wild beasts. It seemed as good a way as any to send Roger to meet his God.' He produced a strange, high-pitched laugh that chilled my blood. 'After the pain my father suffered for his sake, it was the least he deserved.'

An unnerving silence followed this outburst as the echo of his words died away. Sophia, Jerome and I stared at Thomas in rapt horror for a moment.

'And with every member of the college under increasing scrutiny, I was afraid my cover would be at risk. Which was your intention all along, was it not, my friend?' Jerome added softly, raising his head to look at Thomas, who only continued to return his stare, unblinking. I watched them both, still feeling all my nerves taut as a bowstring; I didn't know if Thomas was more disturbing when he was pulsing with manic energy or in this strange new stillness, as if he were a cat waiting to pounce.

'So you went to Mercer's room to get your hands on those papers before Thomas did?' I asked, turning back to Jerome. He made a brief, impatient movement with his head.

'I had no idea that Thomas knew about them. After Mercer threatened to expose me, I knew I would always be vulnerable while those letters – all Edmund Allen's correspondence with Rheims about my mission, and the *Regnans in Excelsis* Bull – were not in my own hands. But I barely had time to search his room before I saw you through the window, crossing the courtyard towards the tower staircase. I had to hide myself up on the roof of the tower before you came in. That was when I knew your true business in the college.' He nodded significantly, planting his hands on his hips.

'I had no *business*,' I said, my heart pummelling at my ribs, 'other than an interest in finding out how a man could have met such a horrific death – an interest none of his colleagues seemed to share. I only wanted to find some clue as to who he planned to meet and why he carried a full purse.'

Jerome cast his eyes down, his face guilty.

'Thomas asked only that I lure Mercer to the Grove that morning. I had told him I felt I should return to France in the circumstances. I asked him to meet me to return some of the money he held for me on behalf of the mission so that I could travel.'

'But then what of Coverdale?' I asked, looking from Jerome to Thomas. 'Did he also find out about Sophia?'

'You had better ask Thomas about Coverdale,' Jerome said, setting his jaw.

'That snake,' Thomas whispered, his soft voice making me jump after his long silence. 'Coverdale petitioned the rector for my removal from the college. He feared I knew too much and thought I would betray them out of revenge. The rector at least had some compassion and let me stay on, but it was Coverdale's fault that I lost my scholarship and had to depend

411

on *his* charity.' He jerked his head towards Jerome. 'Well, James Coverdale learned what revenge looked like. He was ever a coward – he cried like a girl child when I showed him the razor, and pissed himself.'

'So you decided to make a martyr of him too, because you despised his faith?'

Thomas smiled, looking at me from the corner of his eye like a child caught out in some mischief.

'When Jerome sent me to take his longbow and arrows to the strongroom, I had the idea of St Sebastian. I thought if the deaths looked like a pattern, it would frighten them even more. I asked Doctor Coverdale if I could speak privately with him later and he told me he would arrange to leave the disputation early. He feared I had come to bargain with him, but he never expected what happened next.' He was hugging himself tightly, rocking slightly, his mouth wide in a silent laugh. 'I needed those letters too, and I knew where to find them. That room used to be my father's, remember? I thought if I could put them into the right hands, *he* would be finished.' He pointed again at Jerome with a flourish.

'But I don't understand,' I said. 'If you wanted to expose Jerome, why not just tell the rector what you knew, long before this? You could have saved two innocent lives.'

Thomas gave me a scathing look.

'And lose my own? I took you for a clever man, Doctor Bruno. I was dependent on him – don't you see that? I could do nothing until I was assured of another place by some means. And perhaps you do not know the laws of our land. To aid, comfort or maintain a Jesuit is a felony, punishable by death. To live as his servant, to take his shilling to maintain his disguise – what is that if not aiding? And if the law did not kill me, that whoreson Jenkes would have done it first if I betrayed Gabriel. *Gabriel* – ha! He even took the name of an archangel – is that not hubris?'

'The face of an angel,' I murmured, echoing Humphrey Pritchard's words. 'But if someone *else* were to discover him, then you could not be implicated. All you had to do was point them in the right direction, with your quotations and your diagrams.' I let the words hang in the air. Thomas only looked at me, his teeth grinding together unconsciously. 'And poor Ned? Did he also betray your father?'

'*Ned*?' Sophia, who until now had been listening to Thomas's confessions with an expression of increasing horror, suddenly reached out and clutched Jerome's arm. 'Little Ned Lacy, the bible-clerk? He is not dead too?'

I nodded grimly, watching Thomas. Sophia pressed her hands over her face.

'He saw me with Sophia in the library while everyone was at the disputation, before I went to Coverdale's room,' Thomas said, with a shrug. 'I was trying to persuade her not to run away with Jerome.' His brow creased briefly and he rubbed his eyes. 'Then I saw you giving Ned money, I didn't know what to do. If he had not come back early, he would not be dead. It was his own fault.'

'But you couldn't resist visiting a martyrdom on him as well?' I said, my revulsion growing as I watched his apparent coldness. Thomas smiled slowly.

'It was a way of punishing the rector. Didn't you always say, Sophia, that your father loved Foxe's book more than his family? I swore I would make him hate that book. For you,' he added, turning to her with shining eyes. 'It was all for you. One day you will see that.'

'Enough!' Sophia cried, her voice thick with emotion. 'Enough talking, all of you – it is almost full daylight and no doubt they will have the watch out looking for me by now. We must leave, Jerome. What's done is done, and it will all be for nothing if we do not get away while we can.' She pulled urgently at his sleeve.

Thomas suddenly sprang to life as if a fire had been lit under him.

'You will not go to your death, Sophia,' he breathed, planting his feet firmly and fixing her with his furious gaze, his trembling hand still pointed at Jerome. 'You think he will take you safe to France? Five years of training and the best part of his inheritance he has given to this mission – you really believe he will give it all up for you? No – he craves the glory of martyrdom like the rest of them. He means for you to meet with an accident at sea.'

'Your mind is addled, Thomas,' Jerome began, taking a step towards him, his hand held out in a placatory gesture. Thomas sprang away.

'But I will not let that happen,' he cried, his voice high and strangulated, 'and if you will not heed my warning—'

He left the threat unspoken as, instead, he pulled the razor from under his cloak and, in the same movement, lunged at Jerome. I slipped Humphrey's knife from my belt but the Jesuit was soundly trained; before I could move, he had pushed Sophia behind him and aimed a kick at Thomas's outstretched arm. Thomas lost balance for a moment, though he did not drop the razor, but his slip gave Jerome the chance to bend and pull a knife from the side of his boot. Both circled warily, facing one another, eyes locked and weapons drawn, while Sophia stifled a scream and I hovered uselessly at the edge of this duel, wondering how I might intervene. But I did not have the chance; at that moment the door burst open and the servant, Barton, ran into the room, his poker held aloft; Thomas wheeled around with blazing eyes and, faster than you could blink, slashed wildly at the man's arm with his razor before he could strike. Barton howled and dropped the poker, clutching at his wound, and Thomas, seemingly crazed, leapt upon him and slashed at his neck with the razor over and over again; I threw myself at Thomas,

414

wrapping myself around his back and pulling at his arm but he was surprisingly strong for such a wiry boy, and it seemed his fury had lent him supernatural strength. He attempted to shake me off, but I was unable to restrain him and Barton's last guttural cries were drowned by Sophia's screams as his lifeblood gushed from the open wound over the brick floor and his dying breath faded as he clutched at Thomas's cloak and then slumped to the ground.

I let go of Thomas and turned, expecting to find Sophia hysterical from the scene she had just witnessed, but I saw that in the confusion Jerome had seized her from behind and was now holding her with one arm hooked around her chest, his knife pointed at the soft white skin of her throat.

'Put the razor down, Thomas,' he said, slowly and clearly, again sounding as calm as if he were a schoolmaster addressing a room full of mischievous boys. Thomas only stared slack-jawed, his face, arms and hands sprayed with the servant's blood, then he took a step forward and Jerome jerked the knife closer to Sophia's neck; she bit back a cry and squeezed her eyes shut, shaking her head with tiny movements.

'Let her go,' I said, trying to match Jerome's tone of calm authority.

'Let her go? Or what will you do, Bruno?' He kept the knife tilted at her throat, regarding me as if I were a tiresome distraction. 'Did you bring reinforcements?'

'No one knows I am here,' I said, not knowing if I spoke the truth. If Cobbett's messenger had managed to get the bundle of papers to Sidney, would he gather some men and come to look for me at Hazeley Court? How long would it take them to arrive, if he did? But the chance that Slythurst had let any messenger leave the college unhindered was tiny.

As if reading my mind, Jerome shook his head impatiently.

'Well, no matter. They will be too late. Once and for all,

throw your weapons down on the floor or your quest will have been in vain.' He lifted the elbow of the arm that held the knife, as if to plunge it; Thomas gave me a brief glance, then cast his razor on to the floor in front of him, where it clattered in the silence until it became still. I looked at Sophia, who had opened her eyes now and was watching me with an expression of mingled despair, fear and disbelief, then I too threw down my knife.

Jerome nodded.

'Good. Now you will stay here and keep quiet, before anyone else gets hurt.' He was manoeuvring Sophia towards the door that led to the western tower staircase, his knife held in place at her neck. Roughly he wrestled her forward, kicking the door shut behind him; as it swung, Thomas gave a cry of rage and ran at the doorway.

'You will not succeed,' Thomas cried in ragged breaths, racing to follow them; to my surprise, Jerome was forcing Sophia up the stairs instead of down, and as Thomas reached them Jerome kicked out and caught him on the jaw, making him fall back into me, his mouth bleeding.

Undeterred, he picked himself up and launched himself on to the narrow staircase, trying to grab at Jerome's heels as Jerome tried to kick back at him, while I followed close behind, pausing only to pick up my knife from the floor. Somewhere above us, echoing from the curving stone, we suddenly heard Sophia scream as if at a sharp pain, and I slapped at Thomas's ankle from below.

'He has a knife at her back,' I hissed. 'For God's sake, do nothing hasty.'

The climb was relentless; at one point I thought I heard Sophia cry, 'I cannot,' and Jerome answer, 'Trust me,' but the voices were muffled by the echoes. My battered legs began to tremble as we climbed higher, intermittently passing small cruciform windows that offered views over the manor's parkland and forest, and still Jerome forced Sophia upwards, and we followed, until I felt a draught of chill air on my face and understood that he was leading us to the very battlements of the tower. My stomach convulsed slightly as I tried to imagine what he might have in mind, and whether all four of us would return alive.

I emerged through a low doorway behind Thomas on to a platform perhaps twelve feet wide, enclosed by eight crenellated walls the height of a man's chest. Beyond them I could see the carriage drive and the cart track by which I had approached the house, the woods that bordered the path spread out far below us like a green canopy and, behind them, the line of distant blue hills, their peaks misted in the early light. At this height, more than a hundred feet above the ground, the wind was shrill in my ears, slicing across the roof of the tower. On the far side, Jerome once again held Sophia at the point of his knife, his hair whipping over his face. He beckoned to Thomas with his eyes.

'Come, then, Thomas,' he called, 'will you save her?'

Thomas hesitated a moment and I saw his body stiffen as he gathered his resolve, perhaps trying to judge how quickly he could move compared to Jerome. Sophia whimpered softly, her eyes flicking wildly from Thomas to me to the man whose arms now held her close, not for the first time, but now with very different intent; from the confusion and terror in her expression I could tell that she did not know if Jerome was serious or play-acting to trap Thomas. I reached out a hand to restrain Thomas, but in that moment he made up his mind and threw himself once again at his former master, bending to hurl his full weight at Jerome's midriff. The priest, pushing Sophia roughly to the ground, tried to stick Thomas with his knife, but Thomas twisted aside at the crucial moment, grabbing Jerome's raised arm in mid-air. For a moment their two arms were raised aloft in the shape of an arch, locked

417

together and trembling with the force of their opposing efforts, the knife flashing silver as it twisted in the air. Then Thomas jerked a knee sharply upwards into Jerome's groin; the priest yelped and doubled over, the tension in his arm momentarily lost, and in that second's lapse Thomas bit him hard on the wrist, causing him to drop the knife. But before Thomas could pick it up, Jerome had grasped him by the hair, yanked his head back and punched him hard in the face. Thomas attempted to hit back, blood coursing down his nose, but Jerome caught him again with a fist hard in the jaw and Thomas stumbled backwards, dangerously close to the parapet.

Sophia had wriggled away to the shelter of the wall; I crouched beside her and motioned to the stairway, but she shook her head, her eyes glassy with fear and still riveted on the life-or-death struggle before us. Slowly, so as not to attract attention, I reached out and scrabbled Jerome's fallen knife towards my hand, keeping my eyes on the fighting pair all the time. Thomas, now badly bruised and bleeding, mustered one last burst of energy and thrust a hand forward to grip Jerome around the throat; Jerome, his face contorted with rage, let go of Thomas's hair and clamped both his hands around the boy's neck. They swayed together in this oddly intimate dance, matching one another's steps, now one pushing forward, now the other, both choking and gasping through gritted teeth until it seemed that both must expire in the same moment, so fierce and determined were their crimson faces, when Jerome, who had the advantage of weight and strength, managed to force Thomas a few steps further back, into a gap between the battlements. Thomas felt the wall against his back and appeared to tighten his hold on Jerome's neck; Jerome leant all his weight forward, pushing Thomas so that he was hanging backwards through the gap, and for a moment I thought both would fall to their deaths together, when suddenly Sophia leapt to her feet, grabbed Jerome's knife from my hand before I realised what she was doing, and ran across to the fighting pair where she stabbed the knife, just once, into Thomas's right hand, still clamped fast around Jerome's throat.

Thomas cried out and released his grip involuntarily; in the same moment Jerome also let go of Thomas's throat and, bracing himself against the brick parapet, gave Thomas one almighty shove in the chest. With a harrowing scream, the boy flailed for a moment, his hands grasping furiously at nothing, before he toppled backwards and vanished from our sight, that terrible last cry echoing fainter and fainter as he fell seven tiers to the waiting ground. The impact was so dull we barely heard it from the roof; I wanted to lean over and look but kept my distance from the parapet, afraid to turn my back on Jerome. Sophia collapsed into his arms, sobbing and shaking violently. Gently he prised the knife from her fingers and rested his chin on the top of her head, breathing hard in ragged gasps. He looked across at me, the fury drained from his face and in its place only a bone-deep exhaustion. He rubbed his throat and twisted his neck from side to side as if to ease the pain.

'It had to come sooner or later,' he croaked, his voice barely audible. 'He would have been found out eventually, and then he would have taken me down with him.'

'We have killed him,' Sophia sobbed, raising her tear-streaked face from Jerome's shoulder. 'Oh, God – we have killed him! Poor Thomas – he was my only friend once. Will God ever forgive us his blood?' She looked up to the sky, now streaked with bands of blue, the worst of the rain clouds scurrying away toward the horizon.

'He killed three men, Sophia,' Jerome said hoarsely, still rubbing his throat. 'He would have killed me. We are fighting a Holy War, remember. To kill those who oppose God's kingdom is not murder.'

419

'Is that what they teach you at Rheims?' I asked, recovering myself and moving towards the stairs. Now that Jerome was in possession of his knife again I realised how vulnerable I was. I fervently did not want to follow Thomas over the parapet, but it was clear that Sophia could not be counted upon to act against Jerome, and I could not see that there was any chance he might let me walk free.

'And what of Sophia?' I added. 'Would it have been murder to have her killed before she reached France? Is she in the way of God's kingdom?'

Jerome laughed abruptly, wincing as the effort hurt his bruised throat.

'You saw for yourself how troubled that boy's mind was, Doctor Bruno. Once he had dirtied his hands with murder, he began to believe the rest of the world was also bent on killing. He was deluded to the very end.'

He took a step towards me, but before I could reach the stairs I collided with a body; whipping around, I saw that the doorway was blocked by two solid-looking servants in household livery. One of them, a burly man who was a good foot taller than me, grasped my arm and twisted it up behind my back, sending bursts of white-hot pain through my shoulder. This time I offered no resistance. I was not going to fight my way out of this, I realised. It seemed that unless the Jesuit was willing to show mercy, I had very little hope.

# TWENTY

'I will ask you again, Bruno – who else knows you are here?'
Jerome circled me, his eyes infinitely patient.

'No one,' I said through clenched teeth.

'Where are the papers you took from my chamber? The
ones Thomas left for you to find?'

I shook my head.

'I hid them in my room. No one else knows they are there.'

He frowned.

'He is lying,' he said, after a pause, addressing the servants.
'Listen – we have not much time. You –' he motioned to the
second man – 'go now, tell Lady Eleanor to expect a visit
from the pursuivants in the near future, and request her to
send a fast rider to Rowland Jenkes of Catte Street in Oxford,
bring him here as soon as possible. I must get Sophia safely
on the road – her father will have people looking for her by
now. Then I will return to Oxford. This man –' he nodded
towards me – 'should be kept alive until Jenkes arrives. He
travels with the royal party – there must be nothing in his
death that could point to us, any of us. But Jenkes will need
to speak to him first. He will be glad to be reunited with
you, will he not, Doctor Bruno?'

'Sophia, he means to kill you,' I burst out, as Jerome motioned for the servants to manhandle me back down the stairs. 'You may believe he cares for you,' I cried in desperation, 'but you heard with your own ears – he believes he has a dispensation from God Himself to cut down anyone who stands in his way! Do not go with him – you will never see France. Go back to your family, they will understand, I am sure of it.'

The servant tugged again on my arm as a warning, and pulled me back towards the stairs.

'I cannot, Bruno!' Sophia called in a cracked voice, as the servant ushered me roughly through the doorway and on to the staircase. 'I can never go back, not now. Apart from the child, I am a convert to Rome – I would only be tortured in some filthy gaol to betray my friends, and the child would likely die, and then I would end up wishing I was dead.'

'That will not happen,' I called back up the stairs, my voice echoing above me as the servant shoved me in the back of the head. 'I would help you – I have friends—'

'You, Bruno?' Jerome's mocking voice floated down the stairs. 'Oh yes, you have influential friends, I do not doubt it. But they are not here, and you will not be able to reach them, whatever you may have told them already.'

When we reached the tier where the stairwell opened into the grand gatehouse room, the man holding me dragged me out and waited for Jerome to emerge. Sophia followed, her dress dishevelled and her face pale and blotchy. The brief look she cast me was tense with distress.

'Bind him,' Jerome said curtly. He held out his knife towards me. 'Fetch ropes and a cloth to gag his mouth – you may leave him here with me. If he tries to flee he will not get far.'

The servant grunted and released my arm, though from the pain I could barely unbend it. As he disappeared through the door, Jerome advanced on me, holding out his knife.

'Come, Bruno, I would show you something,' he said, almost smiling. 'Please do not make things more difficult by trying to run now – I would have to hurt you and I do not want to do that.'

He beckoned me towards the opposite door into the eastern tower, where he and Sophia had been hidden when we first arrived.

Instead of a stairwell, this door led to a room lit by a tall window in each of the six outward-facing walls. As well as the door leading to the grand chamber, there was another door on the other inner wall, even narrower, leading to a small, low-ceilinged room built into the brickwork where the tower joined the east wing of the house, which I guessed must at one time have been a garderobe or privy. It was now quite empty, the walls of mellow brickwork, lit by two candles in sconces, and the floor of earthenware tiles. In the rear wall of this tiny room was built a recess about the height of a door and of a size that suggested it might once have held a small altar. Leaning against the interior wall of the recess, Jerome pressed his heel hard against the innermost floor tile and stepped back as a trap door concealed beneath the tiles swung soundlessly upwards, its weight beautifully poised on a wooden pivot. The lid was made from two solid blocks of oak nailed together, perhaps a foot thick; when in place its covering of tiles made it invisible, and no priest-hunter, knocking on the surface, would hear any hollow sound from within.

'Welcome to my home from home.' Jerome gestured with his knife. 'Not even five among the servants know this hide is here. It is carved into the very fabric of the house and is made to be undetectable from either side. You will find it surprisingly comfortable.'

'Master Owen's handiwork?' I asked.

Jerome glanced sidelong at me.

'Very good. I see you have learned much, Bruno. The question is – how much have you passed on?'

'I do not understand you,' I said. Jerome gave a little click of impatience, but before he could speak we heard the echo of hurried footsteps on the stairs and the stocky servant returned carrying a length of rope. My stomach lurched.

'Bind his hands before him,' Jerome barked, levelling the knife at my face. 'Make it secure. He can slip through mouse-holes, this one. It would go better for you if you don't resist, Bruno.'

I did not; after the night's events I no longer had the strength left for resistance. My left shoulder was so badly torn from the man's previous attentions that it barely seemed part of me any more; I held out my arms and when my wrists were tied for a second time, the position seemed almost familiar.

'Give me the rope and get gone. Help the household hide any sign of our presence and make ready for the pursuivants,' Jerome told the servant, gesturing for him to hurry. 'I will finish here. Sophia – go to Lady Eleanor, tell her we must have horses made ready. I will ride with you to Abingdon – I have contacts there who may be able to accompany you to the boat. You –' he said, turning to me and nudging me hard between the shoulder blades towards the gap in the recess – 'in there.'

Sophia wavered, as if unwilling to leave me to his mercy. 'Jerome, do not hurt him. He has been kind to me.'

'I'm sure he has,' Jerome replied, stony-faced.

I sat awkwardly on the edge of the gap in the floor, unable to balance without the use of my hands, and took a last look at Sophia's bone-white face, before feeling as best I could with my trussed hands to grip the grooves carved into the wooden lintel above the hold. I slid my body awkwardly through and under the wall; Jerome helped me on with a shove that caused me to land heavily on my damaged shoulder on the brick floor of the vault beneath. He took a candle from the wall and twisted his body through after me, lithe as a cat, guarding the flame with his right hand. Over his shoulder he had looped a length of rope and a piece of cloth.

By the jittery light of the candle flame, I saw that we had landed inside a surprisingly spacious cavity that appeared to have been built into the angle of the wall where the east range of the house joined the eastern tower of the gatehouse; it was high enough for a man to stand in, with a wooden bench placed in an alcove at the far end and beneath this, a small oak chest bound with iron bands. With some difficulty, I pressed my back against the wall and struggled to my feet. Jerome set his candle down on the floor and gestured to the bench; I limped across to sit down, grateful for the brief rest but already feeling my anxiety at being enclosed in a small space rising to the surface. My breathing was growing quicker and shallower and I knew that if he were to shut the trap door and leave me here alone I would forget how to breathe normally altogether. He regarded me with what I hoped might be pity, passing the rope between his hands as if deciding how to proceed.

'You don't like it here,' he remarked, noting my nostrils flaring in and out as I attempted to remain calm. 'I don't like being shut in either, but I have had to master it. Four hours I spent in here once, when there was a raid.' He shuddered at the memory.

'I suppose if the alternative is having your belly ripped open, you learn to bear it.'

Jerome acknowledged the truth of this with a wan smile, then crouched in front of me, staring me earnestly in the eye.

'What have you done with the letters, Bruno? I need to know. Who else have you told about me?'

'I have told you – the letters are in my room. As for you

– I only guessed at your identity tonight and I have not seen anyone since.'

'And I say you are lying,' he said, rising impatiently to his feet. 'Well, it is no matter. Jenkes will have the truth from you. He is quite as skilled as some of the queen's men in that grisly art. Did you know he was a mercenary in his youth? There is not much he does not know about pain – inflicting and enduring it.' He flashed me a significant look and turned away. 'People have had to die to protect my secret, Bruno. If you have set anyone else to hunt me down, my friends and I must at least know where to be vigilant.'

'Three men were killed under my nose in Oxford – my only interest was in finding out what happened. I did not come looking for secret priests.'

'No?' He gave me a long look, the candle lighting his high cheekbones from below so that his face resembled a carved mask whose contours shifted in the dancing flame. 'The Catholic Church has threatened your life – do you not want revenge? Have you not sold your hatred to the Protestant cause to work against the Church that has hunted you?'

'No,' I said simply. 'I hate no one. I want only to be left in peace to contemplate the mysteries of the universe in my own way.'

'God has already laid out for us the mysteries of the universe, or as much as He permits us to understand. You think your way is better?'

'Better than these wars of dogma that have led men to burn and fillet one another across Europe for fifty years? Yes, I do.'

'Then what *is* it you believe?'

I looked at him.

'I believe that, in the end, even the devils will be pardoned.'

'Ah. *Tolerance*.' Jerome pronounced the word as if he had just eaten a bad olive. 'Compromise. Yes, there are many in

426

the seminaries who would advocate the same – failing to understand that this tolerance is equal to saying there is no right or wrong, no truth or heresy. Thank God my order fiercely opposes all such dilution of the faith. Do you not know, Bruno, that the fiercer the persecution inflicted on Catholics and priests in England, the more our numbers flourish? Your tolerance would destroy in twenty days what twenty years of suffering has only served to strengthen.'

'So the holy bloodshed continues,' I said. 'Men and women rushing headlong into the executioner's embrace. Is that martyrdom or suicide?'

Jerome only smiled gently.

'Do you know what we call England on the mission?' He paused for effect. '"Death's ante-chamber." I have never had any doubt as to how it will end for me – but there is a harvest of souls to be gathered first. Perhaps yours among them, Bruno.'

He reached inside his shirt and pulled out a silver chain bearing a small key, then he knelt again at my feet and reached under the bench to pull out the wooden chest. Opening its padlock, he removed two small vials of holy oil and sat back on his heels, looking at me intently.

'I must make this plain,' he said, holding up the bottle so that I could see it. 'You are going to die. Whatever you have or have not already said, everything you have seen this past night makes you a danger to God's work here. But I would not leave you in your final moments without comfort, Bruno.' He held out a hand to me. 'Confess yourself, repent of your heresy, be reconciled to the Church in your last hour, and as a Jesuit I can give you the sacrament of absolution.'

I read his sincerity in his face, and in spite of myself I laughed.

'*You*, Father Jerome – you would absolve me? You, who father a child and would kill its mother and two other men to protect the sanctity of your reputation – you presume to absolve *me*? My heresy was to read a few books of astronomy and philosophy. If you are right, and God weighs our sins in the balance on the Day of Judgement, whose do you think will weigh heavier?'

Jerome lowered his eyes for a moment before returning to meet my gaze defiantly.

'When Lucifer tempted Christ in the wilderness, did he tempt him with women, with sins of the flesh? No. He tempted Him with the sin of pride. He dared Christ to prove Himself equal to God. I have sinned, but mine were sins of the flesh, for which the flesh atones with hard penance. Whereas *you* presume, in the arrogance of your intellect, to remake the fabric of the universe, to rip the Earth from the centre of God's creation where His Word and all the teachings of the Fathers have set it! It is you who is the true heir of the rebel angels, Bruno.'

'I prefer such a lineage to that of Cain,' I replied. 'Even if I wished to be reconciled to the Church, I would not take my absolution from such a man as you.'

'As you wish,' he shrugged, replacing the holy oils in the trunk. When he had locked it, he tucked the key back inside his shirt and stood to face me, hands on his hips. 'It is strange that I should admire you, Bruno, but I feel a curious kinship. In different times I should have so enjoyed the chance to debate with you. I am trained first and foremost for scholarly argument, and you would have been a worthy opponent.' He smiled sadly. 'You and I are similar men, I think, though we stand on different sides of the great divide. For all your talk of tolerance, you will no more compromise than I will. You have endured great hardships for your beliefs, as have I, and you go to your death defiant, just as I will when the appointed time comes. For that I cannot help but respect you, and wish you had been one of us.'

'Then in a spirit of kinship, let me ask one thing of you, Father, in place of my absolution,' I said quickly. He gave me a questioning look and I continued, 'Let Sophia go back home. Do not pursue the course you have set. Save one innocent life, at least.'

Jerome sighed, a great shudder that seemed to wrack his whole body.

'You have not understood, have you, Bruno? She has no home. There is nothing in Oxford for her now. She will be spurned by her family for converting to the old faith, and spurned by the Catholics as a fallen woman.'

'She is a Catholic and a dishonoured woman because of *you*,' I said through gritted teeth, struggling to my feet, though there was little I could do except gesture with my bound hands. 'Is it right that she should be disposed of so that you can walk free? Her sins are your sins, *Father*.'

'Do you think I do not know that?' He grasped my wrists suddenly and held his face close to mine and I saw for the first time the storm of emotion beneath the professional calm.

'You do not seem to feel much remorse,' I remarked.

'Remorse?' He stared at me, then released my hands with a strange, desperate laugh. 'Oh, I can show you remorse, Bruno.' He began unlacing his doublet and I sat back on the bench, watching as he opened his fine silk shirt to reveal a cilice of coarse black animal hair. He unlaced the neck and drew the hairshirt gingerly down over his shoulders, wincing soundlessly as he did so.

'Here is my remorse,' he said, turning away from me.

I looked for a moment at his broad naked back, at the welter of torn, bloody skin, some wounds still livid and seeping where the metal hooks of the whip had gouged great pieces of flesh, others forming scars over older scars. I had seen penitents many times on my travels through Italy, and I was freshly amazed that any living being could inflict such cruelty on their own body in the name of atonement. I drew my breath in sharply and turned away, but he wheeled around to face me once more. Something had broken in him; his eyes shone with fury and tears.

'Is that remorse enough for you? Do you think I did not love her? Do you know how it tore my soul in two, to choose between the vows I have taken and what I felt for her?'

'If you love her, then do not sacrifice her,' I said softly.

'For Christ's sake, Bruno, I am not going to sacrifice her!' he cried, running both hands through his hair. 'She will be safe in France.'

'I think you are lying,' I said.

He took a deep breath, gathering in his turbulent emotions, then fixed me with a severe look.

'Then in that we are equal.' He replaced the cilice, clenching his jaw hard as it made contact with his ravaged skin, then buttoned up his shirt and shrugged on his doublet, watching me all the time. Finally he bent down to retrieve the length of rope from the floor, and with it bound my ankles, not painfully but firmly. 'Goodbye, Bruno,' he said, standing and regarding me sadly before sweeping all traces of tears from his cheeks with a brusque movement. 'I am genuinely sorry it ends this way. I pray God will speak to your soul in these last moments.'

He took the piece of cloth he had brought and moved to secure it around my mouth.

'The trap door does not open from the inside,' he remarked as he did so. 'And the walls are so thick that no one will hear you scream, but just in case.'

'Jerome – wait,' I said, holding up my hand as he lifted the cloth.

'Yes?' His eyes widened, almost touchingly eager, perhaps hoping that I had changed my mind about repentance.

'Leave me the light,' I whispered, hearing the tremor in my voice.

He nodded once before securing the cloth over my mouth, then turned and moved back towards the opening that led to the small garderobe. I watched as his fine leather boots disappeared upwards into the square of daylight, before the hatch slid into place with barely a click, and I was left alone, bricked into the wall of the house, unable to move or speak, feeling that I had been buried alive.

The last I remember was thinking that I would even be relieved to see Jenkes, as I battled the sense that my chest was swelling to bursting point, my breath trapped under my ribs as I was trapped in the priest-hole, the little vision afforded me by the candle blurring and wavering as I lost all feeling in my hands and feet and a strange, welcome light-headedness, almost as if I were underwater, carried me away through the flickering light into blackness.

# TWENTY-ONE

I was returned abruptly to my senses as I hit the brick floor hard on my side. The candle had long burned out but a faint square of light entered through the open trapdoor; I blinked hard but could only make out shadows against the darkness. A pair of strong arms grappled me awkwardly towards the open hatch, where other hands gripped me beneath my armpits and hoisted me upwards into the garderobe. Dazed and half-conscious as I was, I squinted and tried to open my eyes, expecting to look up into the triumphant eyes of Rowland Jenkes, but the man who had pulled me from the hide was dressed in some kind of soldier's uniform I did not recognise. He pushed me roughly down the steps into the chamber, now brightly lit by a sun that was high overhead; I stumbled and came to rest on my knees at the feet of a short, sandy-haired man with a foxy face, a neat, pointed beard and wide moustaches, dressed in a green doublet. He stroked his chin, looked at me with satisfaction for some moments, then nodded. The man in soldier's uniform reached for his dagger and brought it up to my face; I tried to wrench my head away, screaming to no avail through the cloth gag, but the soldier neatly slipped the point of his dagger behind the cloth and cut through it, tearing the pieces from my mouth.

'That's him, sir,' said another voice; I looked up to see the man who had given me passage through the East Gate of Oxford, still in his watchman's livery

'Now,' said the fox-faced man. 'Where is your accomplice?'

I stared up at him, uncomprehending.

'Answer me, you papist dog,' he said, kicking me soundly in the stomach.

'I don't understand,' I gasped, the little breath I had recovered knocked out of me once more.

'What did you say?' The fox-faced man stepped forward with sudden interest, crouching so that his face was close to mine. 'Speak again in the queen's English, you filthy piece of shit.'

'I have no accomplice,' I managed to croak.

'What accent is that you have?'

'I am Italian. But I—'

'As I thought. Sent by the Jesuits in Rome, no doubt. Well, we have found your hiding place now, Padre. I'm afraid not all the Lady Tolling's servants are as loyal as she might have hoped. Do you know who I am?'

'No, but I am no Jesuit—' I began, but the man lifted a hand and slapped me soundly around the face.

'Silence! You will have time enough to make your defence hereafter, when you have told us where to find your friend. I am Master John Newell, County Pursuivant of Oxfordshire. State your name – and do not waste our time with one of your aliases. We will have the truth from you sooner or later.'

Relief flooded over me, despite my smarting face; the man was obnoxious, but at that moment I could have thrown my arms around him and kissed him. His presence here with armed men could only mean that my message had reached

Sidney and he had alerted the authorities – though it sounded from the pursuivant's words as if they had arrived too late to stop Jerome and Sophia from leaving.

'I am Doctor Giordano Bruno of Nola,' I said, attempting to sit up and recover some dignity, 'a guest of the University of Oxford travelling with the royal party.'

'You lie,' he said coldly. 'You are one of Lady Tolling's priests. But where is the other? The servant we persuaded to talk said there was an Englishman, tall and fair. Where is he hiding?'

'He is fled,' I said, my tongue tripping over the words in my haste, 'he travels with a young woman, Sophia Underhill, towards the coast. They will board a ship to France where she will be killed. Hurry, you must stop them!'

The pursuivant laughed unpleasantly.

'It does not take much to make you squeal, does it, Jesuit?' he mocked. 'You will be an easy job for my men. There is the loyalty of papists for you,' he added, looking up, and the men standing about laughed sycophantically.

'I am no Jesuit,' I insisted. 'Where is Sidney? He will tell you who I am – let me see Sidney.'

'Who is Sidney?' asked the pursuivant.

'Sir Philip Sidney, nephew to the Earl of Leicester,' I said, my confidence faltering. 'Did he not call you here, on my instructions? Is he not with you?'

'Sir Philip Sidney?' The pursuivant seemed to find this vastly entertaining. 'Oh, ho! And are we to expect Her Majesty herself to arrive any moment to intervene for you? No, my Romish friend, I was not called by Sir Philip Sidney, nor anyone so grand, but by Master Walter Slythurst of Lincoln College, who had reason to believe a notorious papist and murderer was fleeing the city of Oxford in the direction of Great Hazeley, most likely seeking protection.'

'Oh, God, Slythurst,' I moaned, burying my face in my

still-bound hands. 'He has it all wrong, you must believe me – I am no murderer, nor a papist. I live with the French ambassador in London, for God's sake! I was trying to save Sophia when the real priest threw me in that hide.'

'He *is* bound, sir,' pointed out the young soldier who had dragged me from the hide, somewhat nervously.

'*What?*' Newell snapped around peevishly.

'He was bound hand and foot and gagged in there,' the young man said, his voice wavering now. 'It's just – why would he do that to himself?'

'They have all sorts of ruses you would never dream of,' said Newell, his lips pressed tightly together. He turned back to me. 'You can plead your case before the Assizes when the time comes. A spell in the Castle gaol should clear your head. Meanwhile, you can tell me what you know of Sophia Underhill. Her father alerted the watch yesterday that she had been abducted. Is it the papists that have done this?'

'They are en route to the coast,' I gasped, 'though they went first to Abingdon. Every moment you waste here is a gift to him – you must send your men on the road after them.'

'Don't tell me how to command my men, you cur,' he spat in my face. He motioned to the soldier. 'Arrest this man for the murder of two respected Fellows and one student of Lincoln college, and on suspicion of the murder of a young man thrown to his death from the gatehouse tower.' When I opened my mouth to protest he added, 'and on suspicion of entering this country with treasonable intent to seduce the queen's subjects to the Church of Rome, and with meddling in affairs of State.'

'No! I beg you, send for Sir Philip Sidney at Christ Church College, he will tell you I am innocent,' I cried, as the young soldier untied my ankles, took me by the elbow and heaved me to my feet.

'Oh yes – and with stealing a horse,' added Newell, with malicious pleasure. 'We found an animal of quality, wearing harness of royal colours, tied in the woods by the cart road.'

'The horse is mine – it was lent me from the royal stables at Windsor.'

'Is that so?' His moustaches twitched with cruel amusement. 'I wonder that Her Majesty did not lend you her best carriage as well. Enough of this folly.'

He stalked away through the large chamber over the gatehouse. At the staircase in the western tower he paused and turned.

'Let Sir Philip Sidney come and pay your release from the Castle gaol if he is truly your friend,' he said, as if it hardly concerned him, before addressing the soldier: 'Bring this man down to the courtyard – we will take him back to Oxford with us. Have some of your men stay here to sort the servants into those who will talk willingly and those who will require force.'

The soldier nodded and pushed me forward towards the spiral staircase. As I fought to keep my footing on the narrow stairs, going downwards this time towards the yard, I tried to consider my situation in the best light. It looked bleak, but surely Sidney or Rector Underhill could be called upon to vouch for me. Then I remembered the package of letters, and Bernard's warning to me on my arrival in Oxford, that no man is what he seems. I had trusted Cobbett, but supposing he was yet another Catholic sympathiser? If he had not passed on the cache of letters between Edmund Allen and Jerome Gilbert, there would be no hard evidence to condemn Jerome but my word against his. My nationality and my former religion would be enough to damn me in many eyes, as I had often been reminded since arriving in Oxford. And might Underhill not find it convenient to allow me to shoulder the blame rather than acknowledge the presence of a Jesuit under his very nose for more than a year? Sidney was now my only hope, but if he had not received my message, he would have no idea where to find me until long after I had been thrown into a stinking gaol. On the bright side, I told myself, as I was bundled out through the gatehouse archway into the glare of the courtyard, if Jenkes had reached me before the pursuivant, I would surely be lying in a roadside ditch with my throat cut by now, so there was still hope.

The sun was high overhead, intermittently shadowed by drifts of cloud. Around the courtyard, small groups of servants huddled nervously, whispering to one another as they watched the proceedings, each group attended by two or more armed men. I glanced around, recognising the stocky man who had brought me down from the tower, but he quickly looked away. I wondered if it was he who had pointed the pursuivant to the hide in the first place. If any of the household knew that the pursuivant had the wrong man, they were not willing to speak; presumably their loyalty lay with Father Jerome and they were happy to see me taken in his place.

I was presented with a mounting block and helped on to a dun horse, my hands still tied before me. The lack of sleep and food and the night's various injuries were beginning to tell; my head seemed filled with lead and I could barely sit upright. John Newell noticed how I slumped forward and hit me in the stomach with the handle of his sword.

'Should I have a sign made to hang around your neck, you Italian son of a whore?' he asked, squinting up at me into the sunlight. 'Reading *Seditious Jesuit* – like the one Edmund Campion wore when he was paraded back to London? Make sure he sits upright,' he barked at the soldier who held the horse's reins. 'Or he'll fall off before we reach the end of the carriage drive and we shall never get him to Oxford.'

'He might need a drink to keep him awake, sir, he looks

a bit parched,' the soldier ventured, and I nodded at him gratefully; the man clearly had more compassion than most.

'A *drink*?' Newell looked at the man as if he had just suggested I be provided with musicians and courtesans. 'I see – shall I send for the best of Hazeley's cellars for our dear guest? And, what, shall we roast a goose for him? Pay attention to your business, soldier, and do not tell me mine.'

The soldier lowered his eyes, chastened, daring a quick glance of apology at me. I mouthed 'thank you' at him through cracked lips when Newell had turned away to mount his own horse. He had just walked it around to lead the party that was apparently to parade me triumphantly back to Oxford, when the silence was shattered by a frantic clattering of hooves, and I looked up to see in the distance, at the top of the carriage drive, two horsemen leading a group of perhaps thirty armed men, in different colours from those already gathered in the courtyard. I confess I was astonished that they should think they needed so many reinforcements to subdue a couple of priests, but then I saw the County Pursuivant turn to the captain of his group of men with a look of consternation; clearly he had not been expecting these new arrivals.

It was only as the leading horseman galloped his mount right up to Newell before reining it in with a great whinny and scattering of stones, that I fully understood what was happening and my heart leapt.

'What in Christ's name have you done to my friend, you churl?' Sidney cried, leaping from his horse and running over to me, his sword drawn. 'By God, I'll flog the man who did this with my own hands! Untie him, soldier,' he yelled at the man holding my horse, who moved instantly to obey. I thought Newell might object, but when I glanced at him, I saw that he was eyeing the other horseman, Sidney's companion, with a mixture of resentment and deference.

'My Lord Sheriff,' Newell muttered, removing his hat. 'I have captured a dangerous Jesuit out of Italy, bent on spreading popery and corrupting Her Majesty's loyal subjects.'

'I'm afraid you have not, Master Newell,' said the other man calmly. He wore a broad hat with a feather and his beard was greying; a prominent coat of arms was embroidered on his crimson doublet. He had kindly eyes and a bearing that commanded respect. 'This man is a renowned philosopher and a friend of Sir Philip Sidney here. You have let the real priest escape.'

'My Lord Sheriff—' Newell bleated, but the sheriff waved a hand.

'No matter – my men are already in pursuit of him, thanks to Sir Philip and our Italian friend here. He will not get far.'

Sidney reached out and helped me down from the horse. I rubbed my wrists together, barely able to move my hands; Sidney hooked one of my arms around his own shoulder and led me to his companion, supporting my weight with an arm around my waist.

'Sir Henry Livesey, Lord High Sheriff of Oxfordshire,' Sidney announced, gesturing up at the man on the horse. 'May I present Doctor Giordano Bruno of Nola – not, alas, at his best.'

I attempted a bow, still clinging to Sidney's neck, and the man on the horse smiled.

'I – I had reason to believe Lady Tolling was sheltering a Jesuit priest,' Newell spluttered, looking anxiously at his superiors. 'I found him in a priest-hole – and he is an Italian,' he added, with a defensive air.

'The Holy Office hates this man almost as much as it hates Her Majesty,' Sidney said, casting a withering look at Newell. 'Is it not so, Bruno?' He cuffed me affectionately on my damaged shoulder and I yelped in pain.

'Sorry,' he said, rubbing at the spot no less heartily, but

in a manner I supposed was meant to be comforting. 'Christ alive, you are a wreck, Bruno. We must have someone take a look at that.' He led me towards his horse and heaved me up into the saddle, springing up himself in front of me and gripping the reins.

'I will leave my men here to assist you, Newell,' the sheriff commanded, dismounting and motioning to the captain of his men to move forward. 'I want all the servants interrogated. I will speak to Lady Tolling myself. Kindly take me to her. Sir Philip,' he said, turning to us with a brief bow, 'five of my men will escort you and Doctor Bruno back to Oxford. I am most sorry, sir,' he added, addressing himself to me, 'that you have been so badly mistreated at the hands of the County Pursuivant. Please accept my apologies and rest assured that he will be disciplined.'

Newell blanched; I could barely rouse myself to do more than nod my thanks to the sheriff. Sidney wheeled the horse around and I held tight to his back as we rode up the carriage drive, followed by five of the Lord High Sheriff's armed riders at a discreet distance.

'You have acquitted yourself well, Bruno,' Sidney said in a low voice over his shoulder. 'You have risked your life to track down a murderer and a priest without revealing yourself. The sheriff will take the credit for the arrests, but Walsingham will be told it was down to your tenacity.'

'I had given up hope of seeing you again,' I muttered to his back as he urged the horse to a brisk trot, a wave of exhaustion suddenly flooding over me. 'I thought my message had not reached you.'

'A kitchen boy from Lincoln brought your package in the hour before dawn,' he replied over his shoulder, his voice whipped away by the wind, 'knocking on the gate of Christ Church as if it were the gates of Hell, apparently. He told the porter it was urgent – fought tooth and nail to get to me, they said – but the porter would not wake the dean before first light, and the dean would not wake me until after morning service, the pair of fools, hence the delay. The boy, to his credit, would not part with his package except into my own hands, however the dean tried to coax him. As soon as I saw what was inside, I knew you were in serious danger and had the dean rouse the high sheriff. We had no idea the pursuivant's men would beat us to it.'

'Slythurst sent them after me,' I said, unable to keep the bitterness from my voice. 'He was determined to have those letters.'

'I would guess he is a low-rank informer trying to prove himself,' Sidney said. 'Walsingham has them placed all over the university, though he tends not to notify his people of one another's existence. He thinks it keeps them on their toes.'

'Where are the letters now?' I asked, keeping my voice low.

'Safely on their way to London in the hands of the dean's most trusted messenger,' Sidney said. 'They will be decoded there and used as evidence at the trial. But from the little I could read, they will be enough to see Jerome Gilbert hanged for a traitor.' He paused, turning the horse out of the cart track and back on to the lane that led towards the city. 'The attorney general will likely turn this to our advantage by adding three charges of murder. It will be a useful reminder to the populace of the Jesuits' ruthlessness.'

'But Thomas Allen killed the three Lincoln men,' I protested. 'He confessed it. And now Thomas is dead too.'

'How?'

'Gilbert pushed him from the tower.'

Sidney winced, drawing a breath sharply through his teeth.

'Well then, he is not able to confess now, is he, and that version would have far less public impact than to blame the

441

Catholic priest,' he said. 'Jerome Gilbert. He is the younger son of a wealthy Suffolk family – it was his brother, George, who provided all the funds for Edmund Campion's mission. He fled to France when Campion was executed – his brother must have gone with him.' He shook his head angrily. 'They should have been watched more closely.'

'Will they catch Jerome, do you think?'

'The sheriff has the hue and cry after them on every route out of Oxford. They will not get far.'

'And Sophia?' I whispered anxiously.

'She will be arrested with him,' Sidney threw over his shoulder with apparent unconcern. 'The rest will depend on her. If she protests her loyalty to him, she will likely be taken for questioning.'

'Tortured?' I sat up straighter, leaning close to his ear. 'But she is with child.'

I felt him shrug.

'Then she may plead her belly, if her family will buy her release from gaol until the child is born. That will give her time to decide if her loyalty to Gilbert survives his execution. He will be taken to London to coax from him what more he knows. Where did you find the letters, anyway?' he asked casually, leaning back towards me.

I hesitated, knowing that I was about to risk my credibility in Walsingham's service, if Sophia should insist on telling the truth. But the thought of her suffering the kind of tortures Walsingham had detailed to me made me feel I had no choice.

'Sophia gave them to me,' I said, hearing the hollow ring of falsehood in my own voice. I wondered if Sidney detected it too, because I felt his shoulders stiffen beneath my hands.

'Sophia? Really? Then she betrayed him willingly?'

'Yes. She discovered that he planned for her to meet with an accident on her passage to France. She asked for my help.'

For a few moments, the only sound was the soft squelch

442

of the horses' hooves on the muddy turf and the jangling of the armed riders behind us. Sidney appeared to be weighing this up. After a few moments he craned his head back towards me.

'Is this the truth, Bruno?'

'Absolutely.'

'Then by that action she may just have saved herself. Though it will prove rather awkward if her story differs from yours. Something you may want to think about before you repeat it to anyone else.' He let the sentence hang in the air. I did not miss the note of warning.

'What will happen to Lady Tolling?' I asked, keen to change the subject before he could press me further.

'Her estates will be attainted. She and those Catholics among her household will be imprisoned. If she is willing to inform, she may be spared her life.'

I thought of the tall, elegant woman, so calmly receiving us into her grand gatehouse chamber – a room that would not now belong to her heirs, because of me. Of the six people who had been present in that room, perhaps I would be the only survivor, once Lady Tolling, Jerome and Sophia had been arrested and tried. I could only hope that Sophia would have the sense, once Jerome was arrested, not to try and prove her devotion by following him to martyrdom; for then, in trying to save her, I would have delivered her to a worse death, and Sidney and Walsingham would know that I was too easily moved to pity, that my truthfulness was liable to be compromised by my heart.

'And what of us?' I asked, as the road became firmer and Sidney spurred the horse to a canter, causing me to slip sideways and grab frantically at his shoulders for balance.

'We return to London by river, once you are rested,' he said. 'The palatine is tired of Oxford, but I have persuaded him to stay another day for the luxury of returning by boat.

Once Gilbert is arrested there will be no need for you to testify at the inquest into Roger Mercer's death tomorrow. You had better keep your head down – the less you are publicly associated with the circumstances of Gilbert's discovery and arrest, the better for your cover. But rest assured, my friend – you will be well rewarded,' he added, as if this must be my main concern.

Well rewarded, I thought, as the outlying dwellings of Oxford became visible in the distance. I had narrowly escaped with my life, but others would not be so fortunate, and before I reached London I would have to decide how much I would tell Walsingham of what I knew. I still believed that Jerome Gilbert had intended to remove Sophia as an obstacle to his mission, despite his violent denials and her dogged faith in him, but I found it hard to believe he was a danger to the English state, any more than I believed Lady Eleanor Tolling, with her assiduous care for the missionary priests, was a traitor to her country. And while I would not be sorry to see Jenkes apprehended, would I also hand over good-natured, slow-witted Humphrey Pritchard to the torturers, or earnest Master Richard Godwyn the librarian? Walsingham had warned me that this kind of choice was part of his service, and I needed to repay his faith in me if I were to have any hope of gaining the queen's patronage. Playing politics with the lives of others was part of the path to advancement, but that, as I was just beginning to understand, was the real heresy. The only reward I now wanted was to see Sophia take the chance of escape that my lie would offer her, and not to consider martyrdom as a substitute for love.

# TWENTY-TWO

I was woken the following day by the slamming of my chamber door as Sidney, dressed in a plum-coloured velvet doublet and short breeches with white silk stockings, threw it open without a knock, grinning broadly as he strode across and drew back the curtains with a flourish to let in the full force of the midday spring sun. At his insistence I had returned directly with him and was now lodged at Christ Church College, in an oak-panelled room adjacent to his own, several degrees of luxury above the chamber I had become used to at Lincoln. Here I had a soft bed, woollen blankets, fresh water for washing and a jug of small beer by my bed, though I had barely had a chance to appreciate any of this comparative ease, since I had done nothing but sleep since we had returned from Hazeley Court the previous day.

'And how do I find you this fine afternoon, my adventurous friend?' Sidney asked, pouring himself a cup of beer. I noticed that he was now quite openly wearing an ornamental sword at his belt, despite the university's absolute ban on weapons. Clearly he had decided that the circumstances warranted a breach of etiquette.

I struggled to sit up, feeling my shoulder twinge viciously as I leaned my weight on my arm.

'Is it afternoon already? This shoulder is still bad but I feel rested, I think.'

'So you should, you have been asleep almost a whole day. You have missed all the excitement.'

'Why, what has happened?' I asked anxiously, wincing again as I tried to push myself up on my bad arm.

'Gilbert and Sophia were taken shortly after we found you yesterday, at a house in Abingdon,' he said, taking an orange from his pocket and digging his thumb into the peel, 'and Jenkes is fled. His shop was raided last night but nothing incriminating was found, if you can believe it. His apprentice was taken for questioning but says only that his master has had to travel on business. That snake has slipped through our fingers this time, but at least he will not trouble you again in Oxford.' He tore a curling strip of peel from the orange and let it drop on the stand beside my bed. The scent brought back a sharp memory of that first morning in Roger Mercer's room, the peel under the desk, the faint smell on the pages of the almanac. Might it have been better altogether if I had left that book alone, if I had never caught the scent of orange juice from its covers?

'Sophia and Jerome – where are they?' I asked.

'Father Jerome is on his way to London for some uncomfortable questioning,' he said, seeming more interested in delicately separating a segment of his orange and holding it out to me. His detachment made me uncomfortable. 'Sophia,' Sidney continued, putting a piece of fruit into his mouth, 'is at present under the supervision of her father. It seems they allowed her to be released on bail.' He gave me a long look, one eyebrow raised in what I judged to be a disapproving complicity, before licking his fingers deliberately and turning away to the window. 'Anyway, I came to tell you that there

446

is a messenger arrived at the porter's lodge just now from Rector Underhill himself, inviting you to visit him at his lodgings before you leave Oxford.'

'I will go straight away,' I said, levering myself gingerly out of bed, anxious to speak to Sophia if only to make sure she had decided to confirm my story about the letters. The fact that she had been released into the custody of her father suggested that she had not insisted too vehemently on her loyalty to Jerome, but she may simply have pleaded her belly. How she must have hated me, I thought, when she saw him led away in manacles by the pursuivants. More than anything, I wanted the chance to ask her forgiveness, to convince her that I had acted for her own good. There was little chance she would believe me, but I did not want to leave Oxford with these things unsaid.

'I will go with you,' Sidney said, as I pulled on my breeches and buttoned my shirt in such haste that I had it all awry and had to begin again. 'Jenkes may not be at large, but he has friends who may well have been instructed to see that you don't get back to London and talk. Until we leave tomorrow, you are not to go unaccompanied or unarmed.'

I stopped, midway through pulling on my boot.

'I would like to see the rector alone, though.'

'Don't worry – I won't interfere with your fond farewells. I will make idle chatter with the porter while I wait.'

'Cobbett!' I exclaimed, remembering that if it were not for his brave insubordination on my behalf, Sidney would never have received my message and I would certainly be either murdered or arrested, depending on which of my pursuers had reached me first. I turned to Sidney apologetically. 'I fear I must ask you to advance me some of that promised reward from your father-in-law. Jenkes stole my purse, and I would like to thank Cobbett – it was he who sent the boy and brought you to my rescue, at some cost to himself.'

'Well, then, we shall see what the college cellar may offer a man of such stout heart,' Sidney said with a grin, opening the door for me. 'I never thought I would say this, Bruno, but I shall not be sorry to leave these spires behind me this time.'

'Nor I,' I replied with feeling, remembering with a terrible pang of melancholy how I had once dreamed of making my name in Oxford.

When we reached Lincoln gatehouse, carrying a bottle of Spanish wine Sidney had bought from the cellarer at Christ Church, there was no sign of Cobbett in the little lodge beneath the archway. In his place was a thin-faced man with straggly brown hair who looked up at us suspiciously, then lowered his eyes as he registered the quality of Sidney's clothes.

'Where is Cobbett?' I asked, more brusquely than necessary.

The man shrugged, evidently disliking my tone.

'All I know is he's suspended from duty. They're saying he'll be retired. Who'd'ye want to see?'

'Rector Underhill. He is expecting me. Doctor Bruno.'

Sidney clapped me on the shoulder with unusual gentleness.

'I think I shall take a drink in the Mitre Inn on the corner of the High Street. Find me there when you are done – do not think of going any further without me,' he added, with a warning glance. The new porter glared at me, then motioned me towards the courtyard.

'Ye'll find him in his lodgings,' he grunted, eyeing the bottle of wine. I tucked it tightly under my arm and set off across the courtyard, turning in the middle to glance back with a shudder at the window of the tower room and the doorway to what had been Gabriel Norris and Thomas Allen's room.

The rector's old servant, Adam, opened the door to my knock and almost fell backwards when he saw me, his usual surly countenance replaced by a wide-eyed expression of

448

honest terror. He pulled the door close behind him so that his voice would not carry and stepped out into the passageway.

'I can pay you, sir,' he hissed, clutching urgently at the front of my doublet. 'I have money saved for my old age – it is not a fortune, but you may find a use for it. You know, it was only ill luck that you saw me that night, for I hardly ever go to that place any more, it was only to oblige a friend, but if you must make a report or a list of names, I pray you, take what money I have in my coffers, if only my name might not appear—'

'Peace, Adam,' I whispered back, removing his trembling hands from my clothes and feeling oddly insulted. 'I have no use for your money, nor has anyone asked me for names. But if you will profess a forbidden faith, at least have the courage to be true to it – otherwise what is the point?'

He offered up a limp smile of gratitude, then opened the door for me.

'My master is within,' he murmured, bowing his head.

In the wide reception room where we had dined so companionably on my first evening in Oxford, the rector stood facing the window that gave on to the Grove, hands clasped behind his back. I glanced around at the empty dining table, remembering where Roger Mercer and James Coverdale had sat at that dinner, recalling the deep rumble of Mercer's laughter. Perhaps the rector too was remembering as he looked out over the garden where Mercer had met his terrible death only hours later. Adam closed the door behind me with a click and slipped discreetly through the door to the interior room. Underhill still did not stir from the window; when he spoke, he kept his back to me, his voice flat and unnatural.

'My daughter would speak to you next door, Doctor Bruno.'

I waited, but nothing more was forthcoming, so I followed Adam through the door to the rector's private room, where

Sophia and I had once talked of magic in what seemed like another age.

Now she stood alone by the fireplace, her hands resting on one of the high-backed wooden chairs. Her long dark hair was modestly tied back, though a few curling tendrils had escaped and hung about her face. There was still nothing about her figure, slight in a straight-bodiced dark grey dress, to advertise her condition, save for perhaps a fullness about the bust, but her face seemed thinner, more pinched and drained, and her eyes were puffy with exhaustion and tears.

'The pursuivants caught up with us at a house in Abingdon,' she said, without preamble, and though her face looked so fragile, her voice was as clear and strong as always. 'They asked Jerome what he was. He answered that he was a gentleman and a Christian. Then they tore off his shirt and saw his hairshirt.' She hesitated for a moment to swallow hard, then took a deep breath and continued without looking at me, her voice steady again. 'They arrested him as a traitor, shackled him and took him away. I begged them to take me with him, but I was brought back to Oxford.'

'They shackled you?' I asked, horrified.

'No. They were surprisingly gentle. But then I did not resist them. I was taken to the Castle gaol,' she said, finally raising her head and looking me in the eye, almost defiantly. Then she shook her head and seemed to crumple. 'You cannot imagine it, Bruno, if you have not seen it. Or smelled it. People would not keep animals in such conditions. One low room they have for the poor women, with filthy straw over the floor that stinks of piss and shit, and the walls are so damp there is fungus growing there and the cold goes right inside your bones. I think I will feel that cold for the rest of my life.'

'They put you in such a place? But did you not tell them of . . .?' I faltered and indicated my stomach. She gave a small bitter laugh.

'Yes, I told them, despite the damage to my honour. Jerome said that I should not speak if I were arrested, save to acknowledge my name. Yet I thought they might treat me with more gentleness than otherwise. But it seems it was all designed to frighten me. I was left in that hole for two hours, among the insane and the destitute, crowding around me, pulling at my clothes and hair, women covered in lice and sores and the stink of rotten flesh and human filth all around me –' Finally her voice cracked and I took a step towards her instinctively, wanting to put my arm around her, but she straightened up immediately and glared at me and I realised with a guilty jolt that there was no comfort I could give: I was the enemy.

'Then what happened?' I prompted, trying to cover over my ill-judged show of emotion.

'My father arrived,' she said, shaking her hair back. 'They had sent for him. It seemed he had been told that I was arrested in the company of a notorious Jesuit, but that I had secretly handed over certain damning documents to the authorities, suggesting that my loyalty lay with the forces of Her Majesty's law after all. That being the case, and given the delicacy of my condition,' here she patted her own stomach with a sarcastic smile, 'he was free to stand surety for my release.'

'Then – you did not contradict them?'

'I presumed it was you who had told them the story about the letters,' she said softly, her tone betraying neither gratitude nor anger. 'You gave me a chance to escape, even at the last minute. And the sheriff did me a kindness, I think, in insisting I be thrown in the prison first. Had I not seen that, I might have been stubborn enough to insist on the truth, for Jerome's sake. But two hours in that pit –' She broke off and shuddered, her hand straying absently to her belly in a gesture of protection. 'I feared that even in that short time

I would catch the gaol fever – the air was so dank and full of poisons. And I was afraid for the child,' she added, so quietly I could barely catch the words. 'If its father must die, it should at least have the chance to live.'

'I'm glad,' I said, with feeling.

'I'm sure you are,' she replied. 'It would not have done for your masters to discover that you lied to save a Catholic whore, would it? You played your part very well, Bruno, I never suspected you. But then, you never suspected me, did you? So perhaps you are not so clever as you believe.'

'I do not expect you to thank me,' I whispered. 'You have every reason to hate me. But I only ever acted out of care for you. He would have had you killed, Sophia, on the crossing to France, I am sure of it.'

'You say that only because Thomas put it in your head. Jerome would never have harmed me. He loves me.' A sob caught in her throat and she turned her face away to swallow it down, determined that I should not see the weakness of tears.

'He loved his mission more,' I said. 'Well, it is fortunate that our opposing theories were never put to the test, and you are still alive.'

'Fortunate? Oh yes, I am fortunate indeed,' she said, her voice tight with bitterness. 'I am to be banished by my family, the man I love will die in cruel pain and I will never see him again, the child I carry will be taken from me before I can even give it a name and after that I will be interrogated by the authorities. If it pleases them not to detain me, I will be sent back to live with my aunt, perhaps in time to be married to some rough unlettered farmer or inn-keeper, if one can be found who will overlook my sins. And who is the author of all this good fortune? Why, it is you, Bruno.' Anger flashed for a moment in her beautiful amber eyes, but she was too defeated to sustain it, and the fierce light quickly died.

'Perhaps when you hold your child in your arms, even for a moment, you may hate me less,' I said, looking steadily at her. She brushed a loose strand of hair from her face and met my gaze.

'I do not hate you, Bruno,' she said wearily. 'I hate the world. I hate God. I hate religion and the way it makes men believe that they alone are right.'

'You sound like Thomas Allen,' I said, and instantly regretted what sounded like an attempt at levity. To my surprise, though, she gave a weak smile.

'And we have seen where that may lead. Poor, poor Thomas. No, life is too short for hating.'

'Your faith will not survive interrogation, then?'

She almost laughed then, her face briefly lighting up.

'My *faith*, as you call it, was only ever a way to please him. I would have worshipped the Moon and the Sun and sacrificed a cockerel to the Devil at midnight if that would have made him love me better.'

'I well remember – you asked my advice on it once,' I said. 'But I would advise you not to say as much when you are interviewed.'

'No, Bruno.' She shook her head. 'Have no fear for me on that account. When I saw that gaol today, I knew without doubt that I could never endure years in such a place for love of the pope. For Jerome, yes, but he would not be here to appreciate it, would he? And the child must survive. That is all that matters now.' She fell silent then and stared down at her folded hands for a long while. I didn't dare to move. Eventually she reached into a pocket sewn into her dress and drew out a folded scrap of paper. Stepping across the room towards me, she took my bandaged right hand and pressed the paper into it, holding my hand between hers for a few moments while she looked intently into my eyes. Despite everything, my heart gave a foolish jolt and I was seized by

453

a desire to take her in my arms. The cruelty of the fate that she described reminded me painfully once again of Morgana; I had sentenced a young woman of spirit and beauty to be crushed beneath the wheels of propriety and the injustice of it clutched at my heart. I still clung to the belief that I had saved her life, but I would always live with a tiny kernel of doubt: what if Jerome Gilbert really had meant to escort her to safety in France? I would never be wholly sure and neither would she; that uncertainty bound us together, and I felt an overwhelming sense of responsibility for her. If there was anything I could do to help her now, I determined that I would not let her down again.

'Write to me,' she whispered, glancing nervously towards the door in case her father should overhear. 'Tell me how he died, what he said on the scaffold. That is all I wish. This is the address of my aunt in Kent. I will be taken there tomorrow and I do not think I will ever return to Oxford.'

'Surely your father would not banish you for good?'

She shook her head, her lips pressed tight.

'You do not know my father. If you could do this one thing . . .' She let the sentence trail away and squeezed my hand gently; I tried not to wince.

'I will.'

'Thank you, Bruno.' Her wide eyes roved over mine as if searching for something. 'If you had only come to Oxford two years ago – how different everything might have been. Perhaps we . . . But it is no good dwelling on what might have been. It is too late now for me.' She leaned forward and kissed me softly on the cheek, so gently that I might have imagined the brush of her lips over my skin. She squeezed my hand once more and let go.

As I turned towards the door, my heart so heavy I felt stooped by the weight of it, she whispered, 'Write!' I looked back to see her miming writing on the palm of her hand, her face stretched into a brave attempt at a smile. I nodded and turned my back on her for the last time.

When I closed the door behind me, the rector was still standing in the same position, silhouetted against the window, but he had turned to face the room and kept his arms folded across his chest, his small beady eyes fixed on me.

'So, Doctor Bruno, I have you to thank for delivering the college from a brutal murderer and a seditious Jesuit.' His tone was oddly unemotional, as though all capacity for feeling had drained out of him; I could not tell if he were pleased by this or not, and the ambiguity of his words made me pause.

'You know, Rector, that the two were not the same person?'

'I know that Gabriel Norris – I cannot think of him any other way – is to be charged with the murders of Roger Mercer, James Coverdale, Ned Lacy and Thomas Allen, and with treasonable intent towards Her Majesty's person. I have learned, too, that there are other accusations made against him, perhaps of less interest to the Privy Council but none the less of considerable significance to my own family.'

Here he drew in a great shuddering breath that seemed as if it would wrack his very soul; briefly his eyes met mine and I saw in them a weight of sorrow that I understood would burden him the remainder of his natural life. I also understood, in that moment, that Sophia had spoken the truth; there was a degree of coldness in the rector that would allow him to cut her off for good if he felt it necessary. In his eyes I saw the grief of a man who has already lost both his children. I wanted to intercede with him, to plead on her behalf, but decided to hold my tongue; my interference in the business of this college and especially this family was perhaps sufficient.

'I do not think we will see you in Oxford again, Doctor Bruno,' he said stiffly, holding out a hand for me to shake as he walked across to the main door, the boards creaking under his feet in the silence. 'In the light of recent events, I regret not confiding in you sooner, but here in Oxford we are not accustomed to regarding foreigners as – well, you see my position.' He held the hand out more insistently and I reached out to take it, whereupon he grasped my hand between both of his and fixed me with an imploring stare. Sophia had been fortunate, I thought as we looked at one another, that she had taken all her looks from her mother. Or perhaps not so fortunate; had she been less beautiful, her situation now might be very different.

'Among my many regrets, Doctor Bruno,' he continued, seeming to shrink slightly as he held tight to my hand, 'I could wish I had been a more gracious host and friend to you. Had I known of your connections – but I have much to reprimand myself for, as you may imagine. But perhaps if you have the opportunity to convey to the Earl of Leicester that I have only ever tried to serve him and the university to the best of my ability, that would not be too much to ask? I expect to hear from him concerning these events, and I am not at all sure of how he will receive the news.' His eyes grew wide with fear as he wrung my arm urgently, unaware that he was even doing so.

'I would help you if I could, but I'm afraid you mistake my intimacy with the earl – I have never met him in my life.' Seeing his disappointment, I quickly added, 'but I'm sure that if I discuss these matters with Sir Philip, he will not be ignorant of your loyalty.'

The rector nodded solemnly and released my hand.

'Thank you. It is more than I deserve. You were a most worthy adversary in the debating hall, Doctor Bruno. I only wish we might have had the opportunity again.'

You have a short memory, I thought, as I smiled politely; I was your superior in substance and conduct, though it

456

pleased you to ridicule me before the entire congregation of the university. But that humiliation seemed a trivial thing now.

'There is one favour I must ask of you in return,' I said, as we approached the door. He looked at me with mild surprise. 'I have learned that Cobbett has been suspended from his duties.'

'That is correct,' the rector said. 'Master Slythurst made a most serious complaint that he deliberately disregarded orders to hand over sensitive documents and allowed a thief to escape college who might otherwise have been detained.'

I stared at him, incredulous.

'But surely you know, Rector, that the thief he describes was me? And if Cobbett had not disobeyed Slythurst to get an urgent message to Sir Philip, I would be dead by now, and so would your daughter!'

'Nevertheless,' said the rector, in the same flat voice, affecting to become absorbed in a loose thread on his gown, 'Master Slythurst is a senior Fellow of this college, and as a college servant, Cobbett's duty was to obey his orders, not those of a visitor who had been found removing items from a student's room. For that dereliction of duty he has been punished.'

'Those papers, in Sir Philip's hands, saved your daughter's life,' I said, lowering my voice. 'In Slythurst's hands, they might not have done so in time. Cobbett acted according to his conscience and for this he should be rewarded.'

Underhill stopped picking at his gown and fixed me with a direct stare.

'In your opinion,' he replied, enunciating each word carefully and precisely.

I could not believe what I was hearing.

'His actions saved Sophia from being murdered,' I repeated, more slowly in case he had not understood the first time.

'And your grandchild,' I added deliberately, since this did not seem to provoke a response. 'You do not think that is worth rewarding?'

For a moment he did not answer but continued to look at me with something like pity.

'It has never occurred to you that I might rather have rewarded the man who could have spared my family all this?'

It took the space of a heartbeat for me to comprehend what he was saying; when I did, I could hardly credit it.

'You would have wished me not to interfere?' I shook my head in disbelief. 'You do understand that he meant to kill her? Jerome Gilbert – Gabriel Norris, whatever you want to call him? His intention was to have her drowned on the way to France to spare himself the ignominy of discovery. In time, you and your wife would have received a letter saying she had run away to join a religious order and you would have been none the wiser.'

'And you do not think her mother would have found that easier to bear?' He took a step towards me, and I saw that all his poise was on the verge of shattering; his hands trembled violently and he clasped them together until his knuckles turned white. 'We could at least have gone into our old age benignly deceived. Instead, my daughter is arrested in the company of a Jesuit missionary and escorted back to Oxford by the Sheriff's men. I have to go to the Castle gaol in person to pay for her release, where I find her in the company of thieves and whores. Then I must escort her back to college in full view of all the town, I must endure their jeers and whispers as we pass, as my wife will endure them should she ever venture out of her room again, which is doubtful. I would be a fool to believe the rumours are not already in full flood. I will be known hereafter as the father of a Jesuit's whore, grandsire to a papist bastard. My reputation in the university is finished, and her mother's nerves will not bear this new assault, I fear.'

I looked at him with contempt.

'Better she had been quietly murdered, and your reputation survived unblemished?' I said, through my teeth.

'No doubt you think me a monster for saying so,' he replied, with no trace of apology. 'But you have no children, so you cannot know the pain of losing them. My daughter is dead to me in any case, Bruno. Better she had been lost at sea and her mother spared this shame. Yes, I think so. Better for Sophia, too. She will have no kind of a life after this.'

'And you would rather have gone on harbouring a Jesuit in the college and living well from his fees, if it meant an easy life? Or perhaps you knew about Norris all along?'

'No – that is a lie!' he cried, springing forward. 'I had no idea about Norris. Perhaps that in itself is a grave failing, but I would never knowingly have tolerated an active missionary in the college, it is absurd to suggest so. I pray you, do not repeat that suggestion to your friend Sir Philip. Norris paid his way and he was granted no more or less licence than the other commoners.'

'Norris was recommended for a place here by Edmund Allen,' I said, 'a man you already knew to be a secret Catholic. And Norris never attended chapel – did that not strike you as suspicious?'

'The sons of gentlemen are not used to rising early. It is one of their privileges that they are not expected to.'

'Every dispensation may be bought here,' I said, looking at him with scorn. 'It reminds me so much of Rome. But you knew about the others, too, didn't you?'

He sighed.

'I knew about William Bernard. But everyone in Oxford did – it was no secret that he kept to the old ways, though he took the Oath. But he was a recalcitrant old man and judged harmless. He is fled, by the way, but I don't think there will be too much of a hunt put out for him. To put a

459

white-haired old fellow like that in gaol or stand him on a scaffold does not play well with the people, as the Privy Council knows. And the others – I suppose when I am questioned about Norris I must reveal their names?'

'I do not think that will be necessary,' I said, reeling from his callous words about Sophia. 'The names of the worst offenders are already known.'

He studied me as he reached for the door handle.

'You have too much compassion, Doctor Bruno, to be embroiled in this business. I know that you lied to spare my daughter a public trial. Just as I could have handed the Catholics here, the whole lot of them, over to the pursuivants years ago, but I thought we could all rub along together. I see now one has to be ruthless, and for men like us, it is not in our character. You are like me in that regard,' he added, with a hint of self-satisfaction.

'No, sir,' I said quietly, as he held the door open for me to pass. 'I am nothing like you. Had I a daughter, I hope I would not wish for her death rather than my own dishonour.' He opened his mouth as if to protest, but I cut him off. 'She is no whore. She is a woman of mettle, and she deserves your care and protection, not your contempt.'

I left him standing in the doorway, his mouth still gaping wordlessly like a fish, and strode purposefully across the quadrangle of Lincoln College for the last time. At the gatehouse I turned to take my final look, and saw the outline of Sophia at the first-floor window of the rector's lodgings, her figure distorted by the patterned glass, one hand raised in farewell.

# EPILOGUE

## London, July 1583

Under a sky barely touched by the first streaks of dawn, through a thin drizzle that misted on my hair and on the horse's mane, I rode westward out of the ambassador's residence at Salisbury Court along Fleet Street, away from the City of London, a cloak tucked around me against the damp and my chest as tight as if it were bound by iron hoops. I would not have chosen to make this journey, but I had received word from Walsingham that he expected my presence and I thought it better not to argue. Steam clouded from the horse's nostrils in the morning air as I turned him northwards at the great monument of Charing Cross, on to the spur road that led out of London to the open country to the northwest. Here the road grew busier; small groups of people on foot heading in the same direction, chatting eagerly among themselves and sharing drinks from leather flasks, while pie-sellers moved quickly alongside them, calling out their wares to the expectant crowd all making for the morning's spectacle. Nearer to our destination, people had lined the streets, children hoisted on their fathers' shoulders to witness the passing of the procession.

At the place they call Tyburn, a wooden platform had

been erected at the height of a man's head to ensure all the crowd had a clear view. On this scaffold the executioner's table had been set, an over-sized butcher's block all laid out with various knives and instruments and beside it a fire had been lit to heat the water in a large cauldron. Those at the front of the crowd pressed closer, stretching out their hands towards the warmth of the flames; though it was July, the damp had left a chill in the early morning air, and people stamped their feet and rubbed their hands together impatiently as they waited. At the side of the scaffold a wooden gallows had been built and a cart stood empty underneath it. I turned the horse and made my way around the back of the crowd; at the far side, nearest to the gallows, I could see a number of gentlemen on horseback keeping their distance from the jostling throng and guessed I would find Sidney among them. As I guided the horse around, city officials with pikestaffs passed through the crowd at the front, clearing a path through in front of the scaffold.

I found Sidney with a group of young mounted courtiers close to the gallows. Though his companions seemed in high spirits and talked loudly among themselves, he kept his horse reined in tight, making it step impatiently on the spot as he surveyed the crowd, his mouth set in a grim line. Catching sight of me, he nodded without smiling.

'Let us move to one side, Bruno,' he said quietly. 'I am not inclined to be among those who would treat this as if it were a country fair.'

'I had much rather not have been here at all,' I admitted, as we took up a position a little way off from the group of young men.

'Walsingham was adamant that you should attend. He feels it is important that his people fully understand every aspect of their work. Those who fight wars are not spared the sight of gore, and neither are we boys playing at soldiers.

Our struggle is real, and its consequences are bloody.' He turned and fixed me with an earnest expression. 'This execution is your triumph, Bruno. Walsingham is very pleased with you.'

'My triumph,' I repeated softly, as a great cry went up from the crowd and they all stood on tip-toe to watch the arrival.

It was almost fully light when two black horses appeared in the gap between the scaffold and the front row of the crowd as a group of women rushed forward to throw roses and lilies, the flowers of martyrdom, in the path of the horses, the officials jabbing with their pikes at those who pressed in too closely and threatened to impede progress. As if by common consent, the crowd drew solemnly back, the babble of conversation ceased, and the horses' hooves could be heard thudding quietly on the turf as the hurdle they drew behind them carved ruts into the damp ground. I stood in my stirrups and leaned forward, my stomach clenching at the sight.

Jerome Gilbert was bound to the hurdle, feet uppermost, arms crossed over his chest, his head almost level with the ground so that his face and hair were spattered with mud. When the hurdle reached the gallows, two men stepped forward to untie him and his body slumped to the ground like a child's cloth doll; the two men grasped him beneath his shoulders and hoisted him up between them on to the cart. He had been stripped to his undershirt and hose but now, as they lifted him up to an expectant murmur from the crowd, he reached inside his shirt and drew out a handkerchief to wipe the worst of the mud from his face. I winced to see that his left eye was so bruised and swollen he could not open it, but he scanned the crowd frantically with his good eye before throwing the handkerchief into the air, where it was deftly caught by a grey-haired man with a lugubrious face near the front.

'Keep an eye on that fellow,' Sidney whispered. 'Most likely he is another of the Jesuits, or a supporter, come to give comfort in the last hour. Gilbert marked him out to catch the handkerchief.'

'Should we follow him?' I asked anxiously. Sidney shook his head.

'Walsingham will have men in the crowd to shadow all those who dive for relics of his clothes afterwards and any other such business.' He stopped suddenly; Jerome was being held up while the executioner climbed into the cart and fastened the noose about his neck before attaching it to the crossbeam and checking it was secure. I realised that the two men were still standing either side of him because he could not support himself, and my jaw clenched tight; he must have been racked so severely that his legs were beyond use. 'What have they done to his hands?' I whispered to Sidney, indicating the mass of congealed blood as Jerome lifted a hand feebly to try and push his matted hair from his face.

'Torn out his fingernails,' Sidney said, his voice tight, and I could not read anything beneath his outward composure.

A portly man dressed in royal colours stepped up on to the scaffold and unfolded a piece of parchment.

'Jerome Gilbert, Jesuit,' he declaimed in a clear voice that carried across the silent crowd, 'you have been found guilty on four counts of murder and of seducing the people away from the queen's allegiance, of plotting with others in Rheims and Rome to assassinate the queen and of being privy to plans of foreign invasion. What say you?'

With enormous effort, the noose still slack around his neck, Jerome summoned what little strength was left in his ravaged body, raised his head and replied, in a surprisingly strong voice:

'I am guilty only of trying to bring wandering souls back to their Maker. I pray God forgive all those who have been accessory to my death. God save the queen.' Here his eye roved the crowd again and came to rest on me; for a moment we held one another's gaze and he added, his solemn voice carrying over the clearing,

'One day you will stand where I stand.'

'Silence!' called the official, thinking this a threat to the English protestants, but I was gripped by a terrible shudder; I could not escape the chilling sense that he had been speaking directly to me.

I recalled his words in the hide at Hazeley Court: 'You and I are similar men . . . you go to your death defiant, as I will when the appointed time comes.' He had been right about himself, at least, I thought; though his beautiful face had been destroyed by the torturers and he could not stand unaided, in these last moments he was magnificently, fiercely defiant.

The official regarded him with distaste as the assembled throng held its breath.

'As a convicted traitor, your sentence is clear. You are to be hanged by the neck and let down alive, your privy parts cut off, for you are unfit to leave any generation after you, your entrails to be taken out and burned in your sight, your head, which imagined the mischief, to be cut off and your body divided in four parts, to be disposed of at Her Majesty's pleasure. And may God have mercy on your soul.'

Jerome flung his head back so that the summer rain, now falling steadily, filled his eyes and mouth as he cried out to the heavens:

'*In manus tuas, Domine, commendo spiritum meum!*'

And the horses were whipped, and the cart drew away, leaving him writhing on the end of the rope.

He was barely conscious when they cut him down and the two burly men dragged him up the steps to the scaffold; this at least seemed a mercy, I thought, until the executioner flung a pail of cold water into his face and he choked back into a semblance of life, spluttering and flailing wildly as he was lifted to the executioner's table and his clothes stripped from him. As Sidney had predicted, a number of people in the crowd threw themselves forward to try and snatch a piece of the martyr's clothing, and the men with pikes moved in forcibly to push them away from the scaffold.

Like many another man in the crowd, I had to turn away as the executioner raised his knife to slice off Jerome's genitals, but the howl that rent the still air brought tears to my eyes even as the crackle as his severed flesh was thrown into the cauldron made my stomach rise. Yet in that moment, perhaps the most horrific spectacle I had witnessed in my life, I thought of Sophia. 'Unfit to leave any generation behind you' – and yet somewhere in Kent a child of his was growing towards the light, a child that would never know the truth about its father but would carry his beauty into the future. I wondered again, for the thousandth time since my return from Oxford, if I had been right to listen to Thomas Allen's frenzied accusations. Would Jerome really have had Sophia drowned, or might they both even now be alive and well in France if I had not interfered?

'He would have had you killed, Bruno – remember that,' Sidney said in my ear, as if he had read my thoughts. 'But he was a damned fine card player,' he added, barely audible, and I realised that beneath his professional soldier's demeanour, he too was deeply affected by this death. I nodded heavily, and raising my head at that moment I caught sight of Walsingham, mounted on a black horse on the other side of the crowd, his face set grimly as he watched the butchery on the scaffold. As the executioner plunged his knife into Jerome's breastbone to rip him open, and his dying screams echoed to the blank white sky, Walsingham turned and caught my eye across the heads of the people who stood in terrible,

468

threatening silence. He nodded, once, as if in approbation, then turned his attention back to the scaffold as Jerome's heart was held aloft to no other sound than the soft chafing of the wind in the leaves and the persistent drumming of the worm rain.

'Take another drink, Bruno – you look as if you need it.' Walsingham reached over and poured me a glass of wine but my throat closed as I lifted it to my face. I could not scour the smell of blood and burning flesh from my nostrils and though Walsingham's wife had offered us food, I had found myself unable to eat anything.

Now we sat in his private study in his country house at Barn Elms, some miles to the west of London. The sky was still overcast and the room close and gloomy with its dark wood panelling and narrow windows. Sidney stood looking out over the garden, his hands clasped behind his back. He had been unusually subdued since the execution and we had ridden down to Mortlake in almost total silence, each wrapped in our own thoughts. Now Walsingham sat opposite me with his chin resting on his hands, studying me carefully.

'You did well, Bruno,' he said at length, stretching out his legs in front of him. 'The queen has been told of your part in stopping another would-be assassin. It may be that at some time in the future she will feel it appropriate to express her gratitude in person.'

'I would be honoured,' I said, running my tongue around dry lips.

'Something troubles you,' he said gently. I glanced at Sidney but his back was turned. 'You may speak freely here, Bruno,' Walsingham prompted, when I did not reply.

'Did you really believe he was guilty of plotting to kill the queen?' I asked.

He looked at me with great heaviness in his eyes for a long time without speaking, and I remembered how he had spoken at our first meeting of the weight of his responsibility to the kingdom.

'No, I did not,' he said eventually. I saw Sidney snap his head around and rest himself on the window seat, watching with interest.

'The copy of the *Regnans in Excelsis* Bull was old – I do not think Jerome Gilbert brought it with him. Besides, the missionaries do not carry any item that would compromise them, by order of the Jesuit Superior – Gilbert would not have been so careless. It may have belonged to Edmund Allen or one of the other Fellows. It hardly matters now.'

'And you know he did not murder the two Catholic Fellows and the boy at Lincoln College?'

'I know that too.'

'Then,' I looked up at him, seeking reassurance. 'He was executed for crimes he did not commit.'

'Her Majesty's Government does not persecute anyone for his faith alone,' Walsingham said, with a trace of impatience. 'That is the official line, and it is important that the people are reminded of that often, or we shall only make more martyrs. If they believe that these Jesuits are willing to murder for their faith, it helps our cause immeasurably.'

'Then all is propaganda,' I said wearily.

'This is principally a war of loyalties. We must persuade the people that their allegiance is best placed with us, by whatever means we can fashion. You saw their response today, did you not? Usually when the head is struck off, a great cry goes up from the crowd of "Traitor! Traitor!" for they have their sport. But with this Gilbert they witnessed it in complete silence, and that must be a serious cause for concern for the Privy Council. It means the crowd did not approve of what was done today, they found it too barbaric. One more like that and they will turn against us.' He shook his head. 'I have suggested on numerous occasions that they should hang until they are dead, but I have been shouted down. Perhaps now the Council will see reason.'

'It is a brutal way to die,' I agreed.

Walsingham rounded on me, his face agitated. 'Worse than the burnings and massacres they inflict on Protestants? In any case, you told me you saw him kill the boy, Thomas Allen, in cold blood, and you were certain he meant to kill the girl too, though she was with child. And Philip says he would have killed you. So he was not an innocent man, Bruno. Do not pity him on that account.'

'No.' I acknowledged this by lowering my eyes.

'It is a hard thing to witness,' Walsingham said more gently, laying a hand briefly on my arm. 'No doubt you think me barbaric for insisting you watch. But I warned you that entering Her Majesty's service would not be an easy path to tread. I needed you to see that for yourself.'

'He died well,' Sidney cut in abruptly, as if he had been dwelling on it all this time. 'With dignity.'

'He bore himself with fortitude in the Tower as well,' Walsingham agreed, a note of respect in his voice. 'They trained him well in Rheims to endure pain. We did not get one name from him, despite long hours of work.'

I winced to remember Jerome's bloody fingers and tried not to think of what more 'work' might have been carried out on him.

'What will happen to Sophia?' I asked hesitantly, attempting a sip from my glass.

'Underhill's daughter? At the end of her confinement, when she is strong again, she will be questioned.' Seeing my expression, he added, 'It is my belief she will talk willingly, just as she gave up those letters. But she may have other names we can usefully add to those provided by you and Walter Slythurst.'

He fixed me then with an intense look and I dropped my gaze to the floor; I wondered if Sidney had told him about my covering for Sophia over the letters, or if he knew that I had withheld certain names when he debriefed me after my return from Oxford. Perhaps he would have got those same names – Richard Godwyn, Humphrey Pritchard, the Widow Kenney – from Slythurst or Underhill when he questioned them, but I doubted it.

'Oh, please – this Slythurst is useless,' Sidney said scathingly, rousing himself from his perch and striding across the room to pour a glass of wine. 'He missed the priest right under his nose and tried to hand Bruno over to the pursuivants. Do not give him another penny, I say.'

Walsingham sighed.

'He was not the most efficient of my Oxford informers,' he acknowledged. 'He offered his services a couple of years ago to get himself out of debt. He exposed Edmund Allen by very crude means, but that only served to make the other Lincoln College papists yet more hugger-mugger. He is too greatly disliked by his colleagues ever to gain their confidence, so that all his intelligence was largely guesswork based on tavern gossip. In fact I had warned him he could not continue in my service without some news of more note just before you arrived – perhaps that was why he was so keen to prove himself by pointing the finger at any suspect.'

'It might have helped if I had known he was your man,' I said, trying to keep the reproach from my voice. 'I thought him the killer at first.'

Walsingham smiled, but I caught a warning note in his tone.

'Better we all guard our secrets, Bruno. He could have turned out to be the killer. I would not have wanted your judgement wrongly coloured by sympathy.'

'That will not happen, your honour,' I murmured, not quite meeting his eye.

'I trust it will not,' he said brightly. 'For now, Bruno, I need you back in the French embassy. I hear worrying reports out of Paris that the Guise faction is newly strengthened and plotting against our realm. Place yourself close to the ambassador and see what you can find.'

'I will, your honour, to the best of my ability,' I assured him.

'And now,' he said, rising slowly to his feet, 'Philip has some news I hope you will find welcome.'

He looked expectantly to Sidney, who hooked an arm about my shoulders.

'My old tutor, John Dee, has expressed great interest in making your acquaintance, Bruno, and in showing you the treasures of his library. His house at Mortlake lies not a mile from here, and I am to take you this afternoon, if that pleases you.'

'If it pleases me?' For the first time in days I felt myself stirring back into life. Though Sidney had called Jerome Gilbert's execution my triumph, since my return from Oxford I had felt no sense of achievement. In fact, I had felt nothing but intense melancholy at the thought of so many lives wasted for so little, and even my books had failed to animate me; I thought often of Sophia and how her life might be unfolding, and I had begun to fear I might no longer be capable of taking pleasure in anything. Now the prospect of Doctor Dee's library, and the slender chance that he might have some clue as to who had robbed him of the lost book of Hermes Trismegistus all those years ago, pricked my curiosity once more.

Sidney took up his cloak as Walsingham crossed to me, grasping my hand between his, those unfathomable eyes probing mine.

'You have proved your mettle, Bruno,' he said, a note of fatherly pride in his voice. 'Philip told me you risked your own life to bring this priest to justice and the Privy Council is grateful. I hope ours will be a long and happy association.'

I thought it politic not to tell him that I had actually risked my life for a book and a girl. Since I had returned with neither, I thought, I may as well claim it was all for the English state, so I accepted his praise with a sober nod as Sidney held the door open for me. If any good had come from the bloody events I witnessed in Oxford, it had been to convince me that, now more than ever, Christendom desperately needed a new philosophy, one that would draw us together as we passed from the shadows of religious wars into the enlightenment of our shared humanity and shared divinity. It would fall to me, Giordano Bruno of Nola, to write the books that would light this fire in Europe, and with Walsingham's help, I planned to put them into the hands of a monarch with a mind equal to understanding them. When I wrote to Sophia to tell her of Jerome's courage, I would also impress upon her that it was not too late to hope for a better world.

# ACKNOWLEDGEMENTS

I am extremely grateful to Professor Paul Langford, present Rector of Lincoln College, Oxford, for his kind hospitality and to the other Lincoln Fellows who generously allowed me to poke around their beautiful buildings and gave their time to answer my questions.

My thanks also to Gemma Tuxford and Giovanni Tepedino for all their help with Italian translations. Any mistakes remaining are my own.

SJP.

Also available

The second novel in a series featuring the maverick
agent Giordano Bruno

Read an excerpt now

# PROLOGUE

*Mortlake, House of John Dee*
*3rd September, Year of Our Lord 1583*

Without warning, all the candles in the room's corners flicker and feint, as if a sudden gust has entered, but the air remains still. At the same moment, the hairs on my arms prickle and stand erect and I shudder; a cold breath descends on us, though outside the day is close. I chance a sideways glance at Doctor Dee; he stands unmoving as marble, his hands clasped as if in prayer, the knuckles of both thumbs pressed anxiously to his lips – or what can be seen of them through his ash-grey beard, which he wears in a point down to his chest in imitation of Merlin, whose heir Dee secretly considers himself. The cunning-man, Ned Kelley, kneels on the floor in front of the table of practice with his back to us, eyes fixed on the pale, translucent crystal about the size of a goose-egg mounted in fixings of brass and standing upon a square of red silk. The wooden shutters of the study windows have been closed; this business must be conducted in shadow and candlelight. Kelley draws breath like a player about to deliver his prologue, and stretches his arms out wide at shoulder height, in a posture of crucifixion.

'Yes . . .' he breathes, finally, his voice little more than a whisper. 'He is here. He beckons to me.'

'Who?' Dee leans forward eagerly, his eyes bright. 'Who is he?'

Kelley waits a moment before answering, his brow creasing as he concentrates his gaze on the stone.

'A man of more than mortal height, with skin as dark as polished mahogany. He is dressed head to foot in a white garment, which is torn, and his eyes are of red fire. In his right hand he holds aloft a sword.'

Dee snaps his head around then and clutches my arm, staring at me; the shock on his face must be mirrored in my own. He has recognised the description, as have I: the being Kelley sees in the stone matches the first figure of the sign of Aries, as described by the ancient philosopher Hermes Trismegistus. There are thirty-six of these figures, the Egyptian gods of time who rule the divisions of the zodiac and are called by some 'star-demons'. There are few scholars in Christendom who could thus identify the figure Kelley sees, and two of them are here in this study in Mortlake. If, indeed, this *is* what Kelley sees. I say nothing.

'What says he?' Dee urges.

'He holds out a book,' Kelley answers.

'What manner of book?'

'An ancient book, with worn covers and pages all of beaten gold.' Kelley leans closer to the stone. 'Wait! He is writing upon it with his forefinger, and the letters are traced in blood.'

I want to ask what he has done with the sword while he writes in this book – has he tucked it under his arm, perhaps? – but Dee would not thank me for holding this business lightly. Beside me, he draws in his breath, impatient to hear what the spirit is writing.

'XV,' Kelley reports, after a moment. He turns to look up at us, then over his right shoulder, his expression perplexed, perhaps expecting Dee to interpret the numerals.

2

'Fifteen, Bruno,' Dee whispers, looking again to me for confirmation. I nod, once. The lost fifteenth book of Hermes Trismegistus, the book I had come to England to find, the book I now knew Dee had once held in his hands years earlier, only to be robbed of it violently and lose it again. Could it be? It occurs to me that Kelley must know of his master's obsession with the fifteenth book.

The scryer raises a hand for silence. His eyes do not move from the crystal.

'He turns the page. Now he traces . . . it seems . . . yes, he makes a sign – quickly, fetch me paper and ink!'

Dee hurries to bring him the items; Kelley reaches out and flaps his hand impatiently, as if afraid the image will fade before he has time to transcribe it. He takes the quill and, still gazing intently into the stone, sketches the astrological symbol of the planet Jupiter and holds it up for our inspection.

I tense; Dee feels it where his hand still holds my arm, and half-turns to look at me with questioning eyebrows. I keep my face empty of expression. The sign of Jupiter is my code, my signature; it replaces my name as the sign that my letters of intelligence are authentic. Only two people in the world know this: myself and Sir Francis Walsingham, Her Majesty's Principal Secretary of State and chief intelligencer. It is a common enough sign in astrology, and coincidence, surely, that Kelley has drawn it; still I regard the back of Kelley's head with increased suspicion.

'On the facing page,' Kelley continues, 'he traces another mark – this time, the sign of Saturn.' This he also draws on his paper, a cross with a curving tail, the quill scratching slowly as if time has thickened while he watches this unfold in the depths of the stone. Dee's breathing quickens as he takes the paper and taps it with two fingers.

'Jupiter and Saturn. The Great Conjunction. You understand, I think, Bruno?' Without waiting for a reply, he turns impatiently to Kelley. 'Ned – what does he now, the spirit?'

3

'He opens his mouth and motions for me to listen.'

Kelley falls silent and does not move. Moments pass, Dee leaning forward eagerly, poised as if held taut on a rope, balanced between wanting to pounce on his scryer and not wishing to crowd him. When Kelley speaks again, his voice is altered; darker, somehow, and he proclaims as if in a trance:

'"All things have grown almost to their fullness. Time itself shall be altered, and strange shall be the wonders perceived. Water shall perish in fire, and a new order shall spring from these."'

Here he pauses, gives a great shuddering sigh. Dee's grip around my arm tightens. I know what he is thinking. Kelley continues in the same portentous voice:

'"Hell itself grows weary of Earth. At this time shall rise up one who will be called the Son of Perdition, the Master of Error, the Prince of Darkness, and he will delude many by his magic arts, so that fire will seem to come down from heaven and the sky shall be turned the colour of blood. Empires, kingdoms, principalities and states shall be overturned, fathers will turn against sons and brothers against brothers, there shall be turbulence among the peoples of the Earth, and the streets of the cities will run with blood. By this you shall know the last days of the old order."'

He stops, sinks back gasping on to his heels, his chest heaving as if he has run a mile in the heat. Beside me, I can feel Dee trembling, his hand still holding my wrist; I feel him hungry for more of the spirit's words, silently urging the scryer not to stop there, unwilling to speak aloud for fear of breaking the spell. For myself, I reserve judgement.

'"Yet God has provided medicine for man's suffering,"' Kelley cries in the same voice, sitting up suddenly and making us both jump. '"There shall also rise a prince who will rule by the light of reason and understanding, who shall strike down the darkness of the old times, and in him the alteration of

4

the world shall begin, and so shall he establish one faith, one ancient religion of unity that will put an end to strife."'

Dee claps his hands gleefully, turning to me with shining eyes and the excitement of a child. It is hard to believe that this is his fifty-sixth autumn.

'The prophecy, Bruno! What can this be, if not the prophecy of the Great Conjunction, of the ending of the old world? You read this as plain as I do, my friend – through the good offices of Master Kelley here, the gods of time have chosen to speak to us of the coming of the Fiery Trigon, when the old order shall be overturned and the world made anew in the image of ancient truth!'

'He has certainly spoken of weighty matters,' I say, evenly.

Kelley turns then, his brow damp with sweat, and regards me with those close-set eyes.

'Doctor Dee – what is this Fiery Trigon?' he asks, in his own, somewhat nasal voice.

'You could not know the significance, Ned, of what your gifts have revealed to us this day,' Dee replies, his manner now fatherly, 'but you have translated a prophecy most wondrous. Most wondrous.' He shakes his head slowly in admiration, then stirs himself and begins to pace about the study as he explains, resuming his authority, the teacher once more. While the séance occurs, he becomes dependent upon Kelley, but it is not his habit to be subservient; he is, after all, the queen's personal astrologer.

'Once every twenty years,' he says, holding up a forefinger like a schoolmaster, 'the two most powerful planets in our cosmology, Jupiter and Saturn, align with one another, each time moving through the twelve signs of the zodiac. Every two hundred years, give or take, this conjunction moves into a new Trigon – that is to say, the group of three signs that correspond to each of the four elements. And once every nine hundred and sixty years, the alignment completes its cycle through the four Trigons, returning again to its beginning in fire. For the past two hundred years, the planets have aligned within the signs of the Watery Trigon. But now, my dear Ned, this very year, the year of Our Lord fifteen hundred and eighty-three, Jupiter and Saturn will conjoin once more in the sign of Aries, the first sign of the Fiery Trigon, the most potent conjunction of all and one that has not been seen for almost a thousand years.'

He pauses for effect; Kelley's mouth hangs open like a codfish.

'Then it is a momentous time in the heavens?'

'More than momentous,' I say, taking up the story. 'The coming of the Fiery Trigon signifies the dawn of a new epoch. This is only the seventh such conjunction since the creation of the world and each has been marked by events that have shaken history. The flood of Noah, the birth of Christ, the coming of Charlemagne – all coincide with the return to the Fiery Trigon.'

'And this transition into the sign of Aries at the end of our troubled century has been prophesied by many as signifying the end of history,' Dee agrees, thoughtful. He has arrived in front of his tall perspective glass in its ornate gilt frame that stands in the corner by the west-facing window. Its peculiar property is that it reflects a true image and not the usual reversed image of an ordinary glass; the effect is unsettling. Now he turns to face us and raises his right hand; in the glass, his reflection does the same.

'The astronomer Richard Harvey wrote of this present conjunction, "Either a marvellous fearful and horrible alteration of empires, kingdoms and states, or else the destruction of the whole world shall ensue",' I add.

'So he did, Bruno, so he did. We may expect signs and wonders, my friends, in the days to come. Our world will change beyond recognition. We shall bear witness to a new era.' Dee is trembling, his eyes moist.

'Then – the spirit in the stone – he came to remind us of this prophecy?' Kelley asks, his face full of wonder.

6

'And to point to its special significance for England,' Dee adds, his voice heavy with meaning. 'For what can it signify but the overthrowing of the old religion once and for all in favour of the new, with Her Majesty as the light of reason and understanding?'

'I had no idea,' Kelley says, dreamy.

I watch him closely. There are two possibilities here. One is that he truly has a gift; I do not yet discount this, for though it has never been granted to me, in other countries I have heard of men who speak with those they call angels and demons through just such showing-stones, or else a speculum made for the purpose, like the one of obsidian that Dee keeps above his hearth. But in my years of wandering through Europe I have also seen plenty of these itinerant scryers, these cunning men, these mediums-for-hire, who have a smattering of esoteric learning and for the price of a bed and a pot of beer will tell the credulous man anything they think he wants to hear. Perhaps this is snobbery on my part; I cannot help but feel that if the Egyptian gods of time chose to speak to men, it would be to men of learning, philosophers like myself or John Dee, the true heirs to Hermes – not to such a man as Ned Kelley, who wears his ragged cloth cap pulled down to his brow even indoors, to disguise the fact that he has one ear clipped for coining.

But I must be careful what I say to Dee touching Ned Kelley; the scryer has had his feet firmly under Dee's table since long before I arrived in England, and this is the first time Dee has allowed me to take part in one of these 'actions', as he calls them. Kelley resents my recent friendship with his master; I see how he regards me from under the peak of his cap. John Dee is the most learned man in England, but he seems to me unaccountably trusting of Kelley, despite knowing almost nothing of the medium's history. I have grown fond of Dee and would not like to see him hoodwinked; at the same time, I do not want to fall from his favour and lose the use of his library, the finest collection of books to be found in the kingdom. So I keep my counsel.

With a sudden draught, the study door is thrown open and we all start like guilty creatures; Kelley, with surprising quickness, throws his hat over the showing-stone. None of us is under any illusion; what we are engaged in here would be considered witchcraft, and is a capital offence against the edicts of Church and State. It would only take one gossiping servant to catch wind of Dee's activities and we could all be facing the pyre; the Protestant authorities of this island, more tolerant in some matters than the church of my native Italy, still strike with force against anything that smells of magic.

Dusty evening sunlight slants through from the passageway outside, and in the doorway stands a little boy, not more than three years old, who looks from one to the other of us with blank curiosity.

Dee's face crinkles with tenderness, but also with relief.

'Arthur! What are you about? You know you are not supposed to disturb me when I am at work. Where is your mother?'

Arthur Dee steps across the threshold and at once gives a great shiver.

'Why is it so cold in your room, Papa?'

Dee casts me a look of something like triumph, as if to say, *You see? We were not deceived.* He flings wide the shutters of the west window and outside the sun is setting, staining the sky vermilion, the colour of blood.

# ONE

*Barn Elms, House of Sir Francis Walsingham*
*21st September, Year of Our Lord 1583*

The wedding feast of Sir Philip Sidney and Frances
Walsingham threatens to spill over into the next day; dusk
has fallen, lamps have been lit and above the din from the
musicians in the gallery and the laughter of the guests,
the young woman with whom I have been dancing tells me
excitedly that she was once at a marriage party that lasted
four days altogether. She leans in close when she says this
and presses her hand to my shoulder; her breath is laced
with sweet wine. The musicians strike up another galliard;
my dancing partner exclaims with delight and clutches
eagerly at my hand, laughing. I am about to protest that the
hall is warm, that I would like a cup of wine and a moment's
respite in the fresh air before I return to the fray, but I have
barely opened my mouth when the wind is knocked out of
me by a fist between the shoulder blades, accompanied by
a hearty cry.

'Giordano Bruno! Now what is this I see? The great philosopher throwing off his scholar's gown and lifting a leg with
the flower of Her Majesty's court? Did you learn to dance

9

like that at the monastery? Your hidden talents never cease to astonish me, *amico mio*.'

Recovering my balance, I turn, smiling widely. Here is the bridegroom in all his finery, six feet tall and flushed with wine and triumph: breeches of copper-coloured silk so voluminous it is a wonder he can pass through a doorway; doublet of ivory sewn all over with seed-pearls; a lace ruff at his neck so severely starched that his handsome, beardless face seems constantly straining to see above it, like a small boy peering over a wall. His hair still sticks up in the front like a schoolboy hastened out of bed. In all the tumult I have not exchanged a word with him since the morning's ceremony, he and his young bride have been so comprehensively surrounded by high-ranking well-wishers and relatives, all the highest ornaments of Her Majesty's court.

'Well,' he says, grinning broadly, 'aren't you going to congratulate me, then, or are you just here for the food from my table?'

'Your father-in-law's table, I had thought,' I answer, laughing. 'Or which part of the feast did you buy yourself?'

'You can leave your debating-hall pedantry at home today, Bruno. But I hope you have had enough meat and drink?'

'There is enough meat and drink here to feed the five thousand.' I indicate the two long tables at each end of the great hall, spread with the detritus of the wedding banquet. 'You will be eating left-overs for weeks.'

'Oh, you may be sure Sir Francis will see to that,' Sidney says. 'Today, generosity, tomorrow – thrift. But come, Bruno. You have no idea how it pleases me that you are here.' He holds his arms wide and I embrace him with sincere affection; I am the perfect height to have his ruff smack me directly in the nose.

'Watch the clothes,' he says, only half-joking. 'Bruno, allow me to introduce you to my uncle Robert Dudley, Earl of Leicester.'

He steps back and gestures to the man who stands a few feet away, at his shoulder; a man of about Sidney's own height, perhaps in his mid-fifties yet still athletic, his hair steel grey at the temples but his face fine-boned and handsome behind his close-clipped beard. This man regards me with watchful brown eyes.

'My lord.'

I bow deeply, acknowledging the honour; the Earl of Leicester is one of the highest nobles in England and the man who enjoys greater influence over Queen Elizabeth than any alive. I raise my head and meet his shrewd appraisal. It is rumoured that in their youth he was the queen's only lover, and that even now their long-enduring friendship is more intimate than most marriages. He smiles, and there is warmth in his gaze.

'Doctor Bruno, the pleasure is mine. When I learned of your courage in Oxford I was eager to make your acquaintance and thank you in person.' Here he lowers his voice; Leicester is the Chancellor of the University of Oxford, charged with enforcing the measures to suppress the Catholic resistance among the students. That the movement had gathered so much momentum on his watch had been a matter of some embarrassment to him; my adventures with Sidney there in the spring had helped to disarm it, at least temporarily. I am about to reply when we are interrupted by a man dressed in a russet doublet, with a peasecod belly so vast it makes him look as if he is with child; the earl nods politely to me and I turn back to Sidney.

'My uncle likes the idea of you. He's keen to hear more of your outrageous theories about the universe.' I must look anxious, because he elbows me cheerfully in the ribs. 'Leicester's friendship is worth a great deal.'

'I am glad to have met him,' I say, rubbing my side. 'And may I now pay my respects to your bride?'

Sidney looks around, as if for someone to deal with this request.

'I dare say she is here somewhere. Giggling with her ladies.' He does not sound as if he is in a hurry to find her. 'But you are needed elsewhere.'

He turns and bows to my companion, who has discreetly withdrawn a couple of paces to watch us from under lowered lids, her hands modestly clasped together. 'I am borrowing the great Doctor Bruno for a moment. I will return him to you at some stage. There will be more dancing after the masques.' The girl blushes, smiles shyly at me and obediently melts away into the brightly coloured, rustling mass of guests. Sidney looks after her with an expression of amusement. 'Lady Arabella Horton has her sights set on you, it seems. Don't be fooled by all the fluttering lashes and simpering. Half the court has been there. And she will soon lose interest when she learns you are the son of a soldier, with no capital but your wit and a pittance from the King of France.'

'I was not planning to tell her that immediately.'

'Did you tell her you were a monk for thirteen years?'

'We had not got around to that either.'

'She might like that – might want to help you make up for lost time. But for now, Bruno, my new father-in-law suggests you might like to take a turn in the garden.'

'I have not yet had the chance to congratulate him.'

But it is clear that this is business. Sidney rests a hand on my shoulder.

'No one has. Do you know, he disappeared for two hours altogether this afternoon to draft some papers? In the middle of his own daughter's wedding party?' He smiles indulgently, as if he must tolerate these foibles, though we both know that Sidney is in no position to complain; financially, he needed this marriage more than young Mistress Walsingham, who I suspect entertains greater romantic hopes of it than her new husband.

'I suppose the great machinery of state must keep turning.'

'Indeed. And now it is your turn to grease the wheels. Go to him. I shall find you later.'

12

On all sides we are pressed by those who wish to congratulate the bridegroom; they jostle, aggressively smiling and attempting to shake his hand. In the mêlée I slip away towards the door.

Outside, the night air is hard-edged with the first frost of autumn and the grounds are quiet, a welcome relief from the celebrations inside. In the knot-garden close to the house, lanterns have been lit and couples walk the neatly cultivated paths, murmuring, their heads close together. Even in the shadows, I can see that Sir Francis Walsingham is not to be found here. Stretching my arms, I strain my head back to gaze up at the sky, the constellations picked out in bright silver against the ink-blue of the heavens, their arrangement different here from the sky above Naples where I first learned the star-patterns as a boy.

I reach the end of the path and still there is no sign of him, so I set off across the open expanse of lawn, away from the lit paths, towards an area of woodland that borders the cultivated part of the garden at the back of Walsingham's country house. As I walk, a lean shape gathers substance out of the shadows and falls into step beside me. He seems made of the night; I have never seen Walsingham wear any suit other than black, not even today, at his daughter's wedding, and he wears still his close-fitting black velvet skullcap, that makes his face yet more severe. He is past fifty now and I have heard he has been ill this last month – one of the protracted bouts of illness that confines him to his bed for days at a time, though if you enquire after his health he swats the question away with a flick of his hand, as if he hasn't the time to consider such trifles. This man, Queen Elizabeth Tudor's Principal Secretary, though he may not seem an imposing figure at first glance, holds the security of England in his hands. Walsingham has created a network of spies and informers that stretches across Europe to the land of the Turks in the east and the colonies of the New World in the west, and the intelligence they bring him is the queen's first line of defence against the myriad Catholic plots to take her life. More remarkably still, he seems to hold all this intelligence in his own mind, and can pluck any information he requires at will.

I had arrived in England six months earlier, at the beginning of spring, sent by my patron King Henri III of France to stay for a while with his ambassador in London in order to spare me the attentions of the Catholic extremists who were gathering support in Paris, led by the Duke of Guise. I had barely been in England a fortnight when Walsingham asked to meet me, my long-standing enmity with Rome and my privileged position as a house guest at the French embassy making me ideally suited to his purposes. Over the past months, Walsingham is a man I have grown to respect deeply and fear a little.

But his cheeks are hollowed out since I last saw him. He folds his hands now behind his back; the noise of the celebrations grows fainter as we move away from the house.

'*Congratulazioni*, your honour.'

'*Grazie*, Bruno. I trust you are making the most of the celebrations?'

When he converses alone with me, he speaks Italian, partly I think to put me at ease, and partly because he wants to be sure I do not miss any vital point – his diplomat's Italian being superior to the English I learned largely from merchants and soldiers on my travels.

'Out of curiosity – where did you learn our English dances?' he adds, turning to me.

'I largely make them up as I go along. I find if one steps out confidently enough, people will assume you know what you are doing.'

He laughs, that deep rolling bear-laugh that comes so rarely from his chest.

'That is your motto in everything, is it not, Bruno? How else does a man rise from fugitive monk to personal tutor to

14

the King of France? Speaking of France –' he keeps his voice light – 'how does your host, the ambassador?'

'Castelnau is in good spirits now that his wife and daughter are newly returned from Paris.'

'Hm. I have not met Madame de Castelnau. They say she is very beautiful. No wonder the old dog always looks so hearty.'

'Beautiful, yes. I have not spoken to her at any length. I am told she is a most pious daughter of the Catholic Church.'

'I hear the same. Then we must watch her influence over her husband.' His eyes narrow. We have reached the trees, and he gestures for me to follow him into their shadows. 'I had thought Michel de Castelnau shared the French king's preference for diplomatic dealings with England – so he claims when he has audience with me, anyway. But lately that fanatic the Duke of Guise and his Catholic Leaguers are gaining strength in the French court, and in your letter last week you told me that Guise is sending money to Mary of Scotland through the French embassy –' He pauses to master his anger, quietly striking his fist into the palm of his hand. 'And what need has Mary Stuart of Guise money, hm? She is more than generously provided for in Sheffield Castle, considering she is our prisoner.'

'To secure the loyalty of her friends?' I suggest. 'To pay her couriers?'

'Precisely, Bruno! All this summer I have laboured to bring the two queens to a point where they are prepared to hold talks face to face, perhaps negotiate a treaty. Queen Elizabeth would like nothing better than to give her cousin Mary her liberty, so long as she will renounce all claim to the English throne. For her part, I am led to believe that Mary tires of imprisonment and is ready to swear to anything. That is why this traffic of letters and gifts from her supporters in France through the embassy troubles me so deeply. Is she double-dealing with me?'

15

He glares at me as if he expects an answer, but before I can open my mouth, he continues, as if to himself:

'And who *are* these couriers? I have the diplomatic packet intercepted and searched every week – she must have another means of delivery for her private letters.' He shakes his head briskly. 'While she lives, Mary Stuart is a banner to rally England's Catholics, and all those in Europe who hope to see a papist monarch back on our throne. But Her Majesty will not move pre-emptively against her cousin, though the Privy Council urges her to see the danger. This is why your presence in the French embassy is more crucial to me than ever, Bruno. I need to see every communication between Mary and France that passes through Castelnau's hands. If she is plotting against the queen's sovereignty again, I *must* have hard evidence that incriminates her this time. Can you see to it?'

'I have befriended the ambassador's clerk, your honour. For the right price, he says he can give us access to every letter Castelnau writes and receives, if you will guarantee that the documents will bear no evidence of tampering. He is greatly afraid of being discovered – he craves assurances of your honour's protection.'

'Good man. Give him all the assurances he needs.' He clasps my shoulder for a moment. 'If he will obtain for us an example of the ambassador's seal, I will set my man Thomas Phelippes to create a forgery. There is no man in England more skilled in the arts of interception. In the circumstances, Bruno, I do not think it prudent that you should be seen so much with Sidney,' he adds. 'Now that he is so publicly tied to me. Castelnau must not doubt your loyalty to France for a moment.'

Even through the dark, my face must betray my disappointment; Sidney is the only person I truly consider a friend in England. We had first met years ago in Padua, when I was fleeing through Italy, and renewed our friendship in the spring, when we had travelled to Oxford together on Walsingham's business. The adventures we shared there had only served to bring us closer. Without his company, I will feel my state of exile all the more keenly.

'But I have found you another contact. A Scotsman named William Fowler – you will meet him in due course. He is a lawyer who has worked for me in France, so you will have plenty to talk about.'

'You would trust a lawyer, your honour?'

'You look amused, Bruno. Lawyers, philosophers, priests, soldiers, merchants – there is no one I will not make use of. Fowler is well connected in Scotland, both among our friends and those loyal to the Scottish queen, who believe he is a friend to their cause. He has also insinuated himself with Castelnau, who believes Fowler to be a secret Catholic unhappy with Her Majesty's government. He has the knack of making himself all things to all men if necessity demands. Fowler is well placed to convey your reports from inside the embassy without you compromising your position.' He pauses and lifts his head; strains of music and laughter drift faintly towards the house and he seems to remember the occasion. 'For now, this is all. Come – we should be merry today. You must rejoin the dance.'

We turn to face the lit windows across the lawn, his hand lightly on my back. Out here, so far from the City, clean night scents of earth, grass and frost carry to us on the breeze. Even the Thames, running its sluggish course beyond the line of the trees behind us, smells fresh here, so far to the west of London. We are only a mile from Dee's house; I am surprised that he has not been invited. He is, after all, Sidney's old tutor and a friend of sorts to Walsingham. As if reading my thoughts, the Principal Secretary says, casually.

'You are spending a good deal of time in Mortlake lately, I hear?' It is not really a question.

'I am writing a book,' I explain, as we begin to move slowly together in the direction of the music. 'Doctor Dee's library has been invaluable.'

'What manner of book?'

'Of philosophy. And cosmology.'

'A defence of your beloved Copernicus, then.'

'Something like that.' I did not want to say too much about the book I was working on until it was completed. The ideas I was attempting to put forward were not just controversial but revolutionary, far beyond the theories that Copernicus had proposed. I wanted at least to have written it before I was obliged to defend it.

'Hm.' A heavy silence. 'Be wary of John Dee, Bruno.'

'I thought he was your honour's friend?'

'Up to a point. In matters of cartography, or ciphers, or the reformation of the calendar, there is no one in the kingdom whose knowledge I prize higher. But lately his talk runs much on prophecies and omens.'

'He believes we are living in the end times.'

'We are living in times of unprecedented turbulence, that much is certain,' he replies brusquely. 'But Her Majesty has enough to fear without Dee whispering these apocalyptic forecasts in her ear because he wants to make himself indispensable to her. As do we all, I suppose, in our way,' he concedes, with a sigh. 'But then his influence filters down even to the Privy Council chamber and suddenly she will not allow any decision without first consulting a star-chart. It makes the business of government very difficult. Besides,' he lowers his voice, 'it is my firm belief that Almighty God has written some secrets into the Book of Nature that are not supposed to be unlocked. From what I hear, Dee's newest experiments come dangerously close to crossing that line.'

There is no point in asking how he knows of Dee's experiments; Walsingham's eyes and ears encompass all of Europe and even the colonies of the New World. It should be no surprise that he knows what goes on a mile from his own house. Yet Dee has been so scrupulous about secrecy where his scrying is concerned.

18

'There are some at court who feel he has too much influence over Her Majesty, and must be removed from favour,' Walsingham continues.

'Your honour included?'

His teeth shine briefly in the dark as he smiles.

'I have a great respect for John Dee, and I would not do anything to hurt his reputation. The same is not true of some others on Her Majesty's Privy Council. Lord Henry Howard is publishing a book, I am told, to be presented to the queen – a fierce attack on prophecy and astrology and all those who claim to tell the future, calling them necromancers, accusing them of speaking with demons. He does not mention Dee by name, but the intent is clear enough . . . If Dee can be tainted for witchcraft, so much the worse for those of us known as his friends – me, Sidney, the Earl of Leicester. The Howards are dangerously powerful, and the queen knows this well enough. You may like to mention this to Dee the next time you are using his library.'

I incline my head to show that the warning is understood. As I bow and prepare to take my leave, I glance up to see a figure haring across the grass to us, a short riding cloak flapping behind him. He drops breathlessly to his knees at Walsingham's feet, and even in the thin silvered light I can make out the royal ensign on his livery, beneath the spattering of mud that shows he has ridden hard to get here. He mutters something about Richmond, a matter of urgency; there is alarm in his bulging eyes. I step away discreetly so that he may deliver his news privately, but Walsingham calls me back.

'Bruno! Wait for me a moment, will you?'

I stand a little way off, stamping my feet against the chill and rubbing my hands while the man rises to his feet and imparts his news in frantic bursts, Walsingham canted over to receive it, his hands still folded immobile behind his back. Whatever news this messenger has brought from the royal household must be serious indeed to interrupt a man's family wedding feast.

At length, Walsingham murmurs a response, the messenger bows and departs in the direction of the house with the same haste. Walsingham raises his hand to beckon me over.

'I am needed at Richmond Palace on a most grave matter, Bruno, and I want you with me. It will be preferable to disturbing the celebrations. We must leave quietly, without attracting attention – that fellow is gone to instruct the servants to make a boat ready. I will tell you as much as I know while we travel.' His voice is tight but controlled; if something distressing has befallen Her Majesty, Walsingham is the man she relies upon to bring order, discipline, calm.

'Will you not be missed?' I gesture in the direction of the wedding feast. He laughs, briefly.

'So long as I leave my steward in charge with the keys to the wine cellar, I doubt anyone will notice. Come, now.'

He leads me around the back of the house and through the garden to the little wharf where lights are bobbing gently, reflected in the black water. I must wait for him to tell the messenger's tale in his own time.

# THE
# GIORDANO BRUNO
## SERIES

---

'Impossible to resist' *Daily Telegraph*

---

### HERESY

The country is rife with plots to
assassinate Queen Elizabeth and
return the realm to the Catholic faith.
Giordano Bruno is recruited by the
Queen's spymaster and sent undercover
to expose a treacherous conspiracy in
Oxford – but his own secret mission
must remain hidden at all costs.

### PROPHECY

When Mary Stuart's supporters scheme
to usurp Queen Elizabeth's throne,
spymaster Francis Walsingham calls on
Giordano Bruno to infiltrate the plotters.
The proof he seeks is within his grasp.
But a young woman's murder could
point to an even more sinister truth…

## SACRILEGE

Giordano Bruno is being followed
by the woman he once loved – Sophia
Underhill, accused of murder and on
the run. With the leave of the Queen's
spymaster, Bruno travels to Canterbury
to clear Sophia's name – but a series of
mysterious crimes strike the city.

## TREACHERY

Sir Francis Drake is preparing
a daring expedition against the Spanish
when a murder aboard his ship changes
everything. Giordano Bruno agrees
to hunt the killer down, only to find
that more than one dangerous plot is
afoot in Plymouth's murky underworld.
And as he tracks a murderer through
its crime-ridden streets, he uncovers
a conspiracy that threatens the future
of England itself.

## CONSPIRACY

Paris is on the edge of catastrophe,
and Bruno is drawn into a dangerous
web of religious politics and court
intrigue. On the trail of a killer with
an awful secret, which threatens the
royal houses of France and England,
Bruno must expose the truth –
or be silenced for good…

# THE NO.1 *SUNDAY TIMES* BESTSELLER

## PARIS, 1585.

### UNITED BY FEAR. DIVIDED BY BLOOD.

## A KING WITHOUT AN HEIR

Heretic-turned-spy Giordano Bruno arrives in Paris to find a city on the edge of catastrophe. King Henri III lives in fear of a coup by the Duke of Guise and his fanatical Catholic League, and another massacre on the streets.

## A COURT AT WAR WITH GOD

When Bruno's old rival, Father Paul Lefèvre, is found murdered, Bruno is drawn into a dangerous web of religious politics and court intrigue. And watching over his shoulder is the King's mother, Catherine de Medici, with her harem of beautiful spies.

## A DEADLY CONSPIRACY IN PLAY

When murder strikes at the heart of the Palace, Bruno finds himself on the trail of a killer who is protecting a terrible secret. With the royal houses of France and England under threat, Bruno must expose the truth – or be silenced for good…